Little Bitty Lies

ALSO BY MARY KAY ANDREWS

The Fixer Upper

Deep Dish

Blue Christmas

Savannah Breeze

Hissy Fit

Little Bitty Lies

Savannah Blues

Little Bitty Lies

A Novel

Mary Kay Andrews

An Imprint of HarperCollinsPublishers

LITTLE BITTY LIES. Copyright © 2003 by Whodunnit, Inc. All rights reserved. Printed in the United States of America. No part of this book may be used or reproduced in any manner whatsoever without written permission except in the case of brief quotations embodied in critical articles and reviews. For information address HarperCollins Publishers, 10 East 53rd Street, New York, NY 10022.

HarperCollins books may be purchased for educational, business, or sales promotional use. For information please write: Special Markets Department, HarperCollins Publishers, 10 East 53rd Street, New York, NY 10022.

FIRST HARPERLUXE EDITION

HarperLuxe™ is a trademark of HarperCollins Publishers

Library of Congress Cataloging-in-Publication Data is available upon request.

ISBN: 978-0-06-198002-2

10 11 12 13 14 ID/RRD 10 9 8 7 6 5 4 3 2 1

Dedicated with love and thanks
to Nanny, a.k.a. Martha L. Winzeler,
who allowed herself to be adopted by a family
who can't imagine life without her wisdom,
friendship, and foolishness

Acknowledgments

Little Bitty Lies owes a whopping big thanks to the following folks who helped with research questions, advice, and general assistance: Ellen Tressler, who explained how mortgages work; Susie Deiters, who shared the original chicken salad recipe; Mickey Lloyd, who knows crime; Sue Hogan, who knows medicine; and Jeannie Trocheck, who knows insurance. Any errors or blunders are my fault and not theirs. I also owe a huge debt to the best damn editor in New York, Carolyn Marino, and to Stuart Krichevesky, the best damn agent in the world, who believed I could get away with murder. Thanks, guys.

Little Bitty Lies

1

Mary Bliss McGowan and Katharine Weidman had reached a point in the evening from whence there was no return. They had half a bottle of Tanqueray. They had limes. Plenty of ice. Plenty of time. It was only the Tuesday after Memorial Day, so the summer still stretched ahead of them, as green and tempting as a funeral home lawn. The hell of it was, they were out of tonic water.

"Listen, Kate," Mary Bliss said. "Why don't we just switch to beer?" She gestured toward her cooler. It had wheels and a long handle, and she hauled it down to the Fair Oaks Country Club pool most nights like the little red wagon she'd dragged all over town as a little girl. "I've got four Molson Lights right there. Anyway, all that quinine in the tonic water is making my ankles swell."

She thrust one suntanned leg in the air, pointing her pink-painted toes and frowning. They looked like piggy toes, all fleshy and moist.

"Or maybe we should call it a night." Mary Bliss glanced around. The crowd had been lively for a Tuesday night, but people had gradually drifted off—home, or to dinner, or inside, to their air conditioning and mindless summer sitcom reruns.

Bugs swarmed around the lights in the deck area. She felt their wings brushing the skin of her bare arms, but they never lit on Mary Bliss, and they never bit either. Somebody had managed to hook up the pool's PA system to the oldies radio station. The Tams and the Four Tops, the same music she'd listened to her whole life—even though they were not her oldies but of a generation before hers—played on.

She and Katharine were the only adults around. Three or four teenaged boys splashed around in the pool, tossing an inflated beach ball back and forth. The lifeguard, the oldest Finley boy—Shane? Blaine?—sat on the elevated stand by the pool and glowered in their direction. Clearly, he wanted to lock up and go to the mall.

"No," Katharine said, struggling out of her lounge chair. "No beer. Hell, it's early yet. And you know I'm not a beer drinker." She tugged at Mary Bliss's hand.

"Come on, then. The Winn-Dixie's still open. We'll get some more tonic water. We'll ride with the top down."

Mary Bliss sniggered and instantly hated the sound of it. "Well-bred young ladies never drive with their tops down."

Katharine rolled her eyes.

The Weidmans' red Jeep stood alone in the club lot, shining like a plump, ripe apple in the pool of yellow streetlamp light. Mary Bliss stood by the driver's door with her hand out. "Let me drive, Kate."

"What? You think I'm drunk?"

"We killed half a bottle of gin, and I've only had one drink," Mary Bliss said gently.

Katharine shrugged and got in the passenger seat.

Mary Bliss gunned the engine and backed out of the club parking lot. The cool night air felt wonderful on her sweat-soaked neck and shoulders.

"I can't believe Charlie gave up the Jeep," Mary Bliss said. "I thought it was his baby. Is it paid for?"

"What do I care?" Katharine said, throwing her head back, running her fingers through the long blonde tangle of her hair. "My lawyer says we've got Charlie by the nuts. Now it's time to squeeze. Besides, we bought it with the understanding that it would be Chip's to take to Clemson in the fall. I'm just using it as my fun car this summer. We're having fun, right?"

"I thought freshmen weren't allowed to have cars on campus," Mary Bliss said.

"Charlie doesn't know that," Katharine said.

Mary Bliss frowned.

"Shut up and drive," Katharine instructed.

The Winn-Dixie was nearly deserted. A lone cashier stood at the register at the front of the store, listlessly counting change into her open cash drawer. Katharine dumped four bottles of Schweppes Tonic Water down on the conveyor belt, along with a loaf of Sunbeam bread, a carton of cigarettes, and a plastic tub of Dixie Darlin' chicken salad.

"Y'all got a Value Club card?" the cashier asked, fingers poised on the keys of her register.

"I've got better than that," Katharine said peevishly, taking a twenty-dollar bill from the pocket of her shorts. "I've got cash money. Now, can we get the lead out here?"

The fluorescent lights in the store gave Katharine's deeply tanned face a sick greenish glow. Her roots needed touching up. And, Mary Bliss observed, it really was about time Katharine gave up wearing a bikini. Not that she was fat. Katharine Weidman was a rail. She ran four miles every morning, no matter what. But she was in her forties, after all, and the skin around her neck and chest and shoulders was starting to turn to corduroy. Her breasts weren't big, but they were beginning to sag. Mary Bliss tugged at the neckline of her own neat black tank suit. She couldn't stand it the way some women over thirty-five paraded around half naked in public—as if the world wanted to see their goods. She kept her goods tucked neatly away, thank you very much.

Mary Bliss made a face as she saw Katharine sweeping her groceries into a plastic sack.

"Since when do you buy chicken salad at the Winn-Dixie?" she asked, flicking the tub with her index finger.

"It's not that bad," Katharine said. "Chip loves it, but then, teenaged boys will eat anything. Anyway, it's too damn hot to cook."

"Your mother made the best chicken salad I've ever tasted," Mary Bliss said. "I still dream about it sometimes. It was just like they used to have at the Magnolia Room downtown."

Katharine managed a half-smile. "Better, most said. Mama always said the sign of a lady's breeding was in her chicken salad. White meat, finely ground or hand shredded, and some good Hellmann's Mayonnaise, and I don't know what all. She used to talk about some woman, from up north, who married into one of the Coca-Cola families. 'She uses dark meat in her chicken salad,' Mama told me one time. 'Trailer trash.'"

"She'd roll over in her grave if she saw you feeding her grandson that store-bought mess," Mary Bliss was saying. They were right beside the Jeep now, and Mary Bliss had the keys in her hand, when Katharine shoved her roughly to the pavement.

"What on earth?" Mary Bliss demanded.

"Get down," Katharine whispered. "She'll see us."

"Who?" Mary Bliss asked. She pushed Katharine's hand off her shoulder. "Let me up. You've got me squatting on chewing gum."

"It's Nancye Bowden," Katharine said, peeping up over the side of the Jeep, then ducking back down again. "She's sitting in that silver Lexus, over there by the yellow Toyota. My God!"

"What? What is it?" Mary Bliss popped her head up to get a look. The Lexus was where Katharine had pointed. But there was only one occupant. A man. A dark-haired man. His head was thrown back, his eyes squeezed shut, his mouth a wide O, as if he were laughing at something.

"You're crazy, Katharine Weidman. I don't see Nancye Bowden at all." She started to stand. "I'm getting a crick in my calves. Let's go home."

Katharine duck-walked around to the passenger side of the Jeep and snaked herself into the passenger seat. She slumped down in the seat so that her head was barely visible above the dashboard. "I'm telling you she's in there. You can just see the top of her head. Right there, Mary Bliss. With that guy. Look at his face, Mary Bliss. Don't you get it?"

Mary Bliss didn't have her glasses. She squinted, tried to get the man's face in better focus. Maybe he wasn't laughing.

"Oh.

"My.

"Lord."

Mary Bliss covered her eyes with both hands. She felt her face glowing hot-red in the dark. She fanned herself vigorously.

"You're such a virgin." Katharine cackled. "What? You didn't know?"

"That Nancye Bowden was hanging out in the Winn-Dixie parking lot giving oral sex to men in expensive cars? No, I don't think she mentioned it the last time I saw her at garden club. Does Randy know?"

Mary Bliss turned the key in the Jeep's ignition and scooted it out of the parking lot, giving the silver Lexus a wide berth. She would die if Nancye Bowden saw her.

"It's called a blow job. Yes, I'm pretty sure Randy knows what Nancye's been up to. But you can't bring yourself to say it, can you?" Katharine said, watching Mary Bliss's face intently.

"You have a very trashy mouth, Katharine Weidman. How would I know what perversion Nancye has been up to lately?"

"I guess y'all were down at Seaside when it happened. I just assumed you knew. Nancye and Randy are through. She moved into an apartment in Buckhead. He's staying in the house with the kids, at least until school starts back in the fall, and his mother is watching the kids while Randy's at work. Lexus Boy is some professor over at Emory. Or that's what Nancye told the girls at that baby shower they had for Ansley Murphey."

"I had to miss Ansley's shower because we took Erin down to Macon for a soccer tournament," Mary Bliss said. "I can't believe I didn't hear anything, with them living right across the street. The Bowdens? Are you sure? My heavens, that's the third couple on the block. Just since the weather got warm."

"Four, counting us," Katharine said. "You know what they're calling our end of the street, don't you?"

"What?"

"Split City."

2

Mary Bliss put on the turn signal as she approached her driveway. Katharine reached over and flipped the signal off, spilling the drink she'd mixed for herself on the way home from the club. By Mary Bliss's count, it was Katharine's seventh gin and tonic of the night.

"You always do that," Katharine said. "Who are you signaling for? It's nearly midnight. There's nobody around. Six hundred eighty-seven people live in Fair Oaks, and six hundred eighty-five of them are in bed, asleep. We are the only ones in this damn town who are awake. We are the only ones who even have a goddamn pulse."

Mary Bliss flipped the signal on again and completed her turn. "By my count, it's six hundred eighty-four. Parker's probably still up, waiting for me to come home. And you forget, at least one of our neighbors is still awake, over there fornicating in the parking lot at the Winn-Dixie. Besides, it's the law, Katharine. Suppose somebody came careening down the street behind us? Like an ambulance or a fire truck? They could rear-end us, big as anything. You may drive like a bat out of torment anytime you like, but when I'm behind the wheel this is how I drive. Safe."

"You do everything safe," Katharine grumbled, mopping the gin and tonic off the Jeep's seat with her bathing suit cover-up. "You're the only woman I know who'll insist on a seat belt in her coffin. And if you want to get technical, Miss Priss, what Nancye Bowden was doing in that Lexus was not actually fornicating, as far as I could see."

"I'm glad you're thinking of my funeral and Nancye Bowden's sex life when your own life is such a wreck right now," Mary Bliss said. "You really are a mess, Katharine. No wonder Charlie left. I'm surprised it took him this long."

"Ha!" Katharine said, braying unattractively. "Charlie likes round numbers. He wanted to wait until we'd been married exactly twenty years. Not nineteen or twenty-one, but twenty. That way he could tell his

therapist he'd given it two decades and the whole thing
was hopeless. It makes him less of a bad guy, don't you
see?"

Mary Bliss turned off the ignition and unfastened
her seat belt. "He's not all that bad a guy, you know.
Charlie is a decent human being. I still think you two
could have worked things out, if you'd just tried a little
harder. Now look at you. You're a wreck. Charlie's in
therapy. Chip's unhappy. Doesn't it feel like your whole
life is turned upside down?"

Katharine pretended to be hurt. "Hey. You're my
best friend. You have to be on my side. Why is it so
hard for you to believe that I'm better off without the
jerk? Anyway, I *like* upside down. I've had normal.
Normal sucks."

"I just wish you'd tried couples counseling," Mary
Bliss said.

"Hey," Katharine said loudly, determined to get
Mary Bliss off the therapy track. "Did I tell you what
I did today?"

"You mean yesterday," Mary Bliss said, checking
her wristwatch. "It's officially past midnight. And
I shudder to think about what you did."

Katharine giggled. "I called Grimmy. Actually, she
called me first. Looking for Charlie. He won't return
her calls. He's been out of the house two months, and

he still hasn't broken it to his mommy that he's getting divorced. Keeps saying her poor old heart won't take it. Which is a load of crap. Grimmy's just playing possum. That old biddy will be playing bridge tournaments when we're all dead and in the grave. Charlie just doesn't want to admit to Grimmy that there's trouble in paradise."

"You didn't tell her, did you?" Like everybody else in town, Mary Bliss McGowan was terrified of Katharine's mother-in-law. Sarah Grimes Weidman, known to all as Grimmy, was eighty years old, and as far as Mary Bliss knew, nobody had ever gotten the better of her. "Didn't Grimmy have bypass surgery last year?"

"Sure did," Katharine said. "And then she went on a cruise to Alaska with the Sojourner's Sunday School class at Fair Oaks First United Methodist six weeks later. I'm tired of everybody tippy-toeing around that old bag. So when she called yesterday, I told her, 'Look, Grimmy. You and Charlie need to have a chat. He's got some important news to share with you.'"

Katharine fished around in her plastic cup until she found the slice of lime. She sucked on it loudly. "Know what Grimmy thought? She thought maybe Charlie lost a big wad in the stock market. Talk about denial. She still thinks Chip was born two months premature. The world's only eleven-pound preemie."

She shook her head. "Gawd. So I said, 'Grimmy, here's the deal. Charlie's left me and I'm divorcing his ass. He's moved in with his girlfriend. Your son is pushing fifty and he's living with a twenty-nine-year-old named Tara. And here's the rest of the news flash: I am not a natural blonde, and I haven't been a virgin since I was fifteen. Also—Chip didn't go to Woodward Academy because he wanted to play lacrosse, he went because his grades weren't good enough to get into Westminster, and we couldn't afford to donate a new library so they'd bend the rules.'"

"What did she do?" Mary Bliss's voice was hushed.

"She hung up. Ten minutes later, she called back, tried to disguise her voice, and asked for Chip. So I hung up on her. It felt so good, I called her back and hung up again as soon as she answered the phone."

"That's awful," Mary Bliss said. "Even if it is Grimmy. What if she'd had a heart attack? Wouldn't you have felt guilty?"

"No way," Katharine said, shaking her head vehemently. "I hope she does blow a valve. When she dies, all the Coca-Cola stock goes to Chip. And he's not speaking to his dad right now."

"You want my advice?"

"No, I do not."

Mary Bliss plunged ahead. She'd been offering Katharine unsolicited advice ever since the day they'd met at the Fair Oaks Country Club swim meet, when Chip was seven and her own daughter, Erin, was six, and Mary Bliss had taken Katharine aside and tactfully suggested that a thong bathing suit was not appropriate for youth-oriented events. Not club-sponsored ones, anyway. Katharine had laughed in her face, told her not to be such a biddy, and offered her a wine cooler. They had been friends ever since. Katharine never took her advice, but it made Mary Bliss feel better to be the voice of reason.

"Clean up your act, Kate," Mary Bliss said. "Don't alienate Charlie's friends and family. Stop leaving those obscene messages on his answering machine. Stop ordering all that Victoria's Secret stuff and putting it on his American Express card just to piss off Tara. Face facts. Charlie's not totally over you. Why else would he still be coming over for Sunday supper? It's not like he comes to see Chip. Chip doesn't even speak to his daddy. Charlie comes over because he wants to see you. To keep the door open."

Katharine made a disparaging, pooting noise. "That ship has sailed, honey. You and I both know he's freeloading off me because Tara the bitch-whore can't even fix microwave popcorn. And this is his way of keeping her guessing. But I'm not guessing anything. Trust me, M. B., it's over."

"You're telling me you wouldn't take him back? Right now? If he showed up at your door and said it had all been a hideous mistake, and he wanted to take you to Paris and prove how much he still loved you?"

"Not even if he showed up with a twelve-carat diamond and grew a twelve-inch penis and knew what to do with it," Katharine said. She jiggled the ice in her cup impatiently, wanting to fix herself another drink, but knew it would just get Mary Bliss on a jag about her drinking.

"Talk about denial," Mary Bliss said. "Face it, sugar. It's not over yet. You've only been separated a few months. You and Charlie are right for each other. You're too screwed up for anybody else. It's destiny, Katharine. Besides, you know my theory about marriage."

Katharine deliberately crunched a piece of ice, knowing it set Mary Bliss on edge, just as did gum-smacking or finger-tapping. "Which cockeyed theory is that? The one that says if a man makes more than a hundred thousand a year and has full medical and dental coverage, you're morally obligated to have sex with him more than once a pay period?"

"I never said that," Mary Bliss said. "Don't be crude."

"Spiritual commitments? Children of broken homes inherit a legacy of shame and guilt?"

"You know what I'm talking about," Mary Bliss said, ignoring the ice-crunching. "A marriage is like a pet poodle. Poodles have a certain life expectancy. But lots of times, the poor thing just keeps on ticking and takes a licking. It may be old and blind and make tee-tee all over the rug in the den, but it has a life force of its own. It doesn't matter when you think it's over. It's not over until it's all played out. And your marriage isn't all played out yet, Katharine. Believe me, I've seen it happen so many times. Right now, you're hurt and upset, so you're trying to strike out at Charlie. But really, you're only hurting yourself."

"Gawd," Katharine said, fumbling around on the floor of the Jeep for the gin bottle. "What do you call that figure of speech? An anachronism? That's the worst kind of anachronism I ever heard. Comparing marriage to an incontinent poodle."

Mary Bliss had been an English major. "It's called an analogy," she said.

Katharine found the bottle and shakily poured more gin into her plastic cup. The tonic bottle had rolled out of reach, so she didn't bother with the niceties. She was tired of niceties, and she was even more tired of well-meaning advice. "That's the worst damn aneurysm in the history of Western civilization." She knew she was drunk and she knew she was slurring her words. Sloppy drunk. Stinking drunk for the fourth night in a row. She felt great.

She steadied herself and held her cup at a distance, to signal that she had something important to say.

"My marriage is nothing like some damn Pekinese. For your information, Mrs. McGowan, my marriage is dead. Flatline. No pulse, no brain activity. Certainly no sex activity. Go on inside now, Mary Bliss. Tell Parker McGowan what a lucky man he is. Hell, give him a blow job while you're at it. I can drive home. It's only a block."

Mary Bliss grabbed the drink out of Katharine's hand and threw it out the window of the Jeep. "Stop it. You're revolting. Just leave the car here and walk home. I'll walk with you."

"No way," Katharine said. "Charlie cruises the neighborhood every night, after he thinks I've already gone to bed. If the Jeep isn't there, he'll start calling and raising hell. If he sees it over here, he'll think I'm over here boo-hooing to you and Parker."

"Maybe he'll think you miss him," Mary Bliss said. "Maybe he's already come to his senses. He wouldn't go looking for you unless he missed you, idiot."

"He's the idiot," Katharine said, yawning. "He misses the Jeep, not me." She reached over and opened Mary Bliss's door. "Shoo. Go home. Parker probably thinks you've been abducted by aliens."

Mary Bliss reached for her beach bag. "Parker knows I'm with you. And he agrees with me that you and Charlie should get back together. He even told Charlie that."

Katharine climbed over the console and into the driver's seat. Nimble as anything, despite her advanced state of intoxication.

"You know the problem with you, Mary Bliss? You keep assuming that everybody else's marriage is like yours. You have no idea what a real marriage is like. You and Parker are like Ozzie and Harriet, Mary Bliss. You're a couple of dinosaurs."

"Nice aneurysm. Maybe so," Mary Bliss said. She blew Katharine a kiss. "Sweet dreams, Kate. And don't forget to lock up."

3

All the lights were on, the television in the den was blaring, and the CD player in the kitchen was blaring Erin's current favorite music, some sort of gangster rap whose nasty lyrics made the large vein in Mary Bliss's forehead throb in indignation.

She walked through the house, switching off lights, the television, and the CD player. She set the burglar alarm in the kitchen, put some dirty dishes in the dishwasher, and turned it on.

The bedroom was dark. She could just see the green glow of the clock radio. Twelve-thirty. She felt her way to the closet, dropped her damp bathing suit and shorts in the hamper there, and pulled on a clean cotton nightgown.

In the bathroom, she brushed her teeth and creamed her face with moisturizers, frowning at the memory of

Katharine's wrinkled neck. Mary Bliss's mother's skin had been magnolia-smooth until she was in her fifties, until the time the cancer began eating its way through her body and her skin grew translucent and waxen yellow. Mary Bliss peered into the mirror, to see if she could find any trace of her mother there. Her eyes were certainly Mama's—hazel-green, dark-lashed, with surprisingly strong, dark eyebrows.

But the nose was Daddy's—stubby, no-nonsense, a workingman's nose—her lips full and lush, Harker lips, her mother informed her, pursing her own narrow lips, a sign that Harker lips were not a desirable family trait.

Erin was a McGowan through and through, everybody said. Meemaw had peered through the glass in the Piedmont Hospital nursery and just crowed with delight at the sight of her long, narrow granddaughter. "Look at those feet! She's got her daddy's feet for sure."

Mary Bliss never said as much, but she'd done a complete inventory and found several of her own family traits in her infant daughter—the folds of her ear, the long neck, the high forehead, even Mary Bliss's own thick, dark hair. She'd watched anxiously as Erin grew and changed, anxious that those small traces of Mary Bliss's own family, all dead and gone now, would remain in her own child.

She switched off the bathroom light and made her way easily to her side of the bed. She pulled back the sheets on the big four-poster bed. No pillows. She smiled to herself. Parker had stolen them again. He was such a pillow hog.

"Honey?" she whispered tentatively. She pulled herself close to the warm, drowsing form in the middle of the bed. "Park? You awake?"

But the smell was all wrong. Perfume instead of antiperspirant. And long, thick hair, curled over a bare shoulder.

"Mommy?" Erin's voice was groggy. "Where's Daddy?"

4

She sat on the floor of Parker's closet, held the note in her hand, and dialed Parker's cell phone number. No answer. She dialed again, squinting at the readout window on her own phone to make sure she hadn't made a mistake. But the number was correct, and nobody was answering.

Mary Bliss put the phone down again and looked at the note.

The bastard hadn't even bothered to use a whole sheet of paper. It was written on the back of a junk mail envelope.

"MB," it said.

"I'm gone. Mama's all paid up at the nursing home. Tell Erin I'll call when I'm settled. You are a good woman, and I'm sorry things didn't work out. Sincerely, A. Parker McGowan."

"Mama?"

Mary Bliss crawled to the door of the closet. Erin was wrapped in the big comforter, huddled in the middle of the king-sized bed. Her dark hair stood on end. One side of the oversized T-shirt had slipped off her slender shoulder, and the hazel eyes were clouded with sleep and confusion. Again, as always, her daughter reminded her of a just-hatched duckling. Mary Bliss thought she felt a jagged pain ripping through her right ventricle. It was only love.

"Did you forget again? That Daddy was going out of town?"

Of course. Out of town. Way out of town.

"Stupid old me," Mary Bliss said, grimacing, giving herself a comic knock on the head. "Katharine made me drink gin and tonic at the pool tonight. You know how your mama gets when she drinks likker. Of course Daddy's out of town. Dallas, I think. What time did you get home, sweet girl?"

Her lies came out smoothly, easily. Mary Bliss swallowed and felt the bile rising in her throat. They were just little lies.

"The movie got out at ten," Erin said. "But Lizbeth had to have her quarter-pounder and fries, so we went to McDonald's afterwards. I swear, that girl must have a tapeworm. And she never gets a zit or gains a pound. I hate her guts. And she told me tonight that she has a crush on Andrew Gilbert. Oh my God! Can you believe that? Last year he asked her out every day, and she wouldn't even look at him. When we got home tonight, I came in here to watch Letterman. The cable's messed up in my room. Guess I fell asleep. Are you sure Daddy's in Dallas?"

A fine bead of sweat raised itself on Mary Bliss's upper lip. She looked down. Her cotton gown was soaked, clinging to her chest and arms. She had to catch her breath, had to think.

She stood up and walked unsteadily to the bed, catching the bedpost with her right hand, grateful for the support.

"Honey, to tell the truth, I can't keep it all straight. You know Daddy. He's always on the move. With the holiday and all, Libby must have forgotten to fax me his itinerary. I'll check in the morning."

Erin nodded and yawned widely. "Okay if I sleep in here with you? It's so hot in my room. I think you need to get the air conditioning people over here. I won't wake you when I go to work in the morning."

Erin had a summer job at the Gap. It paid better than lifeguarding at the club, which she had done last summer, and she also got a discount on clothes.

"You better wake me up," Mary Bliss said, easing down into the bed. "I can't sleep all day long, you know. Just because it's summer. Teachers have stuff to do too."

It was an unspoken rule in the McGowan house. Whenever one of them was away, Erin usually slept in the big bed upstairs. None of them felt this was odd or inappropriate, even though Erin was seventeen, going to be a senior this year at Fair Oaks Academy. Anyway, it was mostly Mary Bliss who ended up sharing the bed with Erin. Parker's software consulting business seemed to take him out of town two or three weeks of every month.

She waited until Erin's breath grew soft and sweet and regular, then peered over the mound of pillows her daughter had stacked up, like a moat surrounding a castle.

Erin had been a fretful baby, never sleeping through the night until she was nearly four. Now, though, she seemed to be catching up on all those lost hours. She slept as late as she dared on school mornings, liked a nap in the afternoons, and slept 'til noon most Saturdays.

Mary Bliss kissed her fingertip and planted it tenderly on the top of her daughter's head.

She took the note, crumpled and damp with her own sweat, and read it again. She swept her hands through the row of clothes hanging on Parker's side of the closet. His dress shirts, slacks, suits, sport coats, and ties were undisturbed. The shoe trees poked out of the line of wingtips and loafers. She opened the top drawer of the dresser. Neat balls of dark dress socks. But no white socks. She opened the next drawer down. His underwear had been cleaned out. Same with his shorts and T-shirts. She looked again at the row of shoes. No tennis shoes. He'd packed, all right, but not for business.

She flipped off the closet light and tiptoed downstairs to the den.

Parker had laughed at her when she told him this was her dream house. It was just a little cottage, really, a Craftsman bungalow on the nicest street in Fair Oaks. The house had been a shabby mess when they'd bought it, just before Erin was born. Parker always meant for them to move out of Fair Oaks and into Druid Hills, which he considered a nicer Atlanta neighborhood. He wanted them to join the Druid Hills Country Club, one of the more exclusive golf clubs in town, like the Piedmont Driving Club, or Ansley or the Peachtree Golf Club.

Parker had talked about taking up golf, once his business was doing really well. Fair Oaks Country Club was nice enough, but in the past it didn't really have the glamour of the better-known clubs. The price of in-town housing in Atlanta had skyrocketed in the past five years, and now Fair Oaks was considered an enclave of exclusivity. Suddenly their cozy little four-bedroom, two-bath on the big half-acre lot was worth maybe ten times what they'd originally paid for it. It made Mary Bliss dizzy to think about it.

This den was supposed to be their little boy's room. She'd waited, kept Erin's crib there, along with the toy chest and the changing table. Then she hit thirty, and then Parker hit forty, and she knew there would be no second child. She'd fretted about it but knew better than to bring up the subject of infertility with Parker, who liked things just the way they were, thank you.

When Erin was twelve, Mary Bliss had found a leather sofa on sale at Rich's, and she'd had some bookshelves made and refinished Parker's granddaddy's desk from the textile mill, hand-polished the old walnut until it shone like satin.

She sat at the desk now and looked around. No papers in the fax machine. No light blipped on the message machine. The desktop had been swept clean. Hospital-clean. So it was true. Parker was gone.

She felt that jagged pain in her chest again. What if she had a heart attack? Right now—with Parker gone

Lord knows where, and Erin upstairs, sound asleep in their bed?

No, it wasn't a heart attack, she decided. It was panic. Dread. Again she felt the same wave of nausea that had swept over her upstairs, where she'd crouched on the floor, reading the note by the closet light.

Gone. Gone where? And why?

Their life together was seamless as far as she knew. No major fights, no money worries. Mary Bliss taught at the public school, kept house, cooked, did volunteer work at the church and Erin's private school. She visited Parker's mother, Eula, once a week at the Fair Oaks Assisted Living Facility. They had dinner parties, went on vacation. Damn it, this was not a broken home. She had a normal, happy marriage. Didn't she?

The problem was, one half of the marriage equation was gone and unavailable for polling.

She found herself praying, whispering aloud. "Please don't let it be true. Please don't let it be true." Mary Bliss clamped her Harker lips together to make the praying stop.

The bank statements were neatly bundled together with rubber bands in the bottom drawer of the desk. When they'd first married, Mary Bliss had kept the household bills. She was good at it; liked toting up numbers, making a budget, keeping their little family ship afloat. But a year ago, Parker had insisted that his computer software could do a much better job of all that, so she'd reluctantly handed over the bill-paying to him.

It had hurt her feelings, his taking away her job, but she'd gone ahead and handed over the checkbook, and after a few months of not worrying over how many ATM withdrawal charges they were paying, Mary Bliss found she did not miss bookkeeping quite as much as she'd expected.

Everything was on the computer, she was sure. The problem was, Mary Bliss didn't know where. She knew how to play solitaire and blackjack on the computer, knew how to pick up e-mail messages from Parker and her friends and former Agnes Scott classmates, but she had no idea where everything else could be.

She looked at the bank statements. For the first two months of the year, the balances in their checking, savings, and money market accounts looked fine. The checking account balance was a little low, but Parker did that intentionally because the bank didn't pay interest on checking.

In March, the balance on all the accounts seemed to start dropping dramatically.

She skipped ahead to the most recent statement. May. It had been mailed only two days earlier. She looked at the number on the last sheet of paper and blinked. This had to be wrong. But the right account number was listed at the top of the sheet.

One time, a year ago, Parker had called from the airport in San Diego and asked her to call the computerized phone number to move some money around in their accounts. "It's strictly for idiots," he'd said when she'd protested that she didn't know how. "Just listen to the instructions and punch in the codes when you're given the prompt."

She looked at the May statement again, found the telebanking number at the top of the first sheet. She dialed the number, followed the prompts, and listened, her pencil poised.

Zero. Zero in checking. Zero in savings. Zero in their money market account.

She heard a snapping noise and looked down. She'd broken the pencil in half.

5

Mary Bliss barely made it to the downstairs powder room. After the first spasm of nausea subsided, she managed to kick the door shut with her foot so that her retching wouldn't echo through the house. She had no idea how long she stayed like that, sprawled on the cold tile floor, hugging the commode, bleating and sobbing and cursing and praying.

Finally, she got to her feet, scrubbed her face with cold water, and rinsed out her mouth with a tiny sample bottle of mouthwash she found in the cupboard under the sink.

The woman in the mirror stared back at her with red-rimmed eyes and skin gone pale under the summer tan.

"Christ," she moaned.

After a while, she forced herself to go back to the den. Parker had made no attempt to hide what he'd done. She found the stack of bills tossed in the top drawer of the desk, the dunning notices paper-clipped to the front of each envelope. Atlanta Gas Light. Georgia Power. Southern Bell. Cablevision. Fulton County Tax Assessor's Office. Piedmont Savings and Loan. Visa, American Express, Talbot's, Land's End.

When she'd opened all the envelopes, faced all the facts, the desktop was littered with the pieces of paper that traced their lives for the last four months. The special dinners at Babette's Café and Bones. Erin's prom dress, $240 from Nordstrom's. Four steel-belted radial tires for the minivan. Two black canvas Voyager suitcases from Land's End, and six cotton pique sports shirts, for a total of $377.86.

But there were no other clues. No plane tickets or hotel reservations or rental cars. Nothing to explain Parker's treachery, his decision to steer their little family ship smack into the shoals of humiliation and despair.

Mary Bliss reached across the mound of paper and picked up the framed photo by the telephone. It was an old black-and-white snapshot. Parker, his mama and daddy (bless his heart, Grampa Mac had his hands full with Eula), and Mary Bliss, holding baby Erin, standing in front of the cottage at the Cloister. The photo was taken right before Grampa Mac got sick. He'd taken them all to the Cloister for Easter that year. There was a palm tree in the background, and they were all tanned, smiling, looking, Mary Bliss always thought, a little like a southern version of the Kennedys. In the photo, Mary Bliss had Erin tilted toward the camera; Parker's hand rested lightly on the nape of Mary Bliss's bare neck, while Mary Bliss looked up at Parker in something like adoration, and one strap of her sundress had fallen off her shoulder. Grampa Mac was smiling down at the baby, and Eula, she stared straight ahead at the photographer, lips bared in the closest thing she could get to a grin.

It was the last picture they had of Grampa Mac. The leukemia had been deadly but quick. Bless his heart. Al McGowan didn't have a mean bone in his body. What would he say about his only son leaving her in a mess like this?

She took the photo and whapped it hard against the edge of the desktop. The glass splintered into a bazillion pieces. With the edge of her hand she swept them over the edge of the desk and into the trash can.

Parker's slot in the garage was empty, nothing but a small grease stain where the Lexus should have been. She leaned against the garage doorway and closed her eyes, smelling the garage smells—gasoline and weed killer and fertilizer. Where had he gone? Had he simply driven off, leaving them behind like a pile of old newspapers?

"You're a good woman," Parker had written. Good for what? Leaving?

The cicadas droned on and on. Out on the front porch, Mary Bliss tucked her legs under her and used the weight of her body to rock the old wicker chair in time to the rhythm of the whirring insects.

It was only slightly summer, technically, but the heat on the porch was already a damp blanketing presence. Her gown stuck to her back and legs, and her hair was soaked with sweat. Soon the county would start the water restrictions. Her lawn, her perennials and ferns, were already wilting in anticipation. And her tomatoes, the Early Girls, could not stand a drought right now. She got up, walked around to the side of the house, and turned on the sprinklers.

Then she rocked and listened to the soft swish of the water hitting the parched grass. A mosquito flitted around her head, and a moth danced around the porch light. Gradually, the navy velvet sky lightened, then washed into purple, then peach. The streetlights switched off, and slowly she saw porch lights flicker on at the house across the street. Fifteen minutes later, the house next door was lit up too. Discreet little FOR SALE signs had sprouted on the lawns at the Gasparinis and the Weidmans, like the first toadstools of summer.

Fair Oaks taxes were sky-high, and everybody sent their kids to private schools. A divorce usually meant a reshuffling of finances. Mary Bliss still couldn't believe Katharine intended to sell her house. It was the biggest and oldest in the neighborhood, but Katharine said it was a mausoleum, and she intended to buy one of the new condos being built at the back of the old Connelly estate.

Directly across the street, even the pearly morning light was not kind to the Bowdens' house. It looked more than a little tatty. The lawn needed mowing, weeds were as high as the azaleas in the pine island, and four or five days' worth of newspapers were piled in a heap by the front door. Randy Bowden's little green Saab backed slowly down the driveway and out onto the street. Mary Bliss scrunched down in the rocker so that Randy wouldn't catch sight of her. She felt sorry for him, that was for sure. Did he know what his wife was up to in that Winn-Dixie parking lot last night?

It wasn't until the Saab was out of sight that she remembered to feel sorry for herself. Parker was gone, and from the look of things, so was all their money.

The morning quiet was split by the throb of a bad muffler on a rusted white Cadillac that came rattling slowly down the street. She knew without even looking that this was not a vehicle owned by a Fair Oaks resident. Sure enough, when the car rolled past, she saw a dark, sinewy arm extended from the driver's window, and she saw the rolled-up newspaper go sailing onto the Bowdens' front yard, plonking onto the sidewalk near the pine island, not far from the other, yellowing newspapers.

The arm extended again, and the newspaper sailed over the top of the Cadillac, landing neatly at her own curb.

At least Parker had cut their grass before leaving. He'd been meticulous about their lawn, lavishing it with iron supplements and fertilizer, aerating twice a year, spring and fall, trimming and weeding until it was the deepest green on the block.

The McGowans had won "Yard of the Month" so many times from the Fair Oaks Garden Club, it had gotten embarrassing.

Now, with Parker gone, how long would it be before the neighbors were tsk-tsking under their breath about *her* weeds, *her* scraggly azaleas, and *her* yellowing stack of newspapers? When a yard in Fair Oaks went to hell, it was the first sign, she thought, that a marriage was on the rocks.

"Welcome to Split City," she told herself.

6

"You're late," Katharine said, glancing at the thin platinum watch on her deeply tanned wrist.

It was past ten. During the summer, when school was out, they had a Coke date every morning, alternating houses.

She frowned as she assessed Mary Bliss's appearance. "You look like shit on a shingle," she said, holding the back door open to let Mary Bliss enter. "And I'm the one with the hangover."

Mary Bliss pinched her lips together to hold back another wave of nausea. She dropped down into one of the high-backed chairs in Katharine's breakfast room. "I didn't sleep very well last night. I almost didn't come over this morning." She blinked rapidly in the strong sunlight that poured in through the wall of windows overlooking the Weidmans' rose garden.

Katharine poured two Diet Cokes into cut-glass highball tumblers, then added a slice of lime to each. She reached into the refrigerator and pulled out a tray of Sara Lee cheese Danish, which she'd already sliced up and arranged on one of her mother's Wedgwood platters, with a garnish of strawberries and fresh mint leaves.

Mary Bliss managed a wan smile at the snack. "You've got style, Katharine. That's one of the things I've always admired about you. You manage to make Sara Lee look like something out of *Gourmet* magazine."

"I always thought you thought I was kind of trashy," Katharine said, popping a strawberry into her mouth.

"Trashy-talking," Mary Bliss said. "But you do everything with such elegance, I forgive you."

She took a sip of the Diet Coke. It felt good on her dry throat. Another sip.

"Ask me why I didn't sleep last night."

"Was it Parker's night for a double-header?" Katharine wagged her eyebrows, trying to look like Groucho Marx. She came off more like Bette Midler doing Groucho Marx.

Mary Bliss's face crumpled. Her upper lip started to tremble, then her chin, then her hand shook so badly that she spilled Diet Coke all over the tile-topped table.

"What? What is it?" Katharine asked, taking the glass from her friend's hand. "Darlin', tell Kate. What's the matter? Do you want another Coke? They had twelve-packs at the Citgo for a dollar ninety-nine."

Mary Bliss shook her head violently, and the tears came again. She was sobbing and trying to cover her face with her hands, and she'd smeared her lipstick badly, making her look like a three-year-old who'd gotten into her mommy's makeup.

Katharine was startled. Except for the lipstick, Mary Bliss wasn't wearing any makeup, which was totally un-M.B.-like. She never, ever left home without base smoothed over her face and a light coating of mascara and concealer.

"Tell me," Katharine said, grabbing her friend by the wrist. "Please, hon, you're scaring me. Is it Erin? Is she all right?"

"It's Parker. He's left me. Note in the closet. And there's no money."

Katharine got up from the table and went to the kitchen cabinet. She brought out a handful of pill bottles, squinting at the label on each until she found the one she wanted. She opened it, shook a small blue tablet

into the palm of her hand. She opened another bottle
and took out a red-and-blue capsule.

"Take these," she said, shoving the pills into Mary
Bliss's hand.

"Drugs?" Mary Bliss was appalled.

"Shut up and swallow," Katharine said. She picked
up her own Diet Coke and held it to Mary Bliss's lips.
"Drink it down, now."

Mary Bliss did as she was told. She squeezed
her eyes shut. As the pills slid down the back of her
throat, she had a vision. The beginning of a down-
ward spiral. She could see it now, drugs and Diet
Coke. Valley of the Dolls, in Fair Oaks, Georgia.

Still, she needed some help in coping this morning.
This once wouldn't make her an addict, would it?

She swallowed, then burped a little from the car-
bonation.

"What was that?" she asked, reaching for a napkin
to mop her face. "Halcion? Ativan?"

"Midol," Katharine said. "With a diuretic chaser.
Don't hate me for telling you this, but I *am* your best
friend. And I think you're retaining water, Mary Bliss.
Now. What's this shit about Parker?"

7

Katharine's kitchen was trashed. Empty Diet Coke cans littered the stylish black-and-white tiled floor. The Sara Lee had lasted only five minutes into Mary Bliss's detailed accounting of her disastrous financial situation. Katharine had pulled out a box of Gino's frozen mini-pizzas, a bag of ranch-style Doritos, and a jar of peach salsa. The salsa made her thirsty, so Katharine whipped up a batch of banana daquiris in the blender. She ate and drank while Mary Bliss talked. The awfuller the story got, the hungrier and thirstier Katharine got.

Once the diuretics kicked in, Mary Bliss talked and cried and peed and kept drinking all of Katharine's expensive bottled water, but she wouldn't eat a thing.

By noon, they were both nauseous and exhausted.

After a while, they moved into the den, where they lolled on the matching sofas facing Charlie Weidman's big-screen TV, which was tuned to *Oprah*, but with the sound turned down.

"You're really broke?" Katharine asked again. "And you're sure he's really gone?"

Mary Bliss nodded. "That's why I was so late. I called the branch manager at the bank to have them double-check the computers. I called the mortgage company too, and the 'customer courtesy' line kept me on hold for forty-five minutes. When the girl finally got on the line it took her about a minute to tell me that Parker hasn't paid the house note since February. Then I called Libby. You know, Parker's assistant. She was as shocked as I was."

For the first time that morning, Mary Bliss cracked an honest-to-God smile.

"At least I know he didn't run off with Libby. I was always sort of secretly jealous of her, if you want to know the truth. Parker used to talk about what a terrific-looking neck she had. Like Audrey Hepburn's. And she wore the cutest clothes. You know, Ann Taylor, that kind of thing.

"Anyway, the office phone had been disconnected. I called her at home. Libby was as hysterical as I was. When she got in to the office this morning, the building manager was having the janitor haul their files and stuff into storage. They wouldn't let her in. Said Parker was three months in arrears. And Libby's paycheck bounced. Her bank said Parker's business account was closed on Friday."

"What about your stocks and bonds and stuff?" Katharine asked.

"Not good," Mary Bliss said. "I called our stockbroker. He was surprised to hear from me. Parker told him I had malignant bone cancer and that's why he was liquidating our accounts. Because the insurance company wouldn't pay for the bone marrow transplant, because it's considered experimental."

"The son of a bitch," Katharine shouted. "Parker Son-of-a-Bitchin' McGowan. No offense, M. B., but I never would have thought he had the balls for something like this. I mean, to give you bone marrow cancer. Jeez. That is cold."

"I know," Mary Bliss said, sniffing. "This from a man whose idea of a walk on the wild side was ordering chocolate jimmies on his fat-free frozen yogurt."

Katharine drummed her long nails on the top of the cocktail table. Mary Bliss gave her a look, and Katharine put her hands in her lap.

"He's cleaned out checking and savings, sold your stocks, and the house could go into foreclosure at any time. Credit cards?"

"Maxed out."

"Your car?"

"Paid off," Mary Bliss said. "Of course, the book value on a ninety-eight minivan with eighty thousand miles on it isn't much."

"At least you've got your wheels," Katharine said grimly. "What about insurance?"

Mary Bliss sighed. "I've got health insurance coverage for me and Erin through the school system. And there's my life insurance policy through school too. Parker always said it cost too much to have us on his company plan. Although, he had Eula on the plan, of course. As vice president of the company. Cute, huh?"

"He's a pig," Katharine said.

"It's just semantics now," Mary Bliss said. "The company's kaput. Anyway, his note said Eula was taken care of. So that's something, I guess."

"Don't teachers get paid all summer, even though school's out?"

"Oh yeah," Mary Bliss said. "My paycheck might just cover this month's light bill."

"The weasel. The fucking weasel. What did you tell Erin?"

"Just that he was out of town on business. She thinks he's in Dallas."

"Any idea where he might really be?"

"The Lexus is gone. And he ordered two suitcases and some sport shirts from Land's End. You know Parker, he hasn't bought his own clothes since we got engaged. I checked with the mail-order people. He had the stuff delivered to his office. That's about all the detecting I was up to this morning."

An uneasy silence fell over the den. On the big-screen TV, Oprah was hugging a small, squirming wheelchair-bound child. Katharine's finger-drumming stepped up. She cleared her throat.

"Another woman?"

"I don't know," Mary Bliss said. "It was the first thing I thought of. A man like Parker, he's used to being taken care of. First Eula took care of him, then me, then Libby. Just at the office, though. But who? Who else could he have been carrying on with?"

She gave Katharine a searching look.

"You'd have told me if you knew something, wouldn't you?"

Katharine looked hurt. "Are you kidding? Didn't I just tell you about the water-retention thing? Wasn't I the one who let you in on the fact that your ankles are just the teeniest bit beefy for capri pants? M. B., if I'd even suspected what the prick was up to, I would have been all over him like white on rice. But he was too damn sneaky. I didn't have a clue. And I'll tell you what. If anybody would have known, it would be me. I sense things. You know that."

And Mary Bliss did. Katharine had an amazing ability to look at a man and know what kind of low-down behavior he was indulging in. Even with Charlie, she'd suspected months and months before she'd found the first shred of evidence.

Now they were both drumming their fingertips.

"You want my lawyer's phone number?" Katharine asked, breaking the silence.

"For what?"

"For the divorce, fool."

Mary Bliss lifted her chin, steely-eyed. She felt calm for the first time that morning. "No divorce," she said. "I want him dead."

Katharine patted her hand. "I know, shug. For what he's done to you, and to Erin, and to women everywhere, I want him dead too. I want Parker McGowan hurt. I want him stoned and stripped, and dragged naked through the streets of Fair Oaks. And we can do that. My lawyer is the most vicious, ruthless woman you have ever met in your life. She even scares me. She will put an ass-kicking on Parker that he will never forget."

"It's not enough," Mary Bliss said quietly. "Dead won't even be enough."

Katharine nodded again. She had felt this same way, the first time she'd seen Charlie get in that woman's car outside his office. She'd even had a handgun, a little .22 that she'd bought after a couple of break-ins in Fair Oaks, in the car that day. It was right there in her Prada handbag. She'd gotten the pistol, clenched it in her fist, thought seriously about shooting Charlie, and his little slut, right then and there.

But she hadn't been fast enough. And anyway, she'd never actually learned how to fire the thing. But the will, the intent, was there. After she'd found her lawyer, Gina Aldehoff, Gina told her lots of her clients wanted to kill their ex.

"But there's no future in homicide," Gina told her. "Divorce is better. No stains. Trust me, it'll be just like that country music song."

Katharine didn't listen to country music, and she was shocked that her Harvard-educated lawyer did.

"What song is that?"

"I'll get you the CD," Gina said, grinning. "It's called, 'She Got the Goldmine, I Got the Shaft.'"

8

Mary Bliss clenched her fists so tightly that she could feel her nails cutting into the flesh of her palms, feel the warm blood oozing from the tiny cuts.

She'd been reciting scripture to herself all the way over to the Fair Oaks Assisted Living Facility, trying to keep herself calm, trying to figure a way to make Parker's mama tell her what she knew.

"Keep sweet," she kept telling herself. "Just keep sweet."

Now, Eula McGowan was lifting the lid of the CorningWare casserole, frowning down at its contents, as though she had not seen the same food hundreds of other times.

Oh no. Now, unbelievably, she was holding it up to her nose, sniffing, actually sniffing, like an old bloodhound. Come to think of it, Eula's fleshy, wrinkled face did remind Mary Bliss of a bloodhound.

Mary Bliss smiled at the notion. Eula, a bloodhound. The old bitch.

She found it weirdly amusing that Eula gave herself credit for Mary Bliss's cooking skills.

Eula had made it clear from the start that Parker had married beneath himself.

Eula had taken it upon herself to educate Mary Bliss about the fine points of cooking. She had drawn up a list on the back of a brown paper sack. Duke's mayonnaise. Heinz ketchup. Luzianne tea bags. White Lily all-purpose flour. Swan's Down shortening. Chicken of the Sea chunk white tuna. Martha White grits. Dixie Crystal sugar. Campbell's cream of mushroom soup. These were the keystones of any good southern cook's kitchen, according to Eula.

Not that Eula could cook. Not on your life. That was Lena's job. In Eula's time, no white woman of means did anything more in the way of cooking than an occasional trifle at Christmas, or maybe some peanut brittle, something like that.

Mary Bliss watched while Eula stared down at the banana pudding, trying not to look too eager. The old woman frowned down at the meringue, as though she could smell something . . . off.

"How am I supposed to eat all of this," she fussed, waving her liver-spotted hand at the banana pudding casserole. "Think I'm some kind of field hand or something?"

Mary Bliss forced her lips into a smile but knew it was more of a grimace. Her jaw muscles ached from the effort of smiling and trying to be pleasant.

"The nurses can put it in the refrigerator for you, Meemaw. Then you can have some whenever you like."

"Hah!" Eula said, snorting. "They keep urine samples in Dixie cups in that icebox. I wouldn't eat anything out of there if they paid me."

"All right," Mary Bliss said slowly. "I'll leave the pudding and your dinner in this little cooler right here. Maybe you'd like to share with Mrs. Caldwell next door, or some of your other visitors."

Other visitors, Mary Bliss thought. What a laugh. Eula was such a nasty old witch, she had no visitors other than family. The other women in her bridge club down in Griffin were either dead, in a nursing home themselves, or relieved at not having to put up with Eula McGowan anymore.

"Verlene Caldwell has the worst gas in the world," Eula was saying. "Smokes like a chimney too. Give that woman bananas and there's no telling what might happen. This whole place could go up in a cloud of smoke."

Be nice, Mary Bliss repeated to herself. You've got to be nice to Parker's mama. Be nice, and she'll tell you what she knows. But Mary Bliss wanted to throttle Eula, wanted to conk her over the head with the goddamn banana pudding dish. Wished she'd put ground-up glass in with the bananas.

Or poison. Ant poison. She'd read about a woman over in Anniston, not far from where Mary Bliss had grown up in Alabama, who'd killed off most of her family with Ant-Rid. The woman had killed her first two husbands, her stepmother, her mother-in-law, and a second cousin. Mary Bliss thought the lady had put the Ant-Rid in with some home-canned chow-chow. Or maybe it was watermelon-rind pickle.

Forty-two hundred dollars a month. That's what it cost to keep Eula McGowan in a private bedroom and bath at Fair Oaks Assisted Living. Another six hundred a month for all the medicines keeping her shriveled old heart beating. Mary Bliss had no idea what the doctor's bills came to. Parker's insurance company always paid those bills.

Now there was no company. And Parker had vanished. Just like the Home Depot stock and the Vanguard mutual fund.

Mary Bliss spooned a mound of pudding into the flowered china dish she'd brought from home and handed Eula a spoon.

The old lady didn't miss the slight tremor in her daughter-in-law's hand. She dove into the food, shoveling it into her face as fast as she could, inhaling the fumes of home cooking and counter-ripened bananas.

Mary Bliss folded her hands in her lap, willing herself to be calm.

"Meemaw," she said slowly. "Where's Parker?"

Eula turned the spoon over and licked it with a huge pink tongue that reminded Mary Bliss of cured fatback. She wanted to gag.

"Gone," Eula said, pudding spilling out of her mouth.

"I know that," Mary Bliss said. "He left me a note. Did he tell you where he was going? I'm really worried about him, Meemaw. This isn't like him."

"Worried about money, I 'spect," Eula said, enjoying Mary Bliss's misery.

Mary Bliss's face reddened. She'd been trying so hard. So very hard.

Slowly, she stood up from the molded plastic visitor's chair, and she closed the swinging door that led to the hallway.

She knelt down on the linoleum floor beside her mother-in-law's wheelchair. Her face felt hot, and her breathing was rapid. She put her face very close to Eula's, and she took Eula's skull and held it tight between her two hands. Now the shaking had stopped. She could feel the little bird-bones beneath her fingers.

Eula's cataract-milky eyes bulged, and on the purple-tinged network of veins on her forehead, one throbbed crazily. Mary Bliss put one thumb on either side of Eula's temples, and she asked Jesus Christ, her personal savior, to keep her from doing this terrible thing she felt driven to do. Failing that, she asked the Lord to keep her from getting caught and thrown in prison, sodomized by girl gangs and prison guards, and then being given that lethal injection they talked about on the news.

Georgia, as Katharine had already reminded her, was full to bursting with lesbian girl gangs, and after all, this was a death penalty state.

Pausing from prayer, Mary Bliss felt moved to speak.

"Old lady," she whispered in a hoarse voice. "My house note comes due in two weeks. Erin's first-semester tuition is due in a month. Your sorry, no-account, spineless she-goat of a son has milked us dry and disappeared into thin air. There's no money left. He's cashed in his life insurance policy and taken off somewhere. Now. If you don't tell me exactly where Parker is, right this New York minute, I'm going to squash you like a mealy bug."

Eula wheezed like a pawnshop accordion.

Mary Bliss kept her grip tight and tried to remember the name of Katharine's lawyer, just in case Meemaw stroked out, just to spite her.

"Island," Eula gasped.

"What was that?" Mary Bliss asked, leaning closer. She let her thumbs rest loosely on the tips of Meemaw's ears.

"Some island," Eula said, sucking in air as quickly as she could. "That's all I know. That's all he told me. An island." Her hands clawed for the nurse's buzzer, but Mary Bliss clamped her own hand down on top of Eula's.

"You better be telling me the truth," Mary Bliss said. "I'm friends with every nurse and aide over here. There's not a one of them who wouldn't hesitate to do me a favor. Any favor. You understand what I'm talking about here, Meemaw?"

Eula nodded once.

"All right, then," Mary Bliss said. "Enjoy your dinner. And if you hear from Parker, I better hear from you right quick. It's not only me he's abandoned, you know. There's your granddaughter too, you know. Erin. If you don't care about me, you might think about her. She's the only grandchild you've got. The last McGowan."

Eula winced as the door to her room slammed behind her departing daughter-in-law.

Somehow, after leaving Meemaw's room, Mary Bliss managed to pull herself together. She'd checked with the Fair Oaks Manor business manager, and Parker had been truthful about that, at least. Meemaw's bill was all paid up for two more years.

When she got home, Mary Bliss checked the answering machine, poured herself a Diet Coke, and listened. There were two messages from bill collectors, one from Katharine, and one from Nancye Bowden.

"Mary Bliss," Nancye had said. "You've got to call me. Right away."

The last person she felt like talking to was Nancye Bowden. Besides, Erin would be home from work by six o'clock. Mary Bliss fixed her daughter's favorite supper, chili-roni and tossed salad with bleu cheese dressing, and a pan of corn bread.

She herself could not eat. But she found a half bottle of chilled white wine in the refrigerator, which she swigged out of the bottle while dialing Katharine's number.

Katharine picked up on the first ring. She'd had caller ID installed on her phone when she'd first suspected that Charlie was fooling around on her. It was how she'd discovered that when Charlie called to tell her he was playing a round of golf with a client, he was really calling from that bitch-whore Tara's apartment.

"What did you find out?" Katharine demanded. "Did she tell you anything?"

"Meemaw's playing senile," Mary Bliss reported. "I threatened to rip the nitroglycerin patches right off her arm if she didn't tell me what she knew, but I don't think she believed me."

"Didn't she tell you anything at all?" Katharine asked.

"Island. He told her he was going to an island. Or so she claims."

"The prick," Katharine said. "I could kill him myself."

"Not if I get to him first," Mary Bliss said. She thought she heard a car in the driveway. "Listen, Erin's home. I've got to go. Remember, not a word to anybody. I mean it too, Katharine. Not anybody."

"As if I would," Katharine said. "Anyway, nobody would believe it. Parker McGowan running away from home. And at his age."

9

She was peering out the window, watching a black sedan with tinted windows pull into her driveway, then back out and leave, when the phone rang.

"Mom?" Static on the line. Erin must be using her cell phone. "Just wanted to let you know I'm going to the movies with a couple of girls from the store. Then we'll probably go to Starbucks afterward. I'll be home around midnight. Okay?"

Mary Bliss looked at the chili-roni casserole on top of the oven. "But I fixed dinner already. Your favorite. Anyway, didn't you just go to a movie last night?"

"Mo-om. It's summer. There's nothing else to do. Anyway, just put dinner in the fridge. I'll take it to work for lunch tomorrow. Is that cool?"

"I guess," Mary Bliss said. "What are you going to see? Not another of those horrible slasher movies, I hope."

Erin giggled. "I'm nearly eighteen, Mom. Too old for Disney. It's the new Mel Gibson movie. Don't worry, there's hardly any slashing at all. And I won't be late. Did Daddy call?"

Mary Bliss gulped and thought about what to say.

"Haven't heard from him," she said, her voice gay, even carefree.

"Well, did you figure out where he went? Did you ask Libby?"

Mary Bliss's throat constricted. "No, uh, Libby was out of the office all day." Which was true.

Erin sighed. "What a rat. Daddy was supposed to take me to buy tires for the Honda tomorrow. Guess it'll have to wait for next weekend."

"Probably," Mary Bliss said. She added new tires to the growing list of expenditures in her head. She'd have to find the money for the tires somehow. Couldn't have Erin running around Atlanta on bald Firestones.

"Drive careful," she said, and Erin promised, and they hung up.

Mary Bliss went into Parker's office and got the big atlas down off the bookshelf. She took it back to the kitchen table, got the bottle of white wine out of the refrigerator, and filled up an iced tea glass with it.

She was running a finger down the map index, paused at the Azores, when someone rapped smartly at the back door.

Mary Bliss whirled around in her chair and saw a tall man in a white baseball cap standing there. The door was unlocked, of course. She was so used to leaving everything unlocked. Maybe that was where she'd gone wrong. Maybe she should have locked up tight, kept Parker at home where he belonged, instead of taking off for some island somewhere. But the door was unlocked, her husband was gone, and suddenly she felt incredibly vulnerable.

"Mary Bliss?" The man's voice was apologetic. "It's me, Randy Bowden. I didn't mean to scare you."

"Randy," she said, her voice giddy. "Of course you didn't scare me. My mind was just a million miles away is all." Literally.

Her cheeks flaming, she got up and opened the door for her neighbor.

"How in the world are you?" she asked, her voice high and squeaky, taut with nervous tension.

Randy was in a bad state and they both knew it. There were deep circles under his eyes. His graying blonde hair was shaggy under the cap, and his shorts and T-shirt hung baggily on his already lanky frame. He'd lost at least five pounds since Memorial Day weekend, when she'd last seen him at the country club.

"I'm all right," Randy said. It was his stock phrase. People didn't know what to say to somebody whose life had gone to hell. "How are you?" he asked, for lack of anything better to say.

Mary Bliss stood there, unable to answer. She was rooted to the kitchen floor. She didn't want him in her kitchen, didn't want his naked pain so close, so close it could be catching, like cooties, or cancer, or the plague. Go on back across the street, she wanted to tell Randy Bowden. We'll both wave and pretend nothing bad has happened to either of us.

"Would you like a glass of wine?" she said finally, gesturing toward the bottle on the table. She took the atlas and shoved it under a stack of cookbooks on the shelf.

Randy looked around the room. "Is, uh, Parker at home?"

She stared down at the table. He knew. He had to know. And if Randy Bowden knew, it must be all over Fair Oaks that Parker McGowan had run off and abandoned his family. Everybody at the club, everybody on her block, even the big-haired lady at the dry cleaners and the girls on her tennis team, even that pimply, hormone-charged lifeguard at the pool knew that Mary Bliss's husband had discarded her like an empty cigarette pack.

"No, um, Parker's out of town on business. Can I take a message for him?" The lie came easily, and she took a long sip of wine.

Now it was Randy's turn to blush. His pale blue eyes blinked rapidly behind the tortoiseshell-framed eyeglasses. He shifted from one foot to the other, ran a pale tongue over his lips.

"Maybe, if you don't mind, I'd love a glass of wine. If it's not any trouble."

"No trouble," she said smoothly, and was glad to occupy her hands getting down a proper wine glass, a paper napkin, pouring and handing it to him.

The two of them nearly emptied their glasses in one embarrassed gulp.

Randy leaned a bony hip against the kitchen counter.

"Actually, Mary Bliss, you're the one I really need to talk to. It's kind of embarrassing. In fact, it's embarrassing as hell. Could I have a little more of that wine?"

She nodded and poured it out, hardly spilling any.

"You know Nancye and I are separated, right?"

She nodded and looked down at her wine glass, then up at Randy. "Somebody mentioned it yesterday," she said. "I'm always the last to know about these things. I'm so sorry, Randy."

For some reason, it was important that she let him know that she hadn't been gossiping about him. Even though, of course, she had. But everybody in Fair Oaks was talking about the Bowdens. And that was understood. In a small town like theirs, juicy gossip was the coin of the realm.

Randy pushed his glasses up higher on the bridge of his nose. He'd lost so much weight, even his glasses were too big.

"She walked out. Just up and walked out on all of us. My lawyer says I can't get custody of the kids without a fight. He says it's gonna get nasty." He laughed, but he didn't smile. "I didn't think things could get any nastier than they already were. Guess I was being naive. Right now, we've got joint custody. But, uh, Nancye's behavior has gotten kind of, uh, you know."

"Really?" Mary Bliss coughed. "I had no idea."

He picked at his thumbnail. Mary Bliss knew he worked in downtown Atlanta, doing something at the bank that used to be C&S but was now called something else. His hands were unusual for a banker, though, callused, red, crisscrossed with cuts and scrapes.

"God," he blurted. "I can't do this." He sighed. "I was going to ask you to do something for me. It's disgusting. So, never mind." He shook his head, jerked abruptly away from the counter, and knocked over the wine glass. He grabbed for it, but it fell to the floor, shattering into bits.

"God," he exclaimed. "I'm sorry. What a moron."

"It's nothing," Mary Bliss said, running to the sink for paper towels and a whisk broom. She was babbling, trying to make him feel better. "Just an ugly old cheap wine glass you got free with a ten-dollar purchase. At the Winn-Dixie."

She clapped her hands to her mouth as soon as the words had escaped. Winn-Dixie. He must think she was awful.

"I'm so sorry," Randy said, stooping now, holding out the dustpan. "I'll replace this. I think we've got a set of these glasses at the house. Nancye goes to Winn-Dixie all the time. I think she likes the meat."

Mary Bliss gasped, then started to choke. Thank heavens Katharine wasn't here. She would be rolling on the floor, hooting and screaming with laughter. Katharine had a very smutty mind.

The more she thought of Katharine, the more her unintentional faux pas worked on her. She started to giggle but clamped her lips shut, trying to suppress the laughter. Poor Randy would think she was a mental case. The giggle kept welling up, and now tears were streaming down her face, and oh, God, she thought she might wet her pants.

Randy sat back on his heels, astonished. He hadn't expected anybody, especially one of Nancye's friends, to sympathize with him. Nancye was telling everybody in town that he was abusive, drank too much, was a control freak. Everybody loved Nancye. She was the life of every party. People were choosing up sides, avoiding him. What other lies had his wife been telling on him?

Mary Bliss stood up, her knees pressed together. She fanned her face with her hand. "I'm sorry, Randy. I really am. I shouldn't drink wine this early. What was it you were going to ask me? Please." She touched his arm. "I'd like to help. I can tell you're in pain."

He took the dustpan full of glass bits and dumped it in her trash can. "Has Nancye called you? Mentioned anything to you about me?"

Her eyes widened. "She left a message on my answering machine today. I haven't called her back yet. Why? What's going on?"

"She's called all our friends. Practically everybody in Fair Oaks. Even people we don't know very well. I'm surprised she waited this long to call you."

"We're not really that close," Mary Bliss explained.

"Close enough to hear her scream when I beat her?" Randy asked, gazing straight at her. "Close enough to see her run from the house in her nightgown to get away from her abusive husband?"

"What on earth are you talking about?"

"That's what she told her lawyer. That's why she's calling up all the people who live around us. To get somebody to go on the record that I used her as a punching bag."

"That's absurd," Mary Bliss said. "I never heard anything like that. In fact, I always thought you two were such a darling couple. I used to tell Parker, 'Look how Randy Bowden holds hands with Nancye when they go for a walk.' I saw the two of you, last year, at the Sinclairs' Christmas party, slow-dancing to Johnny Mathis singing 'Twelfth of Never.' The way you held her, I felt so, oh, jealous, I guess. Parker's not very demonstrative like that. Not in public."

"The Sinclairs' party," Randy said. "How could I forget? She told our pastor I got mad at her for dancing with Charlie Weidman that night and slugged her in the stomach in the car on the way home," Randy said.

"Nancye danced with Charlie at that party?" Mary Bliss said, surprised.

"Nancye likes to dance."

In all the years she'd known him, Mary Bliss had never seen Charlie Weidman dance. Not ever. That

Nancye Bowden must be quite a piece of goods. Quite a piece, Katharine would say.

Mary Bliss chewed her bottom lip.

"Never mind," Randy said, moving toward the back door. "It's not your problem. It just bugs me, you know? The idea that you and Parker might think I was that kind of guy. Nancye and I had our problems, but I swear to God, I never lifted a hand to her. It was never anything like that. Not even when we were separated last time."

"You were separated before?" This man was full of surprises.

"Four years ago, right after Christmas," Randy said. "Nancye told everybody I was up in Charlotte, at a bank training seminar. We didn't even tell the kids, actually. It only lasted about five weeks."

A training seminar, Mary Bliss thought. That's what she could tell anybody who asked about Parker. He was out of town. At a seminar. But Nancye Bowden had already used that fib. She'd have to come up with something better. More original. That would be a challenge. To make up bigger lies than Nancye Bowden, the town slut.

"I think it's horrible, that she would accuse you of physical violence," Mary Bliss said. "If she calls me back, I'll tell her straight out. I'll call her a liar right to her face. And I'll tell that to your lawyer too, if you want."

"Thanks," Randy said. "Thanks for believing me. I hope somebody else will too." He opened the back door and walked outside.

"And I'm gonna have her kicked off the carpool too," Mary Bliss called out, watching him plod up the driveway, back toward his own house.

Damn tootin'.

10

Making lists kept the crazies at bay.

She'd always kept lists, ever since she was old enough to write. Boys I like. Mean girls at school. Books I want to read someday. Foods Parker won't eat. Erin's Christmas list. Emergency contact numbers.

First thing, Mary Bliss made a list of all the marital casualties in Fair Oaks over the past five years. Alphabetically. It was the schoolteacher in her, she guessed. Wynnie and Robert Adair. Debra and Paul Ammerman. Nancye and Randy Bowden, Sidney and Kip Dubinsky. Rebecca and Mike Killaney.

She stopped when she got to Patti Mitchell and Jake Myers. "The hippies on the hill," everybody in Fair Oaks called them, because they both drove battered Subarus and had a solar heating unit on their roof. Patti had kept her maiden name and she never shaved her legs or wore a bra and she was always running around recycling all the time. Parker said they were probably never married anyway, so technically, maybe they weren't divorced. Feeling defiant, Mary Bliss decided to include the hippies on the hill, listing them as Mitchell-Myers.

So many more couples, she had to get out the city directory to remember all the names. Still, there were bound to be marital fatalities she didn't know about. People who were older than the people the McGowans ran with. People who were younger. Childless career couples, "yuppie scum," Charlie Weidman called them, couples who were too busy to join the club or socialize with their neighbors, who only thought of Fair Oaks as a "desirable in-town zip code."

And then there were the people who lived in the Oaks, which was the high-priced cluster home development Manning Jelks had built on the site of the old Fair Oaks Dairy property. The Oaks was a "gated community" with a security hut at the entrance and a guard who would call ahead to see if you were expected. It had great big houses on teeny-tiny lots, everything new and shiny, from the brass doorknobs to the close-mown Bermuda sod at front. All the houses were made of that pale-pink European stucco, and they all had rear entrances to the garages. Although it was only a couple blocks from her own house, Mary Bliss didn't really know anybody who lived in the Oaks.

The streets over there all had theme names like Live Oak and White Oak and Red Oak and Pin Oak. "Oakies" was what the people in Fair Oaks called them. They might join the Fair Oaks Country Club, but they were still separate, had their own book clubs and tennis teams and supper clubs, their own lives. Their domestic difficulties were unknown to the rest of Fair Oaks.

Mary Bliss decided more research was necessary. She wrote down "The Oaks???" and continued working her way through the alphabet.

When she got to the Weidmans, she put her pencil down. Mary Bliss hated to give up on Charlie and Katharine. To put them on the list was an omen, she decided. The divorce wasn't final yet. Things could still change.

Without the Weidmans, she came up with seventeen couples who'd called it quits. There were 320 families listed in the Fair Oaks City Directory. Mary Bliss was terrible with math, but if she got the calculator out of Parker's desk, she could probably figure the percentages. She was cross-referencing the list by street when Katharine rattled the back doorknob.

"Boo!" Katharine said as Mary Bliss unlocked and opened the door. "When did you start locking the barn door?"

"After the stallion ran away," Mary Bliss said, locking the door after Katherine. "Aren't you scared, without Charlie living there?"

"Scared he might come back," Katharine said, picking up the nearly empty bottle of wine and giving her a questioning look. "Anyway, I'm not living alone. Chip's a man."

"Chip's going back to school in August. And you told me yourself, he's never home."

"I like having the house to myself," Katharine said. "I have a rich fantasy life, you know."

Mary Bliss gave her a searching look.

"What?" Katharine said. "I'm free, white, and twenty-one, aren't I?"

"I don't want to know," Mary Bliss said, shaking her head and folding her arms across her chest.

Katharine smiled dreamily. "My favorite fantasy is the one where I'm asleep, and I wake up, and some thug is breaking into my house, rifling through my lingerie drawer. I stifle a scream, he turns around, looks at me. I'm naked, did I mention that?"

"I just assumed," Mary Bliss said.

"He walks slowly toward the bed, climbs in, and ravages me."

"Would he be masked?" Mary Bliss asked.

"With a black silk scarf."

"Would you be tied up?"

Katharine ripped the top off the half-pound bag of peanut M&M's she'd brought along. She shoved a handful of candy into her mouth and considered while she chewed. She'd brought along a bottle of wine also. Katharine was an extremely thoughtful friend. Now she poured glasses for both of them.

"Maybe not. I think that would be sick and depraved. I only have healthy, normal fantasies, you know. This would be what you would call consensual ravaging."

"I've thought about that myself," Mary Bliss confessed, emboldened by all the wine she'd been sipping. She tried an M&M, but it tasted like chalk, so she spit it into the trash.

"Only my guy breaks in while I'm in the shower. With the bathroom all steamed up, and he takes his clothes off, and gets in the shower with me, and we soap each other off, and I can't really tell what he looks like, what with the steam and all. And we do it, standing up, right there in the shower."

"That's pretty good," Katharine said admiringly. "Is there music?"

"Al Jarreau. 'Masquerade.' Erin gave me the CD for my birthday a couple of years ago."

"This shower fantasy of yours. Is it actually original to you? I mean, no offense, but wasn't that a made-for-TV movie a couple years ago? With Valerie Bertinelli?"

"Absolutely not," Mary Bliss said proudly. "You know I only watch PBS."

Mary Bliss tried to flip the pages of her notebook so that Katharine wouldn't see her divorce list and think she was having a breakdown.

"I've been thinking about places Parker could have gone."

"Good," Katharine said, nodding and chewing. "We need to know where he is. So we can hunt him down and kill him."

"Me personally?"

Mary Bliss was raised Methodist. Spiritually-wise, she felt underprepared to break the First Commandment. After all, it was the first thing she'd ever learned to write, in Sunday school. Thou Shalt Not Kill. Emotionally, however, she could kill Parker right this second, with her bare hands.

"Who did you have in mind?" Katharine asked.

Mary Bliss just looked at her.

"Mary Bliss, I love you like a sister, but if I ever *do* kill a man, it would be Charlie Weidman, not Parker McGowan," Katharine said.

They sipped their wine and Mary Bliss idly flipped the pages of the atlas, looking for likely island destinations. Bora-Bora didn't seem likely. Long plane trips made Parker's ankles swell. Catalina was off the coast of California, and Parker thought everybody in California was crazy.

"What if I just *said* he was dead?"

"Huh?"

"I meant to tell you. Randy Bowden was over here a little while ago. And he told me that he and Nancye were actually separated once before, about four years ago. And Nancye was too embarrassed to tell anybody the truth, so she just said he was away at a banking seminar."

"He told you that?"

Mary Bliss nodded emphatically.

"I wonder why he came back?" Katharine said. "I remember that time he was gone. The rumor going around was, she had an affair with the boys' Little League coach while he was supposedly up in Charlotte."

"Wouldn't surprise me," Mary Bliss said. "But that's not the point. The point is, I could just tell people Parker was dead. Like Nancye told people Randy was in Charlotte, instead of the Days Inn in East Point. It wouldn't be too hard to make Parker seem dead."

"I'll say," Katharine said, a little too quickly.

"Don't be mean," Mary Bliss said. "Listen. I could have a nice funeral. We could make your mother's chicken salad, maybe some tomato aspic and those little tea cakes. Parker despises aspic, so it would be my chance to use that *Southern Living* recipe. Nothing too showy. Afterwards, I could collect his life insurance, and I could pay all the bills and Erin and I could stay right here in Fair Oaks."

Katharine's jaw hung slack in disbelief. "Let me get this right. Just *say* he's dead? But he's really not?"

She took the wine bottle and hid it behind her chair. "That's enough wine for you, Mary Bliss McGowan. You're starting to scare me."

"You're the only one who knows he's run off," Mary Bliss pointed out. "Everybody else will think he went out of town on business, like he always does. And then he'll just . . . die."

"What about Meemaw?" Katharine said. "Aren't you forgetting about her? She knows the truth. And she'd never let you get away with that kind of thing."

"Alzheimer's disease," Mary Bliss said, a glint coming to her eyes. "You know how Meemaw is. She's always been a terrible liar, and everybody knows it. Her memory's not what it used to be. And she makes up the most incredible stories. Last week she told everybody in the nursing home that she'd been Ethel Merman's understudy on Broadway. She kept belting out *There's No Business Like Show Business* during crafts class. Parker and I had been talking about having her moved over to the memory-impaired unit. That's nursing-home talk for Senile Street."

"You'll never pull one over on that old lady," Katharine said. "Besides Meemaw, what about his secretary? She knows Parker closed the business."

"Libby? She's so naive, she'll believe anything I tell her. I'll just say he closed it down because he was depressed," Mary Bliss said quickly. "Having a midlife crisis." She was making this up as she went along, enjoying herself. It was sort of fun. More fun than worrying about how she and Erin would live on a teacher's salary.

"I didn't want to say anything before," Mary Bliss said, her tone hushed. "But Parker had a gambling problem. He was deeply in debt."

"Parker McGowan?" Katharine giggled.

"He was leading a double life. A lot of those 'consulting trips' of his were really to Mississippi," Mary Bliss said. "The blackjack tables."

"Now I know you've lost your mind," Katharine said. "Nobody would believe that."

"But that part is really true," Mary Bliss insisted. "He really did love to go to Tunica to play blackjack. I never told you because I was embarrassed. I mean, how low-rent. Tunica. Not even Vegas or Tahoe or Atlantic City. He went on these chartered bus trips."

"Nice try," Katharine said. "But it's not working for me. Even if it is partly true."

"I can show you the credit card receipts," Mary Bliss offered.

"Not good enough," Katharine said. "Reporting your husband dead is serious stuff, hon. Once you do it, you can't take it back. You've gotta come up with a story that will stick. Something tragic, yet believable. And a body. What are you going to do about a body? And how about this—what if Parker changes his mind? Decides to come back and give marriage another shot? Or if he comes back and files for divorce?"

"He's never coming back," Mary Bliss said. "You don't really know Parker. What he's like inside. He must have been planning this thing for months. Years maybe. He took his contact lenses. Left his prescription glasses, all his business suits, still in the closet. I know Parker McGowan. He's gone for good. So as far as I'm concerned, he's dead."

"But how?" Katharine repeated. "How does he die?"

"Violently," Mary Bliss said. "He owes me that much."

11

"It's stuffy in here," Mary Bliss said, fanning her face with her hands. "Or is that just me?"

Katharine shrugged. "Aren't you too young for menopause? How old are you, anyway?"

"I'm thirty-eight, and no, I'm not going through menopause." She got up and checked the air conditioner thermostat. "I'm roasting in here."

"It's Georgia," Katharine reminded her. "Summertime."

"I can't breathe," Mary Bliss said. "Let's go outside."

"Its ninety-two degrees outside, with about eleventy-hundred percent humidity," Katharine said. "And what about the mosquitoes? You can't see the sky for the swarms of mosquitoes."

Mary Bliss opened the cupboard under the sink and handed Katharine a bottle of bug spray. She got two

Diet Cokes out of the refrigerator and handed one to Katharine. "We drank all the wine. Here. Let's go play in the sprinklers."

They stepped outside and proceeded to mist themselves all over with the bug spray.

Katharine looked around appreciatively at Mary Bliss's house.

It was a shingled bungalow, painted the darkest gray Mary Bliss could find, with the trim picked out in bright white, and the doors painted a glossy black. The McGowans' house stood a little ways up a hummock, with a porch stretched across the front, with two big water oaks shading it. Mary Bliss kept red terra cotta planters on the porch steps brimming with ferns and green and white caladiums, and when the garden was overflowing, she left a basket by the front door, full of crookneck squash and zucchini and tomatoes, for any neighbors to help themselves to.

A sidewalk ran past at the bottom of the hill, and many was the night that Mary Bliss and Katharine sat up on the porch, hidden in the dense shade, trash-talking whoever was walking by. And they never even knew they were being discussed.

In the back, Mary Bliss had fenced the vegetable garden with a little cedar fence, and she'd hung a hammock between two sweet gum trees, and the sprinkler, an old-cast iron one she'd found in the garage when they'd moved in, swirled around and around, curved arms lowering and lifting with each rotation of the sprinkler, spraying the still evening air with the warm, sulfur-scented droplets.

Katharine leaned back against the back stoop and watched as Mary Bliss unbuttoned her sundress, let it fall around her ankles, and then stepped daintily out, as though she were in the better sportswear dressing room of the long-gone downtown Rich's department store.

Mary Bliss ran toward the sprinkler, whooped as the cold water splashed her, then ran in circles—letting it soak her, stopping to thrust her hair into the spray, then skipping around, turning and whooping some more.

If this wasn't a sight. Mary Bliss McGowan gone wild. Well, not wild enough to get teetotally naked, but certainly, she was running around in her Vanity Fair bra and modest white hip-hugger panties like an eighteen-year-old Chi O after her first kamikaze party. If the Shipsteads next door decided to come out on their backyard deck for some reason, they would get an eyeful of a nearly naked Mary Bliss McGowan.

"Are you drunk?" Katharine called.

"No," Mary Bliss answered. "Come on, Kate, come get wet. It's wonderful."

"You ever hear of a bathing suit?" Katharine asked. "Or better yet, the shower in the privacy of your own home?"

"I'm getting baptized," Mary Bliss said. She stood directly in front of the sprinkler, thrust her arms wide open, threw back her head, and opened her mouth wide, letting the water run in and sluice down her face.

"Baptized." Katharine shook her head, smiling. Maybe there was hope for Mary Bliss yet. Maybe marriage to Parker McGowan hadn't zombified her as totally as Katharine feared.

"In the name of the Father. And of the Son. And of the Holy Spirit," Mary Bliss hollered, thrashing her wet hair this way and that. She was standing on her tippy-toes, hugging her arms across her chest. "I christen me, Me."

She opened her eyes and smiled radiantly. Her hair was plastered to her head, her panties and bra transparent from the water.

She ran over to where Katharine sat on the porch stoop and shook her head like a dog, spraying Katharine with water.

"Stop," Katharine laughed, holding up a hand to shield her makeup from melting. "You're drunk or crazy, I don't know which."

"Neither," Mary Bliss said. "Guess what? I know how to do it. I know how to get rid of Parker."

"I can't wait to hear," Katharine said.

Mary Bliss grabbed her hand and tugged her to a standing position. "Come on," she insisted. "You've got to get baptized too. Then I'll tell you."

12

"I've been baptized," Katharine protested, but she was already unzipping her shorts, pulling her T-shirt over her head. "Anyway, I'm Catholic, and we're not into total immersion."

"This is sprinkling, Catholics believe in sprinkling, don't they?" Mary Bliss asked. Suddenly she had an answer to everything.

Katharine cringed as the first spray of cold water sliced across her face, chest, and thighs.

"Come on," Mary Bliss said. "You've got to keep moving. Do like I do."

So Katharine Weidman, age forty-five, found herself doing some kind of rain dance in the backyard of her best friend's house—wearing nothing but her black lace thong panties and Wonderbra.

When they'd danced and laughed themselves near dead, they went inside and put their dry clothes on again.

Katharine made a face when she saw the lukewarm casserole of chili-roni; instead she ordered beef Kowloon and garlic prawns and hot-and-sour soup from the Chinese delivery place up the street, and charged it to Charlie's Visa.

"So?" Katharine asked when they were down to the fortune cookies.

Mary Bliss adjusted the towel covering her hair. "Hmm?"

"The plan. You said you had a plan, for taking care of Parker. I got baptized, now I want to hear your plan."

"Accidental death," Mary Bliss said. "It's the best way."

"And what about a body? No insurance company is going to pay death benefits without a body."

"I know," Mary Bliss said. "So it has to be an accident where the body is never found. But nothing too sensational, you know? Nothing where there would be a big police investigation. So that lets out something like a plane crash or a fire or something like that."

"What's left?" Katharine asked.

"Well . . . ," Mary Bliss said. "Do you ever watch that Discovery Channel on cable?"

"No," Katharine said firmly. "I am not interested in the mating habits of sperm whales, or quantum physics or snowstorms in the Himalayas or any of that kind of thing. Anyway, I thought you only watched PBS."

"And Discovery," Mary Bliss said. "It's very educational. Anyway, a couple of years ago, when Parker first started traveling so much, I saw this true crime–type program. You know, it's not only science and nature on there. Anyway, this time I was watching, it was a show about this cute little married couple from Oklahoma. The wife was this kind of plain-looking girl, and the husband was a big brawny type. Anyway, they got married, and on their honeymoon, they went on one of those windjammer sailing trips, down in the Bahamas. They were way out at sea, and a big storm came up, real suddenly. And the husband radioed for help, that something had gone wrong with the sails, but all of a sudden, a big wave swept over the boat, swamped it, and the boat broke in half, and they were both swept into the water."

"I bet I know what happened," Katharine said, out of patience. "The wife drowned, and the husband survived. Is that what happened?"

"Just let me finish," Mary Bliss said, taking her own sweet time. "No, Miss Smarty-pants. Actually, the wife was able to grab a life jacket. When the Coast Guard came out looking for them, they found her, passed out from the heat and all, but they never did find him."

Katharine gave her a fishy look. "The husband died? Are you sure you got that right?"

"Dead sure," Mary Bliss said defiantly. "And when she got back to Oklahoma, or wherever it was that they lived, she cashed in a two-million-dollar life insurance policy they'd taken out, just before the wedding."

"What's the catch?" Katharine asked. "Are you telling me she planned the whole thing?"

"Yes, ma'am," Mary Bliss said. "It was her idea to take the sailing trip. They took a weekend sailing school together, down in Florida, a couple of months before the wedding. And that's where she met the other guy."

"There was another guy?" Katharine asked, sitting up straighter. "You didn't say there was another guy."

"She had to have an accomplice," Mary Bliss explained. "So she seduced this sailing instructor she met down in Florida. His name was Lars. When the couple went out on the windjammer, Lars followed them in another boat. And when they got far enough out to sea, she fixed her husband a drink, and of course she'd put some kind of tranquilizer or something in it, so he got real woozy. And when he'd about passed out, she radioed Lars on the other boat."

"What happened next?"

"Lars got on the sailboat's radio and acted like he was the husband. And when the wind really picked up, they just sort of slid the husband overboard. And he sank like a rock. So the wife puts on her life jacket, and they did something to the sail, to break it somehow, to make it look like the wind did it. Then the wife got on Lars's boat while the storm was really bad, and when it died down, she got on the life raft and acted all stunned and confused."

"What about Lars?"

"He got on his own radio and contacted the Coast Guard, and they told him they'd heard the distress call and were on the way. So he backed on off and let them rescue her."

"Slick," Katharine said. "But, how did they get caught?"

"It turns out neither of them was as bright as they thought," Mary Bliss said with a sigh. "The husband's mother was a real bitch. She never liked the wife. The mother-in-law hired a private investigator. He started following the wife, and of course found out everything."

"And they got caught."

"Lars turned state's evidence," Mary Bliss said. "He told the police it was all the wife's idea. She got a life sentence, Lars got six to fifteen."

Now Katharine sighed. "Good story. But, hon, let's face it, they got caught. You don't want to do anything like what they did."

"No," Mary Bliss said. "My plan is different. I just got it from thinking about that program. I was thinking about a scuba diving accident. Down in Cozumel."

Katharine thought about it.

"I didn't know Parker liked to scuba dive."

"We took lessons years ago. At the Y. We both got certified, we even went on a couple dive trips to the Cayman Islands. We've even still got our equipment, up in the attic."

"Why Cozumel?" Katharine asked.

"I saw another program," Mary Bliss started to say.

Katharine held up her hand. "Just cut to the chase, please. I can't take another of your shaggy dog stories."

Mary Bliss stuck out her tongue. "In Mexico," she said deliberately, "they have a very lax and corrupt law enforcement. You can get anything you want down there for the right amount of money. Like a death certificate for a hundred bucks."

"Is that so?" Katharine asked.

"I saw it on the Discovery Channel," Mary Bliss said.

"This could work," Katharine said. "It really could work. We go down to Cozumel, check into a nice hotel. One that has filtered water. You don't want to get Montezuma's revenge. We do some shopping, buy some nice silver jewelry, then buy the fake death certificate and fake Parker's death."

"We?" Mary Bliss's eyebrow was raised way up near her hairline.

"You've got to have an accomplice," Katharine pointed out. "And I was born to do this."

13

Mary Bliss considered the remains of the Chinese takeout in their neat cardboard boxes. Half a container of fried rice, most of the shrimp, and two limp-looking egg rolls. In a former life, she would have tossed them in the trash with the empty Coke cans.

But that was before her baptism into the Church of the Necessary. She'd been sprinkled with the cold water of reality, and now, as she looked down at the leftovers, she saw her checkbook balance and the contents of her billfold and was born again. Doctored up with a little stir-fried chicken and maybe some soy sauce, there was enough here for a meal for herself and Erin.

Carefully, she scraped the rice and shrimp into little Tupperware dishes and nestled them on the top shelf of the refrigerator. She avoided looking too closely at what those shelves held. Whatever was there would have to do until payday. No more quick trips to the grocery store to pick up some nice steaks to grill, or a pretty piece of salmon to poach. When she and Parker had married all those years ago, she'd been an expert at the art of making do, tutored by her mother, the world's thriftiest single mom.

She and Parker had lived off of meatloaf stretched with oatmeal, tuna-noodle casseroles, and grilled cheese sandwiches. Most of the dishes she cooked came out of a little red tin file box her mother had filled with index cards on which she had laboriously printed out dozens of her favorite recipes.

Meemaw had fussed at Mary Bliss about making Parker live off of "poorhouse rations," but Parker had proclaimed himself a lucky man to have such a clever bride.

Somewhere along the way, she'd discarded most of those old, grease-spattered recipe cards, counting them too greasy, too fatty, too "tacky" compared to the gourmet fare served up at the Fair Oaks Supper Club and the fancy restaurants Parker favored.

Mary Bliss gazed around her kitchen, and she wondered what had become of her red recipe tin. When had she last seen it? She squatted on the floor beside the bookshelves that held her fancy cookbooks, letting her fingers trail across the spines of *The Joy of Cooking* and *The Silver Palate* and various Junior League cookbooks she'd acquired over the years. She thought about the quiches, the salsas, the pasta salads she'd produced from those books. Her own mother had laughed out loud the first time Mary Bliss had offered her a taste of the pasta salad she planned to serve to her Sunday school class.

Mary Bliss could see Nina now, her hair neatly combed, the sensible shoes and silver-rimmed glasses. Her mother had been old before thirty, had lived a quiet life of church and work at the elementary school cafeteria, never caused a fuss, and at the age of not quite fifty, she got sick and died quietly in a matter of weeks.

She'd never even seen Erin, Mary Bliss thought. Never held her only grandchild. And Erin had never known any of her mother's kin. The McGowans were all the family she knew.

Erin. Mary Bliss stood up, looked at the kitchen clock. It was nearly midnight.

She thought back to her glib planning session with Katharine. It had been fun, delicious, really, to talk about how to kill off Parker. Another quick stab of pain in her ribs. Erin. How would she tell her daughter?

Everybody said it. Erin was her daddy's girl. The light of his life. It was the family joke. For her sixteenth birthday, Parker had had a ring made for her, an opal, her birthstone, surrounded by tiny diamonds. And on the inside of the ring, he'd had engraved DLP. Daddy's Little Princess.

What would Daddy's Little Princess say when Mary Bliss told her Parker was gone? That he'd emptied the family coffers, left them high and dry? Gone with the wind? Never to return?

No. It was no good. She could not think of how to form the words. Abandoned. Cars were abandoned. Houses were abandoned. But not families. Not this family.

The ugly thought seeped into her head. It was happening again. Her own daddy, James Clewitt, had abandoned his family. Had told her mama he was going to Florida to look for work. Drove away in a 1968 green Ford Falcon. And that was that. Never to return.

For a long time, Nina told everybody, including Mary Bliss, that James was away, working in Florida. A big government job. When she was in the sixth grade, old enough to ask questions, Nina had sat her down and served up the truth.

"He's gone, and he's not coming back. I've done divorced him. And that's what you need to do too. Just divorce him from your mind. You're a big girl now, so you're just going to have to handle it. I know you loved him. I loved him too. But the truth is, your daddy was sorry. He couldn't help himself. He was just sorry."

Mary Bliss set her chin. She couldn't tell Erin what her own mother had told her. Not Erin. Parker had not only abandoned them, he'd stolen their future, which made him sorrier than her own daddy, but it wouldn't do to tell that to Erin, who adored Parker.

No. Her only hope of preserving the life they'd so carefully built for their daughter was in taking Parker's life. It had to be, she told herself. The insurance policy would pay off the outstanding bills, help them get on their feet. And the title insurance would pay off the mortgage on the house, in the instance of Parker's death. So that was it. Parker was dead.

She cleaned up the kitchen, glanced at the clock again, and frowned. Close to midnight. And no sign of Erin.

Mary Bliss went to the den and switched on the television. The news was over, and David Letterman's guest was some hip young movie star she'd never heard of. She yawned and stretched out on the sofa, willing Erin to come in the door so that she could lock up the house and get to bed. She had a long day tomorrow, what with planning Parker's demise and all.

The den was warm. Erin was right. The air conditioning wasn't working properly. Mary Bliss yawned and closed her eyes, just to shut out the reality pressing in around her on every side.

When she woke, David Letterman had been replaced with somebody she didn't recognize, another talk show host interviewing another hip celebrity.

She got to her feet, went to the kitchen. It was after midnight. Twelve-forty, to be exact. Where was Erin? Had she come in while Mary Bliss was napping?

Mary Bliss checked the driveway. Erin's car wasn't there. She ran upstairs to Erin's bedroom, where the rumpled bed was empty.

Her heart was pounding. In her own bedroom, Mary Bliss sat down on her bed, forced herself to think. Where could Erin be? She picked up the telephone and dialed her daughter's cell phone number, but got no answer.

She was overreacting, she knew. If Parker had been home, that's what he would have told her. "Calm down. She's fine." But Parker was gone, and her daughter was out there somewhere.

Mary Bliss went back downstairs, found her address book. She bit her lip as she dialed the Wilkersons' phone number. But Stephanie Wilkerson was sound asleep and didn't have a clue about Erin's whereabouts.

Mary Bliss walked to the window and looked out across the street. No lights were on at the Bowdens' house. But she knew Josh's bedroom was at the back. And she knew Josh was as much a night owl as Erin was. According to Erin, Josh only needed a few hours of sleep a night. He regularly stayed up 'til three or four in the morning, talking with friends on the Internet, strumming his guitar, or reading.

Mary Bliss didn't approve of letting a child—no matter if he was a senior in high school—stay up 'til all hours of the night. But Nancye Bowden pretty much allowed her oldest son to do whatever he liked, and Randy had never challenged her authority on raising the kids.

She knew Josh had a private phone line, and she looked in the neighborhood directory for it. There it was, Bowden, children's phone.

She dialed it, and Josh picked up on the first ring.

"Erin?" His voice was husky.

"What?" Mary Bliss was taken aback.

"Oh," he said. "Hi, Mrs. McGowan. I thought you were Erin. I've got caller ID."

"No," Mary Bliss said. "That's why I'm calling. Erin's not home yet. Her curfew's at midnight, and it's nearly one now, and I'm getting pretty concerned. Josh, do you have any idea where she might be at this time of night?"

"Well," he said cautiously. "She's been going to see a lot of movies, I know."

"No movie gets out this late," Mary Bliss said, getting cross. "She said she'd be with some girls from work, but I don't know any of their names. Did she tell you who she'd be with tonight?"

Erin and Josh had become inseparable earlier in the spring. Josh and Erin had gone to school together since first grade, but Erin had always considered Josh something of a geek. That had all changed somehow after Christmas break.

Erin swore it wasn't a boyfriend-girlfriend thing. "We're just buddies," she'd told Parker when he pressed her for details. "He's like a brother, you know?"

"I forget the girl's name," Josh was saying. "Did you try Erin's cell phone?"

"Yes, it must not be working right," Mary Bliss said. "Are you sure you can't think of anybody she might be with?"

"No, ma'am. Hey," he said excitedly, "you want me to get in my car and go looking for her?"

"At this time of night? Your daddy would skin me alive if I sent you out like that."

"He's asleep," Josh said. "Anyway, if you're worried about Erin, you could come with me."

"That's all right," Mary Bliss said. "I'll just wait up for her. I'm sure she'll be home pretty soon. It's not like her to be this late."

"Okay," he said. "Well, good night."

Mary Bliss went downstairs and checked the garage and the driveway again. She tried to sit down but discovered it was impossible to stay still. If she was still, she started to think about all the possibilities. Traffic in Atlanta was impossible. All those giant eighteen-wheeler tractor-trailers, and those gigantic SUVs, could mow down a little Honda like the one Erin drove and not even know it. And crime was on the upswing. Just last month, a young girl had been abducted from Phipps Plaza, the nicest mall in town. They still hadn't found the girl's body. Another thought occurred to her. Parker was gone. What if he'd spirited Erin away too? What if he'd abducted her only child?

She felt the sweat drying on her neck, felt suddenly chilled to the bone. No, she insisted to herself, it wasn't possible. Parker had been gone nearly two days. Stop this nonsense. Erin was just out with her friends, having such a good time she'd forgotten all about curfews and such.

Do something, she commanded herself. Get busy. She went into the kitchen, snapped the light on. The room was already spotless. Nina had taught her to never go to bed with a messy kitchen.

But what about the refrigerator?

The shelves were crowded with half-empty jars of pickles, nearly empty bottles of salad dressings and ketchup, plastic bags full of limp vegetables.

Mary Bliss ran a plastic basin full of warm soapy water. She pulled on a pair of yellow rubber gloves, cleared everything from the shelves, and started working, scrubbing at the shelves with a plastic bristle brush, tossing out jars and bottles past their usefulness.

She was lining the salad dressings up on the door shelf when she heard the kitchen door open.

She whirled around. Erin stood there, eyes wide.

"Mama? What's wrong? Why are you doing that?"

Her throat caught. Her child was home. She should have felt flooded with relief. Instead, she felt hot rage welling up in her chest.

"Erin! Do you know what time it is?"

Her daughter's shoulders sagged. "I'm late, huh?"

"It's two o'clock in the morning! Do you know how worried I've been?"

"I'm sorry, Mama," Erin said, starting toward her, setting her pocketbook on the kitchen counter. "I guess I lost track of the time."

"Lost track?" Mary Bliss's voice bounced off the high ceiling of the kitchen. "I thought you were dead. I thought you'd been kidnapped, or were lying on the side of a road somewhere. I've been out of my mind."

Erin wrapped her arms around Mary Bliss's neck, but her mother pulled away from the embrace.

"Where in God's name were you at this hour of the night?"

"I told you I was going to the movies with Jessica. And to Starbucks," Erin said, getting defensive. "I don't understand why you're so upset."

Mary Bliss peeled the rubber gloves off and flung them in the sink. "You don't understand? You can't think why I'd be worried when you're two hours past curfew and you haven't called?"

"I tried," Erin cried. "The damned thing doesn't work." She pulled the cell phone out of her purse and showed it to Mary Bliss. "See? It doesn't even get a dial tone."

"I don't care," Mary Bliss said, tossing the phone back at her. "There are pay phones. Or you could have borrowed your friend's cell phone. Just who is this Jessica? I've never met her. And Josh didn't know where you were either."

Erin's face turned pink. "You called my friends? You were checking up on me? Mama, how could you?"

"How could *you*?" Mary Bliss demanded. "You know the rules. You know how I worry. I don't even know this Jessica person's last name."

"It's Lassiter. Jesus H. Christ! I don't know why you're making such a big deal out of this. After Starbucks I went over to Jess's house and we were watching a video and I lost track of time. God. You'd think I'd killed somebody."

"Don't talk to me in that tone of voice," Mary Bliss snapped. "I'm your mother. And you will respect me."

"Fine," Erin said, her face a sullen, white mask. "Whatever. I guess I'll just have to respect you and let you ruin my life. God, I wish Daddy were home. He never gets like this. He understands that I'm old enough to have a life."

"That's enough!" Mary Bliss said. Her face was on fire, her heart was beating like a snare drum, she was near tears. "Your daddy isn't home. It's just you and me tonight, Erin. And if you want to be treated as an adult, you'll have to understand that it's your responsibility to be home on time, and to let me know exactly where you are and who you're with. You know the rules. I expect you to follow them."

"Whatever." Erin whirled around and stomped toward the hallway. "If you're done now, I have to get up and work tomorrow morning."

Mary Bliss clenched her hands at her sides. "And don't make any plans for the rest of this week, young lady. You're on restriction."

"A week?" Erin shrieked. "Goddamn! I'm not believing this."

Mary Bliss put her hands over her ears. She couldn't listen to any more. She sank down into a kitchen chair. She could not remember another time when she had been this angry at her only child.

Looking down at the table, she saw Erin's cell phone. Hesitating only a moment, she picked up the phone and dialed the house number. Instead of a ring, she got a recorded announcement.

"Call your service provider regarding your current account balance."

Mary Bliss stood up, closed the refrigerator door, and went to the sink to splash cold water on her face.

She looked around the kitchen, seeking comfort in its familiar sights and smells. But nothing looked like it had looked earlier. The cold overhead lights cast harsh shadows on the room, and for the first time she saw the bits of peeling vinyl flooring, the worn paint finish on the cupboard doors, and the wallpaper seams that were coming unglued. She snapped off the light, sighed, and went upstairs.

14

Mary Bliss sat up in bed and looked wildly around the darkened room. A scratching sound was coming from the window. Instinctively, she reached over to grab Parker. She came up with a handful of pillowcase, but nothing else.

Then she remembered. His side of the bed was empty. She glanced at the neon dial of the clock radio. It was 5:45 A.M. Still dark. On a normal morning, they would both be fast asleep, but Parker would have one ear cocked for the six o'clock alarm. He'd always been an early riser.

She held her breath to see if the noise would go away. But the scratching sound continued. It was metallic, slightly hollow. She made herself count to three. Slowly, she slipped out of bed and edged over toward the window.

When she was only inches away, she saw in the half-light a fallen pine tree limb that had become snagged on the roof of the dormer window. A branch hung down and scratched against the window screen.

Nothing. It was nothing. She should go back to sleep. But she knew sleep wouldn't come.

Mary Bliss pushed her feet into her slippers and turned on the bedroom light. Quickly, she made up the bed. Parker hated an unmade bed, and she herself had gotten used to making it the minute her feet touched the floor in the morning.

As she plumped the pillows on his side, she scolded herself for caring how they were arranged. Parker had two firm pillows, and a softer, down one, that he liked to put on top of the stack of pillows on his side of the bed. Who cared what he liked, she asked herself, punching the pillow, leaving a satisfying fist-shaped depression in it. She could leave the bed unmade all day if she liked. Commandeer his side, hog all the covers she wanted, never have to put the toilet seat down in the morning, ever again.

She sank down onto the spread and smoothed out the depression in the pillow. It was too late. After all these years, she had molded herself to Parker's likes and dislikes, habits and tics. She could no more leave a bed unmade than she could leave a greasy pot soaking overnight in the kitchen sink. It just wasn't in her.

She scuffed out into the hallway and saw Erin's bedroom door ajar. She walked over and peeked inside. The clothes that Erin had been wearing the night before were strewn around the floor, along with empty Coke cans, CDs, a laptop computer, and some paperback books.

Erin had flung herself on top of her covers, wearing only a worn T-shirt over her panties. The bedspread lay in a pile on the floor at the foot of the bed. Mary Bliss stepped into the room, thinking to cover her daughter. But the air was still and hot. The air conditioning, she thought.

She bent down and kissed her daughter's sweat-dampened hair, then went quietly out, gathering dirty clothes as she went. It was early. She could run a couple loads of laundry, read the newspaper, gather her thoughts before Erin came downstairs. She was sure her daughter would understand why her breach of curfew was such a serious issue, and they would make things up. Even laugh about the nasty fight of the night before.

After she started the first load of laundry, Mary Bliss fixed herself a cup of coffee and took it out to the front porch. She sat down in the rocker and watched again as Fair Oaks came to life.

By eight, she had washed, dried, and folded three loads of laundry. She'd read the newspaper, clipped coupons, and fixed a sack lunch for Erin, with a Tupperware container of the chili-roni and another of the salad, along with a can of Coke.

At nine, she went back outside to surreptitiously water her tomato plants. The watering ban had been announced the day before, and since her house was an even number, she wasn't really supposed to water until tomorrow. But it was already a scorcher, and there had been no rain in days. The hell with watering restrictions, she thought, unrolling the hose and dragging it out to the fenced-in garden plot.

She knew she really should change into proper clothes, shorts, and T-shirt, and surely a pair of sneakers. But there was something deliciously subversive about gardening in her thin cotton nightgown. Parker would hate this, her, outside, barely dressed. But she loved the cool feel of the grass on her bare feet, imagined she could hear the dry clay soil lapping up the water as she sprinkled it over the parched tomato and squash vines.

Mary Bliss was bending down to pick a clump of dandelions out of the grass when she heard a polite cough.

She stood up quickly. A man stood in the driveway, staring at her, a smile on his face.

"Mrs. McGowan?" he called.

She took two steps in his direction, then stopped and looked down at herself. Water from the hose had splashed all over her gown, making it nearly transparent. Her hands were filthy, her hair uncombed. Not to mention that she was basically undressed. Good Lord!

"Mrs. McGowan?" he called again. "Sorry to barge in on you like this."

She held up her hand. "I'm sorry. Could you go around to the front door? Let me just dash inside and get dressed. I wasn't expecting company this early."

"Sure," he said, half laughing. "Or I could come back a little later."

"It'll just be a minute," Mary Bliss said. She ran-walked to the kitchen, her face in flames.

She took a look out the kitchen window and saw the car the man had come in. It was a navy-blue sedan, and there was some kind of gold shield emblazoned on the passenger-side door. It looked sort of like a police car, but not a Fair Oaks police cruiser. Those were dark green and tan. She saw the man sitting behind the wheel of the sedan, gazing off in the direction of the street.

Upstairs, she hurriedly threw on a pair of khaki slacks and a cotton blouse and tied on a pair of sneakers. She heard the sounds of the shower running in Erin's bathroom. After she'd combed her hair and washed her face, she ran back downstairs and opened the front door.

The man was still looking out at the street, the windows of the car rolled down.

Was he a cop, Mary Bliss wondered? All the Fair Oaks cops were in their early to mid-twenties. This man was much older, with blonde hair streaked with silver. His face was tanned, ruddy, even, and she could see he wore a neatly trimmed beard. He wore dark sunglasses, so she couldn't see his eyes. He looked vaguely familiar.

She stepped out on the front porch and waved in his direction. But he was still staring out at the street.

Finally, she walked up to the passenger side of the car. The gold seal on the door was something official, but she couldn't tell what it was.

"Excuse me," she said. He whipped his head around, surprised.

"You can come in now," she said. "I'm decent."

"Oh, I wouldn't say you were *indecent* out in the garden," he drawled. She blushed, noticing he had nice, even teeth, and the sunglasses failed to conceal the smile lines that radiated out from the corners of his eyes.

"It's Mary Bliss, right?"

"Yes, that's right," she said. "Have we met?"

"Not really," he said, getting out of the car. If he was a cop, he was in a weird kind of undercover, including white tennis shorts and a faded raggedy T-shirt. His legs were deeply tanned and muscular.

"I've seen you at the club, but never got around to introducing myself." He stuck out his hand. "I'm Matt Hayslip."

She shook his hand, which swallowed her own. "At the club? Fair Oaks, you mean?"

"I play tennis with Parker. Doubles," Hayslip said. "In fact, it's Parker I'm really huntin'. We had a tennis date this morning. At nine. I tried calling his office, and his cell, but got no answer. Is he around?"

She dropped his hand, because her own palms were beginning to sweat. Profusely. "No. He's out of town. On business."

Hayslip frowned. "The SOB. This is our standing date. I can't believe he didn't let me know."

Parker had a standing tennis date? Mary Bliss tried not to seem surprised. Now that she thought about it, yes, she had seen this man at the club, though from afar.

"It's a consulting thing," she said. "It came up sort of suddenly, so maybe it just slipped his mind."

"Still," Hayslip said, glancing around the yard. "The answering machine at the office didn't pick up. And usually I can get him on his cell phone."

"His assistant quit this weekend," Mary Bliss said. "Parker's been in a tizzy about that, so things are in sort of a mess, you might say. And then this trip came up. Unexpectedly," she added again, and it sounded lame even to her.

Hayslip was staring up at the house. He was making her edgy, and she hadn't done anything wrong. Except lie to her daughter. And threaten her mother-in-law's life. And then there was the off-day watering.

"Are you in law enforcement?" It came out all wrong.

"What, now?" He laughed. Very nice teeth, she thought again. He was actually sort of attractive. She wished she'd put on some lipstick. And this shapeless shirt did nothing for her figure. But if she'd fixed herself up, that would have made him suspicious, wouldn't it?

She gestured at the emblem on the car door.

"Oh, that," he said. "I guess it does look kind of official. Actually, I'm retired from real law enforcement."

She raised an eyebrow.

"I did my thirty with the Georgia Bureau of Investigation, and got out once the politicians started running the show. These days I'm sort of a fancified rent-a-cop. Southern Utilities Corp. I'm director of security."

"How nice." This man really was making her very edgy. There was something dangerous here. "Well,

I do apologize on Parker's behalf, for making you miss your tennis match. And I'll tell him you came by to see him."

"When will he be back?" Hayslip asked. "We're supposed to play Sunday, in the club round-robin."

"Oh." Oh God, would he never leave?

"It's still up in the air," Mary Bliss said. "The client is having problems integrating his new software with the parent company's mainframe."

She had no idea whether this made sense, but it did seem like something Parker might have said in the past.

"Hmm. Who's the client?"

"The client?" Her voice cracked a little.

"Yes. The client. Is it a big company?"

What did he care who the client was? Why didn't he just fold himself back into that official car and go away? Why didn't he mind his own business? And what kind of job did he have that he could play tennis at nine o'clock on a weekday morning?"

"It's his biggest client," Mary Bliss said finally, at a loss for any names. "But Parker doesn't ever name names. He believes in strict confidentiality."

Hayslip took this in, frowned some more, then nodded.

"Well, if he calls, will you let him know I'm wondering about this weekend?"

"Absolutely," Mary Bliss said. "I'll tell him as soon as he calls. Although, to tell you the truth, I wouldn't plan on this weekend. Apparently, this mainframe thing is a real bear."

"Apparently," Hayslip said. Now he was staring across the street again. What was it with this guy?

"That house over there," he said finally, pointing in the direction of the Bowdens. "Have the owners moved out?"

"No," Mary Bliss said quickly. "They're having some family issues, that's all. Why do you ask?"

"No reason," Hayslip said.

He had the door of the car open. Good. Maybe he would leave now.

"I like this street. I've been halfway thinking of house hunting over here."

"Where do you live now?" Mary Bliss asked. "Not far, I imagine, since you belong to the club."

"No, not far," Hayslip said. "I've got a townhouse over at the Oaks. It's all right, but I miss having a yard."

The Oaks. That explained why she hadn't met him before. He was an Oakie. She didn't know any Oakies. And she wasn't aware that Parker knew any. But there were a lot of things about Parker she didn't know, weren't there?

"With this drought we're having, you should be glad you don't have a yard," Mary Bliss said. "I spend half my day dragging a hose around, trying to keep my pathetic little garden alive."

"It looks good to me," Hayslip said. "Must be all that illegal watering you're doing."

She started to protest, but he gave her a snotty little smile, and a mock salute, and closed the door and backed down the driveway.

Mary Bliss blinked in the bright morning light. Who was this man? She heard a car start then, and as she turned around, Erin's little Honda came whipping down the driveway.

"Erin!" Mary Bliss called.

Her daughter stuck her head out the window of the car. "Thanks for the lunch, Mom. Gotta go, or I'll be late for work."

"We need to have a talk, young lady," Mary Bliss started, but Erin had rolled the window of the car up again, and she was at the bottom of the drive.

"And you're still on restriction!" she called.

15

On Monday morning, Mary Bliss realized she must have made it through the weekend. But she couldn't remember how. She was feeling vague and unfocused—right up until the air conditioning repairman gave her an estimate of fourteen hundred dollars to install a new chiller/condenser.

After he'd left, Mary Bliss emptied the silverware drawer in the dining room. The pieces clanged against the top of the mahogany sideboard as she slipped them out of their mothproof bags and counted them out. The final total was impressive. She had twelve place settings of Frances I sterling silver, a dozen assorted serving pieces, including one strange five-pronged fork she'd never figured out a use for, and ten demitasse spoons.

She ran her fingers slowly over the smooth silver surface of the spoons and knives, held the cool bowl of a soup spoon against her neck. As she traced the whorls and lines of the design, she remembered the first Christmas she had opened one of the pink-wrapped boxes sent by Parker's aunt Lily, who lived in Charleston.

Aunt Lily wasn't a real aunt. She was Parker's godmother, widowed and childless. Together, she and Eula had decided it was a scandal that Parker's young bride had never registered for a silver pattern. Eula and Lily had picked out Frances I as being suitable for a modern young couple. And every Christmas, right up until her death, Aunt Lily, who Parker said was so rich she couldn't move without tripping over sacks of money, sent Mary Bliss exactly one place setting of "her" silver. The silver came in the same thin wrapping paper, accompanied by a Christmas card that Aunt Lily recycled by whiting out the previous sender's name and substituting her own.

For her birthdays, Eula gave Mary Bliss the serving pieces. Frances I was not a pattern Mary Bliss would have chosen. And in the early years of their marriage, when money was so tight, Mary Bliss had gotten nauseous at the sight of the pink box under the Christmas tree, thinking of how much sterling silver cost, and what she could have done with the money instead.

But Frances I had stood by her—through inexorably long visits from Aunt Lily, through the dinner parties and buffets she and Parker had hosted over the years.

She felt a pang as she slid the forks and spoons back into their gray silver-cloth compartments. She would miss Frances I. But she had a perfectly serviceable set of stainless steel to eat off of. And although she'd always intended for Erin to inherit her wedding china and silver and crystal, Erin, at least at this age, had zero interest in the finer things of life. Given the choice, her daughter would definitely have chosen a new chiller/condenser over twelve place settings of Frances I.

With a chiffon scarf tied over her hair and dark sunglasses, Mary Bliss barely recognized herself in the sun-visor mirror.

Incognito, she thought. She was going incognito.

She'd passed Citizen's Pawnshop many times on her way into downtown Atlanta. It was tucked in the corner of a strip shopping center on Ponce de Leon, between a vacuum cleaner repair shop and a Hispanic grocery store. There were pawnshops closer to her house, but Mary Bliss had a horror of being recognized.

A dark-skinned Mideastern-looking man stood behind the counter of the pawnshop. He was polishing the lens of a large camera and muttering to himself in some foreign language. The shelves of the store crowded in around her, lined with musical instruments, amplifiers, televisions, stereos, computers, even a large, badly tarnished brass bedstead and a hideous crystal chandelier as big as a bathtub.

"Yes?" he said, glancing up at Mary Bliss only briefly before returning his attention to the camera.

She cleared her throat. "You, um. You buy things as well as sell them, is that how it works?"

"Yes? What you got?" His eyes swept over her, and she felt her face redden.

"Silverware. Sterling silver flatware. Frances I. There are twelve place settings, and some serving pieces, and ten demitasse spoons, and, of course . . ."

"Show me," he said, setting the camera down.

"Well," she said, hesitating.

"You don't want to sell, forget it." He picked the camera back up and muttered to himself again.

Mary Bliss hoisted her canvas tote bag onto the counter with a loud thud.

She heard a long, low growl and felt hot breath on her ankle.

"What in heaven's name?"

A huge German shepherd placed its muzzle directly on top of her shoe and looked balefully up at her.

The pawnshop man glanced over the counter at the dog. "BooBoo!" he said sharply.

The dog's ears pricked up, but he didn't move. He was still staring at Mary Bliss.

"Get off, BooBoo," the man called. "Stupid bastard."

The dog stood up slowly, swished its tail, and wandered to a far corner of the shop.

"Stupid bastard," the man repeated. "Oh," he said, seeing the look on Mary Bliss's face. "Sorry. My ex-wife's dog." He pulled the tote bag toward him. "Let me see what you got."

He unwrapped the silver-cloth bundles and started taking the pieces from their compartments, holding each one up to the light, turning it this way and that.

It took him fifteen minutes to examine all of Mary Bliss's silver. Occasionally he would stop and write something down on a scratch pad of paper. When he was done, he looked at the pad, did some addition, and sighed.

"Business sucks," he said. "Nobody wants silver. Nobody wants to polish it. People eat off plastic. They want to throw things away, not polish them and put them back in a drawer. I give you twelve hundred dollars."

She felt like he had slapped her across her face. Tears rose up in her eyes. "This is very fine sterling silver," Mary Bliss said, feeling defensive. "People will always want lovely things in their home. Southerners, especially, love silver. Why, this silver would cost at least five hundred dollars a place setting, even at an antique shop."

"You love it so much, why don't you keep it?" he asked, shoving the bundle back at her.

"I have to have fifteen hundred dollars," Mary Bliss said, gritting her teeth. "I looked it up in a reference book. This is Frances I. Five hundred a place setting is what it sells for. That doesn't even take into account the serving pieces and the demitasse spoons."

"Too bad," the man said. He picked the camera up and looked through its lens.

"You're saying you won't buy it?" She felt a surge of panic. The temperature in the kitchen had been eighty-six degrees when she went downstairs in the morning. By that night, when Erin got home, the place would be like an oven.

"I told you, business sucks."

"How much?" Mary Bliss repeated. "Surely you can do a little better than twelve hundred."

He picked up the five-pronged serving fork, pinged it with a fingernail.

"Say . . . thirteen hundred."

"Thirteen-fifty." Mary Bliss could not believe she was standing here, in this cheesy pawnshop, dickering over her wedding silver.

"You're nuts."

But he got a clipboard with a sheet of paper on it and gave it to her. "Fill this out," he told her. "And take off the glasses and that scarf." He nodded toward a small wall-mounted camera on the wall behind him. "For business purposes. We like to see our customers, you know?"

"It's not stolen!" she cried. "Is that what you think, that I stole this silver?"

He shrugged. "Lady, I don't know you. You don't know me. And that's a lotta expensive silver you got there."

She felt her shoulders sag as she removed the glasses. "It was a wedding gift. And a Christmas and birthday gift. For a lot of years."

"You love it so much, why you sell?"

Mary Bliss filled out the blanks with precise block lettering. "I need the money." She looked right at the camera then. "There's been a death in the family."

16

Mary Bliss was poring over the help-wanted ads in the newspaper when Erin walked into the kitchen and went immediately to the refrigerator.

Huge sigh. "We're out of skim milk."

"I'm sorry," Mary Bliss said quickly. "I'll get some today."

"Whatever." Erin ducked into the pantry and came out with the cardboard Pop-Tarts box. "And this is the last Pop-Tart, too. When was the last time you went grocery shopping?"

The last time there was money in my checking account, Mary Bliss wanted to snap. Instead she bit her lip. "I'll go today."

"Whatever," Erin said. She picked up her purse off the kitchen counter and started toward the door. "What about my phone?" she asked. "Did you find out what the problem was?"

Mary Bliss knew what the problem was. "I'll try to get it taken care of today. You know how those phone places are. Customer service is deplorable."

"The people who work there are all a bunch of retards," Erin sneered. It was the closest they'd come to agreement all week.

Erin was headed out the door, without a good-bye.

"See you tonight," Mary Bliss called over her shoulder.

"It'll be after nine," Erin said. "Coach called a special practice."

Erin was on a select soccer team, but the season was over.

"In June?" Mary Bliss asked.

"There's a big invitational tournament in September. He's all spazzed out about getting us in condition."

"You're in great condition," Mary Bliss said, annoyed. "You run nearly every night, work out at the gym. It seems to me this soccer team is taking up every minute of your time."

Erin shook her hair over her shoulder, a sign of her own annoyance. "You know what Daddy says. Sports are great for girls. Keeps 'em off the streets and out of trouble."

"As if you'd be on the streets," Mary Bliss muttered.

"You never know," Erin said. And she was out the door and gone.

Mary Bliss turned back to the classifieds.

The pickings were pretty slim. She couldn't, in good conscience, take a full-time job, knowing she'd be starting back to school in mid-August. But it was only June. She was broke, and a part-time job seemed the only answer.

She skimmed over the ads for advertising sales, computer programmers, data entry clerks, and HVAC technicians. She had no idea what an HVAC tech did, but she was pretty sure it would be out of her realm of experience.

She paused when she came to an ad with large bold print: PRODUCT DEMONSTRATION HOSTESS. It was the word *hostess* that caught her eye. Everybody said she was an amazing hostess. She loved to cook, loved to entertain. Of course now she'd be entertaining without her Frances I flatware, and if she didn't find some employment soon her repertoire would be reduced to instant oatmeal and squeeze cheese.

"Energetic people-magnet needed to demonstrate exciting new food products. Self-starter. Flex hours. No experience necessary." All of that sounded good.

But it was the last line of the ad that sounded best: "$22.00 per hour."

Her hands were shaking as she punched in the phone number in the ad.

A man's voice answered. He identified himself as Jeff Robertson. Yes, he said, the position was open. Yes, he'd be willing to talk to her. Today? Excellent. An hour from now? Perfect.

"If we come to an agreement on your employment, would you be willing to start today?" he asked.

Mary Bliss's eyes filled with tears. After paying the bills, she was down to $12.32 in her checking account.

"Absolutely," she said.

She flew up the stairs and stood in the closet, staring at the clothes rack. What did a product demonstration hostess wear? A dress seemed too Sunday-schoolish, slacks and a blouse seemed too casual. After some false starts, she found the right look. Her navy poplin blazer, crisp white blouse, and starched and creased khaki slacks, with blue cork-soled sandals. She tied a bright print scarf around her neck, fastened little gold hoops in her ears, and stood back from the mirror.

Yes. Perfect. Not too dressy, not too casual. Although . . . she did look a little like the first mate on the Love Boat.

She shook the doubts out of her head and took the stairs two at a time. For the first time since she'd found Parker's note, she felt good. She felt strong, energetic, businesslike. No more crying and hand-wringing for Mary Bliss McGowan. She was now, she told herself, a full-fledged product demonstration hostess.

She exited the interstate at Windy Hill Road in Cobb County, made the right turn, and started watching for Windy River Crossing, the office park she was supposed to report to.

The park was a maze, but she found building 300, and office suite 15B, with relative ease. The sign on the door said MARKET CONCEPTS.

Mary Bliss straightened her scarf and her spine and opened the frosted glass door.

The room was small, with a single desk against the back wall. The man sitting there looked up. "Mrs. McGowan?" His voice cracked. For a moment, Mary Bliss considered leaving. Man? This was a kid, barely twenty. He still had acne on his cheeks. His head was shaved nearly bald. He wore wire-rimmed glasses with tinted blue lenses and he had a white-blonde goatee and a small silver stud piercing his left nostril. He wore a white golf shirt with the Market Concepts logo embroidered on the breast.

"I have an appointment with Mr. Robertson," Mary Bliss told the kid.

"That's me," he said, gesturing toward a plastic laminate chair opposite the desk. "Great. Let's talk product placement."

Mary Bliss sat. The chair wobbled.

He had her fill out an employment application, and while she scribbled, he watched silently, stroking his goatee as though that would make it grow.

"Drugs?" Robertson blurted.

"What?" Mary Bliss nearly dropped her pen.

"Do you do illegal drugs? Our client stores won't tolerate substance abuse," Robertson said. "You'll be subject to random drug testing at any time."

"I've never used illegal drugs," Mary Bliss said, her face reddening.

"Police record?" he asked. He leaned forward. "We'll run a check on you, you know, so it's best if you just tell me the truth."

"I don't do drugs and I've never even had a parking ticket," Mary Bliss exclaimed. She shoved the clipboard holding her application across the desk toward him.

"Ever take a lie detector test?" he asked, cocking his head to one side to appraise her reaction.

"No!" She stood up, her entire body fairly quivering with indignation. "I understood the job I was applying for was as a product demonstration hostess, not

Supreme Court justice. I resent the implication that I might be some sort of lying, cocaine-snorting master criminal. I'm just a woman. A woman with a family who needs a job." Her upper lip was really quivering now, and she could feel a sob working its way up from her chest.

She swallowed the sob and squared her shoulders. Goddamn this little peckerwood, she thought. He had a job that paid twenty-two an hour. Fine. She would get the job, pick up her paycheck, and pay her bills. And someday, this little peckerwood and all his peckerwood brothers would be mighty sorry they ever messed with the likes of Mary Bliss McGowan.

"Do I get the job or not?" she asked, looking down at him, speaking in a voice that she hoped sounded imperial.

"Sure you get the job, Mary Bliss," he said. "Nothing personal. I have to ask, you know. You're hired. Absolutely."

"Good," Mary Bliss said, still frosty. "When and where do I report?"

"Bargain Bonanza Club has a new store opening today down in Riverdale," Robertson said. "Go on down there and ask for the manager. Mrs. Peabody."

"Um." She hesitated. "When do I get paid? I've, uh, had a death in the family, and some pressing bills are due."

"Whatever," he said, sounding way too much like Erin. "Your pay period ends on Friday. We'll have a check for you then, if your paperwork gets processed on time."

"Who processes the paperwork?" she asked.

"You're looking at him," Robertson said, puffing up a little.

"Good," Mary Bliss said, giving the little pecker-wood the look she gave her students when she explained her classroom rules. "I'm a very responsible employee. I expect the same from my employer. And I'll need that paycheck on Friday. Absolutely."

An hour and half a tank of gas later, she parked the car in front of the new Bargain Bonanza Club down in Riverdale, Georgia.

A giant blue hot-air balloon bobbed in the sky above the store. Yellow banners proclaimed GRAND OPENING! The parking lot was thronged with cars and shoppers, and heat shimmered from the vast expanse of asphalt and automobiles.

A teenaged girl with a bad perm stopped her just inside the front door. "Membership card?" she asked.

"I'm not a member," Mary Bliss said.

The girl whipped a square of cardboard from the clipboard she was holding. "If you'll fill this out, we can get your membership started today," she said, offering a smile. She wore a bright blue vest and a name badge identifying her as Mystee.

"I don't need a membership," Mary Bliss said, smiling back. "I'm from Market Concepts. I'm the product demonstration hostess."

The girl looked her up and down. "For real?"

"Why not?" Mary Bliss asked.

"I dunno," Mystee mumbled. "You just look different from most of them."

"I'm supposed to see Mrs. Peabody," Mary Bliss said. It was nearly two o'clock. She didn't want to be late for work on her first day.

"You mean Imogene," Mystee said. "Just go over to customer service and ask somebody to page her."

"Thank you," Mary Bliss said.

"I like your outfit," Mystee said. "Like that chick on that show on Nickelodeon. You know, the one where they all go on a cruise and get it on."

"*Love Boat*?" It was the scarf. Mary Bliss started to unknot it.

"Yeah," Mystee said. "Julie, that was the chick's name. You look just like Julie. Really retro."

"Thanks a bunch," Mary Bliss said. She stuffed the scarf in her purse.

17

Mary Bliss stopped at the jewelry counter and checked her appearance in a small mirror. She'd bitten all her lipstick off during her interview with Jeff Robertson. Now she carefully applied another layer of Raspberry Glacé.

"Can I help you?" The woman on the other side of the counter had closely cropped hair and a huge smile. Her name tag proclaimed her "Your Sales Associate— Queen Esther."

"Oh. No, no thanks," Mary Bliss said quickly. "I was just fixing myself up a little. I'm actually reporting for a job."

"Where? Here?" the woman's smile disappeared. "You sure you got the right place?"

Mary Bliss straightened her shoulders. "I'm one of the new product demonstration hostesses."

"You? Honey, you don't look like no sample lady I ever seen."

Mary Bliss didn't know whether it was a compliment or a cut.

"Why not?" she asked.

The watch saleswoman looked her up and down. "You wearing heels? And all dressed up? What you supposed to be handing out today? Caviar?"

"They didn't tell me," Mary Bliss admitted, beginning to feel flustered. "I'm supposed to find Mrs. Peabody."

"She's up there," Queen Esther said, pointing toward the front of the store, where an elevated catwalk looked out over the cavernous warehouse space.

"But don't be calling her Mrs. Peabody. Imogene Peabody likes to be called Miz. And I mean M. S. Peabody."

"Any other advice?"

"Pick you up a pair of sneakers before you go on up there," Queen Esther said. "And tell 'em you're very religious. Can't work Sundays. Otherwise, you be working the shifts the other sample ladies won't take."

"Thank you," Mary Bliss said.

Her feet were already aching by the time she'd climbed the metal stairs to the catwalk. Mary Bliss paused before Imogene Peabody's office door. It actually wasn't an office at all. More like a cubicle. The woman sitting at the desk was talking on the phone, gesturing wildly, cussing a blue streak, oblivious to everything going on around her. She had shoulder-length blonde hair and the deepest tan Mary Bliss had ever seen.

Mary Bliss coughed softly.

The woman whirled around in her chair. "Yes?"

"Miz Peabody?" Mary Bliss said. "I'm Mary Bliss McGowan. Jeff Robertson at Market Concepts sent me over. I'm the new product demonstration hostess."

Imogene Peabody reached into a large cardboard box beside her desk, bringing out a bright blue baseball cap with the Bargain Bonanza Club logo, and a matching bib-style blue apron.

"Here's your uniform," she said, tossing it in Mary Bliss's direction. "Today, you'll be in frozen foods, back of the store. Station D. Tell whoever's at that table that you're relieving them. They'll show you what to do. Don't forget to hand out the manufacturer's coupons with the samples. It's after noon now, so you won't get a lunch or dinner break. Fifteen minutes, that's it. We're staying open 'til ten tonight, because it's grand opening. At quarter 'til, break down the station, wash up all the equipment, and make sure you take the leftover unopened stock and replace it in the walk-in freezers. Got it?"

Mary Bliss blinked. "'Til ten?" she asked. "Mr. Robertson didn't tell me that part. I have a teenaged daughter. I need to be at home when she gets off work. I could stay 'til six, possibly."

"Ten," Imogene Peabody snapped. "Did you bring your own gloves?"

"Gloves?"

Miz Peabody snorted, reached down into the box, and tossed a plastic bag in Mary Bliss's direction.

"You're not allergic to latex, are you?"

"No, I don't think so."

"Good." It was the first time Ms. Peabody had seemed pleased with anything. "Last week, some poor clown put on the gloves, and fifteen minutes later his lips were turning blue and he stopped breathing. He was allergic to latex rubber. You believe that?"

"That's terrible," Mary Bliss said. "Was he all right?"

"How should I know?" Ms. Peabody said, shrugging. "We had to get somebody from paper products to finish dishing out the party pizzas. It was a hell of a morning, I'll tell you."

"I'm sure," Mary Bliss said. "Will there be anything else?"

"Time card," Ms. Peabody said. She handed one to Mary Bliss. "Punch in as soon as you get here, punch out when you're ready to leave. Make sure you check the schedule to see what time you're on tomorrow."

Mary Bliss remembered Queen Esther's advice. "Ms. Peabody? I need to let you know about my religious concerns. I'm a very strict Methodist. And it's absolutely against my religion to work Sundays. I hope that will be all right."

"No." Ms. Peabody didn't look up again. "It's not all right. We all work on Sundays. Got that, Mrs. McGowan?"

Mary Bliss threaded her way through the frozen food section until she found station D, which turned out to be a card table with a cutting board, a toaster oven, and a large cooler full of frozen food.

The product demonstration hostess at station D was actually a host. He looked to be in his early sixties, and the name badge pinned to his blue apron said ART.

"Hi, there," Mary Bliss said, adjusting the bill of her baseball cap so that he could see her face. "I'm Mary Bliss. I'm your replacement."

"Great," Art said. In a minute, he'd stripped off the apron and tucked his own cap in the back pocket of his slacks. "Did they tell you the drill?"

"Only to hand out the manufacturer's coupons and to replace the unused stock in the walk-in freezers,"

Mary Bliss said. "Just what is it I'm going to be demonstrating."

"Right there," Art said, gesturing toward the cooler, which was stacked with colorful blue-and-white cardboard boxes. "Mrs. Korey's Kod Kakes."

"Fish sticks?" Mary Bliss felt her body sag.

"I guess it's fish," Art said. "It sure smells fishy. But I couldn't guarantee it's real cod. Anyway, here's what you do."

He pointed toward a small cutting board and a knife on the card table. "Cut the Kod Kakes into quarters, and toast them in the toaster oven for about five minutes. And don't forget to keep putting out the cocktail sauce." Mary Bliss noted that there was a two-gallon jug of Mrs. Korey's Kocktail Sauce on the card table. "Without the cocktail sauce, they really are inedible."

"Oh," Mary Bliss said. "I don't have a lot of experience with fish sticks. Are people really willing to try these? Are they big sellers?"

"Not by themselves," Art said. "But with the manufacturer's coupon, a carton of eighteen only costs about a dollar ninety-nine. That's a lot of fish stick for the money. Mostly the people who buy them are your immigrant-type consumer."

"I see," Mary Bliss said.

People were starting to line up in front of the station. The timer on the toaster oven dinged.

"Your Kod Kakes are done," Art said. He lowered his voice. "Did they tell you about your quota?"

"Quota?" Mary Bliss whispered. "Mr. Robertson didn't say anything about a quota."

"The bastards," Art said. "That's how they figure your pay. It's all based on the number of samples you hand out."

"The twenty-two an hour isn't straight salary?"

"Twenty-two bucks an hour?" Art snorted. "Is that what he told you he's paying?"

"Yes," Mary Bliss said. "Isn't that what you make?"

"I make eight bucks an hour," Art said. "And I'm the highest producer in the company. God, I can't believe they're trying that trick."

"Excuse me, but I would like to try a Kod Kake." A short squatty woman in a bilious green-and-gold sari was at the front of the sample line.

"Oh yes," Mary Bliss said. She fumbled with the toaster oven door, finally punching the knob that made the door spring open.

"I gotta go," Art said.

"Wait," Mary Bliss pleaded. "You said something about a quota system. What did you mean?"

"Just this," Art said, slinging his apron over his shoulder. "You gotta move a lot of Kod Kakes. You know what I mean? Empty out the cooler you got, and refill it as soon as it's empty. Keep moving that fish, that's all. Cause it's all about the numbers. And take it from me. You can forget that twenty-two an hour Robertson promised you." He gave a hearty laugh. "That's a good one. Twenty-two an hour. I gotta remember to tell that to the missus when I get home."

18

At nine o'clock, Mary Bliss gave in and took her fifteen-minute break. Her stomach was growling and the muscles in her calves screamed in pain.

She limped into the employee lounge and sank down into a Bargain Bonanza blue plastic chair. The first thing she did was kick off her pumps. The second thing she did was put her head down on the table and close her eyes.

"Tough night, huh?"

Mary Bliss lifted her head. Queen Esther was sitting across the table from her, eating cottage cheese from a Tupperware dish.

"My calves feel like they're on fire," Mary Bliss said, reaching down and massaging first one, then the other.

"Told you to get you some sneakers," Queen Esther said. She held up a cherry tomato. "Want one?"

Mary Bliss hesitated, then stuffed the tomato in her mouth. "Thanks. I'm starved. I didn't realize I'd be working so late, and I didn't pack any lunch."

"You giving away samples," Queen Esther said. "Whyn't you just help yourself to some of that?"

"I'm not that hungry," Mary Bliss said. "I'm demonstrating Mrs. Korey's Kod Kakes. They're absolutely disgusting."

Queen Esther wrinkled her nose. "I was wonderin' what that smell was. Girl, you might wanna get those clothes you got on dry-cleaned after today."

Mary Bliss sighed. Another expense.

Her new friend shoved her brown bag across the table toward her. "There's a homemade brownie in there, and an apple. Help yourself. My mama packs me enough dinner for an army."

"Thank you so much," Mary Bliss said, diving into the brownie.

"Other than being starved and your feet hurtin', how you doin' out there?" Queen Esther asked.

Mary Bliss rolled her eyes. "I can't even *give* those fish sticks away. I've only gone through one carton, this whole night, and that was because this weird Pakistani woman kept coming back for seconds and thirds. I finally gave her the whole box, plus about a dozen coupons."

"Lady got on this puke-colored wraparound dress, talk with an accent?" Queen Esther asked.

"Yes," Mary Bliss said, surprised. "Is she a regular customer?"

"Wouldn't call her a customer," Queen Esther said. "Far as I know, she don't never buy nothin'. Just walks around the store with an empty cart, eating samples. Calls herself Fatima. You ever hear a name like that?"

"I've heard it, but I never met anybody named that," Mary Bliss said. She'd never met anybody named Queen Esther before either, but she kept that to herself.

"I don't know what I'm going to do about these damned Kod Kakes," Mary Bliss said, rubbing her toes now. "The product demonstration host I took over for, this guy named Art? Right before he left, he said something about my pay being tied to the number of samples and coupons I hand out. The man who hired me never said anything about that."

"What did he say?"

"Just that I was hired," Mary Bliss said. "The classified ad said twenty-two dollars an hour. I just assumed that was what the pay would be."

"Twenty-two dollars an hour? For real? I bet the manager of this whole store don't make twenty-two dollars an hour."

"Art said he's the company's top producer, and he only makes eight dollars an hour," Mary Bliss said. "I guess the ad was just a come-on. I can't believe I was stupid enough to fall for it."

"Sounds too good to be true, it usually is," Queen Esther said. She scraped up the last of the cottage cheese from the plastic tub with a plastic fork, then snapped the top back on the tub. "Guess I better get back on the floor. I need to sell me three more of them Liz Claiborne watches so I meet my quota for the night."

"Can I ask you something?" Mary Bliss said. "How do you do that? How do you make people want to buy something?"

Queen Esther tapped her head with her forefinger. "It's up here. I make up my mind how good those watches are, and every person comes within shoutin' distance, I tell 'em what a great buy they are. I make it a game, see? Like tonight, I told myself, Esther, girl, you ain't going to dinner 'til you've sold six watches. It took me 'til nine o'clock, but I did it."

Mary Bliss sighed. "At least your watches look good. And they don't stink to high heavens."

"That's true," Queen Esther said. "Course, unless you got motivation, you ain't got nothin'. You motivated, Mary Bliss McGowan?"

"I'm motivated," Mary Bliss said grimly. "I'm flat broke, my husband's gone, and I'm about to lose my house if I don't make some money in a hurry."

Queen Esther whistled softly. "Girl, you in a mess. Sound like you need to make them Kod Kakes disappear."

"How?" Mary Bliss wailed. "People won't even come down my aisle."

"You gotta get rid of 'em, right? Queen Esther gave her a broad wink. "Think about it. Use your head, girlfriend."

At nine-fifteen, Mary Bliss trudged back to station 4. The frozen food department was deserted, except for an elderly man who was studying the frozen pizza case.

Mary Bliss popped a Kod Kake into the toaster oven and started rehearsing her sales pitch.

When the toaster oven dinged, she took the Kod Kake and arranged it on one of the little paper cupcake liners. She carefully spooned Mrs. Korey's Kocktail Sauce all over the fish stick. At least the spicy red sauce disguised the smell somewhat. But it needed something else. Something to make it look palatable.

Mary Bliss had an idea. She darted over to the produce aisle and grabbed a handful of parsley. Then she snatched a lemon from the citrus fruit display. Back at station 4, she sliced the lemon into thin wedges, one of which she slid under the fish stick. She pinched off a sprig of parsley and put it on top of the pool of Kocktail Sauce.

"Oh, sir," she called out. The elderly man turned around and looked at her quizzically.

"Can I interest you in sampling an exciting new appetizer?" Mary Bliss made her voice sing. "This is our very newest product. And I'd love for you to try some."

The man wheeled his cart forward a little. He wore a sweat-stained yachting cap on the back of his head, and little wire-framed eyeglasses perched on the end of his weather-beaten nose. "Is it free?"

"Oh, yes, sir," Mary Bliss called. *Come closer,* she thought fiercely. *Come see what I've fixed for you, old man.*

He did her bidding, wheeling the cart right up to station 4.

"What is that, fish?" he asked.

Mary Bliss was thankful for the lemon wedges. The sharp smell covered up the fishy odor of the Kod Kakes.

She offered the doctored-up fish stick with a flourish. "It's called Mrs. Korey's Kod Kakes. Fresh-caught all-natural seafood from the bracing blue waters of New England. I just know you're going to love them."

In actuality Mary Bliss had no idea where Mrs. Korey got the kod for her Kakes. It could have been from a roadside ditch in Lower Alabama or a nuclear waste dump in Arkansas for all she knew. But what she did know was that she had to make this man like Mrs. Korey's fine fish sticks.

The old man took one. He nibbled on the edge, smacked his lips a little. "Not bad." He chewed vigorously. Mary Bliss turned her head so that she wouldn't have to watch. She should have felt guilty, she knew, but she didn't.

"Wouldn't you like to try another?" she said, as he polished off the first one.

"Don't mind if I do," the old man said happily.

Mary Bliss placed two fish sticks in the toaster oven. "It'll just be a couple minutes," she told him. "They're best when they're hot and crispy right out of the oven."

The toaster dinged, and Mary Bliss prepared the fish sticks, slathering them with sauce, two lemon slices, and a small forest of parsley.

The old man chewed noisily, and Mary Bliss busied herself cleaning up her station. "Yummy, aren't they?" she asked.

He nodded, working his jaws.

"And we've got an amazing manufacturer's coupon we're offering tonight," Mary Bliss continued. "With the coupon, you're going to get a carton of eighteen Kod Kakes for a dollar ninety-nine."

He smiled widely, and small crumbs of breading spilled down his already soiled white sport shirt.

Mary Bliss felt herself on a roll. "I see you were doing some comparison shopping on those pizzas," she said boldly. "But, you know, these Kod Kakes are a much better bargain. Do you live alone?" she asked the man.

"With my son," he said, wiping his mouth with a paper napkin.

"Mrs. Korey's Kod Kakes are individually wrapped for freshness," Mary Bliss said. "So you can cook just one, or three or four, if you and your son are dining together."

"That's true," the old man said. He picked up one of the cartons of Kod Kakes and squinted, looking at the fine print on the back of the box.

"And another thing," Mary Bliss said. She was determined to make this her first sale of the night. "It's a proven fact that cold-water fish like our Kod Kakes are full of natural fish oils, which is proven to reduce the risk of plaque and gingivitis and arteriosclerosis."

"That so?" he looked up at her, clearly impressed with her medical know-how.

"Oh yes," she said airily. She opened her cooler and let her hand rest delicately on the lid. "Nutritionally speaking, as well as economically, our product is clearly the best bargain in frozen food products. Only a dollar ninety-nine for eighteen delicious Kod Kakes. Of course, this is a grand-opening special, and they're going fast, as fast as, well, Kod Kakes." She giggled unashamedly.

"How many boxes would you like?" she asked, giving him a flirtatious little wink.

"Four oughta do it," he said, blushing a little.

Mary Bliss handed him a wad of coupons. "Oh, take six," she insisted. "It's such a wonderful buy, I'd hate for you to miss out on it. And I just know your son is going to love them too."

When he'd wheeled away, with his cart stacked high with Mrs. Korey's Kakes, Mary Bliss pumped her fist in the air and did a little victory dance.

She'd made her first sale. Suddenly, her calves didn't hurt and her stomach wasn't churning. She cleaned up her station, shoved the rest of the Kod Kakes in the big walk-in freezer, and limped over to the time clock. It was five minutes to ten. She'd earned her first paycheck. Not the twenty-two an hour she'd been promised, it was true, but it was a start.

Tomorrow, she promised herself, she'd have it out with that peckerwood Jeff Robertson. And she'd definitely ditch the shoes.

19

Mary Bliss stripped. She stood under the shower and soaped herself with the expensive Crabtree and Evelyn lavender soap she'd been saving for a special occasion. She washed her hair with the grapefruit and mint shampoo her hairdresser had talked her into during her last visit, conditioned with honey-coconut crème rinse, and then loofahed her body until her skin was nearly raw.

When she was convinced that all traces of Mrs. Korey's Kod Kakes had been banished from her body, she took her Love Boat cruisewear and placed it in a plastic bag, which she tightly knotted and deposited in the trash can outside the house. Then she put a brick on the top of the can, to keep the neighborhood marauding cats from tearing into her fish-scented clothing.

Erin's car had been in the driveway when she arrived home at ten forty-five, but her daughter didn't respond to Mary Bliss's polite knock at her bedroom door.

Mary Bliss was too tired to fret about her daughter's feud with her. She slipped between the sheets of her bed and fell into a deep and dreamless sleep.

When the phone rang in the morning, she was still in a kind of death-sleep.

"Mrs. McGowan?"

Mary Bliss rubbed her eyes and yawned. "Yes?"

"Jeff Robertson here."

"Who?" She looked at the clock radio. Good God. She'd slept 'til ten. Unheard of.

"Jeff Robertson at Market Concepts. Your employer. Remember?"

"Yes?" Mary Bliss said. She got out of bed and found her robe, which she wrapped around herself. Coffee. She needed coffee before she could deal with the likes of Jeff Robertson.

"I was just looking at the sales report from yesterday," Robertson continued. "And I gotta say, Mrs. McGowan, I'm extremely disappointed."

Erin's bedroom door was ajar, and Erin was gone. Mary Bliss leaned against the door frame and rubbed her eyes. It had been two days since she'd had a real conversation with her daughter. Parker was gone, and now Erin was somewhere else too. God. How did you get through to a teenaged girl?

Mary Bliss gripped the phone tightly as she walked downstairs.

"Mrs. McGowan, do you understand what I'm telling you?"

She sighed. "You said something about disappointment?"

"That's putting it mildly. Six boxes. That was the total sales output for your shift last night. That's, like, pathetic, Mrs. McGowan. Really pathetic."

Mary Bliss spooned instant coffee into a cup and put the kettle on to boil. Instant coffee. Now that was pathetic.

"Mr. Robertson, do your sales figures show what the product was that I was demonstrating?"

"Of course. It's right here in the report faxed over here this morning."

"What does it say there?"

"Mrs. Korey's Kod Kakes. Eighteen-count cartons. Sales price, with coupon, a dollar ninety-nine. That's an awesome price. Your product should have been flying out of the store at that price last night."

Mary Bliss wanted to scream. "Have you ever tasted these Kod Kakes before, Mr. Robertson? Have you ever smelled them? Well, I have. And let me tell you, they are not fit for human consumption. The one person who did buy them was a near-blind eighty-year-old who only bought them because he lives on a fixed income. I'll probably burn in hell for making him buy them."

"Not my problem," Robertson said. "Look. These sales figures of yours, they're not gonna cut it, you know? You totally are nowhere near where you need to be with your quota."

"You never mentioned a quota to me. You never said my salary would be tied to sales. What's going on here, Mr. Robertson? What about my twenty-two dollars an hour?"

"Who told you that was your salary?"

"You did," she shouted. "The ad in the paper specifically said twenty-two dollars an hour."

"No." He sounded calm now. "If you'll look closer, it said 'Up to twenty-two dollars an hour.'"

"Are you telling me I'm *not* making twenty-two dollars an hour?"

"Hell no, you're not making that kind of money," Robertson said. "Selling six cartons a night? You oughta be paying us. Your salary is directly tied to productivity. Here's the deal, Mrs. McGowan. You are in that store to move product. You got that? Now. Art? You met Art? He's a person who moves product. He sold forty-eight cartons of Mrs. Korey's Kod Kakes yesterday. We had to have more product sent out from the distribution center, just for Art."

The kettle started to whistle. Mary Bliss felt herself start to boil over too.

"Listen," she said, pouring water over the coffee crystals and stirring it with a teaspoon. "Don't you dare compare me to somebody else. I worked my tail off last night. I don't know how Art got anybody to buy that stuff. Nobody would even come down my end of the aisle after I started heating it up in the toaster oven."

"Never mind that now," Robertson said. "You'll have a new product tonight. And I expect a lot better performance from you. Or we'll have to rethink your situation."

"Is that a threat?" Mary Bliss was astounded. She'd worked one night, and already they were threatening to fire her. She'd never been fired before, not in her entire life. Unless you counted Parker's firing her as his wife.

"No," Robertson said. "It's a promise. Get my drift?"

"Perfectly," Mary Bliss snapped. She went looking in the refrigerator for half-and-half. There wasn't any. There wasn't any milk either. She closed the refrigerator and walked over to the pantry. She could use evaporated milk in a pinch. But she didn't have any evaporated milk either. And she couldn't drink her coffee black. She just couldn't.

"Imogene Peabody is expecting you out at Riverdale at noon," Robertson was saying.

"Was there anything else, Mr. Robertson?"

If she didn't get some caffeine in her system right quick, there was no telling what she might do or say. She opened the freezer and pawed through the boxes of frozen peas and desiccated-looking chicken parts.

On the top shelf she found a quart container of fudge-ripple ice cream. She peeled off the lid. The carton was technically bare, with just some smidgens of fudge ripple still clinging to the bottom of the carton. She wished Parker were around. She would throttle him with her bare hands. Which were now shaking badly. Parker was the one who was always putting empty cartons of food back in the pantry or the refrigerator. He never ate sweets in front of her, always saying he didn't even like them. But somebody had eaten a whole carton of ice cream, and it wasn't Mary Bliss, and it wasn't Erin. Parker was a closet snacker. Another of his least attractive features. She must remember to make a list of them.

Mary Bliss scraped up the last of the ice cream and let it melt into the hot coffee. She was admiring the way the smooth white cream dissolved into the black coffee. Like a little mini whirlpool in a mud puddle.

"Noon, Mrs. McGowan. You've got that, right?"

"'Til when?" Mary Bliss asked. "Not 'til ten o'clock again. I really have to be home tonight, Mr. Robertson. You can't expect me to work a ten-hour shift just like that. I have a teenaged daughter and a house to take care of."

"Not my problem," Robertson repeated. "That's the problem with women like you. Always all these lame excuses about kids and stuff. You never hear Art with an excuse."

"I need to get off at eight," she said firmly. "I have a family emergency."

"Family emergency," he said mockingly. "Everybody has a family emergency. All right. Just this once. But it's the last time we arrange schedules just for you. There are other people to consider, you know."

"Thank you," Mary Bliss said. Robertson hung up. "Asshole," she added.

When she'd finished her coffee and eaten some buttered toast, she walked slowly back upstairs, back to Erin's room.

She'd told Robertson she had a family emergency. It was true. Her life was coming unglued. She needed to reach Erin, needed to heal things between them.

She sat down on Erin's bed, picked up the faded pink crib quilt with the appliquéd bunnies draped across one of her pillows. The quilt had been a baby gift from Lyle, her college classmate. It had once had a bright-pink satin binding, but Erin had loved the binding to tatters.

Mary Bliss rubbed the quilt against her cheek. It smelled like her daughter. Like soap and perfume and maybe even a little hint of baby powder.

She stood up and made the bed, folding the crib quilt and tucking it neatly beneath Erin's pillow. Then she walked around the room, scooping up dirty laundry, putting away the folded clothes that hadn't quite made it into the dresser drawers. With a tissue she wiped off the top of Erin's mahogany dresser, sending small dust flurries sailing into the air.

The room needed a good dusting and vacuuming, but there wasn't time today. There didn't seem to be time for anything she really needed to do.

Back in the master bedroom, she started to make her own bed, then stopped, suddenly, when she spied the small yellow scrap of paper on Parker's side of the bed.

It had been written in script, in a bright-pink felt-tip pen. "Mommy. I'm sorry I was a bitch. I love you. Erin." She'd drawn a little heart at the bottom of the slip, and a flower beside that.

Mary Bliss smoothed out the paper and touched it briefly to her lips before tucking it carefully in her jewelry box.

After she'd dressed in jeans and sneakers, she ran downstairs and went back to the freezer. She put some chicken pieces in the refrigerator to thaw for supper, a goopy chicken cheese casserole with cream of mushroom soup. With rice and frozen peas, it was her daughter's idea of a feast. When had she last fixed a real meal and shared it at the table with Erin?

She left a note on the kitchen table. "Erin—I've got a job. Tell you all about it at dinner. Love you bunches. Mom."

20

Mary Bliss spread newspapers on the kitchen table, got out the Wright's silver cream and one of Parker's raggedy old T-shirts, and set to work on his grandmother's silver tea service.

It was heavy Sheffield silver, Victorian, with a dizzying combination of chasing, engraving, raised whorls, and monograms. She hadn't thought about the tea service when she'd pawned her flatware, maybe because she'd really never considered it to be hers. It was McGowan silver, and Eula had made it clear, when she'd handed it over on her and Parker's first anniversary, that she expected it to be handed down to the McGowan children. But things had changed. She didn't expect to be hosting tea parties anytime soon.

She was working the edge of the teapot with an old toothbrush when Katharine kicked open the kitchen door with her sandal.

"Hey, shug," Katharine called out. Her arms were loaded with Publix grocery bags. "Give me a hand here, will you? I've got a bunch more out in the car."

"What's all this?" Mary Bliss asked, setting the bags down on the counter.

"Emergency assistance," Katharine said.

"I can't . . ."

"Never mind telling me you can't accept charity. You've already pawned your wedding silver and you're down to digging change out of the sofa cushions, I know for a fact. It's just a little temporary help."

"Katharine," Mary Bliss started. Her face was beet-red. She'd had a series of humiliations in the past week, but this was possibly the worst.

Mary Bliss's mouth had a sharp metal taste. She remembered another time, back in her mama's house, when an anonymous neighbor had left a sack of groceries on the front porch of their ramshackle wood-frame house. Her own daddy had been gone two weeks by then. Her mother had borne the shame in silence, thinking no one else knew. They'd eaten biscuits and cane syrup for breakfast and supper, and Mary Bliss's mama saw to it that she got a free hot lunch at school.

She'd been the only white child in her whole school to get the free hot lunch.

Word of their plight had gotten out. After that, a brown paper sack showed up on their porch every two weeks, for nearly a year, until her mother, who was by then working two jobs, had left a little note on the porch, telling their anonymous friend, "Thank you, but we're making out now."

"I know you mean well," she said, trying to find the right words, the ones that would not offend her friend.

"Stop it right now," Katharine said, holding up her hand like a traffic cop. "Don't say another word. Just get your butt out to the car and start bringing in groceries."

When they'd unloaded the Jeep, the counter was covered with food. Katharine had bought lavishly: steaks, roasts, chicken, wine, imported cheeses and olives, cleaning and paper supplies, even the current issue of *People* magazine.

"This is too much," Mary Bliss protested. "You must have spent a couple hundred dollars on all this food."

"Closer to three hundred," Katharine said cheerfully. "You know I can never remember to clip coupons or check the specials. I just buy what I want. Always have."

Mary Bliss put the milk in the refrigerator and started stashing paper towels under the sink.

"I'll pay you back, I swear. I got a part-time job. And I'll get my first paycheck Friday."

Katharine opened a carton of Diet Coke and took out two cans. "This is a gift. Not a loan. Anyway, you wouldn't be paying me. You'd be paying Charlie. I charged it all on his American Express card. Don't you just love modern times? Charging groceries on American Express? What a concept!"

Mary Bliss sighed. She sliced up one of the limes Katharine had bought, squeezed them over two glasses of ice, and poured the drinks. "You're making matters worse, charging up all those cards. His lawyer's not gonna put up with it, Katharine."

"Shi-ii-it," Katharine said, making it a three-syllable word. "It's part of my budget. My lawyer told Charlie I need seven hundred dollars a week for groceries. He has no idea what groceries really cost. But hey, what's this about a job?"

"I started yesterday," Mary Bliss said. "I'm a product demonstration hostess. This week they've got me down at a new Bargain Bonanza Club in Riverdale. I hand out samples and free coupons."

"Sounds awful," Katharine said. "How much are they paying you?"

"Not enough," Mary Bliss admitted.

"How much is not enough?"

"Probably around six dollars an hour," Mary Bliss said. "If I can get people to try the product and buy it. Yesterday didn't go so good. My product was nasty. Mrs. Korey's frozen Kod Kakes."

"Gross," Katharine shuddered. "You can't really be serious about this, Mary Bliss. I mean, for God's sakes. A sample lady?"

"Why not?" Mary Bliss said sharply. "It's honest work. I've never been afraid to work. Not ever."

"Aw, don't go getting your little blue-collar feelings hurt now," Katharine said. "This makes no sense. You're a college-educated professional, Mary Bliss. You don't belong in a store where they sell toilet paper by the mile. And you're gonna be paying for gas, not to mention insurance and upkeep and wear and tear on the car. Plus you're gonna be taxed for your income. And just how much income could it be?"

"It's better than nothing," Mary Bliss said. She took a sip of the Diet Coke, trying to wash away the metallic taste of poverty.

"I don't know why you keep resisting the obvious solution to all this," Katharine said. She was leafing rapidly through the *People* magazine, flipping pages with only a glance.

"It's the only solution," she said, staring up at Mary Bliss. "Parker McGowan has to die. And honey, it needs to happen pretty damn soon."

"No," Mary Bliss said. "It would be wrong."

"Talk about wrong," Katharine said. "Here you sit, flat broke. And there he is, off on some goddamned island paradise. And you can bet he's got a woman with him too. Think he went off by himself? Hah! You know what happens when a man says he's leaving to find himself? He finds himself, all right—with another woman."

"We don't know that," Mary Bliss said. But it was what she'd been thinking.

"Hey," Katharine said, running a finger over the silver teapot. "What's with the silver tea service? You giving yourself a party? Or are you fixing to hock that too? Honey, Parker left you. He lied to you and he stole from you, and he took everything, including your dignity."

"I've still got Erin," Mary Bliss said. She took her time putting the rubber gloves on. Then she picked up the toothbrush again and started working the edge of the teapot with it. "Erin's the most important thing." Tears started to well up in her eyes. She rubbed at one and got silver polish in it, then started to cry for real.

"Katharine," she said, her voice cracking. "It's so awful. All we do lately is fight. And I can't stand that."

Katharine got up and tore a paper towel off the roll she'd just unloaded from one of the grocery sacks.

"Hell, Mary Bliss, fighting with your kid is nothing. Chip and I nearly killed each other his senior year of high school. We still fight like crazy, although not as much since Charlie left. I think Chip's afraid I'll go all psycho mama on him, because of the divorce and all. But listen. Even when things were at the worst, I always knew he didn't mean nothin' by it. Sometimes, I just take that big old nineteen-year-old, and I wrap my arms around him and hang on for dear life. He's two inches taller than Charlie now, did you know that? But he'll never be too big for me to love on. And he knows it too. So don't you worry about the fussin', cause that's all it is. Just fussin'."

"I don't know," Mary Bliss said. "It's not just little squabbles. It's different this time. Erin has changed. It's like every day she's building a brick wall between us."

"Have you tried talking to her?" Katharine asked. "Does she know that's how you feel?"

"I can't get her to stand still long enough to talk," Mary Bliss said. "She works, then she stays out late with friends. Or she's at soccer practice. That darned coach of hers has practically taken over her life."

Katharine reached across the table and grasped Mary Bliss's hand.

"You've got to face facts now, Mary Bliss," she said. "Parker has taken off and left you. And sweetie, I know it's hard, but Erin's a big girl now. Next year she's a senior, and then she's gone too. And you'll be here. Alone. That's why you have got to quit ignoring this situation. You have got to do something drastic. Or you're going to lose the house and everything else."

Mary Bliss eased her hand away from Katharine's. "I can't do it, Kate. I can't lie to my child. I can't tell her her daddy is dead. She'd never forgive me."

"What other choice do you have?" she demanded. "Bringing home six bucks an hour? Get real. It's all falling down around your ears, Mary Bliss. How will Erin feel when you tell her you can't afford for her to finish her senior year at Fair Oaks Academy? What's she gonna say when you have to sell the house? Or when you have to sell one of the cars to pay the rent? Face facts. That child has never wanted for anything in her life. But unless you do something quick, you're both headed for the poorhouse."

Mary Bliss shook her head violently.

"No. We're not moving and Erin's staying at Fair Oaks. There's another way. I've been avoiding it. I'd rather take a beating, but you're right about one thing. My back is against the wall. So I'll just have to go on and go."

"To Mexico?"

"No," Mary Bliss said. "Closer than that. Fair Oaks Assisted Living Facility."

"Eula?" Katharine gasped.

"It's the only way."

Assisted Living Facility."

21

Eula thought women who wore blue jeans out in public were harlots, or worse. Mary Bliss slipped on a cotton dress and a pair of sandals, and she packed her blue jeans and polo shirt and sneakers in a tote bag, because she still had to go be a product demonstration hostess later in the day at Bargain Bonanza.

She was heading down the hallway at the Fair Oaks Assisted Living Facility when a voice stopped her.

"Mrs. McGowan?"

Mary Bliss turned. A tall thin woman in pink nurse's scrubs hurried toward her. "Could I have a word with you?"

It was Anissa, who had been helping to take care of her mother-in-law since Eula had moved into the nursing home.

"Hey, Anissa," Mary Bliss said. "Is everything all right?"

"Well, probably," Anissa said. "I was wondering. Is something upsetting your mother-in-law?"

Mary Bliss thought about that. How much should she say?

"Not that I know of," she said finally. "Why? Is something wrong with Eula?"

Anissa frowned. "She's been difficult the last few days. Won't eat meals with her friends like she usually does. Refuses to go to Bible study or crafts time. And there's something else."

Anissa lowered her voice. "I hate to be telling you this, but your mother-in-law used some very unpleasant language last night to Hidalgo, the nurse's aide on the late shift."

Mary Bliss tightened her grasp on the handle of her food basket.

"I don't know what to say," she said. "I do apologize. It's so embarrassing. Eula was raised in a fairly closed society. We've tried to talk to her about her language, but . . ."

Anissa rolled her eyes. "Honey, they were all raised in a different time. We try to just ignore their ways, but when our folks drop the n-word all the time, it's hard on us, you know?"

"I am *so* sorry," Mary Bliss said.

Anissa patted her arm. "I know y'all don't talk like that or think like that. And I'm sure Eula doesn't mean anything by it. But Hidalgo, she's not used to having people cuss her and accuse her of stealing from them."

"She did that? Oh God. I'll talk to her. I promise."

Anissa nodded. "She's slipping some, you know?"

Mary Bliss was taken aback. "Physically? Has her doctor said anything?"

"Her blood pressure's been up," Anissa said. "She hasn't been sleeping too good, says her chest is giving her pains."

"But she's all right? Physically?" Mary Bliss asked. What would she do if Eula got really sick? How would she reach Parker?

"The doctor changed her meds, and he's giving her something to sleep better. Ambien. I don't think it's anything drastic. But I wanted you to know she was cuttin' up."

"I appreciate it," Mary Bliss said. "And I'll talk to her about her language."

She knocked lightly at the door to Eula's room, but when there was no answer, she pushed the door open. Eula was asleep, her face pressed flat against a pillow, her mouth open, and a thin line of spittle glistened on her chin.

"Eula?" Mary Bliss whispered.

She tiptoed closer to the bed. Eula didn't look much different. Her iron-gray curls were flattened on one side, and the hollows of her eyes were deep with shadows.

Mary Bliss put the basket of food on the bedside table and looked around. The room was a mess. Clothes had been flung over a high-backed chair, and a trash basket was overflowing. It smelled funky too. Like dirty socks. It wasn't like Eula to put up with a messy room. Maybe she really was slipping.

She went to the janitor's closet at the end of the hall, got a broom and a sponge mop and a bucket of lemon-scented cleaner, and came back and went to work.

Mary Bliss worked quietly. She swept and mopped and hung up clothes in Eula's closet. She was going through the laundry, sorting things into a plastic bag to take home.

"You stealing from me?" Eula's voice crackled with anger.

Mary Bliss dropped the plastic bag, startled. "Meemaw, you're awake. How are you feeling?"

Eula was struggling to sit up. Her cotton nightgown hung from one bony shoulder, exposing the top of her pale, shriveled breast. The thought occurred to Mary Bliss. *Someday I'll look like that too.*

"Good thing I did wake up," Eula said. "I reckon you already ransacked my purse."

"Meemaw," Mary Bliss said, shocked. "You were asleep. The room needed tidying, and I want to take your laundry home to wash it. You know I would never . . ."

"Steal? Why not? Everybody else in this place is a thief. They're robbing me blind. Think I don't know that? Especially that little spic girl. I ran her off last night."

"Meemaw! You shouldn't say words like that. Nigger. Spic. The words are demeaning. And ugly."

"That girl doesn't understand a word of English," Meemaw said, waving away Mary Bliss's protests. "Anyway, why can't they get some nice white folks in here to take care of me?"

"The people who work here are very nice," Mary Bliss said. "Nice white folks and black folks and brown folks. And you need to stop talking so ugly to them. It hurts their feelings."

"Who cares?" Eula said. "Put the television on, will you? I want to see what Guy Sharpe says about the weather. If we don't get some rain soon, I swear I'm gonna dry up and blow away."

Mary Bliss decided not to point out to Eula that her favorite weatherman had been retired from channel 2 for at least ten years.

Instead, she lifted the pie out of the basket and set it on the bed tray. She cut a slice and put it on the flower-sprigged china plate she'd brought from home. She poured the iced tea into a glass and placed it beside the pie plate, then she slid the rolling table over next to Eula's bed.

"Look, Meemaw," she said. "I brought you a treat. Coconut custard pie from the women's circle cookbook. And home-brewed sweet tea. Your favorites."

Eula had her eyes closed, her head tilted back on the pillow. She opened one eye and grunted. Then she opened the other.

"Treat. Huh. More like a bribe."

But her hand found the electric controls for the hospital bed, and she raised herself to a sitting position.

"Bribe? What's that supposed to mean?" Mary Bliss asked.

"Think I don't know what you're up to? You come sidling in here today, all nicey-nice, mopping and bowing and sweeping. Where were you yesterday? Wednesday? I waited all day, and you never came. Say what you mean to say, girl. Get on with it. I don't want to miss the weather report."

Mary Bliss had been steeling herself for this moment.

"I'm sorry about yesterday. I have a new job and I had to work. All right. Yes. I do need to talk to you. About Parker. Have you heard from him?"

Eula's lips pressed into a tight line. "No."

Mary Bliss looked at her warily. She never could read Eula McGowan. Was she lying? There was just no telling.

"I'll get right to the point. Parker left us in a bad way, Meemaw. He hasn't paid the bills. Emptied out all our accounts. *Our* accounts," she emphasized. "Joint checking and savings. Investments. Erin's college money. It's all gone."

Eula didn't blink. She slowly took a bite of pie, then followed that with a gulp of tea.

"I'm going to lose the house if I can't pay what we owe," Mary Bliss continued. "I've taken a part-time job, but it's not nearly enough. It'll just barely buy groceries. And Erin's tuition for Twin Oaks Academy is due next month. It's eleven thousand dollars, Meemaw. And I don't have it."

Eula ate another bite of pie.

"You'll manage," she said finally. "That's one thing I always did give you credit for, Mary Bliss. You might not be much in the brains or the looks department, but I always did say you were a good manager."

Mary Bliss felt something stirring in her chest. Around the esophagus area. She was shocked when it came out as a laugh. She laughed. She did! She laughed so hard she got stomach cramps.

Eula took another swallow of tea, then set her fork on the edge of her plate, clearly horrified at Mary Bliss's seeming hysteria.

Mary Bliss finally got up and went into Eula's private bathroom, which she had just finished mopping. When she had peed and washed her hands and blew her nose, she came back out.

"Sorry," she said, emerging a few minutes later. She managed to stifle one last snigger.

"There is something bad wrong with you, girl," Eula said.

"Yes," Mary Bliss readily agreed. "You're right, Meemaw. There is something bad wrong with me. I'm at the end of my rope. I'm here, asking you for help. If not for me, for Erin. You do love Erin, don't you?"

"What kind of fool question is that?" Eula snapped.

Mary Bliss dabbed at her eyes with a tissue. "Will you at least loan me the money for Erin's tuition?" she asked. "It would be a loan. I'd pay you back."

Eula stabbed at the pie with her fork, smearing the creamy yellow filling all over the plate.

"I'm an old lady," she said, not looking up. "I'm old, and I'm sick. I'm not sleeping well. My chest hurts. My only child has gone. But you, you're young, Mary Bliss. You're healthy. And you've got *your* child at home with you. You'll manage. I always did."

"I see," Mary Bliss said. So that was it. The metallic taste was back in her mouth again. She wanted to gargle with some of that disinfectant, to make it go away. She picked up her basket and left Eula's room.

She stopped in the visitor's rest room in the nursing home lobby to change into her work clothes. As she was about to leave, Anissa stopped her.

"How did she seem to you?" Anissa asked, concern on her face. "Any better, did you think?"

Mary Bliss had to clamp her hand over her mouth to keep from laughing out loud again. Once she started, she was afraid she wouldn't be able to stop. She took a deep breath. "No better, no worse. Eula McGowan never changes."

22

Imogene Peabody seemed surprised to see Mary Bliss.

"Oh," she said, looking down the rim of her half-glasses. "You came back."

"Yes, ma'am," Mary Bliss said, lifting her chin.

Meemaw wasn't going to give her a dime, she knew now. Had probably known it deep down all along. Nobody else could, or would, help her out of her predicament. She thought of the storybook she'd read to Erin every night when she was still lap-sized. *The Little Red Hen.* Nobody would help the little red hen feed her chicks. Not the rooster, who was long gone. Not the cow, not the pig, not the sheep . . . nobody.

"All right," Mary Bliss told herself. "I'll be like the little red hen. I'll just do it my own self."

Ms. Peabody scanned the clipboard on her desk. "Your first day didn't go too well, did it?"

"It was a disaster," Mary Bliss said.

"You're on station G today. Produce department. You're off at nine tonight."

"All right," Mary Bliss said. She tied the strings of her blue apron and straightened the bill of her baseball cap. "I brought my own gloves today," she said, pulling them from the pocket of her jeans.

"Swell," Ms. Peabody drawled.

Mary Bliss turned to leave the cubicle, all set to plant the wheat and harvest and grind it and bake it into bread all by her own self. And take care of her chick. All by her own self.

"Ms. McGowan?"

Mary Bliss stopped thinking about wheat. "Yes, ma'am?"

"Bargain Bonanza has decided to immediately discontinue the sale of Mrs. Korey's Kod Kakes."

"Really? Why?"

"Consumer feedback." Was that a glint of amusement in Ms. Peabody's eyes?

"Virtually everyone who bought that product yesterday returned it to the store this morning. It wasn't very pretty, I can tell you. Cases and cases of the stuff, and naturally, the Kakes had started defrosting. We had to disinfect the consumer service area, and then truck the remaining Kod Kakes out of the store."

"My goodness," Mary Bliss said. She was starting to feel a little better. "Can I ask what you did with all those fish sticks?"

Ms. Peabody's lip twitched slightly. "It's supposed to be highly confidential. But, since you were involved, I guess I can tell you. Half the product went to the Clayton County Animal Shelter."

Mary Bliss shuddered, thinking about all those helpless puppies and kittens, subjected to Mrs. Korey's Kod Kakes. "And the other half?" she asked.

"Do you know anyone in New Jersey?"

"No. Why?"

"Let's just say there's a certain toxic waste dump outside Trenton that's going to require quite a bit of backfill in the near future."

Mary Bliss's feet felt lighter as she sped toward the produce department. Maybe her career as a product demonstration hostess wasn't doomed after all.

Station G was another card table, covered with a green plastic tablecloth. Big tubs of cream-covered stuff were stacked in the cooler beside the station, and Art, the man she'd met the day before, was emptying bags of baby carrots and celery sticks into a tiered plastic tray on the table.

"Well, look who's here," Art boomed when he saw Mary Bliss. "You came back."

"Yes," Mary Bliss said. "Did you hear about the Kod Kakes?"

"Shhh," Art said, putting a finger to his lips. "What Kod Kakes?"

"Right," Mary Bliss said. She could take a hint. "What are we demonstrating today?"

"Zippee Dip!" Art said joyously. "It's great stuff. Wonderful. Low-fat. Low-calorie. A tasty addition to any healthy snack."

He showed her how to use a funnel to pour the dip from the half-gallon tubs into little fluted paper cups, and instructed her to let shoppers take a handful of carrots and celery to dip into their own individual cups of Zippee Dip.

"Wouldn't it be easier to just put the dip in a big bowl and let people help themselves?" Mary Bliss asked, eyeing the mess Art had made on the tabletop. Glops of Zippee Dip spotted the table and the floor around station G. Art's thick-lensed glasses were spattered and his blue apron was streaked with the stuff.

"Good God, woman!" Art said. "Everybody dipping into one communal bowl? Haven't you completed your hostess hygiene class? Think of the implications."

After Art had gone, Mary Bliss did her best to clean up the area with the paper towels she found stashed under her card table. During a lull in business, she surreptitiously tasted the Zippee Dip. It had a vaguely sour-cream-and-chives taste. Nothing like delicious, Mary Bliss decided, but nowhere near as aggressively nasty as the Kod Kakes.

For hours and hours she poured dip, pushed carrots and celery, and cheerfully handed out coupons to the shoppers who ebbed and flowed through the produce department. Slowly, the cooler beside her emptied, and each time she saw a shopper add a tub of Zippee Dip to their cart, she felt a little zing, heard the ka-ching of money in the bank. Jeff Robertson still hadn't told her what her quota was, but she was positive she was close to meeting or surpassing it.

She was funneling dip into the paper cups when she felt a presence beside her. She looked up and almost dropped the tub.

"Randy!" she said. "What are you doing down here?"

"Bargain hunting," Randy Bowden said, gesturing toward a cart filled with food. "These grand opening specials are pretty good. And you know how it is with teenagers. They never stop eating. So what are *you* doing down here, Mary Bliss?"

"Oh, just keeping myself busy," she said, trying to sound happy and carefree. "Parker's out of town on a consulting job for most of the summer, so I thought a little part-time job would keep me from getting bored."

She could feel her face burning with shame and wondered if he really believed she was only working as a lark. And how must she look, with that goofy baseball cap and apron, not to mention the elbow-length rubber gloves?

"Careful," he said, steadying her hand with his. "You're spilling."

A lavalike puddle of dip was spreading over the card table. She busied herself mopping it up, to hide her embarrassment at having her cover blown.

He stuck a finger into one of the paper cups. "Zippee Dip, huh? Is it any good?"

"It's not bad," Mary Bliss said. "Try it with a carrot."

Randy took a baby carrot and plunged it into a cup of dip. He chewed slowly, thoughtfully.

He was not really so pathetic, Mary Bliss thought, watching him eat. He had nice brown eyes, and the glasses made him look intelligent. His hair had been trimmed since the last time she'd seen him, and he'd gotten some sun, so he didn't look as pale or needy. He was dressed in a good summer-weight suit, not the baggy shorts and T-shirts she usually saw him wearing around the neighborhood. He looked like a handsome young banker. No sign of divorce cooties.

And she looked like a loser, Mary Bliss thought.

Randy took another carrot and dipped it in his cup. "I like it," he decided. "And anything that will get Josh to eat a vegetable has got to be a good thing, don't you think?"

"Sure," she said. "I guess girls are different from boys. Erin loves vegetables. Especially carrots. I'm going to buy some for her before I leave tonight."

"Then I'll do the same," Randy said. He took two tubs out of her cooler. "Do you get a commission or something, if I buy more?"

"No," she said. "But it helps me make my sales quota."

"Anything to help the cause," he said, laughing. And he added another tub of Zippee Dip to his cart. And another.

"What time do you get off?" he asked, trying to sound casual.

She checked her wristwatch. "Another half an hour, thank God. I wore comfortable shoes today, but my feet are still about shot."

"I'm just about done shopping, myself," Randy said. "Want to get some dinner, after you get off?"

"Dinner?" *Was he asking her for a date?*

Two little pink spots appeared on Randy's cheeks. They were actually quite appealing. "That'd be all right, wouldn't it? I mean, Parker wouldn't care if we had dinner together, would he? Just two neighbors sharing a meal, right?"

She considered it. Erin wasn't speaking to her. God knew she was getting tired of eating by herself.

"What about Nancye?" she asked. "What would she think?"

"Good question," Randy asked. "Knowing Nancye, she'd probably assume we're sleeping together. She thinks because she's sleeping around, I must be doing it too."

"Oh."

"Would that bother you?" His voice was gentle, his brown eyes just the shade of Hershey's milk chocolate. There was a tiny spot of blood on the collar of his white shirt, probably from where he'd nicked himself shaving.

Would it bother her? To have Nancye Bowden thinking the same thing about her that she thought about Nancye? But she *knew* the slutty things Nancye Bowden was doing. And she, Mary Bliss, wasn't planning on any bad behavior in the Winn-Dixie parking lot. All she wanted was a real dinner, with a person who didn't despise her. Maybe some quiet conversation. And a chance to forget that the wolf was at her door.

"I'd love to have dinner with you," she said. "Where were you thinking of going?"

"My place," he said. "I bought a dozen steaks over in the meat department. Rib-eyes. And I'll pick up some baking potatoes, and they've got some frozen cheesecakes on special."

"Great," Mary Bliss said. "But you have to let me bring the wine. And I'll fix a salad too. You know, Zippee Dip is a great substitute for sour cream on baked potatoes. And it makes a wonderful salad dressing too."

23

She was singing in the shower, humming along, shampooing her hair, when she heard the phone ringing in the bedroom.

She grabbed a towel and ran for the phone, catching it on the fourth ring. She was out of breath, naked, and shampoo was dripping down into her eyes.

"Mary Bliss?"

It was Randy. "Do you guys have any charcoal over there? Like a dope, I forgot to buy any. Guess I'm still adjusting to buying groceries. And bachelor life in general."

"We've got a gas grill, so I never buy charcoal," Mary Bliss said.

"That's okay. I'll just run over to the Jiffy Mart. Can you think of anything else we need? Do you like steak sauce?"

"Oh, don't bother with going to the store," Mary Bliss said. "It's getting pretty late. Why don't you bring the steaks over here? It's just as easy to cook at my place."

"What? And pass up the chance to show you what an appalling housekeeper I am?"

"I'll take your word for it," Mary Bliss assured him. She felt lighthearted, close to happy, but maybe not quite.

"Okay, it's your house, then," he said. "How soon should I come over? I've pretty much got everything ready."

"Give me fifteen minutes to dry my hair and set the table," Mary Bliss said.

She was still humming while she dressed: loose drawstring pants, a sleeveless top, even a little eye makeup. She decided her feet deserved to go bare for a while, after all they'd been through that day.

They'd eat in the kitchen, she decided, taking plates and glasses out of the cupboard. The dining room seemed too formal. Too datelike.

She was washing lettuce for the salad when Randy knocked at the back door.

Kicked at it, really, since his hands were full.

"You'll have to light the gas grill," she said apologetically. "I've always been afraid the thing might blow up on me."

"So you're willing to experiment with me? Thanks a lot."

"You're a man," Mary Bliss said. "All men like to play with fire."

God. Was that her? Was she flirting?

He did manage to get the grill lit; she poured the two of them a glass of wine and took it out to the little brick patio, where Randy was sitting on one of her Adirondack chairs.

It was full dark. They could hear the soft cooing of mourning doves coming from the trees at the back of the yard, and the thrumming of cicadas, and the hum of tires on the street out in front. Mary Bliss had a wind chime hanging from the eaves of the back porch, and its ringing kept time with the slight breeze blowing through the treetops. When the wind shifted, you could smell the night-blooming jasmine Mary Bliss had planted on the fence around her vegetable garden.

"This is nice back here," Randy said, looking around at the expanse of lawn and flowers, shrubs and vegetable patch. "Who's the gardener?"

"Me, I guess," Mary Bliss said. "Parker usually keeps the grass mowed when he's home, but I've been having to do it lately."

"Me too," Randy said, and they both laughed companionably.

"I'm an outlaw," Mary Bliss said. "I've been watering on off days. You won't turn me in, will you?"

"You can have my water," Randy said. "My lawn is so far gone, I've given up on trying to get it to stay green. Anyway, if I watered it, it would just grow, and I'd just have to keep cutting it."

"It's not that bad," Mary Bliss said, but they both knew she was being charitable.

"I can't seem to get things together with her gone," he said suddenly, staring down at his wine glass. "Our house is the biggest dump on the block. I guess people are starting to complain."

"It's not that bad," Mary Bliss said.

"Yes, it is," Randy said. "But there's so much to do. Get the kids to school and baseball practice, make sure there's food in the house, clean clothes, the bills are paid. Not to mention my job. I never realized how much work there is to keeping a family going."

"It's a lot," Mary Bliss said, thinking of her own recent struggles.

"You don't want to hear me bitch and moan," Randy said, straightening up. "Let's see about those steaks."

She went inside to get everything else ready.

"Hope you don't mind 'em overcooked," Randy said, bringing in the tray of steaks. "Guess I lost track of time out there."

She'd put candles on the table. Should she light them? What was the protocol for a married woman entertaining her nearly divorced next-door neighbor?

"Wow," Randy said, looking at the table, set with her everyday china and a little vase of red-and-yellow zinnias she'd cut earlier in the day. "Do you always fix things so nice?"

What the hell. She decided to light the candles.

They were just spooning the Zippee Dip over their salads when Erin came in through the garage door.

"Hey there!" Mary Bliss said brightly.

"Mom?" Erin looked from her mother to Randy. "Hi, Mr. Bowden."

There was a question in her voice.

"Dad?" Josh Bowden stood behind Erin. His voice had the same question.

"Look who's here," Randy said. "Where have you kids been?"

"We went to Blockbuster after I got off work, to rent a DVD," Erin said. "It's the new remastered *Star Wars*. What are you two doing?"

"Having dinner," Mary Bliss said. "I ran into Randy at Bargain Bonanza. He was buying steaks, and I was selling salad dressing, so we decided to join forces."

"There's lots more steak at the house," Randy said, his voice a trifle too jolly. "Why don't you kids join us?"

"We ate," Josh said.

"I don't eat steak," Erin added, her voice flat. "We're just going to go in the den and watch the movie. That's okay, isn't it?"

She was giving Mary Bliss an accusing look. We'll watch the movie while you two make out in here, it seemed to say.

Now she had Mary Bliss feeling all defensive about an entirely innocent dinner. "Restriction normally means no company, Erin. You know that."

Her daughter's face clouded.

"But since Josh is here, I guess it's all right."

"Thanks." Erin's voice dripped sarcasm. "We're gonna make some popcorn. Unless that's against the rules?"

Mary Bliss wanted to smack her. "Go right ahead."

Randy offered the little plate of carrots and celery sticks Mary Bliss had so carefully arranged. "If you're hungry, try some of these veggies and Zippee Dip."

Josh looked down at the cup of dip. "Gross. No thanks."

"You might have to learn to like it," Mary Bliss said. "Your dad bought a couple gallons of it today."

"Oh yeah," Josh said. "Hey, Dad. Mom's over at the house. She needed to get some stuff. She wants to know if I can go up to the lake with her this weekend."

"What lake?" Randy asked, pushing at the bridge of his glasses.

Josh shrugged. He looked so much like his father, tall and lanky, with the same light-brown hair and milk-chocolate eyes. "I dunno. Some lake up in the mountains. A friend of hers has a house up there. And a boat. We're gonna go water-skiing and stuff like that."

Randy grimaced. "What friend? What's his name?"

"God. I don't know," Josh said. "It's just a lake. No big deal. Can I go or not?"

Erin was watching them both with interest. She saw the look that passed between her mother and Randy.

"Fine," Randy said. "Just make sure to leave a phone number where I can reach you."

Now it was Erin and Josh exchanging a look. They popped their popcorn in the microwave while the grown-ups ate their dinner in silence.

The steak was overdone. But the potatoes were warm and buttery, and the Zippee Dip was surprisingly good on it.

"I take it Nancye's friend is a man-type person?" Mary Bliss asked after the kids were in the other room.

"You could say that," Randy said wryly. "I'm assuming it's this professor over at Emory. According to the kids, he's old enough to be Nancye's father. And rich, of course."

"What does Josh think of him?" Mary Bliss asked. "Is he step-father material? Or has it gotten that serious yet?"

"Josh doesn't talk a lot to me about his mother," Randy said. "I guess he wants to protect me. Or he's so angry at both of us he can't bring himself to talk about it."

Mary Bliss nodded sympathetically. "What's happening with the divorce settlement? Is she still trying to keep you from getting custody of the kids?"

Randy dipped a bit of steak in the salad dressing. "She's done a complete turnaround. Now she doesn't want the kids and she doesn't want the house. Just a big old pile of my money. And my retirement benefits."

"Wow. Why the change of heart? Did the kids convince her they want to stay with you?"

He sipped some wine. "No. I think the folder of photographs and the sworn affidavits from the PI I hired to tail her helped convince her to let the kids stay with me."

"Photos." Mary Bliss let the word sit there. So he knew. And Nancye knew he knew.

"Photos," Randy said. He stood up abruptly.

"Dessert?"

Mary Bliss was astonished. She hadn't even finished her steak.

Just then the back door swung open. "Mary Bliss," Katharine called, sticking her head in the door. "We need to talk. Right now."

But she stopped talking when she saw Randy Bowden, scraping his plate in Mary Bliss's sink.

He was still dressed in his suit pants. He'd removed his tie and unbuttoned his collar, and the sleeves of his white dress shirt were rolled to his elbows. He looked pretty damned at home.

"Hello," Katharine said. She gave Mary Bliss an accusing look. "I didn't know you had company."

"Hey, Katharine," Randy said. "Looks like the whole neighborhood is around tonight. Josh and Erin just came in to watch a movie."

"Yeah," Katharine said, a bit of malice in her voice. "And I saw Nancye's car parked in your driveway too."

Mary Bliss could have kicked her.

"She's picking up some things for her new apartment," Randy said. "Want some dessert? It's chocolate praline cheesecake. We've got nearly a whole pie here."

"No, thanks," Katharine said, leaning against the kitchen counter. But she did pour herself a glass of wine. Clearly, she intended to stay for a while.

Mary Bliss decided to ignore her. She finished her steak, poured herself another glass of wine.

Randy sat down across from her and looked miserable. They each ate a small slice of cheesecake, while Katharine worked on opening another bottle of wine.

"I'd better go," Randy said finally.

"Coffee?" Mary Bliss offered.

"Better not," Randy said. "If Nancye's still over there, I should go supervise. There's not much left for her to take, except for my easy chair and my bed linens. But she's probably loading those up even as we speak."

He gathered up his platter and barbecue tools, said good-bye, and left.

From the other room, Katharine and Mary Bliss heard Erin and Josh laughing uproariously at something.

"What the hell is he doing here?" Katharine whispered.

Mary Bliss started to load the dishwasher. "He came over here to screw me," she said flippantly. "We started here in the kitchen, then we moved upstairs to my room, then we were getting ready to do it in the den when the kids came in. So we stopped and grilled some steaks. What the hell do you think he was doing here?"

"It doesn't matter what I think. I know you wouldn't do anything skeezy with Randy Bowden," Katharine said hotly. "This just looks bad, M. B. I mean, Nancye's car is right across the street. She knows Randy's over here. By tomorrow morning, all of Fair Oaks will know you two are an item. And do I need to remind you that you're still married? God. You're ruining everything."

"We are not an item," Mary Bliss whispered, her eyes blazing. "It was a perfectly innocent dinner. He was shopping at Bargain Bonanza, and he ran into me, giving out samples of Zippee Dip. He was hungry and lonely, and so was I. And that's all there is to it."

"Oh yeah?" Katharine said. "You're wearing eye shadow, Mary Bliss. And lipstick. I haven't seen you this fixed up all summer. And another thing. What was he doing at the Bargain Bonanza way down in Riverdale, when there's one not five miles from here?"

"He was shopping for the kids," Mary Bliss said. "And we have all these grand-opening specials down in Riverdale."

"Bullshit," Katharine said. "They offer those specials at all the stores when they open a new one. He followed you down there. He's hot for you, Mary Bliss. He's single, and he's on the prowl, and the lonely lady across the street is all of a sudden looking mighty good."

"You're disgusting," Mary Bliss said, throwing down her dish towel. "Go home, Katharine."

"No way," Katharine said. "Forget about Randy for now. We've got something more serious to discuss."

24

M ary Bliss clanked china noisily as she shoved plates and cups into the dishwasher. She scrubbed with indiscriminate fury at the remnants of the Zippee Dip on the kitchen table.

"What?" Katharine asked. "Why are you so pissed at me?"

Mary Bliss had to think about that. "I was in a good mood," she said finally. "For almost an hour, I thought about something other than my own problems. Then you come slamming in here, and I'm right back where I started. My life is lousy. And you reminded me of that."

"*Sorr-Ree.* Guess I'll hit the road if that's the way you feel about it." But Katharine didn't look particularly sorry.

"Never mind," Mary Bliss said. "Finish your wine. It might be the last bottle I buy around here."

"That's sort of what I came over here to tell you," Katharine said. She glanced nervously toward the door. "Can the kids hear us?"

"Probably not. Most of the time Erin doesn't hear or see me," Mary Bliss said. "As far as she's concerned, I'm invisible."

"Me too," Katharine said. "Why is that? In my time, I'll have you know, I was what my mother called a real head-turner. Men crashed cars into oncoming traffic looking at me. Construction workers fell off their scaffolding trying to get a good look at my legs. And now? I sit in a restaurant for forty-five minutes before a waiter will even approach to ask if I want something to drink. And I happen to know my legs are still damn good. And I'm still damn hot."

"I know." Mary Bliss patted Katharine's hand. "It's the middle-age curse. You're still hot to trot, but there's nobody to saddle you up."

"Yeah. They're all hanging around McDonald's, hoping to score with the french fry girl," Katharine said. "Let's go outside, okay? I don't want to take the chance of Erin overhearing us."

Mary Bliss fixed herself a glass of iced tea and followed her friend out to the patio.

"All right. What's so top secret?" she demanded.

Katharine leaned against the wrought-iron table, sipping her wine. "More bad news, I'm afraid. My lawyer called tonight. Charlie has canceled my credit cards. All of them. American Express. Visa. Discover. Rich's. Macy's. Saks. Neiman Marcus. Lord & Taylor. I'm toast, M. B."

Mary Bliss blinked. She could not fathom Katharine without her credit cards. The woman even put Domino's Pizza on a charge card.

"Won't your lawyer fight it? Wasn't that part of your separation agreement?"

"It was supposed to be," Katharine said. "But I guess I got a little carried away last month. So he's canceled the cards and put me on a budget. Fifteen thousand a month. Can you believe it?"

Mary Bliss did not even attempt to list all the things she could do with fifteen thousand a month.

"It doesn't sound that unreasonable," Mary Bliss said. "And you knew it was coming, didn't you?"

"That doesn't make it any easier," Katharine said sharply. "Especially now."

"Why now?"

Katharine lowered her voice to a whisper. "Because of Mexico," she said. "We've got to book our trip tonight, before the cancellation goes through. My lawyer got me a twenty-four-hour grace period. So we've got to do it tonight."

Mary Bliss blinked. "I told you, Mexico is off. Definitely. So let's drop the whole thing."

She turned abruptly and walked over to the vegetable patch. In the moonlight, she examined her tomato plants, dug a bare toe into the parched clay soil. It was already bone-dry again. She walked over to the side of the house and turned on the faucet, uncoiling hose as she marched back toward the garden.

"Are you out of your mind?" Katharine asked, now at her side. "I'm talking about life and death and you're watering your damn 'maters?"

"They'll dry up and die if I don't get them sprinkled," Mary Bliss said, pointing the stream of water at the base of the Early Girls.

"Let 'em," Katharine said. "My God. You can buy tomatoes for fifty-nine cents a pound."

"Not these," Mary Bliss said stubbornly. "No store-bought tomato ever tasted like these."

"You are truly nuts," Katharine said.

"No," Mary Bliss said. She stared down at the garden, watching the water soak into the ground. "Not nuts. Just determined. I made this garden. I rototilled it and hauled in good soil and rotted manure. I fertilized it. I weeded it. And now, by God, I've gone too far to give up. I will have homegrown tomatoes this year."

"But possibly no home," Katharine reminded her.

"I'll cross that bridge when I come to it," Mary Bliss said.

She jerked the hose away from the vegetable patch and started walking around to the front of the house.

"Now where are you going?" Katharine wanted to know.

"Front yard. I ordered those caladium bulbs from a nursery in Florida. They cost two dollars apiece. And I'm not letting a hundred dollars worth of caladiums burn up in this drought."

She stood in a circle of yellow light thrown out from the porch lamps and gave the caladiums a good long drink. Katharine stood silently by and watched.

"Now what?" Katharine asked again.

"The Boston ferns by the door," Mary Bliss said, mounting the porch steps. "Potted plants dry out unless you water 'em every day."

"Who cares?" Katharine muttered.

"I care," Mary Bliss said.

A red-and-white UPS envelope was leaning against the front door. It hadn't been there when she'd gotten home and checked the mail.

"What's that?" Katharine asked as Mary Bliss picked it up.

"Overnight package," Mary Bliss said. "Addressed to Mr. and Mrs. Parker McGowan."

"From who?"

"Whom?" said Mary Bliss, ever the schoolteacher.

"Yeah, who's it from?" Katharine asked.

Mary Bliss turned the envelope over and read the airbill. "Consolidated Mortgage. I never heard of them before."

"Another bill?"

"Of course," Mary Bliss said. She looked at the envelope with distaste. "Just when I thought it couldn't get any worse."

Katharine grabbed the envelope. "Burn it. There's no sense opening the thing and worrying yourself sick about something you have no control over."

Mary Bliss shook her head and gently took the envelope back. "No. I need to know what it is. Anyway, if I did burn it, I'd feel twice as bad as I already do, knowing something else is hanging over my head."

She pulled the paper tab on the envelope and slid out the contents: a letter clipped to a legal-looking document. As she skimmed the letter, her face paled. She sank down to the porch floor, her back to the door, knees drawn up to her chest. "I can't believe it," she said, flipping over to the legal documents.

"What?" Katharine asked. "What does it mean?"

"It's the end," Mary Bliss said. "Parker has dug me a hole so deep I'll never crawl out. I'm going to lose the house. Everything."

"Let me see that," Katharine said, snatching the letter away. She was a fast reader. When she got to the last paragraph, she sat on the floor beside Mary Bliss and wrapped her arms around her.

"Is this legal? Is it what I think it is?"

"It looks like it," Mary Bliss said, picking the letter up, running her finger down the crisply typed paragraphs. Her finger jerked in a spastic motion.

"He's refinanced the house," she said shakily. "For eight hundred and twenty-five thousand dollars. Can you imagine that? For my little starter cottage? Cash-out, it says. I think that means they handed him a check for something like that much money. And Parker handed them a note that says we'll pay them back in one big balloon payment. The whole thing is payable August first."

"Less than two months away," Katharine said. "But it can't be legal, can it? Isn't your name on the title?"

"It was," Mary Bliss said. She flipped over to the legal documents. "This is a copy of the loan agreement. It says I gave Parker power of attorney to sign for me."

"Did you?"

"No," Mary Bliss said. "Look. He did this way back in January. He'd been plotting this all along. The letter says this is the fourth notice of the loan coming due. And the mailing address on the agreement is a post office box in Atlanta."

"That's how he did it, the rat bastard," Katharine said. "No telling what all else is in that post office box."

The porch light switched on, and the door opened a crack.

"Mom?" Erin stood over them, looking puzzled. "What are you guys doing out here in the dark?"

Josh stood beside her, staring at the two of them.

"We were just talking," Mary Bliss said. "You know. Girl talk."

"Where's my dad?" Josh asked.

"Oh, he went home a while ago," Mary Bliss said.

"Christ," Josh muttered. "Bet he and Mom are fighting again."

"We were gonna make a run up to the Kwik Trip for some Cokes. We're out, you know. Is that all right?"

It was on the tip of her tongue to say no. Instead, Mary Bliss nodded. "Come right back, though. You're still on restriction."

"Oh yeah," Erin said. "I nearly forgot. Not."

She closed the door harder than was necessary.

"See?" Mary Bliss said.

"What I see is a great big old fraud," Katharine said. "You're not gonna let Parker get away with this, are you? He must have forged your name to that power of attorney thing. Hey. I know. I'll call Charlie. He's got a soft spot for you. He'll take care of this."

Mary Bliss was silent. A moth fluttered around her head, and she batted it away with one hand. "Look at this thing," she said, handing it to Katharine. "See? Charlie signed it. He was the closing attorney. He can't represent me."

Katharine let out a long breath. "The son of a bitch. He must have been in on it. I'll kill the son of a bitch."

"No, Kate. You're right. Charlie wouldn't deliberately hurt me. I bet Parker tricked him into doing it. It's not his fault."

"Well, somebody deserves to be killed," Katharine said. "What can you do? Want me to get my lawyer on Parker's ass? Get her to throw an injunction on him or something like that? She hates men. I think she might be lesbian. Lipstick lesbian, though. She's got a thing for spike heels and slit skirts."

"We don't know where he is," Mary Bliss said. "I can't sue him if I can't find him. And I can't even afford to hire somebody to track him down."

They both sighed in unison.

"I do know one thing," Mary Bliss said, a little while later. She clenched her hands tightly together in her lap. "I won't let anybody take my house away. I just can't. When I was a little girl, and my daddy left? Mama couldn't afford to keep our house. We lived with my granny for a while, before Mama got a job. Granny lived through the Depression. She used to tell me stories about people who got evicted. Back then, if you were poor and homeless, they sent you to this awful place. Granny called it the poor farm. And it was a real place. I've never forgotten that. Never forgotten the day we had to pack up and leave our house. I'd never seen my mama cry before that day."

Mary Bliss rubbed her own eyes wearily, then stood up. She dusted off the seat of her linen pants and squinted in the bright light.

"Come on," she said, offering her friend a hand.

"Where to?" Katharine asked, struggling to get up without spilling any wine.

"Upstairs," Mary Bliss said. "I need you to help me pick out an outfit."

"For what?"

"Parker's funeral," Mary Bliss said.

"Goody!" Katharine squealed. "Cozumel, here we come. I can already taste the margaritas."

25

Friday morning, a week later, Mary Bliss was zipping her suitcase shut when the doorbell rang. She froze, startled. Her shoulders sagged. This was it. Everything was off. And after all their careful planning. She'd gotten time off from work, left emergency numbers at the nursing home, even arranged to have Randy Bowden water her garden while she was gone. Katharine's flight had left hours earlier. Erin was at work, not due home at all, since she'd arranged to spend the weekend at Jessica's while her parents frolicked in the surf in Cozumel.

"What now?" she said aloud. She yanked the suitcase off the bed and trundled it down the stairs behind her. She had exactly an hour and a half before her flight to Miami left Hartsfield. No telling what midday Friday traffic would be like.

Mary Bliss ran to the first-floor landing and looked out the window. She could just glimpse the back end of a car she didn't recognize parked in her driveway. Was it another bill collector? They'd started getting bolder, leaving messages on the answering machine, sending registered letters. But this was the first one who'd come knocking at her door.

And she had neither the time nor the nerve right now to deal with one more pressing problem. Peeking around the sidelight by the front door, she caught a glimpse of her visitor. He wore a khaki-colored ball cap that left his face in shadows. He was dressed in jeans and a golf shirt, and he kept glancing around. He pressed the doorbell again and she jumped, stifling a near scream.

Definitely a bill collector, she decided. She picked the suitcase up and tiptoed to the kitchen and out the door to the garage. After she loaded the suitcase in the trunk, she checked her purse to make sure she had everything, the travel itinerary, the packet of money Katharine had loaned her, her passport, and an economy-sized bottle of Lomotil.

Mentally she reviewed the plan she and Katharine had gone over so painstakingly. It had seemed like such a fantasy, planning it out with a bottle of wine. But it was real. She was doing this. There was no other way out. She was going to Mexico married and coming back a widow.

She checked her watch. Ten minutes had passed. The doorbell had stopped ringing five minutes ago. She heard an engine start and felt her body go limp with relief.

He was gone. Now it was time for her to leave. She pressed the button on the automatic garage door opener and carefully backed her car out of the driveway.

She was at the bottom of the driveway, glancing over her shoulder to make sure there was no oncoming traffic, when she heard a pounding on her window. She looked up, startled. The man in the ball cap stood right beside her car.

"Mrs. McGowan? Mary Bliss? I thought nobody was home."

She squinted in the bright light. His face was somehow familiar. Silver hair, tanned face, but something was missing. She put the car in park and rolled down the window.

"I'm sorry . . . I'm in a hurry. I'm late for an appointment."

"You don't remember me, do you? Matt Hayslip? Parker's tennis partner?"

"Oh," Mary Bliss said. The cop. Retired, but still. She felt her face flush and her pulse quicken. What did he want? Why was he snooping around her house?

"Guess you didn't recognize me without the beard," he said, chuckling. "I had a girlfriend one time, accused me of hiding behind it. I generally shave it off in the summertime."

"Yes," Mary Bliss said faintly. "I guess it was the beard that threw me."

"Say. I still haven't been able to get hold of Parker," Hayslip said in a friendly way. He had his hand on the window frame, his face right at eye level with hers. "I've left messages on your home phone. Didn't you get them?"

The skin on the back of her neck was prickling, and not just from the June heat. She had gotten in the habit of fast-forwarding over all the messages on the machine, listening only for Erin's or Parker's voice.

"I'm sorry," Mary Bliss repeated. "Parker's still out of town. I told him you called, but he's been so busy."

"Going on a trip?" he asked, gesturing toward the seat beside her.

She glanced over. Damn. She'd left the plane ticket and the hotel brochure in plain sight on the seat. Her heart was beating so rapidly that she was certain he could see it, pumping her chest up and down.

"Yes," she said brightly, covering the hotel brochure with her free hand. "That's why I'm in a hurry. My plane leaves in an hour, and you know how traffic can get."

"Cozumel, huh?" he said. "It's great down there. Should be beautiful this time of year."

She repressed a scream.

"Should be," she agreed, glancing at her watch. "Guess I better head out now."

"Parker meeting you down there?" he asked.

She simply stared at him.

Now it was his turn to blush. "That sounds pretty damned nosy, doesn't it? The reason I ask is, there's another tournament coming up, and the competition looks pretty decent. I think the two of us could win this one. But the entry deadline is today."

"I don't know what to tell you," she said. "He is meeting me in Cozumel. It's our first weekend together in ages. I'll give him the message, but I can't make any promises."

"Just the two of you, huh? A romantic weekend for two? That's nice. Maybe you could call him on his cell phone," Hayslip suggested. "I know he'd hate to miss an opportunity like this."

"I would," Mary Bliss said, "but it would be a waste of time. As far as I know, he's in the air right now. Maybe you should consider finding another doubles partner. It being so late and all."

Hayslip shrugged. "We make a great team, you know. He's got that killer backhand, and I play a pretty decent net game. The two of us could clean up in this tourney."

Mary Bliss could feel the minutes ticking away. "Well . . . I'll just leave that up to you boys. I'll ask him to call you, all right?"

Then she made a bold move. She rolled up the electric window and gave him a bye-bye wave.

"Wait," he said, pounding the window again.

She rolled it down an inch. "I'm sorry, but this is the last flight out today. I really have to go."

He reached in his breast pocket, pulled out a business card, and handed it to her. Her blood froze when she saw the gold embossed shield on the card.

"Just have him call me," Hayslip urged. He stood up and pounded the roof of her car. "You two have a great time down there in Cozumel now, you hear? Don't do anything I wouldn't do."

By the time she parked her car at the airport, ran through the terminal, and made it onto her Delta flight, Mary Bliss was limp with exhaustion and anxiety.

She tried to read the in-flight magazine but couldn't concentrate. Tried to nap, but every time she closed her eyes she had a vision of Matt Hayslip, standing in front of her, the tanned face frowning, and instead of a business card it was a pair of handcuffs that he was holding out to her. How had she thought him attractive the last time? The man was a menace, even though without the beard he looked ten years younger.

When the flight attendant came by with the drink cart, she decided to treat herself to something more substantial than a Diet Coke. The wine was vinegary and tepid, but it smoothed down the frayed edges of her nerves.

In Miami she had to run the length of the airport to get to the AeroMexico gate. The flight was packed and she was wedged into a window seat next to a fleshy Hispanic woman who fell asleep as soon as she sat down, her head lolled over onto Mary Bliss's shoulder.

When the drink cart rolled around this time, Mary Bliss held up two fingers. Who knew when or if the flight attendant would come this way again?

She pulled down the seat-back tray and left one minibottle there, while she poured the other into the plastic cup she'd been given.

Great, she thought. I'm a criminal and a lush. My daughter has only one parent, and she's impaired. And the police are already after me.

She fell asleep to that happy thought, lulled there by her third glass of wine and the companionable snoring of her seatmate.

The landing jolted her awake. She sat up and winced at the sharp pain when she tried to straighten her neck.

The Hispanic woman was awake too now, yawning widely. Mary Bliss looked down at herself and cringed when she saw the drool stains on her new cotton blouse.

They were seated near the rear of the plane, and it seemed to take forever before she could finally stand up and stretch a little.

God, she was tired and hot. She had a cramp in her neck and her head was starting to throb from all that cheap wine.

BIENVENIDOS A COZUMEL! The sign in the baggage claim area was printed in flowing pink script. She collected her single suitcase and looked around the terminal. Katharine said the package deal included a free shuttle bus from the airport to her hotel, but she hadn't mentioned where to find the shuttle bus.

Mary Bliss's high school Spanish was limited to phrases like "*¿Donde esta la biblioteca?*" and "*Pasame el pan, por favor.*"

She couldn't remember the word for shuttle bus. So she wandered around the terminal until she finally ventured outside. The heat hit her like a shovel upside the head.

Atlanta had been hot, but Cozumel was scorching. She looked up and down the road in front of the terminal, at the row of motley taxis, vans, and buses.

Finally, a battered seventies-era VW bus chugged up to the curb. La Casa Blanca, the name of her hotel, was painted on the door.

The driver, a wizened Mexican woman in her seventies, with a long silver braid that hung down her back, got out, looked at Mary Bliss and her suitcase. "¿Señora McGowan?" The ash from the cigarette in the corner of her mouth dropped on top of Mary Bliss's new canvas espadrilles.

Mary Bliss stepped backward, startled.

"¿Señora McGowan?" the woman repeated.

"*Sí*," Mary Bliss said finally.

The woman gestured toward the van, then threw her cigarette to the pavement, stubbing it out with a battered red Converse sneaker.

"*Andale*," she said.

26

Cigarette smoke filled the bus. Mary Bliss managed to crank her window halfway down, and she poked her head out the side of the bus in search of fresh air.

The asphalt road was lined with palm trees, and the skies overhead were azure blue. If she craned her neck, there were places where she could see traces of glistening green water beyond the lush green tree line. She thought of the travel brochure. Cozumel—Paradise on Earth. This would be a nice place to vacation, she thought. Maybe sometime in another life.

The VW bus chugged on along the road, passing people on rickety bicycles, more cabs, buses, and even motor scooters. Her driver was busy singing along to the radio, spewing smoke and snapping her fingers to the music.

In fifteen minutes, they turned into a drive lined with a low white wall. Brilliant purple bougainvillea spilled over the walls and more palm trees swayed above. So far, so good, Mary Bliss thought.

The driver was chattering away in Spanish now. Mary Bliss caught words like *bonita* and *ristorante*, but the rest was just noise.

The bus stopped abruptly in front of a long, low, white stucco building. It had a red clay tile roof and a red tile patio entrance filled with pots overflowing with a riot of red, yellow, and purple flowers. There was a tile mosaic rug in front of the courtyard entrance that picked out La Casa Blanca in blue and green tiles.

"Okay?" The old woman turned and looked over her shoulder at Mary Bliss. Bits of cigarette ash showered down on her wrinkled blue work shirt. "Señora McGowan? Okay?"

"*Sí,*" Mary Bliss said, scrambling to get out, once it was clear her driver's duties didn't include unloading or carrying baggage.

She wheeled the suitcase along behind her into the expansive wood-beamed lobby area. Tables were dotted around the tile floor, and people sat at them, sipping cold drinks and eating something that smelled wonderful.

Mary Bliss's stomach twinged. She hadn't eaten all day.

"*¡Bienvenidos!*" said the young woman behind the reception desk. "Welcome to La Casa Blanca. My name is Sofia. Can I help you?"

"Yes, Sofia," Mary Bliss said, relieved to hear English. "I have a reservation. McGowan?"

Sofia tapped the keys of a computer in front of her and smiled. "Yes. Your husband checked in around noon."

"Oh." This was news. She tried not to look flustered. "Oh, good. His flight was on time, then."

"Yes," Sofia beamed. She reached in a drawer and brought out a large brass key and tucked it into a cardboard envelope, which she pushed across the counter to Mary Bliss.

"Your room is four twenty-seven. And here is a coupon for a complimentary drink in our patio bar, and a ticket for our fiesta breakfast in the morning."

"How nice," Mary Bliss said. Her stomach twinged again. She really must eat. And soon.

The soles of her espadrilles were quiet as she walked down the red tile corridor to her room. She paused in front of the door to 427. What had Katharine been up to? Had she really posed as Parker McGowan?

The phone was ringing as she unlocked the door. She fumbled for the light switch, dropped her suitcase, and lunged across the king-sized bed to grab the phone.

"¡*Bienvenidos*, Mary Bliss! ¡*Besame mucho!*" Katharine was cackling like a madwoman. "Do you love it? Do you absolutely love it?"

"Where are you?" Mary Bliss demanded, slipping off her shoes.

"I'm on the house phone right now. You walked right by me not two minutes ago," Katharine said. "The gorgeous blonde in the big black straw hat? Sitting at the table with the biggest pitcher of margaritas in Mexico?"

"You're in disguise?"

"Damned straight. Wait 'til you see what I bought for you. And guess what? I found an old Diner's Club card Charlie forgot about. We're in the money, honey."

"You'll get us both arrested."

"Relax. I've just been using it for cash advances. No paper trail."

"God," Mary Bliss said, leaning back on the pillows of the bed and looking around. The room was simply furnished, tile floor, flowered spread and drapes, a large comfortable armchair, and a desk. It looked and smelled reasonably clean, and the air conditioner was humming along, sending waves of chilled air into the room. "What have I gotten into?"

"Stop it right now," Katharine said. "Come on out to the lobby now so we can discuss the plan. We've got a lot of work to do, in only a little bit of time. I've ordered us some chimichangas or some such thing, and if you don't hurry out here, I'm gonna get likkered up on these margaritas and start taking advantage of all the horny men who have been walking by giving me the eye."

"Food?" Mary Bliss said hopefully. "I'm starved."

"Well, get your ass out here. And change that blouse. It looks like somebody slept in it."

27

Katharine's description of herself had, of course, been accurate. Her brief, gauzy yellow skirt was slit to reveal her long, tanned legs, and the matching yellow halter top left little to the imagination. Most of the platinum-blonde wig was hidden under the broad-brimmed black straw hat.

"This is your idea of incognito?" Mary Bliss asked, sitting opposite her at the table.

"I'm wearing dark glasses," Katharine said.

"And very little else," Mary Bliss pointed out.

Katharine poured her a margarita and shoved a basket of tortilla chips in Mary Bliss's direction. "Do you want to lecture me, or shall we discuss the plan?"

Mary Bliss removed the bottle of Lomotil from her purse and took a hefty swig. She wiped her mouth with a napkin and eyed the margarita. "Is it safe to drink that? The water and all? You know how my stomach gets."

"They have their own filtration system here at the hotel. Listen. We've got to get going here. You're supposed to pick up your dive boat at ten A.M."

Mary Bliss nibbled at a tortilla chip. "The desk clerk tells me my husband checked in early this afternoon. You know anything about that?"

"He works at one of the bars in town," Katharine said. "Pablo and Paul's. He's American. Sort of an aging beach bum hippy type. Very cute. I gave him five bucks and a pair of sunglasses. He checked in as Parker. We met at the beach bar after I checked in. We're supposed to meet again for a drink later this evening."

"Will he be Parker tomorrow too?" Mary Bliss whispered.

"Of course," Katharine said. "I told him we're playing a trick on my husband. Poor thing. He's adorable but totally clueless. I think it really is true about drugs frying your brain."

Mary Bliss took a wary sip of margarita. "Can he drive the boat?"

"Absolutely. He grew up in Florida. Although, you'll have to drive it after you drop him off down the beach. That's not a problem, right?"

"I guess not. I've driven your boat up at the lake tons of times."

"Right," Katharine said. "You're a great little pilot."

"What about the death certificate? That's the part that's really got me worried."

"Dinky knows some people. That's the advantage of being an aging doper. You have all kinds of low-life contacts."

"Who's Dinky?"

"The bartender. Parker's stand-in. Pay attention here, Mary Bliss."

"I *am* paying attention," Mary Bliss said hotly. "You never told me his name was Dinky."

"Well, it is. Dinky Davis. And listen, that Discovery Channel stuff is bullshit. Dinky says it's not all that easy to buy a death certificate."

"What?" Mary Bliss exclaimed.

"Calm down. He says it's not easy . . . but it's not impossible either. He knows a guy who knows a guy. We have to meet him at eleven o'clock."

"Tonight?" Mary Bliss sagged down into the chair. "God. I'm wiped out. You have no idea of the kind of day I've had. All that running around and packing. Making up a lie about a doctor's appointment so I could get out of work. And then, that cop friend of Parker's showed up at the house, just as I was leaving. I had to sneak out the garage door. And he still ran me down, stopped me in the driveway."

"What cop friend? You didn't mention any cops," Katharine said, her voice rising.

"Not a real cop," Mary Bliss said quickly. "He's a retired GBI agent. Now he's director of security for Southern Utilities. He keeps coming around, looking for Parker. Turns out they were doubles partners."

"How much does he know?"

"Just that I was going away for the weekend. He saw the plane ticket sitting on the front seat of my car," Mary Bliss admits. "Don't worry about it. He just wanted to know whether Parker would be back in town in time to play in some tennis tournament."

"I don't like it," Katharine said darkly.

"I don't love it my own self," Mary Bliss admitted. "But he's harmless. I'm sure of it." She wished she felt surer.

"What's he look like? Is he cute?"

"Cute? Don't ask me a question like that. You know I don't look at men that way. He's older. Probably around fifty. That kind of blonde hair gone silver, like Robert Redford. Athletic-looking. He had a beard the first time he showed up, but today he'd shaved."

"See? You do look at men that way. You just won't admit it. Christ, Mary Bliss, loosen up, will you?"

Mary Bliss took a long drink of margarita. She fixed a steady gaze on her friend. "I'm down here in a strange country, faking my husband's death, buying phony death certificates, going on a boat ride with some scuzzball you picked up in a beach bar. That's about as loose as it gets with me, Katharine."

"So far," Katharine said, giving her a broad wink.

A giant neon green cactus sprouted out of the squat cement block building that was Pablo and Paul's. Crowds of writhing drunken people spilled out onto the sidewalk in front of the nightclub and the street, their screams of hilarity barely audible above the bass thump of rock-and-roll music pouring from the roof-mounted speakers.

"Wait," Mary Bliss said, grabbing the door of the cab she'd just gotten out of. "Take me back to the hotel. I'm not going in there."

Katharine grabbed her by the shoulders and pushed her away from the cab. "You're going," she said sternly.

The cab sped away and Mary Bliss tucked her purse tightly under her elbow and clamped it to her side. "We'll be mauled in that crowd," she wailed. "Look at them," she said, pointing at a cluster of teenaged boys who were casually demonstrating precision peeing on the side of the building. "It looks like spring break in Panama City."

"I know," Katharine said, grinning and adjusting her blonde wig. "All that youthful exuberance. Isn't it divine? Just keep your head down and follow me."

She bulldozed through the throng of partyers, with Mary Bliss's hand attached to the waistband of her skirt.

Inside it was even more crowded. Maybe a thousand people were jammed into the warehouse-sized room, seated at long tables, milling around the horseshoe-shaped bar and dancing on the elevated glass dance floor to what Mary Bliss recognized as an old Bee Gees tune. The ceilings were festooned with dozens of gaily-colored piñatas, sombreros, more neon cactuses, and neon Dos Equis signs.

"Oh, good," Katharine said, wedging herself closer to the bar. "There's Dinky."

"Where?"

"Right there," Katharine pointed. "With the pony-tail."

Mary Bliss looked. She saw a short red-faced guy dressed in a Hawaiian shirt. He wore wire-rimmed glasses and was nearly bald on top with a long, stringy gray rattail curving over his shoulder. He held the clear plastic hose of a drink pourer high over his head and seemed to be shooting liquor into the gaping mouth of a middle-aged woman in a lime-green tank top whose arms were being held by three of her female friends.

"Good Lord," Mary Bliss said. "That's your idea of cute?"

"Work with me here," Katharine said. "He speaks English and he doesn't ask a lot of questions. And he comes cheap."

"You said the magic word," Mary Bliss agreed.

"There's a table over there, against the wall," Katharine said, pointing again. "You go stake it out. I'll let Dinky know we're here. And when the waiter comes, get me another margarita. No salt."

Mary Bliss winced at the idea of margaritas. The white wine and her earlier margarita had given her a bad buzz, although she had to admit they had also helped settle her nerves a little.

By the time Katharine made it back from the bar, her margarita was on the table and Mary Bliss was sipping from a tall bottle of lukewarm Coke Classic that had cost six dollars, three times the price of Katharine's drink.

"The guy should be here any minute," Katharine said, glancing at her watch. "His name is Estefan."

"How much should I tell him?" Mary Bliss asked.

"Nothing," Katharine said. "According to Dinky, he'll bring a blank death certificate. It'll be all signed and notarized, with the spaces for name and time and date and cause of death left blank."

"That's it? And Dinky says it'll look authentic?"

"It'll *be* authentic," Katharine assured her. "The guy works in the office of the medical examiner here in Cozumel. It's totally legit-looking."

"And I just hand him three hundred dollars? In cash?"

Katharine lowered her voice. "There's a little more to it than that. The cost is actually eighteen hundred dollars."

"Eighteen hundred!" Mary Bliss was outraged. "I don't have that kind of money."

"Shhh!" Katharine shushed her, although they could barely hear themselves above the Bee Gees' greatest hits blaring from all sides. "That's for everything. Including Dinky's cut. I told you that Discovery Channel thing was bogus. Anyway, don't go getting your knickers in a twist about the money. Thanks to the Diner's Club cash advances, I've got that part covered. Now listen. You give him four hundred up front. He'll show you the death certificate, as a gesture of good faith. Tomorrow, after the uh, accident, you'll come back to the hotel, report Parker missing, ask the hotel people to call the police."

"Then what?"

"Then the police will come. They'll ask you some questions, you'll tell them your story—sobbing hysterically, of course. They'll make a brief search of the waters around the hotel and come back empty-handed. The investigating officer will walk you back to your room. He'll be very sympathetic. You'll be very generous."

"How generous?" Mary Bliss's eyes narrowed.

"Four hundred. And try to be discreet, for Pete's sake."

"Jezebel?" A middle-aged, hatchet-faced Mexican man stood at the table, his hand lightly touching Katharine's bare shoulder.

"Estefan?" Katharine looked up, flashing her best winning smile.

"Jezebel?" Mary Bliss repeated.

Katharine shot her a warning look.

"Estefan, sit right down," Katharine said, gesturing toward an empty chair. "Can we get you something to drink?"

"No, but thank you," Estefan said. His English was perfect and unaccented.

"This is Lolita," Katharine said.

Mary Bliss's left eye twitched slightly. "How do you do?" she managed to say. She wasn't sure how this type of transaction was handled. She'd never gone shopping for a death certificate before.

Estefan nodded politely. "Be assured that you have my condolences."

He pulled a smudged white envelope from the inside pocket of the threadbare sport coat he wore and slid it across the table to her.

Mary Bliss covered it with her hand and looked back at him for guidance.

"Take a look," he said softly.

"Right here? What if somebody sees?"

"Don't worry," he said, waving his hand in a gesture of dismissal. "People will just assume you're buying drugs."

She opened the envelope and glanced inside. The document had elaborate gold borders, scrollwork, a lot of Spanish writing, and an official-looking embossed stamp at the bottom. It could have been a death certificate, but then again, it could have been Estefan's marriage license—she wouldn't know the difference.

Mary Bliss pushed it across the table. Katharine gave it a quick look and nodded at Mary Bliss, who took an envelope of cash from her pocketbook and passed it under the table to Estefan. He snatched it out of her hand without the blink of an eye.

"It looks fine," Katharine said. "And you'll fill in all the blanks with the information we give you, right? And see that we get it back before we leave Sunday?"

"Sunday? No, Jezebel. That's impossible."

Mary Bliss started to say something, but Katharine kicked her under the table. "Sunday, yes. Dinky told you that. Lolita and I have to leave Sunday. And we can't go without the death certificate."

"But it's Sunday," Estefan said. "I am a very religious man. And this Sunday is the feast day of my wife's patron saint. We have to make a pilgrimage many miles from here. I won't be back until Monday at the earliest."

Mary Bliss opened her mouth and Katharine kicked her so hard she nearly fell out of the chair.

"Estefan," Katharine said coldly. "Just how religious are you, exactly?"

He thought about that. "Well. Perhaps I could persuade my sister-in-law to accompany my wife on the pilgrimage. But she would need some new clothing for the celebration. In fact, my wife was complaining this morning that she had nothing to wear for her feast day celebration."

Katharine reached into her purse and magically produced a wad of greenbacks. "They have some very nice stores here in Cozumel, I see."

"Oh yes," Estefan said. "And my wife and her sister love pretty clothes."

"I'll bet," Katharine said. The money went under the table and Estefan cheered up immediately.

"It's settled, then," he said, standing up. He gave each of the women a small, courtly bow. "The name of the police officer you will see tomorrow is Jorge. He is very helpful. Very knowledgeable."

Estefan's fingertips trailed across Katharine's shoulders in a tender caress. "Until Sunday."

"Sunday," Katharine said, brushing his hand away. "And Estefan? Only half the cash is in that envelope. You'll get the rest when you bring us the completed death certificate."

He nodded, turned, and melted into the crowd.

Mary Bliss shoved her chair back from the table and began rubbing her bruised shins.

"Jezebel? Lolita?"

"What? You think Mary Bliss sounds more plausible?"

28

H er alarm went off at 8:00 A.M., but Mary Bliss had been up, pacing, since seven.

At eight, she called Katharine's room. The phone rang six times, and Mary Bliss hung up, disgusted. She wondered if Katharine was still asleep, or if she'd even gotten in yet.

They'd split up the night before, shortly after Estefan's disappearing act.

Katharine had summoned the waiter for another round of margaritas, but Mary Bliss had waved him away. "No way," she said firmly. "We're going back to the hotel before you get us involved in any other criminal acts."

"What criminal acts?" Katharine asked. "Just one more drink. C'mon, Mary Bliss. It's our last chance to party in Cozumel. Tomorrow you put on the hysterical widow act. And I'll be right there, in case you need me."

"I need you tonight," Mary Bliss told her. "To go back to the hotel with me and tuck me in the bed. Honestly, Katharine, doesn't all this intrigue exhaust you?"

"Hell no," Katharine said, her eyes gleaming. "I'm having the time of my life. This is better than sex. Well, better than sex with Charlie."

Mary Bliss clapped her hands over her ears. "Too much information!" she cried.

"You go on back to the hotel," Katharine suggested. "I'm gonna stay here, have a little nightcap. I promised Dinky I'd wait 'til he gets off and then ride back to the hotel with him."

"What hotel?"

"Ours, silly," Katharine said. "Remember? He's Parker. We need witnesses seeing him come out of your room together with you in the morning. Like the happy honeymooners you are."

"Absolutely not!" Mary Bliss snapped. "That dirtbag is not coming anywhere near my hotel room. Are you insane? I've only got one bed in there. And I'd rather die broke than let somebody named Dinky spend the night with me."

"Who said he'd be spending the night with *you*?" Katharine said.

"Well, we sure as hell can't have my husband spending the night with you and then leaving my room in the morning," Mary Bliss said. "How's that going to look?"

"You and I have connecting rooms," Katharine said. "Anyway, why do you think I called myself Jezebel?"

Mary Bliss cabbed back to the hotel and locked herself into her room. She showered, scrubbed her face until it glowed red, put on her nightgown, and stuffed cotton balls in her ears before taking the armchair and sliding it in front of the connecting door.

When Katharine failed to answer the phone the next morning, Mary Bliss slammed the phone down and took a swig of Metamucil.

There was a light tapping at the connecting door. The shave-and-a-haircut signal they'd agreed on.

Mary Bliss moved the chair away from the door and opened it. Katharine, fully dressed, quickly slipped inside and shut the door behind her.

"Are you all right?" Mary Bliss asked her, eyeing her warily. "What time did you guys get in last night? Um, how is everything?"

Katharine stood in front of the mirror, adjusting her wig again.

"Fine," she said, sighing. "Although, I know now why they call him Dinky."

29

"I don't want to know!" Mary Bliss shouted, clamping her hands over her ears again.

"You asked," Katharine said, shrugging. "Come on, let's go try out that fiesta breakfast. I'm starved."

"Won't that look bad? If we're seen together?" Mary Bliss asked. Not that she could eat. Her stomach was doing flip-flops. Even the Metamucil was upsetting it.

"You're right," Katharine said reluctantly. "Want me to bring you something? Huevos rancheros, something like that?"

Mary Bliss clutched her abdomen and groaned.

"Never mind," Katharine said. "Coke and soda crackers, right?"

"Right."

At nine-thirty Mary Bliss got dressed. Bathing suit, a white cotton cover-up, and sandals. She put her gear in a canvas tote bag. At nine thirty-five there was a knock on the connecting door.

"About damn time," Mary Bliss said, unlocking and opening it.

"Huh?" Dinky Davis stood in the doorway, shirtless, his hairy paunch flopping over the waistband of a pair of gaudy yellow-and-orange flowered print surfer shorts. He wore a pair of dark sunglasses, his rattail was tucked up under a broad-brimmed straw planter's hat, and he wore a pair of bright-blue scuba flippers on his feet.

"Good Lord!" Mary Bliss exclaimed, clapping her hand over her mouth as soon as the words popped out.

Dinky yawned and scratched his chest. "Hey. You seen Jezebel? She was supposed to bring me another beer."

"Another? It's not even ten o'clock. How many have you had already?" Mary Bliss heard the shrillness in her own voice, but it couldn't be helped.

"Just the two," Dinky said, stepping into her room and looking around. "You got a problem with that?"

Actually, she did have a problem with it. She had a problem with having this strange man in her hotel room—her bedroom, if it came right down to it.

She glanced down at her watch. "We pick up the boat in fifteen minutes. Where the hell is she?"

Dinky scratched his crotch lovingly. "She'll be back."

Mary Bliss blushed and looked away. "We'll have to do something about your clothes."

"Like what?" he asked. "Jezebel said we were supposed to look like we're going scuba diving."

"That's right," Mary Bliss said. "You're supposed to look like my husband. But you're dressed all wrong. Parker would never wear a pair of shorts like that."

"No problem," Dinky said. He reached down and yanked the drawstring on the flowered trunks. They slid down around his ankles and he tried to step out of them, but the flippers got caught up in the trunks and he stumbled and sprawled out on the tile floor.

"Fuck!" Dinky muttered.

"Hello!" Katharine said brightly, stepping through the open connecting doors. She looked down at Dinky, bare-assed, tangled up in the flowered trunks on Mary Bliss's bedroom floor, and back at Mary Bliss, who could not take her eyes off Dinky.

"I see you two have met," Katharine said, handing Mary Bliss a bottle of Coke and a package of crackers.

"I see what you mean," Mary Bliss said, nodding toward Dinky, who had extricated himself from the trunks by removing the flippers.

"She doesn't like my pants," Dinky said, standing up again. He planted a noisy kiss on Katharine's cheek. "Hey. Where's my beer?"

"It's not that I don't like them, it's just that Parker wouldn't wear anything like that," Mary Bliss said hastily, from the bathroom where she had fled.

"She's got a point there," Katharine told Dinky, tossing him a towel. "Sorry. No more beer. It's show time."

"Fuck," Dinky said. He wrapped the towel loosely around his waist.

Mary Bliss went to her suitcase and handed Dinky the stack of clothes she'd packed back in Atlanta.

"Here," she said. "Put these on."

Dinky let go of the towel and it slid to the floor. He held up first a pair of pink-and-white striped seersucker Brooks Brothers swim trunks, and then a pink Polo golf shirt. "You're kiddin', right?"

"She's serious," Katharine said. "As a heart attack. Now get dressed."

"Jezebel? Could you come in here for a minute?" Mary Bliss was hiding in the bathroom again.

She slammed the door shut behind Katharine and locked it for good measure.

"We've got to call it off. This is not going to work," Mary Bliss whispered, her voice fierce. "Did you see him out there? There's something bad wrong with that man."

"Of course there's something wrong with him," Katharine said, laughing. "He's got a dinky little wee-wee. I told you that already."

"That's not what I mean," Mary Bliss said. "He's definitely drunk. And possibly stoned. He can't even put on a pair of pants right. And he looks nothing like Parker McGowan. We can't go through with this. We'll get caught and I'll go to jail for the rest of my life. And Erin will end up in some foster home . . ."

"Calm down," Katharine said. "Middle-aged white women from Fair Oaks do *not* go to prison. Everything will be fine. You just stay right here and drink your Coke and eat your soda crackers. And when I call, you come look. It'll be fine. You'll see."

Mary Bliss put the lid down on the commode, sat down as she was told to, and took a deep breath and a sip of Coke. She took a tentative bite of cracker and tried to think positive thoughts.

"All right," Katharine called finally.

Mary Bliss opened the door.

"Ta-da!" Katharine said, clapping her hands and pointing at Dinky. "Meet the new Parker McGowan."

"Not bad," Mary Bliss said, circling Dinky. "Not bad at all."

The former Dinky Davis had been transformed. There was no sign of the drunken, nude lout who had sprawled on the floor of this room only minutes earlier. In his place stood a somewhat nattily attired Atlanta businessman, ready for a day of Mexican water sports. On his head he wore a white panama hat with a green Master's golf tournament hatband. The pink shirt was stretched a little tightly over the belly, but it was neatly tucked into the pink-and-white-striped shorts. On his feet he wore a pair of new-looking Topsiders. The expensive mirrored sunglasses reflected the surprise in Mary Bliss's eyes.

"I can't believe it," she said, circling him again. "If I didn't know better, I'd think . . ."

"Never mind," Katharine said. "It's five after ten. Get out of here. The boat should be down at the dock."

She gave Dinky a stern look. "You know the plan—right?"

He scratched his crotch and tried to look bored. "Right. My motorbike is hidden down the beach. I swim in to shore, ditch the clothes, meet you back in town tonight, pick up the rest of my money."

"What about the scuba gear?" Katharine prompted.

"Oh yeah. I was gonna say about that. I leave a flipper and my mask and air hose in the water."

"And forget we ever met," Mary Bliss prompted.

"After I get my money," Dinky said.

30

The boat was called the *Miguelita*. It was battered, but painted bright blue with red trim. Black smoke billowed from the noisy outboard motor as it bobbed up and down in the chop of the surf. A young Mexican man stood in water up to his waist and waved at Mary Bliss and Dinky.

They waved back and waded out to meet him, holding the bags containing their scuba gear high over their heads to keep it dry.

Dinky spoke to the man in Spanish, he nodded, and Dinky hoisted himself over the side of the boat, while Mary Bliss struggled valiantly to find a foothold on the slippery wood.

"Hey," she called finally. "Remember me?"

Dinky's head appeared over the side of the boat. He popped the top on a can of beer. "Oh yeah. My wife."

He reached down, hauled her up, and left her flopping around on the floor of the boat like a half-gaffed marlin.

Once she was inside the boat, Dinky called to the Mexican. The man pulled up the anchor and handed it to Dinky, who casually tossed it onto a pile of life jackets near Mary Bliss, who was still struggling to right herself.

"Anchors aweigh!" Dinky hollered, as he pushed the boat's throttle all the way down.

The outboard roared and the boat lurched forward into the waves, sending a shower of water over the bow and completely soaking Mary Bliss.

"Slow down," she screamed, but her protests were lost in the din of the motor.

"Oh Lord." Mary Bliss mouthed the words. Her fingers fumbled as she hastily strapped one of the life jackets over her dripping bathing suit. "Forgive me for what I am about to do."

Dinky Davis's navigational technique was crude but effective. He pointed the bow of the boat on a course parallel with the shore and floored it. The *Miguelita* bounced and shuddered and slammed through the waves. Mary Bliss gripped a brass boat cleat with both hands to keep from being tossed overboard.

Dinky headed the boat north. Gradually, the white sand beaches and string of shoreline hotels disappeared. The terrain turned rocky, and jungle greenery tumbled down to meet the sea. No other boats were visible on the horizon.

Wave after wave poured over the bow of the boat, and the sun beat down on her head. Her eyes burned from the salt water. She could feel blisters forming on her neck and nose. Her carefully wrought plan was being smashed to bits. No sunblock, no bottled water, no skillful maneuvering into just the right position to stage the accident. Mary Bliss hung on to the boat cleat for dear life. Dinky drank an alarming number of beers, throwing the empty cans into the water with maniacal glee.

After an hour of being jounced around like the proverbial Mexican jumping bean, Mary Bliss grabbed one of the life preservers and aimed it at Dinky's head to get his attention.

"Ow. Fuck." He glanced her way and rubbed his head accusingly. "You made me spill my beer."

"Slow down," she screamed. "You'll wreck the boat and kill us both."

"I thought that was the plan," he hollered happily, aiming the boat directly into another towering wave.

But this time something went wrong. The engine faltered and choked. The wave slammed into the powerless boat, lifting it up and up. Mary Bliss lost her grip on the cleat. She heard herself screaming. From far away, she heard Dinky's voice too.

"Fuuuuuuuuuuck."

Then she was out of the boat. She felt herself being hurtled through the air, weightless, for only a matter of seconds. She felt her body hit the surface of the water with an angry smack, felt the burn of the water on her eyes, on her throat as it rushed into her open mouth. A sharp blow at the back of her head was the very last sensation she remembered.

Now she was having a dream. She was drifting through a curtain of green. Schools of fishes darted in and out, showing flashes of silver where the sunlight caught their iridescent scales. She felt a shadow fall over her. Parker? She lifted her head, opened her eyes. The pain was blinding.

"Owww." Water rushed into her mouth and she choked violently.

"Señora?"

When had Parker learned Spanish?

"Señora?" Now she was being dragged on her belly through sand, sharp edges digging into her skin.

Stop, she tried to call. But her throat burned, the words wouldn't come out.

Arms lifted her. Pain. Her head throbbed. Her skin was on fire. Suddenly it was all very clear. She knew

where she was. Hell. She had planned to kill her husband. Failed. And now she was in hell, where she would
burn for eternity. Funny. She had known there would
be flames, but nobody had ever mentioned the sand.

Or the torrent of Spanish flowing over and around
her.

Mary Bliss forced herself to open her eyes and keep
them open.

"Señora McGowan?" A wizened face hovered over
her own, a long, gray braid grazing the flesh of her
neck. It tickled, actually.

Tickled? Mary Bliss was woozy, but she did not
think one could be tickled in hell.

"Yes?" she croaked.

A smile wreathed the mass of wrinkles. Now the old
lady took a long drag from a cigarette, the ash dropping
on Mary Bliss's chest. "*Bueno*," the old woman said.
"*Muy bueno*."

31

Later on, when it was all over and she was back in her bed at La Casa Blanca, cool, clean sheets pulled up to her chin, a thick wad of bandage wrapped around her head, Mary Bliss could recall only pieces of the events that transpired.

"The woman who found me on the beach, it was the old woman who drives the hotel's courtesy bus. She put me in that VW van," she told Katharine, who was hovering about with cold Cokes and painkillers she'd bought who knows where. "God knows how she lifted me, that old lady probably only weighs eighty pounds herself. And she took me into town to that building where you caught up with me. Was it a jail or a hospital?"

"Both, actually. They called it *la clinica*. I guess that's the jail infirmary." Katharine smoothed back

a strand of hair that had fallen over Mary Bliss's eye.
"How's your head feelin', hon?"

"All right," Mary Bliss said, touching it gingerly.
"Mostly pretty numb."

"Good," Katharine said. She popped one of the pain
pills into her mouth and took a swallow of her own
Coke. "Mine is just a throbbin'. You have no idea of
how terrified I've been for the last day and a half. I've
been half out of my head."

"Day and a half!" Mary Bliss tried to sit up, but she
still felt groggy. "What day is today?"

"Night. It's Monday night, Mary Bliss."

"It can't be," Mary Bliss said, sinking back down
into the pillows. "We got on the boat Saturday. Saturday morning at ten o'clock."

"And you washed ashore three miles down the beach
around sunset Saturday," Katharine said. "Although,
of course, I didn't know that then. Had no idea where
you were for a full twenty-four hours, nearly out of my
mind with worry."

"I'm sorry," Mary Bliss said wanly.

"I don't blame you," Katharine said. "It was that
goddamned Dinky Davis."

"Dinky," Mary Bliss said, closing her eyes. She
could hear his voice, the long echoing expletive ringing
in her ears. "What happened to Dinky?"

"You tell me," Katharine said. "He never did show up at Pablo and Paul's on Saturday. I waited and waited. I even went to the bar where he works, kinda asked around. Nobody's seen him."

Katharine leaned in close to the bed. "You did real good with the police, M. B. I don't know what you told 'em, but they believed every word. That woman they brought in to interpret was bawlin' her eyes out after you told them what happened out there. And Estefan showed up here at the hotel last night, just like he promised, with the death certificate. He was acting kind of funny, though."

Mary Bliss was getting sleepy again. "Death certificate?"

"Parker's death certificate. We're all set, Mary Bliss. The doctor wants to check your head again in the morning. He didn't want you to fly until the concussion thing was cleared up. But after that, we're flying back to Atlanta. Just like we planned. Only a little bit later."

"Home." Mary Bliss was so very tired.

"Erin!" Her eyes flew open. "My God. What about Erin? We were supposed to be home yesterday."

"Calm down, now," Katharine said soothingly. "Don't go getting yourself all upset. Erin knows."

"She knows?"

Katharine hesitated. "About her daddy. The inter-preter lady called and told her."

"No," Mary Bliss wailed. "A stranger? A stranger called and gave her the news that her father was dead? How could you, Katharine?"

"I couldn't help it," Katharine protested. "I'm not supposed to be here, right? The police just think I'm an American woman you met here at the hotel. A new friend. I couldn't very well be the one to call Erin and tell her what had happened. It would have spoiled every-thing. And you certainly couldn't tell her. You weren't even really fully conscious until just a little while ago."

"How was she?" Mary Bliss asked, a tear spilling down her cheek.

Katharine bit her lip. "Upset. She wanted to fly down here, but Jessica's mother persuaded her it would be better to stay put, wait for you to get home. Josh Bowden was over there when I called today."

"My poor baby," Mary Bliss said, sobbing. "Erin. I've got to call her."

"No," Katharine said. "I called her this morning myself. I talked to Erin for a long time. She's shook up. But I told her I was flying to Cozumel, and I'd bring you home myself. On Tuesday."

Mary Bliss turned her head and wept into her pillow. "My baby." The words were muffled, but Katharine could make them out just fine. "My baby. I've ruined her life. She'll never forgive me."

Katharine lay down in the bed beside Mary Bliss and wrapped her arms around her best friend. "Shh. Shush now," she crooned. "You didn't ruin her life. You did what you had to do, and it's over and done with. It's going to be all right now. The worst part is over. Tomorrow we go home. And everything's going to be just fine. I promise."

Mary Bliss's body shuddered. Katharine heard her hiccup, then catch her breath. She stroked Mary Bliss's hair. "Shh, baby. Katharine's here. Right here."

32

On Tuesday morning, the manager of La Casa Blanca trundled them tenderly into the back of a shining new white Lincoln and personally drove them to the airport.

"Why is he being so nice?" Mary Bliss whispered.

"They're afraid you'll sue," Katharine whispered back. "That piece-of-crap boat belonged to the hotel. One guest dead, another injured? Honey, they're just waiting for your lawyer to call up and take them to the cleaners."

Mary Bliss nodded. The ache in her head had started to subside. Her doctor spoke very good English, and he had assured her the dizziness and nausea, along with the headache, would soon be over.

She had managed to piece together most of what had happened on Saturday.

Dinky Davis had gotten drunk, and then nearly gotten them both killed. He'd deliberately steered the boat into a killer wave, and the engine had cut off just at the moment of impact. Probably, the doctor told her, she'd been hit in the back of the head by a piece of the boat, which had shattered like a child's toy.

"You were lucky," he'd told her, his voice somber. "And smart. To wear a life jacket. Your husband apparently was not so smart. And not so lucky."

And that's when she remembered. All the life jackets were in the bottom of the boat. Poor Dinky hadn't bothered to put one on.

"My husband," she'd said slowly. "He's really gone, then. Have they found . . . anything?"

The doctor busied himself changing the bandage on her head. "A pair of flippers. Some empty beer cans. And the life jackets, of course. You have my sympathy."

The Lincoln stopped in front of the airport. The manager stepped out, grabbed their bags, and led them inside to the departure gate. Katharine and Mary Bliss trailed along behind him.

He stepped up to the desk and whispered something to the ticket agent. Then he turned, bowed, kissed Mary Bliss's hand, and walked rapidly away.

The agent waved Mary Bliss's proffered ticket away. "Arrangements have been changed," she said softly.

"We have you seated on the next flight. Nonstop to Atlanta. And first class. We thought you might be more comfortable that way."

"First class," Katharine repeated happily. "I think we'll be *much* more comfortable."

The gate agent let Mary Bliss and Katharine board the plane before anybody else, and the flight attendant tucked them into their leather recliner seats and handed them the new issue of *Vanity Fair* and steaming hot coffee.

When she'd gone, Mary Bliss let out a long, troubled sigh. "What have I gotten myself into?"

Passengers trooped down the aisle past them, giving them the kind of resentful looks they'd always given people sitting in their current situation.

"First class," Katharine said. "You were born for first class, Mary Bliss. And so was I, of course." She put her mouth very near Mary Bliss's ear. "You're doing great with the grieving-widow thing. Very convincing. But I know you, Mary Bliss. And I can tell you're having second thoughts."

"That's an understatement," Mary Bliss said, sipping her coffee. "I am scared totally out of my mind. All the time I was in that *clinica*, I kept thinking, any minute now, somebody is going to step up and arrest me. And at the airport, same thing. I won't feel safe until we land in Atlanta. If I'm going to jail, I just want to go to one with flush toilets and running water."

"Stop that talk!" Katharine said. "Parker is dead. Things went even better than we planned. Except for your concussion. That means it was meant to be. God wants Parker dead. Why else would he have arranged that boat wreck like he did?"

Mary Bliss turned and looked at Katharine with amazement. "How can you say such a thing? Parker is *not* dead. We have no idea where he is, and whether he'll show up again. And in the meantime, how can you be so callous about Dinky? The poor man. We suckered him into our plan, and now he's dead. Doesn't that mean anything to you? That somebody died because of our selfishness?"

"We don't *know* he's dead," Katharine whispered. "And anyway, Dinky knew what he was getting himself into. He's the one who got himself drunk. He's the one who didn't bother to wear a life jacket. And he's the one who drove that boat like a maniac and nearly got you killed in the process. If something bad happened to him, it's his own fault as far as I'm concerned."

"You are awful," Mary Bliss said. "You of all people. I mean, you slept with the man just the night before. Doesn't that mean anything at all to you?"

Katharine opened *Vanity Fair* with a flourish. "Not that it's any of your business, because it isn't. But I do feel I should tell you that nothing happened between Dinky and me. Absolutely nothing."

"But," Mary Bliss sputtered. "You said . . . you knew why people called him Dinky. And I saw him too. He really was dinky."

Katharine rolled her eyes. "Honestly. Look. I let him stay in the room with me because I thought, maybe, I should branch out a little, in the romance department, you know? I mean, Charlie and I are almost divorced. And he certainly hasn't been faithful to me. So what was to stop me from having a little fun?"

"Your conscience?"

"Please," Katharine said, guffawing. "Don't confuse me with you. No. What stopped me was a matter of taste. You saw the man. He doesn't even own a car. Dinky just wasn't my type. Not to mention I have no intention of coming down with some nasty sexually transmitted disease. No. Not Katharine Weidman. Now, can we drop this subject?"

"No," Mary Bliss said. "I think you're a big liar. I think you didn't sleep with Dinky because you're still in love with Charlie."

Katharine reached into the seat-back pocket in front of her and brought out a set of earphones, which she placed over her hair with a flourish. "We are not having this conversation."

When the pilot made the announcement that they were entering their approach to Atlanta, Mary Bliss said a heartfelt prayer of thanks. She looked out the window at the city stretched out below. Tiny matchbox-sized cars sped down streets whose straightness and precision looked like a marvel from up above. Pincushion-sized trees dotted the landscape. It reminded her of her wealthy boy cousin's model railroad layout that she had coveted as a child. Looking down now, Mary Bliss coveted Atlanta. Or, to be more precise, she coveted home.

"What's this?" she asked, when the flight attendant arrived at her side with a shiny chrome contraption.

"It's a wheelchair," Katharine said before the young woman could answer. "And it's the doctor's orders, so don't go giving her any sass about it."

"I'm not an invalid," Mary Bliss protested, but people were standing, and she was blocking the aisle, so she gave in out of politeness.

When they were off the plane, there was a courtesy golf cart waiting for them too. "Not a word!" Katharine warned. "Doctor's orders. Besides, I'm whipped. You might not need to ride, but I do."

There was one more surprise: Randy Bowden waited for them in the baggage pickup area. He carried a huge bouquet of yellow roses, and a look of profound grief.

"Mary Bliss," he said, his face lighting up when he saw the cart approach. "You're all right!"

She shot Katharine a look. "I'm fine," she said wearily. "It's just a little bitty concussion. I don't know why everybody has to make such a fuss over me. I'm perfectly capable of walking."

"But Katharine said," he started to say.

"Never mind," Mary Bliss said, patting his hand. "I'm so sorry to inconvenience you this way."

"Not at all," he said. "Josh is outside with the car. I'll just grab your bags and we'll go out and go home. I know you've had a bad time of it."

"Thank you," Mary Bliss said.

"You're welcome," Katharine said, mouthing the words.

33

"Holy crap!" Katharine said, opening the kitchen door.

"Oh my." Mary Bliss covered her mouth with her hands and started to cry.

Every surface in the kitchen was crowded with food. Foil-wrapped casseroles were stacked three high on top of the oven. The counters were lined with trays of cookies and sandwiches, and plastic cake-carriers offered coconut, pound, and chocolate layer cakes.

"There's a lot of stuff in the refrigerator too," Randy Bowden said, setting Mary Bliss's suitcase down. "I hope you don't mind. People kept calling and asking if they could do something. And I had the key, so I kind of let them bring in the food. It wouldn't all fit in your fridge, so there's a bunch of stuff in mine too."

"How nice," Mary Bliss said, her voice faint. "But they shouldn't have. They really shouldn't have."

"Uh, well," Randy said. "You and Parker are special people, Mary Bliss. And with your loss and all, well, people wanted to do something to help out."

"Wonder if Carolyn Meeks brought anything over?" Katharine said, looking around the kitchen. She walked over to the refrigerator, opened the door, and stuck her head in. "She makes those deviled eggs with the little capers on top." Her voice was muffled as she shuffled dishes around the packed refrigerator. "I had some last winter, at the women's Christmas tea. And I would kill for one of Carolyn's deviled eggs right now."

She held out a clear glass dish of eggs, each nicely capped with a sprig of parsley and a sprinkling of capers. "Ta-da!" she said triumphantly. "Deviled eggs to die for!"

"Katharine!" Mary Bliss said, blushing. She felt ill. Her head was throbbing again and the sight of all that food made her queasy, and now Randy and Josh Bowden were looking at her expectantly.

"Oops, sorry," Katharine said. She finished off the egg with one bite and wiped her hands on a paper napkin. "But you know what I meant."

"Where's Erin?" Mary Bliss asked, wanting to change the subject.

Josh and Randy exchanged a guilty look.

"She's at work," Josh said finally. "That's why she didn't come to the airport to pick you up. She said she'd try to get off early tonight, if she could."

"Good," Mary Bliss said. It was all she could think of to say.

There was more polite conversation after that. Josh carried her suitcase upstairs, and Randy told her where he'd put the list of phone messages and mail, and finally, after what seemed like hours and hours, they were gone.

Mary Bliss sat down at the kitchen table. There were at least a dozen condolence cards, and a potted dish garden with a yellow bow and a card from her minister, Dr. Neely.

"You know what's crazy?" she asked Katharine.

"All of it," Katharine said promptly.

"I keep forgetting Parker isn't dead," Mary Bliss said. "I keep reliving the boat accident, and waking up in the hospital and talking to the police, and I keep hearing the doctor telling me my husband hasn't been found. And the rational, sane me knows it wasn't Parker. It was Dinky. But I keep thinking, Parker's dead. I feel like a widow. I feel like I need to dry my eyes and put on a black suit and plan a funeral."

"Then do it," Katharine said. "That's the general idea, remember?"

"What about Erin?"

Katharine started opening the envelopes. "Look, here's one from the Steadmans. They want you to know you're in their prayers."

"My child thinks her father is dead," Mary Bliss said. "We've told her Parker died in a boating accident. So she goes to work? She just drives over to the mall and puts on her Gap name tag and she starts selling summer shorts and tankinis like nothing happened? Two days after her daddy's death?"

"She's a kid," Katharine said. "She's probably still in shock. Kids don't know how to grieve, Mary Bliss. They don't know anything about death, or funerals or any of that. Probably the worst thing that's ever happened to Erin before was not having her socks match."

"She didn't get named to the all-county team her freshman year," Mary Bliss said suddenly. "She was absolutely devastated. Wouldn't eat, wouldn't answer the phone, or leave the house. She lives and breathes soccer. That experience nearly killed her."

"But it didn't," Katharine said. "She got over it. And she'll get over this."

"I wish I believed you," Mary Bliss said. She was tearing open envelopes now, reading the cards, the warm sentiments from neighbors and friends.

"Look," she said, holding one up. "It's from Nancye Bowden. She says she'll never forget Parker, or what a wonderful marriage we had."

Katharine's fingers were hovering over a platter of fried chicken. She decided on a drumstick, picked it up, and started chewing on the fat end.

"Well," she said thoughtfully. "Guess that shows you how much of an authority on marriage Nancye Bowden is."

"I'm thinking about driving over to the mall," Mary Bliss said, pushing the stack of cards away. "I've got to talk to Erin. This isn't normal, her going to work like this. I'll talk to her manager, make him give her the night off. We can have a quiet dinner."

"Don't," Katharine said.

Mary Bliss raised one eyebrow.

"Leave her be," Katharine said.

"I can't."

The phone rang. Mary Bliss stared at it. Katharine picked it up.

"McGowan residence," she said, her voice the model of crisp efficiency.

"No." Mary Bliss was mouthing the words, shaking her head. "I don't want to talk to anyone."

"It's the supervisor over at the nursing home," Katharine said, covering the receiver with her hand. "Eula's having some kind of fit or something."

"Eula!" Mary Bliss grabbed the phone. "This is Mrs. McGowan," she said. "What's happening?"

"Mrs. McGowan? This is Lillian King. I'm the care supervisor for your mother-in-law. I hate to trouble you with this, so soon after the accident, but the doctor feels I should notify you that Eula is experiencing some difficulties, dealing with all this."

"Difficulties?" Mary Bliss rubbed the back of her neck. Her skin felt gritty and damp. She wanted a bath.

"Losing her son," Lillian King said.

"She knows?" Mary Bliss nearly dropped the phone. "Who told her about Parker?"

"I, uh, I don't know," Lillian King stammered. "I assume somebody in the family told her. She's been very upset ever since Sunday. Violent, in fact. We're afraid she might harm herself, or someone else. The doctor has sedated her now, but he wanted me to let you know what's going on with her."

"All right," Mary Bliss said slowly. "I'll be right over."

"Meemaw." Katharine put down the drumstick. "That didn't sound like good news."

"It's not," Mary Bliss agreed. "It sounds like she's pretty worked up about Parker. Who would have told her? I was going to tell her myself, as soon as I got up the courage. But somebody else did it for me."

"Erin?"

"Maybe," Mary Bliss said. "She hates going over to that nursing home. Says it smells like pee and steamed broccoli. But she and Meemaw were close. Maybe she took it upon herself to tell her."

"What kind of fit is the old girl throwing?" Katharine asked.

"Violent. They're afraid she'll hurt herself."

"Cheer up. Maybe she'll take an overdose of sleeping pills or something," Katharine said. "You could have a double funeral."

"Not funny," Mary Bliss said, not bothering to pretend to be shocked. "But I have an idea if she's violent, it's probably toward others. I seriously doubt she's really suicidal. Eula McGowan is a survivor."

"You don't have to go, you know," Katharine pointed out. "She's not *your* mother. Let the nursing home deal with her."

"I have to go," Mary Bliss said.

"I know," Katharine said, getting up. "This chicken's pretty good, you know? I think it must be from Carolyn Meeks too. I understand she uses buttermilk and real lard."

"Take it," Mary Bliss said, gesturing around the room. "Take all of it."

34

Lillian King was explaining that they had moved Eula out of her own room and into something called the intermediate care facility. She gave Mary Bliss a lot of numbers, her blood pressure reading, her EKG readings, even the dosage of the medicine with which she'd been sedated.

Mary Bliss heard the words as they bounced off the narrow hall walls at the Fair Oaks Assisted Living Facility. Lillian King's rubber-soled nursing shoes squeaked as they walked down the corridor. Erin was right, Mary Bliss thought. The place really did smell like pee and broccoli.

The intermediate care facility turned out to be a small three-bed mini-hospital. The only occupied bed in the room held Eula McGowan.

Mary Bliss tiptoed over and looked down at her mother-in-law. She had last seen her only a week ago. But the change was profound. Her skin was slack and sallow. Flesh seemed to have melted off her once-plump arms. A stand next to her bed held a bag of intravenous fluids and a clear tube ran into a needle taped to her forearm.

"Meemaw?"

Eula's eyes fluttered open. She looked at Mary Bliss, then turned her head away.

"Mrs. McGowan? You've got yourself a visitor here," Lillian King said in a loud voice, patting Eula's hand.

"I don't want her," Eula said, her voice faint but stony. "Make her go away." She slapped hard at the nurse's hand.

"See?" Lillian King whispered.

"Now, that's not very nice," she said, chiding the old lady as she would a toddler. "Your daughter-in-law came all the way over here just to see how you're doing."

"Meemaw?" Mary Bliss leaned over. "Erin told you about Parker, didn't she?"

Eula sprang upright. "He's not dead!" she screamed. She struck out at Mary Bliss, arms flailing, landing a slap to the side of her face that left her ear ringing. "Tell them he's not dead. Tell them."

"Meemaw," Mary Bliss cried. "I'm sorry. I'm so sorry."

"Now that's enough of that," Lillian King said firmly. She stepped in and pushed Eula back onto the bed, pinning her arms to her side. The old woman squirmed, tried to push the nurse away, but Lillian King was thirty years younger and fifty pounds heavier.

"Let me go," Eula demanded. She thrashed around the bed, kicking her legs out from under the covers. "I need to go find my son."

"All right, Mrs. McGowan," Lillian King said, her face reddening. "Do we need to put you in restraints again? Is that what we need to do with you tonight?"

"Restraints?" Mary Bliss said, horrified. "Oh no. Don't do anything like that."

"I'll be good," Eula whimpered, the fight drained out of her. She stopped thrashing and crossed her bony arms across her chest. "I promise I'll be good."

"No more hitting?" Lillian King hovered over the bed.

"No more hitting," Eula repeated.

Mary Bliss rubbed her bruised cheek. "I'm sorry, Meemaw," she repeated. "I know you loved him. I know he loved you."

Lillian King took her by the arm and steered her toward the door. "She needs to rest now. This has all been very upsetting for her. As it has for you too, I'm sure."

"Good night, Meemaw," Mary Bliss said dutifully. The door was swinging shut behind them.

"He's not dead, dammit," Eula called out.

After she left the nursing home, Mary Bliss drove home. But instead of pulling into the driveway, she stopped the car at the curb. The timer had turned on the lights in the house. It looked warm and inviting like this, from the street. She looked over at Randy Bowden's house. Somebody had picked up all the old newspapers. A mound of grass clippings were piled at the curb. From the back of the house she heard the drone of a lawn mower. Life was getting back to normal.

She drove on, to the mall. She had to see Erin, had to talk to her.

It was nearly nine o'clock. The mall was empty except for knots of people waiting to get into the movieplex.

A girl she didn't recognize was counting change out of the cash register at the Gap.

"Erin?" The girl had two tiny diamond studs on the left side of her nose. "She didn't come in tonight. There's been, like, a death in the family."

Mary Bliss nodded and left. She drove past the house, but there was no sign of Erin. Where could her daughter be?

She cruised up and down every street in the neighborhood, looking for Erin's little Honda. It was a quiet summer night. She could see flickering blue lights in the windows of some of the houses. Strains of heavy metal music poured from the Bowdens' house. Only a few cars were still parked in the lot at the country club. She recognized Charlie Weidman's black Lincoln there, and a white Sebring convertible she'd been told was Charlie's girlfriend's car. Katharine would throw a conniption if she found out Charlie had brought his girlfriend over here, to the club.

She kept driving. Past Fair Oaks Academy, darkened now that school was out for the summer, past the Winn-Dixie parking lot, past the McDonald's she knew was Erin's favorite late-night stop-in.

On the way home, she happened to glance over at the municipal park where Erin had played Little Kicker soccer as a four-year-old. A blue Honda was the only car in the lot. Mary Bliss slowed and turned in.

The Honda's high beams were on, pointed at the field nearest the street. She could see a lone figure silhouetted in the light, kicking a ball against the net backstop. Mary Bliss held her breath. Erin.

She parked the car at the far end of the lot and walked quietly toward her daughter. Erin had a plastic laundry basket full of soccer balls. One after another, she scooped the balls from the basket and kicked them into the net. Scoop, kick. Scoop, kick.

The ground was littered with the balls. Mary Bliss sat on the hood of her daughter's car and watched.

After half an hour, Erin gathered up all the balls. She was breathing hard as she approached the car, kicking one errant ball in the direction of the Honda.

She stopped short five yards away.

"Mama?"

"Hey there," Mary Bliss said.

"Hey," Erin said. Her voice was expressionless. She walked past her mother, unlocked the trunk of the car, and dropped the basket in, then closed the trunk.

"What are you doing here?" Erin asked, standing by the car door. Her hair was bound up in a ponytail, her face was red and beaded with perspiration.

"Looking for you," Mary Bliss said. "I was worried."

"Don't be worried," Erin said. "I'm all right."

"No," Mary Bliss said. "I don't think you're all right. I'm not all right either."

"Is this about Daddy?" Erin mopped her face with the tail of her T-shirt.

"Honey, of course it's about Daddy. I'm sorry you had to hear about the accident from a stranger. I wanted to tell you myself, but they wouldn't let me talk on the telephone at the hospital. The doctor didn't want to upset me."

Erin cocked her head. "So are you all right?"

"I had a concussion," Mary Bliss said, touching her hand to the bandage on the back of her head. "They think a piece of the boat hit me when it happened."

"But you were all right."

"I was wearing a life jacket," Mary Bliss said. "They think the tide swept me in."

"But not Daddy." Erin's fists were balled up, perched on her hips.

"He wasn't wearing a life jacket," Mary Bliss whispered. "The boat hit a big wave, head-on. Before I knew it, I was being thrown clear. It was an old boat. Probably not even safe, although we didn't realize it at the time. They found pieces of the boat all over the beach."

"But not Daddy."

"No," Mary Bliss said. "Not Daddy."

"Meemaw says he's not really dead," Erin said.

Mary Bliss winced. "I just came from the nursing home. Honey, your grandmother is old, and she's heartbroken. And she's not real clear on a lot of things these days."

"You're saying she's crazy, right? Senile old Meemaw."

"Not crazy. But the doctors have told us she has the beginnings of Alzheimer's disease, and that's a form of senility. Some days, she's fine. Other times, she can't remember her name, can't remember mine. She says awful things. Does awful things. She claims the nurses are stealing from her. Tonight she got so agitated, she slugged me."

Mary Bliss rubbed the knot forming on her cheek-bone. "It's not her. It's the disease. We have to keep remembering that."

Erin scooped up the last soccer ball. She bounced it against the door of the car.

"So, what happens now?"

Mary Bliss caught the ball in midair and hugged it against her chest.

"I don't know," she admitted.

"But you think Daddy's dead, right?"

"That's what I'm afraid of. They searched the waters all around where the accident happened. The police tell me, they said it's unlikely he could have survived the accident."

Erin bit her lip. "Did he drown? Or do they think he got eaten by, like, a shark, or what?"

"God, Erin," Mary Bliss cried. "Don't talk like that."

"I want to know, dammit," Erin said. "He's my dad. I need to know what happened to him. You might not care, but I do. I have a right to know."

"I can't tell you anything else," Mary Bliss said. Her heart was beating wildly. She was sure she could hear her veins pounding blood into her head. "I don't have any answers. And you're wrong about that, you know."

"What?" Erin pushed past Mary Bliss and got in the car. The key was already in the ignition. She started the engine.

"I do care," Mary Bliss said, holding the door open so that Erin couldn't close it. Couldn't shut her out. "I care that he's gone. I loved your daddy."

"Yeah, right." Erin wrenched the door shut and the car jerked forward, leaving Mary Bliss standing alone at the soccer park. She watched the red taillights until they'd disappeared from sight. Then she picked up the soccer ball and walked back to her own car, alone.

35

Standing on Mary Bliss's doorstep on a white-hot Wednesday morning, Charlie Weidman looked miserable. He wore a stylish dark-blue double-breasted suit, bright-blue dress shirt with white collar and cuffs, and pointy-toed Italian-looking shoes. Clearly, somebody else was making his fashion decisions these days. He shifted from one foot to the other, tugged at his shirt collar and blinked rapidly.

"Uh, Mary Bliss?" His face reddened.

"Hey, Charlie," Mary Bliss said. She reached out instinctively and hugged his neck. "Aren't you sweet to come by and see me."

He brightened. "You don't mind?"

"Katharine's the one who's divorcing you, Charlie, not me," she said. "Come on in and get out of this heat."

He followed her through the hall to the living room, loosening his tie as he went.

She seated him on the sofa. "Let me fix you some iced tea. I know you like my tea."

"Oh no," he said quickly. "I just dropped by to see if I could help you out with things. I don't want you going to any trouble for me."

"It's no trouble at all," she said. "I've got a pitcher made and in the fridge. I'll be right back."

In the kitchen she speed-dialed Katharine's number.

When she answered, Mary Bliss didn't give her time to talk. "Charlie's here," she whispered. "Did you call him and send him over?"

"Hell, no," Katharine said. "I haven't talked to him in a couple weeks. I just left a message on his machine at the office about Parker, that's all."

"He says he wants to help with some things," Mary Bliss said.

"Hmm," Katharine said.

"You think he suspects anything?"

"God, no," Katharine said. "He's totally clueless. You know he's always had a soft spot for you. So he probably does want to help out. I'd say let him. No use in us doing all the heavy lifting."

"All right," Mary Bliss said, putting ice in a tall glass and pouring the cold tea over it.

After she hung up the phone, she added a slice of lemon to the tea, cut a slice from Marifae Jones's chocolate pound cake, and put it on a plate.

Charlie was unloading a set of documents from his briefcase when Mary Bliss got back to the living room.

"Here," Mary Bliss said, handing him the plate of cake. "Help me get rid of some of this food people have been dropping by. There's enough cake and cookies in my kitchen right now to feed Pharaoh's army."

"Oh no," Charlie said, waving away the cake like it was a case of the plague. "I'm doing the Atkins Diet. Carbs are like poison to me."

"This isn't carbs, it's Marifae Jones's chocolate cake," Mary Bliss said. "She only makes it when somebody dies."

Charlie looked shocked.

"Well, it's no use pretending somebody hasn't," Mary Bliss said, sitting down in the chair opposite him. "That's why you're here, isn't it?"

"Yeah, that's about the size of it," Charlie said. He broke off a chunk of cake and chewed it appreciatively. "That Jones woman can bake a damned cake, can't she?"

Mary Bliss got a glimpse of his hands. He was wearing a pinky ring with a large diamond on his left hand.

The wedding ring was gone. She had to look away to keep from staring.

"She certainly can," Mary Bliss said, taking a sip of tea.

"Well," Charlie said. "Let's get down to business, then. You know I was Parker's attorney in a lot of matters. I handled y'all's wills and things like that. So I thought I'd go ahead and start the ball rolling on getting that probated. Then, if you'd like, I'll file for your death benefits and all. That sound all right?"

"Fine," Mary Bliss said. "Do you have copies of everything you need? I'm kinda dumb about all this stuff, Charlie. So having you help me out will be a godsend."

"Not a problem," he said, beaming. "I'll need copies of his insurance policies. Do you have 'em here at the house?"

Mary Bliss thought quickly. Should she tell him Parker had already cashed in his life insurance, or let him find out for himself? She decided it would look better if it were a complete surprise to her.

"I'll have to get them out of the lockbox at the bank," she said. "I can do that this morning and drop them off at your office. Is there anything else you need?"

He bit his lip. "I hate to ask, but the insurance company is going to want to know about the body. That could be a problem. Do you have copies of police reports from Mexico, anything like that?"

She nodded and let a small tear roll down her cheek. It was no act. She was scared witless and was getting used to crying at the drop of a hat. "They gave me copies of everything," she said. "And I have a death certificate. Will that help?"

"They issued a death certificate? Even though they never found Parker's body?"

She muffled a sob and simply shook her head yes.

"All right, then," Charlie said. "Yeah, sure. The death certificate should speed matters up considerably. In the meantime, I hate to ask, but since we're old friends, I'm gonna. Are you all right for money?"

Mary Bliss sobbed again and gulped. "I don't know," she whispered. "Parker handled all that. And he's been gone so much lately, consulting and all, I just haven't kept up with things like I probably should have."

"All right," he said, patting her back awkwardly. "Don't worry about it. I don't want you worrying about one little thing, you hear me, Mary Bliss? You get me those insurance papers first thing, and I'll put a bee in their bonnets about a quick payout."

"All right," she agreed.

"One more thing," Charlie said. "What about a funeral? Have you given any thought to that?"

"A little," Mary Bliss admitted. "Dr. Neely sent over a flower arrangement. I've been thinking I should call him, but I just haven't been able to get around to it."

"I'll take care of that too," Charlie said. "What kind of a thing did you have in mind?"

"Well," Mary Bliss said, hesitating. "We don't have a body, so I don't think it's appropriate to have an actual funeral. I guess, I was thinking maybe a nice memorial service? At Fair Oaks First United Methodist. And afterwards, I suppose, we could have lunch over here."

"Absolutely not," Charlie said emphatically. "They can have a luncheon in the church parlor. You don't want a lot of old biddies swarming around here, asking questions and poking and prodding and upsetting you, do you?"

"Maybe not," Mary Bliss admitted. God, Charlie was wonderful. How could Katharine just give up on him like this?

"Don't they have one of those church-lady thingies that takes care of stuff like this?" Charlie asked. "Who would I call?"

"Kimberly Sheffield is president of the women's circle," Mary Bliss said. "I suppose she'd be the one to organize anything. But really, Charlie, I don't want any fuss. It's too awkward."

Charlie handed her a sheaf of papers. "These forms will authorize me to start probating the will and the other things we need to do. Fill 'em out, and drop 'em off with the other things. And you just leave it all to old Charlie, and don't worry. Okay?"

"Okay," Mary Bliss said. She hugged his neck again. He smelled like strong, expensive perfume. The old Charlie smelled like cigars. She thought she would like to have the old Charlie back.

When he was gone, she called Katharine back.

"Tell me everything," Katharine said.

Mary Bliss sighed. "She's got him on the Atkins Diet."

"Ha! That's a laugh. This is a man who thinks Twinkies and Moonpies are one of the major food groups."

"And she's dressing him funny too. He had on a two-tone dress shirt. With French cuffs! Obviously she doesn't know his shirt size, because his neck looked like it was about to explode. And pointy-toed shoes. They looked like those Bruno Maglis O. J. Simpson was wearing when he killed Nicole."

"Gawd," Katharine said. "And to think when he was married to me he never wore anything but Bass Weejuns."

"He's gone uptown now," Mary Bliss said. "And it doesn't suit him. Not at all."

"What else?" Katharine asked. "You're holding something back, I can tell."

"I wasn't going to bring it up," Mary Bliss said. "But he was wearing a diamond pinky ring. On his left hand. And the wedding band is gone."

"I took the damned wedding band away from him," Katharine said, her voice unusually gravelly. "After I caught him with that slut. I damn near ripped his finger off with it. But this is the first I've heard of a pinky ring. Jesus! A pinky ring!"

"You made me tell you," Mary Bliss reminded her.

"I know," Katharine said, sighing. "What else? Is he gonna make all the arrangements?"

"He said he will," Mary Bliss said. "I've got to take all the insurance papers over to him. I'm gonna let him break the news to me that all but one has been cashed in. And he'll file for the death benefits from the one insurance policy my aunt gave us."

"Good," Katharine said. "And he didn't act suspicious at all, did he?"

"No," Mary Bliss said. "He was really so sweet and thoughtful, Katharine. He even offered to take care of the funeral arrangements, which I was totally dreading. Honestly, sweetie, he's too good a man to just throw away like this."

"He needs killing," Katharine said. "He cheated on me, and he lied like a damn dog. He's just lucky I didn't tear his testicles off when I was taking back that wedding ring."

"But you'd take him back in a heartbeat, wouldn't you? Tell the truth now."

"No effin' way," Katharine said. "Now could we please discuss your situation, and not mine? What did Charlie say about the funeral stuff?"

"Fair Oaks First United Methodist. A small memorial service at the church, lunch afterwards in the church parlor."

"Very nice," Katharine said. "I'm impressed. Did you come up with that?"

"It was all his idea," Mary Bliss said. "He's gonna make some little gal a wonderful husband someday."

"I'm hanging up now," Katharine said.

And she did.

36

Organ music swelled sweetly around the flower-scented sanctuary. Fair Oaks First United Methodist Church was packed to the rafters. Mary Bliss sat in the front row, clasping Erin's hand tight in hers. Erin stared straight ahead. On the other side of Erin, they'd placed Eula's wheelchair in the aisle. She was half turned in the wheelchair, her head whipping back and forth as she watched people filing into the church, packing the old golden oak pews.

Her eyes fixed on two teenaged girls in blue jeans and halter tops who seated themselves across the aisle. Mary Bliss recognized one of the girls as Erin's friend Jessica.

Eula glared at them with undisguised malice. "Well, I never," the old lady said in a loud voice. "Pants at a church funeral. And titties flopping around for all the world to see. Right here in front of God and everybody."

"Meemaw," Erin hissed. "Stop! They'll hear you."

"Good," Eula said, smacking her lips with satisfaction. "I've got a lot more they need to hear."

Katharine sat on the other side of Mary Bliss. "I thought you said she'd been sedated," she whispered.

Mary Bliss just shook her head. She'd spent most of the past two days tussling and fussing with Eula and Erin, and she was so exhausted that her body ached. Up until an hour before the service was scheduled to begin, Erin had flatly refused to attend.

"I'm not going," she'd told her mother when informed of the arrangements. "I don't believe in God. And Daddy hated funerals. You know he did. This whole thing's a farce."

It had been Josh who'd changed Erin's mind. He and Randy had come over to the house the night before. Josh had seen the desperation in Mary Bliss's eyes as Erin held forth on the hypocrisy of organized religion, and how sick and twisted almost everybody in Fair Oaks was.

"Look," Josh had said, cleaning the lenses of his glasses on the hem of his shirt, "it's something you do, okay? I mean, you know there's no Santa Claus, but you still open presents on Christmas morning, right? And you know there's no boogeyman hanging around on Halloween, but you still dress up and go to parties and trick-or-treat, right?"

"I haven't trick-or-treated since I was twelve," Erin said, her lips pressed together in disapproval—or denial.

"You know what I mean," Josh said, persisting. "Like, when my granddad died, I didn't want to go to that funeral. It was in this little church down in the boonies, and I didn't know anybody, and it wasn't even air-conditioned. But I went because my mom and my gramma wanted me to. And it wasn't so bad."

Erin had rolled her eyes. "Not so bad? It'll be a freak show!" But Friday morning, Erin had appeared in the kitchen, wearing makeup, a flowered sundress, and flip-flops.

"I'm *not* changing my clothes," she said defiantly when Mary Bliss greeted her.

"I'm not asking you to," Mary Bliss said. "I think you look very nice." Secretly, she thought her daughter's outfit more appropriate for a day at the beach, but at this point she was ready for any compromise that might keep the peace with her daughter.

"And I'm not getting up and saying anything about Daddy," Erin said. Her lower lip quivered. "It's private. I won't talk about him to all those freaky old people."

"I wouldn't expect you to give a eulogy," Mary Bliss said, secretly relieved. "I'm not going to speak either. We'll let Dr. Neely do the talking. Is that all right?"

"I guess," Erin said. She flicked her hair over her shoulder. "I'll see you at church. Eleven? Right?"

"Right," Mary Bliss said. She had hoped Erin would go with her to pick Eula up from the nursing home, but again, compromise was the spirit of the day.

The scene at the nursing home had been another kind of nightmare. Eula was dressed and ready when Mary Bliss arrived. She wore a powder-blue dress, pearls that had yellowed with age, and a matching powder-blue turban fastened with a large rhinestone brooch.

"Meemaw," Mary Bliss said politely. "How nice you look."

"I see you staring at my hat," Eula said. "That slanty-eyed girl in the beauty shop gave me a perm and burned the daylights out of my hair. It's ruint. Just ruint. And don't think I paid her, either. I want you to call up the immigration office and report her. Have her green card revoked."

Yun Lee was the Korean-American woman who ran the one-chair beauty shop at Fair Oaks Assisted Living

Facility. She was in her fifties and had been born and lived in Atlanta her whole life. She considered her clientele of elderly ladies as her personal responsibility in life, charging only twenty-five dollars for hair color, set, and comb-out, an unheard-of price in Atlanta. And Eula had been trying to have her deported since she'd first laid eyes on her.

"I'm sure your hair will be fine," Mary Bliss said, patting her hand. "How are you feeling today?"

"Awful," Eula said promptly. "My bowels are locked up tight. Haven't had a good sit-down since you-know-when."

"What does the doctor say?"

"Give me all kinda pills and nasty-tasting medicine. And none of it works. Look at this," Eula said, thumping her belly. "I'm swelled up like a toad. Cramps and gas something awful. Every minute it feels like I might just explode."

Mary Bliss stepped away from the wheelchair, in the off chance that Eula was right. "Maybe you should just stay in today," she said uneasily. "Get some rest. Maybe eat some bran flakes."

"And have everybody in town talking about me?" Eula's eyes flashed. She'd lost so much weight, her dentures seemed to float loose in her jaws. "Forget it, sister," she snapped. "I'm ready and I'm going. And don't think I don't intend to tell everybody I see that my son Parker McGowan is alive and breathing."

"Oh, Meemaw," Mary Bliss said. She felt helpless. Should she really just walk out and leave her mother-in-law here at the nursing home?

Just then the door to Eula's room opened. Lillian King sailed in with a cart full of medications.

"Hello there, ladies," she sang out. She seemed stunned to see Eula up and dressed.

"Well, what have we here?" she asked, feigning confusion. "Where have you fashionable ladies hidden my patient, Mrs. Eula McGowan? All I see are two beautiful women dressed up for a Beverly Hills movie premiere."

"It's me, Eula, you old fool," Eula said, her dentures clicking. "I've got burnt hair and locked bowels and it's all her fault." She jerked a thumb in Mary Bliss's general direction. "I'm all decked out like this because I'm going to a funeral for my son who ain't even dead. This little missy here thinks she can pull the wool over my eyes, but she's got another think coming, I can tell you."

Lillian King exchanged a look with Mary Bliss. "Now, Eula," she said, her voice soothing. "We know you miss your son something awful. But what you have to remember is that he's in a better place right now.

Don't think of him as dead. Think of him as being in a better place."

"He's in a better place all right," Eula said, wheeling her chair toward the open door. "And it's not at the bottom of the sea in Mexico. He's on some island somewhere, drinking mai-tais and whooping it up with girls who are lots younger and prettier than Miss Ice-Britches here."

Lillian King tsk-tsked.

Mary Bliss just shrugged. "Can you give her anything for the constipation?"

"Maybe a dose of dynamite," the nurse said. "It's all in her head, of course. She has her little movement at eight A.M. every day, like clockwork. But she's been real agitated since she got the news about her son. I was just coming in to give her a little something for the anxiety."

"She's being sedated and she's still this hostile?"

"Oh yes," the nurse said. "This is a good morning for her. Yesterday when I came in, she had managed to dial nine-one-one. She said she was calling the police to tell them her room had been ransacked and her son was being held hostage by slant-eyed terrorists."

"Good Lord," Mary Bliss said.

"She's delusional," Lillian King said. "We see it all the time."

"Eula," she called, stepping out into the hall.

Meemaw's wheelchair was halfway down the hall, and she was wheeling toward the front lobby like a woman possessed. She stopped when she heard her name.

"Just one moment," Lillian King said. "I need to give you your laxatives."

She turned and gave Mary Bliss a broad wink. "Paxil," she whispered. "We just tell her it's her laxative."

"Well, get up here and make it snappy," Meemaw said. "The Women's Circle is having lunch in the church parlor after the show, and I don't want to miss dessert."

Dr. Neely had promised a short but touching service. The church organist, William Isler, had asked Mary Bliss for suggestions, but she'd been so distracted, she'd asked him to pick the music.

Her shoulders relaxed as she heard the strains of a vaguely familiar Bach piece. "Sheep May Safely Graze," she thought, nodding with approval. She glanced over at Erin, squeezed her hand. Erin met her eyes, then looked away.

Eula was busily counting the number of people in the church. "Ninety-eight, ninety-nine," she said, nodding as she ticked off the numbers. Mary Bliss turned to her and made a shushing noise, putting her fingers to her lips.

"That's the president of the Griffin Bank and Trust," she informed Mary Bliss, pointing to a white-haired gentleman entering the back of the church. "My son has lots of important friends, you know."

"I know," Mary Bliss whispered. "But we're in church. I think we need to be respectful."

"Who cares what you think?" Eula said. "That woman with him, she's his second wife. Used to be his secretary, 'til the first wife caught 'em diddling in the bank vault."

Mary Bliss heard titters of laughter in the row behind them, and discreet coughing.

Katharine leaned in close to Mary Bliss. "What time do you think those drugs are gonna kick in on her?"

"Pray for me," Mary Bliss whispered back.

Mr. Isler segued easily into another piece Mary Bliss recognized, a choral piece from Handel. "I Know That My Redeemer Liveth."

"Isn't this nice?" Mary Bliss asked, trying to get Erin to respond to something. Since her outburst the night Mary Bliss had found her on the soccer field, her daughter had been more distant than ever, leaving Mary Bliss to miss even their fights.

"Groovy," Erin said. She gave an exaggerated sigh. "I just want to get this over with."

Dr. Neely drifted up to the lectern and cleared his throat, and the music gradually softened and then stopped.

"Parker McGowan is not gone," he said, his voice booming through the sanctuary.

"See?" Eula said, digging an elbow into Mary Bliss's side. "Even that pie-faced preacher man knows my son's not dead."

Another barely repressed laugh came from behind her. Mary Bliss wished fervently right then that either she or Eula were the one being eulogized.

She allowed herself a tiny, sideways glance to see who was getting such a laugh out of Eula, and when she saw the source, she thought she could feel her blood freeze.

That man again. Matt Hayslip. He was right here, at Parker's funeral, wearing a navy-blue suit and a somber expression. Mary Bliss sat up straight, held her head high, to keep from throwing up.

"Parker McGowan is in the company of angels," Dr. Neely continued. "So although we mourn his loss amongst us, today we gather to celebrate what his life has meant to all of us."

The pastor's voice was loud but soothing. He spoke of Parker's dedication to family, his commitment to business and community. Eula's head nodded repeatedly, then sank onto her chest. When she snored softly, Erin stared, then grinned for the first time in days.

"Thank God for the miracle of modern pharmaceuticals," Katharine whispered.

37

Charlie Weidman came back to the house after Parker's funeral service to deliver the bad news in person.

They'd sat in Parker's den while Charlie gave her the news she already knew.

"I'm gonna just lay it on the line here," Charlie said, his kind face serious. "Things are bad, Mary Bliss. Real bad. I don't know what was going through Parker's head, but he seems to have gotten into some big-time debt. I suppose you know about a lot of the bills that are past due."

She nodded.

"There's just nothin' left," he said, shaking his head again and again in disbelief. "The mutual funds, Erin's college fund, all cashed in within the past year. He cashed in his life insurance, so we can't make a claim on that. And we can't borrow against the house either, because he pulled a fancy deal pulling all your equity out of the house and signing a gigantic balloon note that's coming due by the end of the summer."

"He refinanced the house? Without me knowing about it?" Mary Bliss felt indignant all over again.

Charlie ran his fingers through his graying hair. "He had a power of attorney from you."

"I never signed any power of attorney," Mary Bliss said.

"And I never notarized it," Charlie said. He was starting to look angry. "I hate to speak ill of the dead. Lord knows, Parker was one of my closest friends. But I think he's given you a raw deal. By my estimates, he liquidated your assets and pulled a cool million out before dying."

Mary Bliss blinked back the tears. She had promised herself she was done with crying. But a million dollars? What could he have done with all that money? And why? What had they ever done to make him hate them this much?

"What's going to happen?" Mary Bliss asked. She was opening and closing the drawers of Parker's desk. His pens and paper clips and yellow Post-its were neatly laid out in the top drawer. She slammed it hard. "Will we lose the house?"

Charlie handed her a manila envelope. "This is all that's left, as far as I can see. A life insurance policy from a company I never heard of in Alabama. It was with those papers you gave me. Do you know anything about it?"

Mary Bliss opened the envelope. "My aunt bought us this policy as a wedding gift. She was a spinster lady, and she sold insurance for a living. I'd completely forgotten about this. Do you think it's any good?"

"It's good," Charlie said. "I called the company this morning, before the memorial service. They're sending the paperwork overnight, and I'll get started on it right away."

Mary Bliss turned the pages of the policy. "It's not very much money."

"True," Charlie said. "But it might be enough to tide you over. And there's also the title insurance on the house."

"What good will it do?" Mary Bliss asked. She felt bad for deceiving Charlie, who was being so kind to her, but she'd already made an uneasy peace with her conscience, telling herself the ends justified the means.

"The title insurance pays off the mortgage in the case of death," Charlie said.

"I can keep the house." Mary Bliss smiled and sank back into Parker's desk chair.

"Looks like it to me," Charlie said. "As for the balloon note, I'm gonna have to take a good long look at that. And the liens, too. You're not in the clear, not by a long way. But I'm gonna have a talk with the loan officer who dealt with Parker, see if I can figure out how he pulled this thing off."

"I never signed a power of attorney, Charlie," Mary Bliss said, staring right at him. "And I had no idea he was refinancing the house."

"Damn," Charlie said. "Damn. What was he thinking? This just isn't like Parker. Isn't like him at all. Did he say anything recently, give you any hint about why he would liquidate everything?"

"Nothing," Mary Bliss said. For the first time, she was telling the complete truth. It felt good. "He never said a thing."

"A million bucks," Charlie said, shaking his head. "Wonder where it went? Why he needed the money?"

"I just don't know," Mary Bliss said. She folded her hands on top of the desk. "What about you, Charlie. He was your best friend. Did he say anything to you?"

"I've gone over it and over it," Charlie said. "I've wracked my brain. We played golf a couple weeks ago. He seemed fine. Shot in the eighties. Best he's ever played. We had a couple drinks in the clubhouse, and went on our way."

Mary Bliss found a paper clip stuck in the corner of the desk blotter. She pulled it apart and started straightening out the bends. "What about women? Do you think he was seeing somebody else? A girlfriend, maybe?"

Charlie had the grace to blush. "I swear to God, Mary Bliss. He never said anything about another woman. He was crazy about you. Everybody knows that."

"You were crazy about Katharine once," Mary Bliss said calmly. "But that seems to have changed."

Charlie stood up. "That's different. Katharine and I are not you and Parker."

"Could have fooled me," Mary Bliss said.

"She's a fine woman," Charlie said. "And I intend to do right by her."

"With money," Mary Bliss said.

"She and Chip will never want for anything. She knows that."

Charlie stood up and reached for his briefcase. "It's getting late."

She walked him to the front door and hugged him around the neck. "I'm sorry for making that crack about you and Katharine. It's none of my business. You're a good man, Charlie. And I know you'll do the right thing."

His shoulders slumped a little. "Sure I will."

After he'd gone, Mary Bliss roamed the house, looking for things to put right. By the time she'd worked off her energy cleaning and straightening, it was nearly midnight. And still no sign of Erin, who'd disappeared immediately after the church service.

Mary Bliss looked over at the Bowdens' house. The front porch light was still on. Maybe she was with Josh. The thought made her feel better. Josh seemed to be a steadying influence on her.

She went out on her own front porch and sat in the rocker, tucking her feet up under her. By shifting her weight slightly, she was able to set the chair in motion. The air had cooled a little, but it was undeniably June. Her gardenias were in bloom. Their white star-shape seemed to gleam in the darkness, and their perfume wrapped around her. Her mother had always planted a gardenia bush near the front door. The smell was better than any welcome mat, Nina always said.

Mary Bliss put her head back. Her eyes were dry and seemed to burn with a lack of sleep. She yawned widely. Maybe she would sleep tonight. The worst was over. She'd survived. Survived the trip to Mexico, the boat accident. Telling Erin her daddy was dead. She'd survived Eula and she'd survived the memorial service.

The worst is behind you, she whispered, rocking softly to and fro. *It's all behind you.*

38

After the thank-you notes had been written, the wilted flower arrangements discarded, and the neighbors' Tupperware scrubbed and returned, Mary Bliss allowed herself to go on autopilot.

She worked out a stock response to the polite inquiries. "We're doing fine, thanks." And, "Yes, he was a wonderful man. I guess we'll have to put our lives back together without him now."

She worked at least forty hours a week at Bargain Bonanza, where her skills as a product demonstration hostess grew so highly developed that she was able to force even the most disgusting convenience food on the most disagreeable customer. Her personal best record for amounts of samples dispersed were for Cha-Cha's Chileetos, a pseudo Tex-Mex appetizer that consisted of a spongy miniature corn tortilla wrapped around a mixture of ground beef, refried beans, hot sauce, and processed cheese.

On the Saturday morning she force-fed seventeen cases of Chileetos to unwary customers, the store manager presented her with a bouquet of blue-tinted carnations and a bottle of generic-label champagne. Her photograph was taken and she was named "Product Demonstration Hostess of the Month" for all of the metro Atlanta stores.

Work was good. It took her away to a place where the bills weren't piled up, and her grass didn't need mowing, and her daughter didn't glower at her on the rare occasions they were together. Although—she was shocked at the number of customers who bore a striking resemblance to Dinky Davis.

On Wednesdays, she took dinner to Eula, who continued to tell everyone within hearing distance that her son was not dead. And every day, she hated Parker McGowan a little bit more.

The last week in June, she screwed up her courage and called Charlie Weidman to inquire about the status of her insurance claim.

He'd hemmed and hawed and beat around the bush, until finally she'd laid it on the line for him.

"Charlie, I'm desperate. Erin's tuition was due weeks ago. The mortgage company is sending me registered letters threatening to take my house. What's taking that darned insurance company so long?"

"Maybe we should have lunch," Charlie said.

"I've *had* lunch," she told him. "Just tell me the truth, please."

"All right," he'd said. "Their people notified me last week, they've assigned a case manager to you."

"That'll speed things up, right?"

There was an uncomfortable pause. "Not necessarily. Case manager is just a nice word for an investigator. From the fraud unit."

"Fraud unit?" She choked on the words. Her hands felt icy.

"Now don't go gettin' yourself all upset," Charlie said. "I've spoken to several people at the company, and they assure me it's just a technicality. See, when you have a case without a body, that slows things up."

"It was a boat accident," Mary Bliss said. "I barely survived it myself. And I've got the headaches to prove it." She glanced at her watch. She was working a double shift today, and she wanted to talk to Erin before leaving for work, but her daughter seemed to come and go at all kinds of odd hours these days.

"I know," Charlie said soothingly. "But that, and the fact that the death occurred in Mexico, well, it's a red flag. Nothing against you personally, but that's how they handle these things."

"But they're not handling it," Mary Bliss said. "You know the state Parker left us in. I'm barely holding my head above water. Can't you do something?"

"There is something," Charlie admitted. "I'm not crazy about the idea, but maybe you'll think it's all right."

"What? I'll do anything. Tell me," she ordered him.

"A fella came to see me not long after the funeral," Charlie said. "Real nice guy. He's retired from law enforcement, got some kinda cushy consulting job. He was a friend of Parker's, and he says he's met you a couple times. He's offered to help expedite things."

"Who is it?" Mary Bliss asked. "What does he want?" She felt a sense of dread deepening in the pit of her stomach.

"I've got his card right here," Charlie said. "Hold on a minute."

She waited for what seemed like hours.

"Here we go," Charlie said. "Matthew Hayslip. That name ring a bell?"

"I've met him," Mary Bliss said. "He played doubles with Parker. He was at the funeral. But I barely know him. What's he doing calling you?"

"We met for the first time in the bar of the country club," Charlie said. "I was having a beer waiting for the rest of my foursome. He came over and introduced himself. He said he knew y'all, and asked how you were doing. Seemed real concerned about your welfare. I didn't see any harm in telling him about our problems with the insurance company."

"You talked to him about my finances?" Mary Bliss was incredulous. "Charlie, how could you? That's private. It's confidential. I can't believe you would discuss my business with a total stranger in some bar."

"Aw, Mary Bliss, hold on," Charlie said. "He's not a total stranger. I remembered seeing him at the funeral. Your mother-in-law was bending his ear something awful. And I checked him out. He's an okay guy. Used to be the number two or three guy with the GBI. He's a member at the club. Lives over there in the Oaks."

"I don't care where he lives," Mary Bliss said. "My business is none of his business."

"That's what I'm getting at," Charlie said. "The insurance company can take their own sweet time investigating this claim. In the meantime, you're about broke, right?"

"I don't need help from this man," Mary Bliss insisted. "Can't you call the state insurance commissioner, or my congressman or something? If that insurance policy is good, like you say it is, they should just go ahead and pay me. Is this how they treat all the widows they do business with?" She was really worked up now.

"Just hear me out," Charlie begged. "Matt thinks it might be helpful if we got affidavits from the police down in Mexico. The ones who investigated the accident."

"Why do we need affidavits? You've got the police reports, and the death certificate. You've got my hospital records. And I've got the rental receipt for the boat, and the hotel bill . . ."

"It's not for me," Charlie said hastily. "For the insurance company. These guys want every *I* dotted and every *T* crossed. Like I keep telling you, it's nothing personal. It's just the way they do things."

Mary Bliss looked up at the kitchen ceiling. It needed painting. Everything in the house suddenly seemed to need painting or fixing or pruning or mowing. It was all falling in on her.

"Charlie, listen to me. I can't afford to pay for Matt Hayslip to take a joyride down to Mexico. And I shouldn't have to. Tell him thanks, but no thanks. And then, could you please just keep on the insurance company's back? You know a lot of people, can't you call somebody and make them make the insurance company quit stalling and pay my claim?"

"I'll do what I can," Charlie said. "In the meantime, don't get upset if you get a call from that fraud investigator, er, case worker. If he calls you, contact me right away. I want to be there when and if he interviews you."

"Why?"

"Because I'm your lawyer," Charlie said. "You need somebody on your side, Mary Bliss. And I'm the guy."

"You're the guy," Mary Bliss said softly. "And I appreciate it, Charlie. I really do. I hope you're keeping a record of all the hours you're spending on this. Someday, when this is all over, and I get myself straightened out, I want to pay for every minute of your time."

She was lacing up her sneakers and getting ready to leave for work when she heard the rumble of a lawn mower outside. Mary Bliss went to the kitchen door and looked out.

A shirtless Randy Bowden was pushing his lawn mower through her knee-high fescue. Sweat gleamed on his pale chest, and a goofy straw hat shaded his face. It was his own lawn mower too. Hers had quit functioning weeks ago.

She stood in the doorway and watched him, and smiled.

When he reached the edge of the yard nearest her, she walked up and shouted for his attention.

He turned, smiled, and cut the mower's engine.

"Hey, neighbor," he said.

"Randy, you don't have to do this," Mary Bliss said, blushing. "I actually like cutting the grass."

"But your mower needs a new spark plug. I checked," he said. "And you've been working a lot of hours lately. I've got a vacation day today, so I thought I'd get a little workout." He slapped his washboard-flat belly. "Need the exercise."

"You need your head examined, working in this heat," she said. "Anyway, with this durned drought, it's mostly weeds. I was thinking of turning it into a meadow for the birds."

"Not in Fair Oaks," Randy said. "We got an ordinance against that type of thing, young lady."

"All right," she said, giving in. "I do thank you. I'm working late tonight, but maybe you'd let me pay you back by coming over for supper tomorrow night? You could bring the kids too."

"It's a deal," he said. "But I'm bringing the dessert. And the wine."

"Fine," she said. "I hope you guys like ham. 'Cause I've still got a freezerfull, left over from the funeral."

"Ham, I am," Randy said. He started the mower up and waved her away.

39

Mary Bliss lowered herself into the cool turquoise waters of the pool and squealed with delight.

"God, it's cold!"

"Feels good, doesn't it?" Katharine asked. Her yellow raft bobbed in the waters of the nearly empty pool.

"It feels illegal," Mary Bliss said, adjusting her sunglasses and glancing guiltily around the deck area of the Fair Oaks Country Club. "I'm not supposed to be here." She lowered her voice. "Our dues are in arrears."

"Don't sweat it, sweetie," Katharine said. "Charlie took care of it."

"Oh, no," Mary Bliss said, shaking her head.

"Well, the club does have a widow policy," Katharine explained. "If the head of the household dies, your dues are automatically supposed to be paid. But some bitch on the board of directors was holding up approval of your widow status, and it pissed Charlie off, so he just paid 'em for you."

Mary Bliss ducked her head under the water and let it drip down her face.

"Who?" she asked. "Who hates me that much?"

Katharine took a sip of her piña colada. "I'm not supposed to say. Hell, I'm not supposed to know, if it gets right down to it."

"Tell me anyway," Mary Bliss said. "It's somebody I know, right?"

"You know everybody in town," Katharine said.

"I'll bet it's Carol Kuhn," Mary Bliss said. "She's had it in for me ever since I beat her out for yard of the month two years ago. It's her, isn't it?"

"Can't say," Katharine said, taking another sip of her drink. "It's confidential."

"I know it's her," Mary Bliss said. "Right after they put the sign up in my yard, somebody snuck over in the middle of the night and cut the top off every single tulip I had in bloom. It has to be her. She gives me the evil eye all the time."

"It's just petty stuff," Katharine said. "I'd advise you to rise above it."

"Hey," Mary Bliss said, perching her arms on the end of Katharine's float. "How come Charlie's telling you all this stuff? You guys talking again?"

"You could say that," Katharine said, smirking.

"Friendly talk?"

"I can't say," Katharine said, flipping her eyeglasses up to avoid a tan line around them. "Lawyers are involved, you know."

"You slut!" Mary Bliss splashed water on her. "You're seeing him, aren't you? You're dating your ex-husband. You brazen hussy, you."

Katharine's eyelids flickered for a moment. "I wouldn't call it dating."

"What would you call it?" Mary Bliss asked. She helped herself to a sip from Katharine's foam-insulated cup.

"Dinner," Katharine said. "Just a harmless little dinner. Nothing for you to be concerned about."

"What about after dinner? Did he stay for breakfast too?"

Katharine reached out with one hand and shoved Mary Bliss's arms off her raft.

Her friend sank to the bottom, then swam back up. "I'll take that as a yes," she said.

Katharine paddled lazily away. "I can neither confirm nor deny."

"Does Charlie talk in his sleep?" Mary Bliss asked. "Did he say anything about my insurance claim? I'm starting to get nervous. They've assigned a fraud investigator to the case."

"At *dinner*," Katharine said, "he mentioned the fraud investigator. He seems to think it's all perfectly routine. Speaking of dinner," she added, "the Fourth of July is coming up. I think you should make your first official appearance at the club dance."

"No," Mary Bliss said. "Not a chance. I'm not coming to a dance here with Carol Kuhn staring daggers at me. Besides, it's too soon after the funeral."

"You can come with me," Katharine said. "I'll tell everybody it's therapy for both of us—the divorcée and the widow. We needed to get out, be around happy people to forget our own troubles."

"Why would you want to come with me?" Mary Bliss asked. "This is a setup, isn't it? You've got some evil little plot cooking, don't you?"

Katharine lifted her head off the raft. "I resent that remark deeply," she said. "It's not an evil plot at all. I just thought it would do you good to get out."

"And?"

One corner of Katharine's upper lip twitched slightly. "And, I happen to know that Charlie's girlfriend is going out of town. I think she has tickets to the Muppets on Ice, or something. He mentioned that it might be fun if we ran into each other at the dance."

"Not on your life!" Mary Bliss said. "I'm not going as your beard, Katharine. Anyway, who cares if you see him? He's not married to her. So he's a free man, right?"

Katharine slid off the raft and into the water. She tilted her head back in the water to wet her short blonde hair.

"You don't get it, do you?" she asked. "It's more fun this way. More dangerous. Come on, say you'll go to the dance with me. Please? For your best friend?"

"I haven't been to a dance in ages," Mary Bliss said. "I don't want to go and just sit there and have every- body feeling sorry for me."

"They won't be feeling sorry for you," Katharine said. "We'll have fun. We'll dress slutty and dance with other girls' husbands, and drink too much and dance too much and have a blast. Okay?"

"Absolutely not," Mary Bliss said.

"I'll take that as a yes," Katharine said. "Come on, let's go shopping. Everything's half off at Phipps. And we'll do dinner. My treat."

"Can't," Mary Bliss said. She swam over to the side of the pool and pulled herself out.

She was arranging herself on a chaise longue when Katharine dropped down on the chair next to hers.

"Why can't you? Money? I told you, it's my treat. Charlie gave me back my credit cards."

"So you are sleeping with him."

"I did *not* say that," Katharine said. "Why can't you come out and play tonight? It's been ages, M. B. You've been all sad and depressed. No fun at all."

Mary Bliss adjusted her bathing suit straps, which had fallen down. "It's hard to be fun when your life is caving in," she said. "Anyway, I've sort of got plans."

Katharine leaned over and lifted up Mary Bliss's sunglasses, sticking her face within an inch of Mary Bliss's.

"What kind of plans?"

Mary Bliss flipped her glasses back down again. "No big whoop. Randy came over yesterday and mowed the grass for me. So I invited him and the kids over for dinner tonight. Sorry to disappoint you, but it's just leftover ham and whatever else I can heat up that's been in the freezer since the funeral."

"He's stuck on you," Katharine said. "Don't encourage him."

"I'm not encouraging him," Mary Bliss said. "He mowed the grass in hundred-degree heat. The least I can do is feed the poor man. He's so thin, he reminds me of one of those refugees from Somalia or something."

"He's starving himself so you'll feel sorry for him and marry him and take care of all those snotty-nosed boys of his," Katharine said. "Feed him and send him packing, if you want my advice."

"I don't," Mary Bliss said.

She was setting the table when Erin came in the back door. "What's all this?" Erin asked, pointing at the place mats and the cloth napkins. "You throwing some kind of party or something?"

Mary Bliss bit her lip. "The Bowdens are having supper with us tonight. Nothing special, just ham and potato casserole and a tossed salad."

"Don't set a place for me," Erin said. "I'm not hungry."

"But Josh is coming too," Mary Bliss said. "I thought you'd be pleased."

"I had a late lunch," Erin said.

"We haven't eaten a meal together in weeks," Mary Bliss said, her voice pleading. "Please? Just one nice family meal?"

"They're not my family," Erin said, her voice cool.

"I'm your family," Mary Bliss said, putting her hand on her daughter's shoulder. "And you're all I've got. Please?"

Erin shrugged. "I guess I could eat a salad."

"Thank you," her mother said, beaming. "And I made that strawberry whip parfait you like, for dessert.

I thought it would be nice to have something cool and light."

"Josh is allergic to strawberries," Erin said. "But Jeremy and Jason will scarf 'em up. Those two eat anything that's not nailed down."

Mary Bliss glanced at the clock. "They'll be here in about half an hour. You'd better get a shower."

Erin gave her a quick kiss on the cheek. "Let me make the salad. I'll be right down as soon as I get cleaned up."

When she was gone, Mary Bliss fixed a pitcher of iced tea and found herself humming. She put candlesticks on the table, placing them on either side of a glass jelly jar full of zinnias she'd just picked from her yard. She had nicer flowers, and a nicer silver vase, but she didn't want to give Randy Bowden the idea that this was anything more than potluck.

Erin had switched on the radio before she'd left the kitchen, and now Mary Bliss found herself humming along to a song they were playing on 99X, Erin's favorite station. "It'll take some time," the song went. "But everything will be all right. All right."

40

Dinner went well. Erin ate two helpings of salad, and she snuck a smidge of the ham casserole when she thought nobody was looking. Mary Bliss felt pleased and relieved. She served up little ice cream dishes of the strawberry parfait and poured wine for herself and Randy, and milk for the kids.

Jeremy, the eight-year-old, was spooning up the strawberries as fast as he could, while Jason, his younger brother, seemed intent on studying his surroundings. "Miz McGowan, this is a nice house," he said, pausing to dab milk from his upper lip.

Mary Bliss winked at Erin. "Why, thank you, Jason. I'm glad you like it."

He looked around the kitchen, cozy in the candle-light. "Y'all got a lot of pots!"

"Yes," Mary Bliss agreed. "I guess I dirty up a lot of pots and pans when I cook. Erin's always complaining, because she has to do the dishes."

"Well, that's good," Jason said, smiling in satisfaction. "I guess my mama was wrong."

Randy coughed and Josh coughed, and Jeremy put down his spoon to listen.

"What was your mama wrong about, Jason?" Mary Bliss asked gently.

"Well," Jason said, sitting up straight, proud to be the center of attention. "My mama said Erin's daddy died, and now y'all don't have a pot to piss in. But y'all got bunches and bunches of pots!"

There was a sudden thump from under the table, and Jason howled, bending down to examine his wounded foot.

"Excuse me," Josh said, hopping up from the table. "Guess I better take Jason home, to see if he needs a Band-Aid or something." He yanked his little brother out of the chair and out the kitchen door before Mary Bliss could blink an eye.

Randy's face was beet-red. "I'm sorry, Mary Bliss," he said, his voice low. "You know how kids are . . ."

"I'll clear the dishes off, Mama," Erin said, jumping up too. "Jeremy will help, won't you, buddy? You guys go out on the porch. I'll bet that rain we had when I was driving home cooled things off."

Outside, sitting in the rocker, watching the water drip down from the gutters, Mary Bliss laughed until her sides hurt.

She laughed so hard, Randy Bowden couldn't get a word in edgewise for a full five minutes.

"Oh," she said finally, wiping the tears from her eyes. "That's the funniest thing I've heard in weeks."

"It's not funny. It's appalling," Randy said. She couldn't see his face in the dark, but from the tone of his voice she knew he was mortified.

"Nancye says that kind of thing in front of the boys all the time," Randy went on. "Her language is disgusting. And we won't even discuss her behavior, which has made her the talk of Fair Oaks."

Now it was Mary Bliss's turn to apologize.

"I'm sorry it's so embarrassing for you," she said. "I've had my own share of trouble lately, so I know it's no fun being the subject of petty gossip. But still, you have to admit it's pretty funny. Poor little Jason looking around to make sure Miz McGowan has a pot to piss in."

She covered her mouth with her hand because she felt another fit of giggles coming on.

"It doesn't bother you?" Randy asked.

"A little," she admitted. "But what really bothers me is the fact that Nancye's essentially right. It's no use trying to hide it. I'm broke."

"I'd heard that," Randy said. "Do you mind talking about it? I don't mean to pry, but you're my neighbor, and I care what happens to you, Mary Bliss."

"There's not much to tell," Mary Bliss said. "Parker must have been working on some big business deal. He liquidated all our assets, took out a balloon note on the house, even cashed in his life insurance. And then he died, before he could tell me what he was working on."

"God," Randy said. "I'd heard rumors around town, but I had no idea things were that bad."

"They're bad," Mary Bliss said. "But I think we'll squeak by. Charlie Weidman has been wonderful, helping with all the paperwork and things."

"But," Randy started.

"I think that's all I want to say about my finances for now," Mary Bliss said firmly. "I appreciate your concern, and I really don't mind your knowing, but let's just leave it at that. All right?"

"I could kill Nancye," Randy said darkly.

"I feel the same way about Parker," Mary Bliss said. "That sounds terrible, doesn't it?"

The front door opened. "Mama?" Erin said. "The dishes are all done. I'm going over to Jessica's for a while."

"This late?" Mary Bliss asked, dismayed. "It's nearly ten."

"I don't have to work tomorrow," Erin said. "And I forgot to tell you, I'm supposed to go down to Macon for an all-day soccer clinic. Coach is picking me up at eight, and we're all spending the night down there."

"Overnight?" Mary Bliss stood up. "I don't remember filling out any permission slips for an overnight soccer clinic."

"Mama!" Erin wailed. "It was way back in spring. Remember? Coach gave us our summer workout schedule, and this was on there. God. You're such a space cadet. I'll be back day after tomorrow."

"You never had to go on an overnight clinic before," Mary Bliss protested. She heard a faint inner alarm go off. Part of it was money. Soccer was a ridiculously expensive sport. Every time she turned around, she was doling out money for tournament fees or shin guards or cleats or summer camps.

"This is a specialty camp. For goalies. Don't worry. We're staying in a college dorm down there, and everybody's bringing food from home. Coach says it's the cheapest camp he could find on the Internet."

Mary Bliss was really getting tired of hearing what coach says. Since Isaac Brownlee had taken over coaching the girls' soccer team at Fair Oaks Academy two years earlier, Mary Bliss had endured a steady diet of the gospel according to coach.

Parker loved Isaac Brownlee, of course. He loved that Brownlee took the Fair Oaks team from perennial last-place losers to state runners-up in the space of two short years.

"Look," Erin said impatiently, "I gotta go. Don't worry about getting up with me in the morning. I've got my stuff all packed. See you Friday, okay?"

"Leave me a phone number," Mary Bliss called as the front door slammed behind her daughter.

"Soccer, huh?" Randy said, sounding wistful. "I wish Josh were interested in sports. All he wants to do is sit in his room all day and play computer games and mess with his guitar."

"At least he's home," Mary Bliss said. She watched as Erin's Honda sped down the driveway and out into the street.

"Hard to believe they're going to be seniors," Randy said. "After next year, they'll be leaving home."

"Don't remind me," Mary Bliss said. "The house already seems empty most of the time."

"I've got three guys living with me across the street," Randy said. "But at night, after they're all in bed, seems like I'm the last one in the world still up."

"I see your light some nights," Mary Bliss said.

"You should call me."

"I wouldn't want to wake the boys," Mary Bliss said. "Anyway. I'm probably not very good company nights like those."

"You're always good company," Randy said. "And that's not just fancy words. I mean it, Mary Bliss."

"Katharine says I'm no fun anymore," she replied. "She was bugging me today to go to the country club dance with her. Stag. It sounds hideous, doesn't it?"

"Totally hideous. But I still have to go," Randy said. His voice had a note of hope in it. "I'm outgoing president, you know. So there's no way I can get out of it. If you don't want to go stag with Katharine, maybe, you could, like, ride with me."

"God, no." She said it before thinking. "I don't mean it like that," she added quickly. "I'd love to go with you under other circumstances. You've been a great friend to me, since all this happened. But we both know how gossip spreads in this town. Parker's only been dead a month, and you and Nancye . . . is the divorce final yet?"

"Not yet," he said, sounding mournful. "She told the kids she's engaged, though. Josh came home the other day and told me he went to the Braves game with his new daddy. Nancye's lawyers are still hammering away at me. She gave up on custody of the kids, but she's convinced there's still some more money she can wring out of me."

"She's got a job, doesn't she?"

Randy laughed. "She makes more money than me, if you want the truth of the matter. And the 'new daddy' is supposedly a professor at Emory."

"You know," Mary Bliss said, sounding surprised. "I don't think I ever knew what Nancye does for a living. She's got a PhD, doesn't she?"

"You won't believe it if I tell you," Randy said.

"Try me."

"She's a sex therapist."

Mary Bliss couldn't control the giggles this time.

"Yeah, it always gets a big laugh at the bank too," Randy said. "It seemed a lot funnier before all this happened."

Mary Bliss stood up, stretched and yawned. "Guess I better go in and finish up the dishes Erin probably left me."

He followed her inside. Mary Bliss stopped at the door of the den. "Look," she whispered.

The television was on, playing Erin's *Aladdin* video. Jeremy was curled up on the floor, inches away from the television, fast asleep.

"How precious," Mary Bliss whispered.

Randy picked his son up, cradling him in his arms. "It's the only way he sleeps."

"What? On the floor?"

"In front of the television. I put him to bed, and he cries and fusses until I let him go in the den and turn on the television, and put in a Disney video. *Aladdin* is his favorite."

"Really? I always thought of that as a little girl's movie. It was Erin's favorite too."

"I don't think it's the movie he likes so much," Randy said. "It's Jasmine. Her voice. He told me one night, when he was nearly asleep, 'Jasmine sounds like Mommy.'"

Mary Bliss sighed. "They'll break your heart."

41

"**M**rs. McGowan? Mary Bliss McGowan?" She didn't recognize the man's voice on the other end of the phone. She tensed. Bill collectors called her Mrs. McGowan. The insurance people called her Mrs. McGowan. Anytime anybody called her Mrs. McGowan lately, she'd come to expect the worst.

"Who's speaking, please?" she asked.

"Oh, you don't know me," he said. His voice had a soft, southern accent. "I'm Gerran Thomas? Of Gerran's Gourmet Cuisine? I was at the memorial service for your husband, Parker, last week. My grandmother was old Mrs. McGowan's cook, and Nanny practically raised Parker. The Thomases and the McGowans go way back."

"That's nice," Mary Bliss said, wondering when Gerran Thomas would get to the point.

"Anyhoo," he said, "I digress. I didn't get a chance to speak to you at the luncheon afterwards, so this is a little awkward for me. But I just couldn't not call you. I've got a favor to ask. It's impossible, I know, but call me crazy. Here it is. Ever since I had that chicken salad at the luncheon, I've been absolutely wild to find out who made it. Honestly, it's the best chicken salad I have ever tasted. And I've tasted it all. I've had Swan Coach House. I've had Piedmont Driving Club, I've had Ansley Golf Club. And that chicken salad was the best!"

"I see," Mary Bliss said. But she didn't.

"If you ever tell anybody I said this, I'll deny it to the grave," Gerran Thomas said, "but that chicken salad was even better than my nanny's."

"I'll never breathe a word," Mary Bliss promised.

"I asked around," he continued. "And your neighbor Kimmy said you made it. Is that right?"

"Yes," she said. "The recipe was my best friend's mother's. She took the recipe to the grave with her. I don't know if I got it exactly right, but I think it was pretty close to the way she made it."

"My dear!" Thomas exclaimed. "That salad came directly from heaven."

Mary Bliss laughed. She'd been laughing off and on for two days now. She wondered if she'd passed some kind of milestone.

"I don't know if Mamie made it to heaven," she allowed. "She was married three times, dipped snuff, and cheated at bridge. But you could definitely say it came from beyond the grave. So I'll take that as a compliment."

"You should. Now here's the sticky part. I've got a huge wedding coming up in two weeks. Do you know Braelynn Connors? She's the anchor on channel eleven at five o'clock?"

"I've seen her," Mary Bliss said. "The blonde with the mole?"

"Adorable, isn't she? Anyway, it's seven hundred and fifty people, at the Botanical Garden. *Town and Country* magazine is flying a photographer down to shoot it. Everything has to be perfect. Perfect!"

"I'm sure," Mary Bliss said. She wondered if she was having an out-of-body experience. This man kept talking in exclamation marks, but he didn't seem to be saying anything specific.

"I've got a confession, Mrs. McGowan," Thomas said. "I was a naughty, naughty boy. Heh-heh. I stole a little dish out of your church kitchen, and I took home a sample of that chicken salad of yours. I went right over to the station, and I caught Braelynn in the makeup room, and she tasted it and she agrees. We have to have that chicken salad at the wedding!"

"Oh." Mary Bliss couldn't think of anything else to say.

"I wonder if you would be willing to part with that recipe?"

She looked around her kitchen. At the peeling linoleum, at the damp spot on the ceiling. At the stack of bills on the counter near the phone.

"I couldn't possibly," she said sweetly. "After all, it's not really my recipe to give. Katharine's mother, Mamie, was extremely secretive. And I feel it would be a betrayal if I passed it along to somebody else."

"Darn! That is disappointing," he said. "Braelynn has her heart set on it. We've already changed the menu around just to make room for your chicken salad. I was going to do cold poached chicken breasts with a margarita crème dressing, but now Braelynn won't hear of having that."

"Hmm," Mary Bliss said.

"I've tried my hand at re-creating it," Thomas said. "But it's a bit of a puzzle. That sweet-tangy thing is so tricky. Tarragon, right? And crème fraiche?"

"Not exactly," Mary Bliss said.

"I wonder . . .," he said, letting his words trail off. "Sour cream?"

"No."

"Buttermilk?"

"No."

"You're killing me!" he said, lapsing back into exclamation marks again.

"It's really a sacred trust," Mary Bliss said.

"All right," he snapped. "What Braelynn wants, Braelynn gets. And she wants that chicken salad of yours. So what would it take?"

"I really couldn't . . ."

"Cut the cute stuff, Mary Bliss," Thomas said. "Let's talk chicken salad."

"Well," she said sweetly. "Since you put it that way. The only way this can work is if I make the salad myself."

"No. Absolutely not. Nobody but Gerran does Gerran's Gourmet Cuisine."

"I understand. Good-bye, Mr. Thomas. And good luck with the wedding. I'm sure Braelynn will make a beautiful bride."

"Wait! All right," he said. "What do you want? What will it take?"

"I make the chicken salad myself," Mary Bliss said, her mind racing. "In my kitchen, in my home. I buy all the ingredients myself, fix it all myself. You pick it up the morning of the wedding. And as far as the world knows, it's Gerran's chicken salad."

"No. No. No. Impossible. Health department regulations stipulate that all food sold commercially must be prepared in kitchens inspected by the county health department."

Mary Bliss found that she had recently gained a healthy disregard for regulations of all kinds.

"Who's to know?" she asked. "I'm a very particular cook, Gerran. My kitchen is spotless. You can ask anybody."

"This is very irregular," he fussed. "I could lose my catering license."

"You could just go with the poached chicken breasts with the margarita crème dressing," Mary Bliss offered. "I think I saw a recipe for that in last month's *Family Circle*."

"*Family Circle!*" he shrieked. "That's impossible. I created that recipe myself. The lime peel is candied and gingered and . . . All right. You can make the chicken salad at your house. I'll pick it up that Saturday morning. In an unmarked van, of course."

"Fine," Mary Bliss said. "I think that will work. Just out of curiosity's sake, how much chicken salad are we talking about here, Gerran?"

"That's why I won't work with amateurs," he said bitterly. "How much? How much do you think? We have seven hundred and fifty confirmed. I've got to have a hundred pounds, minimum."

Mary Bliss swallowed hard. She'd nearly killed herself producing ten pounds of chicken salad for Parker's memorial service. This was ten times as much. Maybe she really was having an out of body experience.

"That's no problem," she said smoothly. "I charge twenty-five dollars a pound, of course."

"Of course," he snapped.

"And I'll bill you for the ingredients," Mary Bliss said.

"I'll require an itemized bill," Thomas said quickly.

"Impossible," Mary Bliss said, borrowing his favorite phrase. "The recipe is a secret, remember? If I tell you what went into it, what's to keep you from figuring the recipe?"

"Never mind," he said. "So you'll do it?"

"I'll do it."

42

The Fourth of July was on a Thursday. On Wednesday, Mary Bliss picked her first tomato of the summer. It was a huge red treasure, an old-fashioned variety called Mortgage Lifter, whose seeds she saved from year to year. She put the tomato in her gardening basket, along with half a dozen crookneck squash and a single cucumber, and carried it triumphantly into the house.

Her mama had always aimed to pick her first tomato of the summer by the Fourth. Mary Bliss wished Nina could have been there to see her gorgeous Mortgage Lifter.

She knew what she had to do with that tomato. She washed and peeled it, then carefully cut it into thick slices, which she then salted and peppered and placed on a pretty pink-flowered saucer.

The tomato would be a sacrificial offering to Eula—her own personal act of contrition for the awful lie she'd been living for the past few weeks.

Mary Bliss packed the rest of her offertory—homemade macaroni and cheese and a thick slice of chocolate layer cake, into the small blue cooler. She'd picked a few flowers, some daisies, cosmos, zinnias, and bee balm, and these she wrapped with a damp paper towel before inserting them into a jelly jar and placing them in the cooler.

She dawdled in the kitchen, arranging more flowers in the yellow McCoy vase she kept on the windowsill, putting the extra squash in the crisper drawer of the refrigerator. What she was really doing was delaying her departure for the nursing home.

She dreaded seeing Eula, dreaded hearing her rail against "colored nurses" and "Jew doctors" who were conspiring against her. Most of all, she dreaded facing her mother-in-law, who at every weekly visit reminded Mary Bliss that Parker was alive, somewhere, on an island, and would soon return to free her from this nursing home hell, and to have Mary Bliss thrown in the slammer.

"Don't pay her no attention," Lillian King, Eula's nursing supervisor, advised her the week before. "She's just trying to get you upset. That's part of the disease, bless her heart. She wants extra attention. She tells all kinds of stories. Last week? Said she's gonna replace Ethel Merman on Broadway. She was beltin' out 'No Business Like Show Business' in chapel, while everybody else was singing 'Walk with Me, Jesus.' And in craft shop? You know what she did? Everybody else made themselves a nice little ashtray. Miss Eula? She took that clay, and she made . . ." Lillian King turned her head, embarrassed. "I hate to say what she made, Miz McGowan."

"You can tell me," Mary Bliss prompted.

Lillian King put her hands up to Mary Bliss's ear and whispered. "She made a penis."

"Really?" Mary Bliss was astonished.

"Yeah," Lillian King said. "And you know what? Her memory ain't all that bad."

When she could stall no longer, Mary Bliss went out to load up the car. But a dark sedan was pulling up into the driveway, blocking her in.

It was Matt Hayslip.

He jumped out of the car, leaving the motor running, and jogged over to her.

She rolled the window down. "Hello," she said. No trace of warmth in her voice, she was sure of it.

"Hey there," he said. "How are you getting along?" As though she had all the time in the world.

"Actually, I was just leaving," she said pointedly. "Today's the day I take lunch to my mother-in-law. At the nursing home. It's sort of the high point of the week for her. So I hate to keep her waiting."

"Miss Eula," he said. "We talked at Parker's funeral. Hell of an old lady. Great spirit. Say—why don't you let me drive you over there? I'll bet she'd love to have another visitor."

Mary Bliss was speechless.

"Oh no," she said. "I couldn't ask you to do that. Meemaw's health isn't all that good." She tapped her forehead. "Her memory. Most of the time, it's all she can do to remember who I am. Being around strangers gets her confused and upset."

"Sure," Hayslip said. "I understand. She probably likes her little routine. In that case, I'll just stay out in the lobby and wait on you. Afterwards, we could go out for lunch. That's really why I dropped by. To see if I could take you to lunch."

"Why?" Mary Bliss asked.

"Just to talk," Hayslip said. He opened her car door and flashed her a smile. The creases in the corners of his eyes weren't crow's-feet, you wouldn't call them that on a man. They were crinkles. And they looked friendly. But looks, Mary Bliss knew from experience, could be deceiving. And he didn't look as scary without that beard of his. He had a strong chin. He was used to getting his way, she thought. Well, too damn bad. It was *her* turn to get *her* way.

Now he was tugging at her hand. His grip was firm, his voice teasing. "Come on. When was the last time you had lunch out? You can't just stay holed up in your house forever, you know."

"I'm not holed up," she protested. "I go out. I work, I shop. I work in the garden. I see friends."

"I meant for fun," Hayslip said. "When was the last time you went out for fun?"

"You sound like Katharine," Mary Bliss said. But she found herself getting out of her car, letting herself be led over to his, even buckling herself into that soft black leather upholstery. What was she doing?

"Who's Katharine?" he asked, after he'd stashed her picnic basket in the backseat and was backing down her driveway.

Was she being abducted? But she'd gone willingly. What was wrong with her? Matthew Hayslip was the enemy. A sexy enemy, but the enemy nevertheless. And she was consorting with him. She was losing her grip. Next thing you knew, she'd be belting out show tunes and making obscene crafts from modeling clay.

"Katharine is my best friend," Mary Bliss said. "She came down to Mexico. You know, after the accident. She's been pestering me too, trying to get me to go out."

"Like where?" Hayslip asked. He'd turned the car in the direction of the nursing home without being told which one it was. "Where does she want you to go? The movies, something like that?"

"It's a dance, actually," Mary Bliss said. "The dance at the country club. Tomorrow night."

"Sure," Hayslip said. "That's a great idea. I'm going. You should go too. It's good to get out, see people. Change of scenery."

"I don't think so," Mary Bliss said, shaking her head. "You don't know Fair Oaks. People talk."

"I live here, but I guess I don't know it as well as you," Hayslip said. "But people talk anyway. A country club dance, that seems pretty harmless to me. What's the worst people could say?"

"You don't want to know," Mary Bliss said. "Parker's only been dead a month. It's too soon. Anyway, I just don't feel like going. So I'm staying home. Katharine can just go by herself."

"That's Katharine Weidman?" Hayslip asked.

"You know her?" Mary Bliss asked.

"I know Charlie," he said. "Met him in the grill the other day, waiting on his foursome. Seems like a good guy."

"He mentioned meeting you," Mary Bliss said carefully. "He said you offered to help in getting the insurance company to pay my claim."

"Like you said, Fair Oaks is a small town. Somebody mentioned you were having kind of a financial struggle. I just thought, Parker would hate that, you and your daughter having to go without."

Parker had planned just that, for over a year, Mary Bliss thought, glancing discreetly over at him. He hadn't given a damn about her and Erin. About how they would get along without any money. Now this stranger was taking it upon himself to help her out. What was he up to?

"We're not really in dire straits," Mary Bliss said. "Not yet, anyway. I've taken on a job this summer, and when school starts up I'll have my teacher's salary again."

"What's a teacher make in this state, anyway?" Hayslip asked. "Thirty, forty thousand? A garbageman makes more than that."

"Thirty-nine, five, with a graduate degree, which I have," Mary Bliss said. God! She'd just told this man how much money she made. The next thing you knew, she'd be telling him her bra size. What was it about him?

"Charlie mentioned that Parker refinanced the house. Some kind of squirrelly deal, and the whole note comes due next month," Hayslip said. "Forgive me for prying, Mary Bliss, but that seems like pretty dire straits to me. You'd lose the house, wouldn't you, if the whole note came due all at once?"

"It wasn't exactly a squirrelly deal," Mary Bliss said primly. "Is that what Charlie told you? I wish he hadn't been discussing my private affairs in the bar up at the club."

"Don't get mad at Charlie now," Hayslip said. He was pulling into the entrance to the nursing home. "He wasn't the one who told me you were in trouble. Anyway, he knows I do some investigative work, on a consulting basis. We were just chatting, confidentially. Nobody else was around, and I never said a word to anybody else. It wasn't like we were gossiping about you."

He flashed her an apologetic smile. She felt a slight vibration, a hum, and a wave of heat in her pelvic area. *Danger!* the hum said. *Testosterone overload.*

"I have Erin to think about," Mary Bliss said, ignoring her hormonal thermostat. "How would you like it if everybody in town was talking about your parents like that? The other night, a little child told me his mother told him Erin's daddy took all our money and now we don't have a pot to piss in. Erin was sitting right there! We laughed it off, but how do you think she felt?"

Hayslip frowned. He pulled into a parking space near the door to the nursing home and put the car in park.

"You're a hard person to help, you know that?" he said after he'd turned off the ignition. "What do I have to do to convince you I just want to assist you in getting your claim paid?"

"Tell the truth." There. She'd said it. "Why should you worry about us? You don't even know me. You've never even met my daughter. What's in it for you?"

"It's a puzzle," Hayslip said. He got out, went around the car, and opened her door. "Why did Parker liquidate all your assets? What was he thinking about? And where did all that money go? You two were married, they were joint assets, right? So it's not just his money, it's yours. From what Charlie told me, there's about a million bucks missing. Where did it go? That's a puzzle that interests me. And I'll admit, you interest me too."

That smile again. He was doing it on purpose. It was really quite unfair. *Hummm*, said her pelvis. *Warning! Warning!* She felt her face flush.

"Me?" She raised an eyebrow.

"Is that a problem?"

"I'm not all that interesting," she said, reaching into the car for her picnic basket. "Middle-aged school-teacher. Soccer mom."

Available! her pelvis screamed. This had to stop. She was going to have to look into some kind of hormone reversal therapy. She couldn't remember the last time she'd felt this way in the middle of the day.

"Don't forget the criminal part," he said.

"Criminal?" She nearly dropped Eula's lunch.

"Sure. I caught you watering your lawn illegally. Remember? The first time we met? You were out in your backyard, in that nightgown of yours."

"I was sopping wet, barefoot, my hair hadn't even been combed."

"You were the sexiest thing I've seen in a long, long time," Hayslip said with a wink. He took the basket from her and led the way into the nursing home lobby. "Now that's what I call interesting."

Sexy. Dear Lord. Had Parker ever called her sexy? Had her pelvis ever *hummed* at the sound of his voice? She thought not. She slowed down just long enough to put on a little lipstick. For Meemaw, she told herself.

Eula had parked her wheelchair in the lobby, as close to the front door as she could get.

"Who's this?" she demanded, cradling the picnic basket in her lap, nodding her head toward Hayslip.

"Hello again," Matt said, bending down and taking Eula's hand in his. "I'm Matt. Remember? We met at your son's memorial service."

Eula regarded him carefully, looking him up and down. "The new boyfriend," she said. "You got some nerve sniffing around my daughter-in-law when her first husband ain't even really dead."

"Meemaw!" Mary Bliss exclaimed. Something inside her shriveled up. Probably just her libido.

Hayslip's eyes crinkled deeply. "I'm actually a family friend," he said. "Used to play tennis with Parker."

"And now you're playing footsie with his wife," Eula sniped.

Mary Bliss grabbed the handles of Eula's wheelchair and started down the hall with it. "He is not my boyfriend," she exclaimed, loud enough for everyone, especially the nurses at the reception desk, and especially Hayslip, to hear.

"Not yet," he said. But Mary Bliss was long gone.

43

Mary Bliss looked up when the waitress approached. "White wine," she said quickly. Hayslip laughed and ordered a beer.

"You probably think I'm an alcoholic," she said, putting the menu aside. "Maybe I am. All I know is, after an hour with Meemaw, I need a drink."

"Has she always been like that?" Hayslip asked. He took a roll from the bread basket and offered it to her. She waved it away.

"Like what? Foulmouthed? Mean? Or just senile?"

"The nice word for it is *feisty*," Hayslip said.

"I'm afraid I'm not in a very nice mood," Mary Bliss said. "It's awful, I know, but I've gotten so I just dread spending time with her."

"Then why go?"

"She's my mother-in-law," Mary Bliss said. "Erin's grandmother. With Parker gone, we're her only family. Fair Oaks is a very nice nursing home—it should be, for the amount of money we pay them, but you know how nursing homes are. If a patient doesn't have family looking out for them, they let things slide. The sheets don't get changed, they don't get bathed properly, and they don't eat right. Those nurses know I'll be there every Wednesday, and I drop in other times too, so usually, Eula is very well cared for."

"She's pretty nasty to you," Hayslip said. "Is that part of her senility, or whatever they call it?"

The waitress was back with her chardonnay. Mary Bliss took her glass and took a sip.

"I was never what you would call Meemaw's first choice to become Mrs. Parker McGowan," Mary Bliss said. "In her eyes, marrying me was definitely a step down for her only son."

Hayslip poured his beer into a glass. "What was her objection?"

"The usual," Mary Bliss said. "We were too young. I was from a broken home. And from Alabama! God, that was really unforgivable."

"Does she really believe Parker's alive?" Hayslip asked.

Mary Bliss set her wine glass carefully down on the table. "That's what she says. She insists he's alive, on an island somewhere. Cavorting with native women."

"Sort of like Gauguin?"

"I doubt my mother-in-law knows who Gauguin is," Mary Bliss said. "The doctors say it's part of her dementia. She also insists she's going to appear in a revival of *Annie Get Your Gun* on Broadway. And in the meantime, she can really be very unpleasant."

"And yet you still keep visiting her, cooking for her, seeing after her."

Their food arrived. The waitress set a chef's salad down in front of Mary Bliss and a hot roast beef sandwich in front of Matt Hayslip. He attacked his food immediately. Mary Bliss watched, her appetite suddenly vanished.

"I feel guilty," she said quietly. "She's old, and she's unhappy. She hasn't made any new friends at the nursing home, and her old friends have either died or stopped visiting her. I guess I go because I'm afraid someday I'll be like her. Old and alone."

"You'd never be like her," Hayslip said. "Look at all those people who came to Parker's memorial service. They didn't come for Parker, not really. They came for you."

She speared a piece of lettuce with her fork and nibbled at it.

"You're a good person, Mary Bliss," Hayslip said. "People want to help you. They want to be around you. Is that so hard for you to believe?"

"You don't know me very well," Mary Bliss said, uncomfortable under his steady gaze. She thought of excusing herself to go to the ladies' room, but then what? Where could she hide from this man who would not look away from her?

"I know you better than you think," Matt said. "I'm a cop, remember?"

"I thought you were retired," Mary Bliss said, alarmed again.

"You leave the job, but it doesn't leave you," Hayslip said. "I guess that's why I'm so intrigued with your financial problems. Admit it, aren't you the least bit curious about where all that money went?"

Her temper flared. "Curious? I don't have time to be curious. I've got a daughter to raise, and a house to run, and no money to do it with. My problems may be some kind of elaborate jigsaw puzzle to you, but it's no game to me, Matt. Parker's gone. That much I know. The money's gone too. I don't need somebody solving unsolvable puzzles for me. I need for the insurance people to pay my claim, and let me get on with my life."

She set her fork down on the table and it clanged against the glass top.

He looked up, obviously surprised by her outburst.

"Hey," he said, "it's not a game. I didn't mean it like that. I was just thinking, maybe I could look into things for you. I read the police report from the Mexican authorities. I even checked the weather and the tide charts for that day. And I was wondering about that boat the hotel rented you. How seaworthy was it? It was a relatively calm day that day, according to the reports I read. Seems to me, a wave shouldn't have smashed it up that way. Maybe the hotel is at fault, maybe they're legally liable for Parker's death and your head injury."

"It's nobody's fault," Mary Bliss said, her face stony. "It happened. He's dead. The money's gone. And I don't have the time or the resources to hire lawyers and investigators to run around to Mexico and chase after a lost cause."

Matt reached across the table to grasp her hand, but it was too late. She was standing up, reaching for the pocketbook hanging on the back of her chair.

"I'm sorry," Mary Bliss said. "I'm not hungry. I guess you'd better take me home."

44

Katharine appeared to be dressed in a pale-green bedsheet. Crib sheet, more like it, Mary Bliss thought, appraising the scant amount of material draped revealingly around her best friend. She was also wearing a star-shaped halo-type headband, glittery green eyeshadow, and four-inch spike-heeled green evening sandals, and she carried a green torch.

"I thought this was a Fourth of July party," Mary Bliss said, "not Halloween."

"I'm Lady Liberty," Katharine said, twirling around so that Mary Bliss could get the whole effect.

"You look more like Lady Marmalade," Mary Bliss said. Still, she got out her Polaroid camera and took a snapshot of Katharine standing in front of the flag by her front door.

"Come on and go with me to the dance," Katharine said, her voice wheedling. "It'll be so much fun. Wait 'til you see Charlie. I got him the most adorable Uncle Sam outfit."

"If it's anything like your version of Lady Liberty, I'm just as happy to stay home," Mary Bliss said. "I love Charlie to death, but I don't want to see your ex in stars-and-stripes boxers."

"They're not really boxers," Katharine explained. "You know Charlie. Such an old stick-in-the-mud. I'd say they're more like gym shorts. But with sequins. I got you something too. It's out in the car."

"Never mind," Mary Bliss said hastily. "I'm staying home. And that's final."

Katharine plopped herself down on the porch swing. "Then I'm staying too. I can't have any fun at the country club dance if I know you're stuck home, alone. So it'll be all your fault if I'm miserable company."

"You're not staying here with me," Mary Bliss said. "You're going to the dance. Remember? You're having a clandestine fling with Charlie. Anyway, I'm perfectly happy to stay home tonight. Erin's gone to a concert at Piedmont Park with Josh, so I'll have the house all to myself. I've got watermelon and fried chicken, and I've rented three movies. I'm having my own Meg Ryan film festival. And you are cordially *not* invited."

"You're pathetic," Katharine said.

Mary Bliss stuck out her tongue. "Sticks and stones. Now get off my porch before I call the cops on you."

"Speaking of cops," Katharine said, sitting back down. "I happened to be driving by yesterday, and I saw his car here. What's going on with you two?"

"You never happen to be driving by anywhere," Mary Bliss said. "You were spying on me."

"So? You're a helpless widow. I'm looking out for you."

"There seem to be lots of people who share your opinion that I'm helpless," Mary Bliss said. "Randy Bowden. You. Matt Hayslip. Everybody wants to look after poor old Mary Bliss."

"There's a difference," Katharine said. "I'm just nosy as hell. Randy and Matt want to get in your pants."

"Not true," Mary Bliss said. "Randy feels sorry for me. And Matt Hayslip claims he wants to help me find the money Parker took. But I don't know."

"What?"

"I keep asking myself, why is he so eager to help me?"

"Because you're adorable, in a pathetic kind of way. Sort of like a wet puppy."

"He scares me," Mary Bliss said. "He already told me he's still a cop at heart. What if he starts digging around and finds out the truth? What if he finds Parker? Or, God forbid, Dinky Davis?"

"Dinky is dead," Katharine said with a note of finality. "And how is he going to find Parker? He's disappeared, and he doesn't want to be found. Parker was always a very determined sort of person."

"Not as determined as Matt Hayslip," Mary Bliss said.

"Not as sexy either," Katharine pointed out. "Who does he remind you of more? A taller Richard Gere? Or a younger Cary Grant?"

"He reminds me of somebody who could get me thrown in jail for the rest of my natural days," Mary Bliss told her.

At eight o'clock, just as she was getting ready to watch *When Harry Met Sally*, the doorbell rang. Mary Bliss ran to the front door. "Go away, Kate," she hollered. "I mean it. Get the hell off my porch."

"Mary Bliss? It's Randy. Do I have to get the hell off your porch too?"

She'd already opened the door by the time she remembered what she was wearing. Which was nothing more than one of Parker's old washed-out Brooks Brothers button-down dress shirts. And a pair of panties.

"Hey!" Randy said, blinking. "I guess you're not going to the dance, huh?"

She looked down at herself. The top three buttons of the shirt were long gone. She crossed her arms over her chest and closed the door slightly so that she could attempt to hide behind it. "Afraid not. I made other plans."

He, on the other hand, looked positively festive. Randy wore a pair of white canvas slacks, a navy blazer, and a necktie emblazoned with Old Glory.

"Oh. I was hoping maybe you'd change your mind. You wouldn't have to go with me. That way people wouldn't talk. I thought we could sort of meet there."

"That's sweet," Mary Bliss said. "I like your tie."

"I like your shirt," he said, blushing.

She moved behind the door a little more. "It was Parker's," she said lamely, instantly hating herself for bringing up his name.

"I'm staying home tonight," she said then. "I've got food and movies, and I'm really looking forward to spending time by myself."

"You're sure?" he asked.

"Positive," Mary Bliss assured him. "Some other lucky lady will get to dance with you tonight."

"Angela Patterson, probably," he said darkly. "She always gets lit up at these functions and hits on single men."

"Hey," Mary Bliss said. "She hit on me at the harvest dance last October. I thought it was my perfume."

"Okay," Randy said reluctantly. "Have fun."

She'd just gotten to the part of the movie where Harry and Sally are reunited at the New Year's Eve party when the doorbell rang. Again.

Mary Bliss stayed on the sofa. She turned down the volume on the movie. Her car was in the garage. Maybe, if she stayed very still, whoever was at the door would give up and go away.

Five minutes later, she heard tapping at the kitchen door.

"Dammit," she said crossly. "Can't a person hibernate for one friggin' night?" She padded into the kitchen. She could see the silhouette of a man through the glass in the door.

"Go away, whoever you are," she called. "I'm not going out. I've got a new bowl of popcorn and two more Meg Ryan movies to watch. And I'm not budging."

"I'll bet you're watching *Sleepless in Seattle*," a man's voice called back. "The ultimate chick movie."

It was Matt Hayslip.

"I am not," she said, rummaging around in the hall closet for something to put on over her panties.

Erin's gym bag was on the top shelf. She grabbed it and rummaged around until she found a pair of bright-green Umbro soccer shorts to slip on.

She opened the back door.

Hayslip wore a dark suit and a cartoonish cardboard Uncle Sam hat. *Humm.* There went that vibration thing again. And heat too. Definite heat. God, he looked wonderful. What was the word? Debonair? He stood in the doorway with his arms folded. "It's *You've Got Mail,* isn't it?" he asked, stepping inside, uninvited. "Why do you women love those sappy movies?"

"Why do men wear ridiculous hats to Fourth of July parties?" Mary Bliss countered. "Why do they love gun battles and car chases?"

He removed the hat and set it on her kitchen counter, smoothing his hair back down. "The hat was a party favor. Some drunk woman over at the country club made me put it on. And then she kissed me on the mouth and slipped me some tongue."

"Red hair of a hue not found in nature? Big dangly earrings?"

Hayslip nodded. "With breasts to match."

"That was Angela Patterson," Mary Bliss said. "I'm surprised you left so early. She gets much friendlier as the night wears on."

"That's what I was afraid of," Hayslip said. "That's why I left and came over here."

"I'm very busy," Mary Bliss said. She opened the refrigerator and got out the bottle of chardonnay. She poured herself a glass and pointedly did not offer one to her visitor. She grabbed her bowl of popcorn and walked into the den.

Hayslip came right behind her. She sat on the sofa. He walked over to the coffee table and picked up the cases of the movies she'd rented, reading the titles on the side.

"Uh-huh," he said with a self-satisfied smirk.

"All right, Dick Tracy," Mary Bliss said. "You got me cold. I'm holed up here watching sappy chick movies. You even guessed which movies. Congratulations. You're the greatest detective since J. Edgar Hoover."

"Aren't you going to invite me to stay and watch movies with you?" He was now perched on the edge of the coffee table.

She put the movie on stop. The credits were rolling anyway. Damn. She loved the end of that movie. But that was the great thing about a video. You could rewind and watch a happy ending as many times as you wanted. Which she intended to do. After she got rid of Matt Hayslip.

"No," she said. "This is a private party."

He cocked his head. "Why do you dislike me? Have I done something to offend you?"

"I don't dislike you," Mary Bliss said. "I just don't want any company tonight. And I don't want anybody meddling in my private affairs and going around asking a lot of questions about my late husband. I'm sure you mean well, and I'm flattered over what you said about me the other day, but it isn't really very proper, you know, talking to me like that."

"What? Just because I said you were sexy with that wet nightgown? Is that improper?" He raised one eyebrow. "You really have led a sheltered life."

She stood up suddenly, spilling popcorn onto the floor.

"Now what?" he asked, laughing. "Are you kicking me out?"

"Yes," she said, standing up. "And don't forget your hat."

She followed him to the back door, and before she knew what was happening, he pulled her close. He set the hat gently on the top of her head, tilted her chin, and kissed her. His free hand found the hollow in her back, pressing him to her.

Her body vibrated like a tuning fork struck with a pickax.

"Hey," she said, pushing him away, a little breathless. "What do you think you're doing?"

He grinned. "You don't know? Maybe I should give it another shot."

"Go," she said, shoving him out the door. She locked it behind him and took a deep breath. She stood with her back to the door, her eyes closed, reliving that kiss. She could still feel the lingering heat of his lips and his hands. And then there was that mysterious hum. This was a strange, unexpected development. She had loved her husband her whole adult life, really, yet she could not remember a time when Parker's touch had affected her this way.

When he'd gone, she did rewind Harry and Sally, but she found she didn't have the stomach to watch the ending again. He'd ruined it for her. Damn him, calling her favorite movie sappy.

She turned off the television and went into the kitchen to lock up. Glancing out the kitchen window, she saw the sky to the east lighting up. The Fourth of July dance always ended with the Fair Oaks fireworks show.

Other years, she and Parker had gone to the dance, usually with Charlie and Katharine. Right at midnight, everybody kicked off their shoes and went outside to the pool area, to lie on the pool chairs and watch the show. She and Parker would lie side by side, holding hands, oohing and aahing along with the rest of the giddy, drunken partyers. When, she wondered, had they stopped holding hands?

She was rinsing out her wine glass when the shrill ring of the phone startled her so badly that she dropped the glass in the sink, shattering it.

Mary Bliss grabbed for the phone. She'd always hated late-night phone calls. "Hello," she said haltingly.

"Mary Bliss," Katharine cried. "It's Charlie. I think he's had a heart attack. Come quick. I think he's dying."

"Where?" Mary Bliss said. "Where are you?"

"My house," Katharine said. "Hurry, dammit. He's not breathing right."

"Did you call nine-one-one?" Mary Bliss asked. "Are they on their way?"

"I can't," Katharine wailed. "Charlie's naked."

"Call nine-one-one," Mary Bliss shouted. "If he's had a heart attack it's crucial you get him to the hospital. He could die if he doesn't get medical help right now!"

"He'll die right now if he finds out I let strangers cart him off to the hospital naked," Katharine said. "Couldn't you just come over here and help me get him dressed?"

"I'm on my way," Mary Bliss said. "Now call nine-one-one right this minute."

45

Charlie was sprawled across Katharine's king-sized bed, clutching his left arm and gasping for breath, his face paler than the sheets that barely covered his nude torso. His body was covered with a thin sheen of perspiration.

"How long has he been like this?" Mary Bliss demanded of Katharine, who was flitting around the room in a short black see-through negligee, trying to find Charlie's clothes.

"Maybe ten minutes. Just since right before I called you," Katharine said, picking up a pair of sequin-spangled shorts. "I called nine-one-one like you said. Now hurry up and help me get him into these."

Charlie groaned loudly. Mary Bliss glanced over at him. He'd rolled over onto his side and was trying to sit up.

She ran to the bedside. "Lie still, Charlie," she commanded. "The ambulance is on the way."

"No," Charlie gasped, pointing wildly at the flag shorts. "Not those."

"Find him something else, Katharine," Mary Bliss ordered.

"There *isn't* anything else," Katharine snapped. "He moved out three months ago, remember? I threw out or burned everything he didn't take with him."

She took a step closer to the bed and Charlie groaned again, shaking his head like a rabid dog. "*Noooo.*"

"Just put him in anything," Mary Bliss said. She could hear sirens approaching the house. "How about one of your bathrobes?"

"Nooo," Charlie groaned.

"Chip's clothes! Get a pair of Chip's pants from his bedroom." Mary Bliss sat on the side of the bed and stroked Charlie's forehead. "Stay quiet now, Charlie," she said soothingly. "The EMTs are on their way. Piedmont Hospital's not ten minutes from here. They'll have you fixed up right away."

Katharine ran back into the bedroom, holding a pair of khaki golf shorts. "Here," she said triumphantly.

"Get him dressed," Mary Bliss ordered. "I'll go downstairs and let the EMTs in."

"Right," Katharine said. She flung the sheet off Charlie and started sliding the pants up his bare legs.

Mary Bliss looked away, but not before she caught sight of her best friend's own naked behind bent over her ex-husband.

"And Katharine?" she said gently.

"What now?" Katharine answered.

"You might want to put some clothes on yourself before those guys come charging in here. Unless you want to give them a heart attack too."

The siren's wail was right outside now. Mary Bliss ran down the stairs and into the marble-floored entry hall. She flipped on the outside light and opened the front door just as the ambulance was pulling into the circular drive of the Weidmans' two-story brick Georgian.

"In here," she called as the technicians ran up the walkway. "Hurry. I think he's had a heart attack. He's conscious, but he's struggling to breathe, and I don't think his color looks too good."

The rest of the evening was a blur. She and Katharine stood in the doorway of the bedroom, watching as one EMT shoved what Mary Bliss assumed was a nitroglycerin tablet under Charlie's tongue, while another hooked him to a portable heart monitor, and still another clamped an oxygen mask over his face.

Katharine rode to Piedmont in the ambulance with Charlie, while Mary Bliss raced behind, driving Katharine's Mercedes.

At the hospital, she found Katharine hovering near the admissions desk in the emergency room, harassing the young clerk behind the desk.

"They brought him in fifteen minutes ago," Katharine fumed. "I want to know what's happening."

The clerk, a kid in his early twenties, wearing blue hospital scrubs, was on the phone. "In a minute, ma'am," he said, rolling his eyes at Katharine but otherwise ignoring her.

The two women finally retreated to a pair of chairs nearest the desk, taking turns approaching the clerk for information every ten minutes. After they'd been waiting an hour, the clerk looked up from the phone.

"Mrs. Weidman?" he called. Katharine jumped up.

"What's happening?" she asked. "Can I see my husband now?"

"Not yet," the clerk said, glancing down at some notes on a chart. "They've got him stabilized, and they're assessing the damage. He did apparently have a massive heart attack. They'll move him over to the CICU in about half an hour, and you can probably see him then."

"What's the CICU?" Katharine asked.

"Cardiac intensive care unit," the clerk said. "You might want to go get some coffee or something, maybe call the rest of your family, and then head upstairs.

His doctor should be ready to talk to you when you get back."

It was two in the morning. The hospital cafeteria was closed, but they managed to scrounge enough change from the bottom of Mary Bliss's purse to pay for two cups of weak, lukewarm coffee from the basement vending machines.

"I'm scared," Katharine whispered, as they trudged back down the corridor to the bank of elevators. "Charlie looked so awful. What if he dies?"

"He's not gonna die," Mary Bliss said, slipping an arm around Katharine's shoulder. "This is one of the best heart hospitals in the southeast. And Charlie's young. It's not his time yet."

"He's fifty-one," Katharine said. She rubbed her red-rimmed eyes, smearing her mascara and eye shadow. "Bet you didn't know that. He turned fifty-one in June. I was so pissed at him for leaving me, I didn't even send him a birthday card. He had dinner with Chip that night, but I wouldn't even lend Chip money to buy his daddy a present. God, I've been such a bitch."

"You were hurt," Mary Bliss said. "Brokenhearted."

Katharine nodded. "The bastard broke my heart. So what do I do? I give him a heart attack. Nearly killed him."

"Hush!" Mary Bliss said, shocked. "You did not give Charlie a heart attack. He's fifty-one, a little overweight. Didn't you tell me he's had high blood pressure for the last few years? All of those are contributing factors to heart disease."

"It wasn't the blood pressure," Katharine said, sniffing. "It was the sex."

"Katharine!" Mary Bliss said. "Stop!"

"It's true," Katharine said tearfully. "I went to that dance tonight with a whole big plan. You saw how I was dressed. I even bought myself a pair of green thong panties! I went to the club with the specific purpose of seducing Charlie Weidman. And it worked. After all these years, I knew how to push every single one of his buttons. And honey, I pushed 'em all. I flirted. I rubbed up against him, and while we were slow-dancing, I promised to do things to him that we hadn't done since our honeymoon."

Mary Bliss clamped her hands over her ears. "I do not want to hear this, Katharine."

"I didn't mean to kill him," Katharine said, stabbing at the elevator button. "I just wanted to have some fun. And maybe get a little revenge on that bitch girlfriend."

"You're still in love with him," Mary Bliss said. "It's natural to want him back."

"What I wanted was some honest-to-God sex," Katharine said. "I don't care what anybody says, a vibrator is not the same thing. A vibrator can't scratch your back, or kiss your nipple. A vibrator doesn't have a tongue . . ."

"Stop it right now!" Mary Bliss exclaimed. "We are in a hospital! Don't you have any decency?"

"No," Katharine said. "If I had any decency, I wouldn't have gone down on Charlie on the practice tee tonight. He was a little pale, afterwards, I admit, but we were having such a good time. It was his idea to go back to my place. And afterwards, when he started groaning like that, I just thought, you know, he was letting me know how good it was. But then he went all blue . . ."

The elevator chimed softly, and the doors slid open. An elderly man in a black cleric's collar, white-haired, bent over a walker, shuffled onto the elevator and looked first at the control panel, and then helplessly around at the two women for some kind of direction.

"Lobby?" he said in a wavery voice.

Mary Bliss punched the number 1 on the control panel and the doors slid shut.

"I think maybe it was the Viagra," Katharine continued, ignoring their new companion. "He told me he bought it off the Internet. You're only supposed to take one, but you know Charlie. If one's good, two are better. And he really did have the most amazing woodie. You should have seen it, Mary Bliss. He was so proud of himself."

Mary Bliss clamped her hands over the priest's ears. "Katharine, for God's sake!" she shouted.

The elevator bell chimed softly again. Third floor. "This is us," Mary Bliss said, shoving Katharine off the elevator.

They trooped down to the CICU reception desk.

"Charlie Weidman," Katharine said to the clerk. "My husband. Has he been moved up here yet? Can I see him now?"

Mary Bliss noticed the language. Husband. Katharine was referring to Charlie as her husband. She took it as a sign.

The clerk picked up the phone and called back to the unit. A moment later, she handed Katharine a plastic clip-on visitor's ID tag.

"They've given him morphine for the chest pain, so he's asleep. But you can see him if you don't stay more than a few minutes."

"Come with me?" Katharine turned to Mary Bliss, her voice pleading.

The clerk shook her head. "Sorry. Only family in the ICU."

"She's my sister," Katharine said. She drew her fingertips across her chest. "Cross my heart."

"Uh-uh," the clerk said, eyeing them both. Katharine stood a good six inches taller than Mary Bliss, her frosted blonde hair and blue eyes a telling contrast to Mary Bliss's dark hair and eyes.

"For real," Mary Bliss added.

"Go on, sisters," the clerk said, handing Mary Bliss a visitor's tag. "Five minutes. Then you're outta there."

The two women stared down at Charlie Weidman, who was, as promised, asleep. The heart monitor beside his bed beeped softly, and his face, behind the oxygen mask, seemed peaceful. His color was better, and his breathing was regular.

"See?" Mary Bliss said, nudging Katharine. "He's fine. He's not gonna die at all. So now you can quit feeling guilty about killing him. Come on. Let's go home. I'm beat."

"Hmm," Katharine said. She glanced around Charlie's glass-walled ICU cubicle. The unit seemed quiet. Two nurses at the horseshoe-shaped desk were bent over a computer monitor. Another talked animatedly on the phone.

"Just a minute," Katharine said. Before Mary Bliss could stop her, she'd lifted the sheet covering Charlie, poked her head under it, then surfaced again.

"Damn," she said. "I guess the Viagra wore off."

46

The first thing Mary Bliss noticed was that the house was just as she'd left it. The front porch light was still on and her car was the only one in the garage.

She felt a chill go down her spine. Dear God. It was 2:30 A.M. Where was Erin?

Erin's bedroom was empty, and in its normal state of upheaval. Mary Bliss checked the answering machine, but there were no messages.

Erin had left to go to the free concert at around seven o'clock. She was wearing shorts; a red, white, and blue halter top; and blue flip-flops from the Gap. Atlanta had a strict noise ordinance, no outdoor concerts could continue past midnight. So where was her daughter?

Mary Bliss went out to the front porch and looked over at the Bowden house. All the lights were off.

She could see Josh's beat-up black Chevy parked in the driveway. Erin had planned to drive her group of friends to the MARTA station, take the train to the Midtown station, and then walk to the concert.

She had been relieved at this sensible plan. Parking in the area was nearly nonexistent, and though the neighborhoods surrounding the park had long been gentrified, there was still an alarming amount of street crime in the area. Erin would be with friends, Mary Bliss thought. She'd be with Josh. She'd be safe.

Was Josh home? She went back inside, had her hand on the phone, picked it up, started to dial, hung up. Should she wake Randy up, demand to know where her daughter was at this time of night?

Wait. She dialed Erin's cell phone number. It rang once, then a recording came on, instructing her that the number was not in service. That's right, she thought. She hadn't been able to pay Erin's cell phone bill, and with everything else going on around her, it hadn't been a priority.

"Where are you?" she said aloud.

She tried fixing herself a cup of tea, but when it had brewed, she couldn't stand the tinny taste. She went upstairs, lay down on her bed, fully clothed, but found her eyes would not close.

"Screw this," she said finally.

She got in the car and backed it out of the driveway. Once she was out on the street, she didn't know what to do next. Where should she look? Where would a seventeen-year-old girl be this time of night?

She cruised the streets of Fair Oaks, searching for Erin's little blue Honda. The first place she looked was the soccer field where she'd found Erin the night she'd arrived back from Mexico. But the parking lot was empty.

The lights were off at Jessica's house. All of Fair Oaks, it seemed, was asleep. Except for Mary Bliss McGowan. She turned the car's radio to WGST, the all-news station, listening for any reports of car accidents, or muggings, or any kind of incident at all that might involve her daughter.

When she'd finished cruising the neighborhood, Mary Bliss drove over to the nearest MARTA lot. A train whistle hooted softly as it passed by on the overhead tracks. She could see at a glance that only a handful of cars were parked in the lot, and none of them were Erin's Honda.

She turned up Clifton Road, and then onto Ponce de Leon. The oak-lined avenue was quiet. No cars in sight, no flashing blue lights or sirens. Mary Bliss exhaled a little. A major east-west artery leading from in-town neighborhoods to downtown, Ponce was so narrow, the oaks crowding right to the edge of the pavement, she'd always been terrified of wrapping a car around trees, or worse yet, a utility pole.

She drove past the Krispy Kreme, one of Erin's favorite late-night hangouts. The first place she'd wanted to drive, once she'd gotten her license at sixteen, was to the all-night Krispy Kreme on Ponce. The doughnut joint was brightly lit, the neon red HOT TO GO light flashing, meaning fresh doughnuts were coming off the conveyor belt; and two police cars were parked side by side in the parking lot, officers hanging out their cruiser windows, drinking coffee and gossiping. But there was no blue Honda. She thought, briefly, of turning her car around, approaching the cops, asking for their help in finding her missing daughter.

No. She knew what they'd say. A seventeen-year-old out past curfew was a matter for parents, not police. Anyway, Erin would never speak to her again if she sicced the police on her.

She turned onto Monroe and followed it down to Piedmont Park. The streets surrounding Atlanta's version of Central Park were deserted, except for the occasional dog walker or Rollerblader, but yards, streets, and sidewalks were littered with the debris of ten thousand people devoted to heavy metal rock and roll: beer cans, fragments of Styrofoam coolers, fast food bags, broken lawn chairs, and paper wrappers from sparklers and firecrackers. The smell of cordite hung heavy in the thick, humid air.

The roads into the park were closed and blocked off with Atlanta Police barricades. She felt a wave of helplessness wash over her. She pulled her car into the blocked-off parking lot, put her head down on the steering wheel, and started to cry.

There was no telling how long she'd been there before she heard a light tapping on her window. Startled, she jerked her head up.

A city sanitation worker, dressed in white coveralls, stood beside her car. "You all right, ma'am?" he asked, his young face etched with concern.

"My daughter," she said, her voice faltering. "She came to the concert tonight. But she never came home. I was looking . . ."

"Cops shut the concert down at midnight," he said. He wore his hair in a Mohawk that was dyed hot pink, and he had a tiny tuft of hair on his chin, sort of an embryonic Fu Manchu goatee. He should have looked frightening, or threatening, but he didn't. He looked like somebody's big brother.

"I know," Mary Bliss said. "I've looked all over our neighborhood. I checked the MARTA station where she said she was going to park. I thought maybe, maybe some kids were still hanging out here. She's only seventeen. I'm worried, something might have happened."

"Me and my crew just finished running the big sweeper truck through there," the young man said. "We didn't see nobody. Unless they're hiding out. She wouldn't be hiding out now, would she?"

"No," Mary Bliss said, surprised. "Why would she be hiding out?"

"Dunno," he said. "Me and my old man used to fight and shit. I'd take off, hide out at my buddy's house a day or two, 'til he cooled down."

Mary Bliss frowned. "She's never done that before."

"Maybe she's with her boyfriend," he offered, giving her a sly wink. "Probably, she hooked up with this guy. They'd been drinking, maybe smoking some weed, and they decided to go someplace private. She can't come home drunk or stoned, right? That wouldn't be too cool."

"I'd kill her," Mary Bliss said quickly. "I won't tolerate drugs or alcohol. She's only a child."

"Right," he said. "So that's why she's stayed out all night."

"But where?" Mary Bliss asked.

He grinned. "You'd be surprised the places me and my girlfriend used to crash when we were in high school. Hell, sometimes, we'd sneak in her basement.

We'd be down there all night long, and her parents never even knew it."

Mary Bliss shuddered. Her own basement held a hot water heater, mildewed luggage, and the furnace. The one place Erin wouldn't go was the basement.

Her shoulders sagged. She rubbed her eyes.

"You should just go on home," her new friend urged. "It's not that big a deal. Kids stay out all night all the time."

She was exhausted and she was out of ideas. Maybe he was right. Maybe home was the only place left to go.

"You want my advice?" he asked, straightening and stretching.

"Sure," she said.

"When she does come home, don't go off on her, you know? Don't be screaming and hysterical and threatening to ground her and shit like that."

"She's broken every rule we have," Mary Bliss said stiffly. "She should be grounded for the rest of the summer. If she's alive, that is."

He shook his head in disapproval.

"Say I don't ground her," Mary Bliss said, thinking it over. "If you had a teenager, what would you do if your child stayed out all night and scared you to death like this?"

"Stay cool," he said. "Just stay cool."

Mary Bliss drove home. Erin's Honda was parked in the garage.

She stormed into the house and up the stairs, driven by a white anger. How dare she! The little monster!

Erin's bedroom door was open. The clothes she'd worn earlier in the evening were scattered on the floor. Her daughter was asleep, lying on her side, clutching the Dutch doll baby quilt Mary Bliss had made her while she was pregnant.

Mary Bliss stood over her, her hand opening and closing. Erin's cheek was pink and damp with sweat, her breathing sweet and slow.

Mary Bliss tucked a strand of Erin's hair behind her ear. The monster was home. She turned off the hall light and went to bed.

47

"**S**he's back!" Katharine said, slamming the kitchen door behind her.

Mary Bliss looked up from the morning paper. "Who?"

"The bitch-whore," Katharine said, referring to Charlie's girlfriend.

Katharine stalked over to the refrigerator, got out a Diet Coke, popped the top, and sat down at the table across from Mary Bliss.

"I went over to Piedmont first thing this morning to check on Charlie. I even stopped at the bagel place at Toco Hills to get him one of those marble bagels with salmon cream cheese like he likes. I even went by his condo, to pick up some pajamas and things for him, and there she was, bigger than hell, coming out of the condo, with an overnight bag."

"Maybe she's moving out," Mary Bliss said.

"She's moving, all right," Katharine said. "She's moving in on the kill. She didn't see me, so I went around to the back of the parking lot, and when she got in her car, I followed her. To the hospital."

"Oh," Mary Bliss said. "How do you think she found out so soon? It's only been a day."

"I know how she found out," Katharine said. "The old fool called her."

"Damn," Mary Bliss said. "How'd you find that out?"

"I skulked around down in the hospital cafeteria for about an hour, then I called up to the cardiac unit and got one of the nurses to check to make sure she was gone. And when the coast was clear, I marched myself up there and tore Charlie Weidman a new one."

"Katharine!" Mary Bliss scolded. "He's not supposed to have any stress. The man just had a heart attack."

"While he was in bed with me," Katharine pointed out. "If it hadn't been for me, calling the EMTs and getting him to the emergency room, he'd be laid up there in a bronze casket at Patterson's Spring Hill by now."

Mary Bliss decided to refrain from pointing out that not two days earlier, Katharine had been blaming herself for causing Charlie's delicate condition.

"How did he take being yelled at?" she asked.

"The big baby kept clutching his chest, like he was gonna have another heart attack," Katharine said. "He's just pulling that heart attack crap to keep from having to deal with choosing between me and the BW."

Mary Bliss folded the newspaper in quarters, then put it in the recycling bin by the back door.

"Is that a choice you want him to make in his current condition?" she asked, trying to choose her words carefully.

"Hell, yes," Katharine said. "He's being released from Piedmont next Tuesday. Yesterday when I was up there, he was all lovey-dovey, holding my hand, telling me how he now has something to live for, how he wanted the three of us to be a family again. You know he can't go home to his condo when he leaves the hospital, because the bedroom's on the second floor. He was hinting bigtime about coming back to my house. Idiot that I am, I even offered to bring him home and take care of him."

"Until you saw the BW."

Katharine nodded vigorously. Tears sprang to her eyes, and she swiped at them angrily with a paper napkin. "Damn him."

"Come on," Mary Bliss said, tugging at Katharine's hand. "Get up. Come with me. Forget about Charlie for now."

"I wish I could," she said, blowing her nose loudly. "Where are we going?"

"Upstairs," Mary Bliss said. "To Erin's room."

"I don't need a nap," Katharine said. "I'm fine. What I do need is a hit man."

"For Charlie or the BW?"

"Both," Katharine said. "What are we going to do in Erin's room?"

"We're going to search every damn inch of it until I get some answers," Mary Bliss said.

Katharine followed her dutifully up the stairs. She paused in the doorway. "Wow," she said, taking it all in. "Chip's room was never this bad. What kind of answers are we looking for?"

"Anything," Mary Bliss said. "She stayed out all night Thursday night. I searched all over Atlanta for her. I even went over to Piedmont Park, thinking maybe she'd gotten drunk and fallen in the lake or something. Finally, I gave up and came home at about four A.M. And here she was, sound asleep in her bed."

"All night?" Katharine raised an eyebrow. "Did you slap her butt on restriction?"

"No," Mary Bliss said. "I didn't say a word. What good would it do? She has a job, her own car, her own friends. She hates me. Hardly ever speaks to me."

"Who was she with?" Katharine asked. She inched her way gingerly into the room and started pulling out the drawers of Erin's chest of drawers.

"Josh," Mary Bliss said.

"Did you speak to Randy about that?" Katharine asked. "I can't believe he thinks it's okay for Josh to be staying out all night with his girlfriend."

"I haven't said anything," Mary Bliss said. "Randy's got enough to deal with right now. Nancye's squeezing him for more money, and his little boys are really having problems adjusting to the separation."

"Are you sure you want to do this, Mary Bliss?" Katharine asked. "What if you find out something you don't want to know?"

"I have to know," Mary Bliss said. "I need to know what's going on in her life. If she won't tell me herself, I'll just have to dig around until I figure it out."

"And then what?"

Mary Bliss was on her belly, her head stuck under Erin's bed.

"I'll let you know when I know," she answered, her voice muffled.

While Katharine went through Erin's dresser, Mary Bliss searched her closet, her nightstand, and the mahogany hope chest at the foot of Erin's bed.

She cleaned and straightened as she went, reasoning that she would tell Erin she'd cleaned her room because it was becoming a health hazard.

After three hours, the floor was vacuumed, the bed changed and made, all the clothes folded and hung up or put away.

"I got nothing," Katharine said, sinking down onto the bed. "No diary. No liquor bottle. No rolling papers or roach clips. No condoms, nada."

"Me neither," Mary Bliss said, flopping down beside her. "I even looked in her backpack and her old purses. I didn't even find a pack of matches."

"The kid's clean," Katharine concluded. "Well, not clean, not in the neat sense of the word. She just hasn't left us any clues. Can you think of anyplace else we haven't looked?"

"Her car," Mary Bliss said. "But it's like her sanctuary. When she's not in it, it's locked. And I don't have a key."

"Hey," Katharine said. "We went through something like this with Chip his junior year. He put me through the wringer, staying out all night, skipping school. His grades went down the tubes. I wanted to kill him."

"You never told me about that," Mary Bliss said, staring at her best friend. "I thought Chip was the model student."

"It was humiliating," Katharine said.

"What was he up to?" Mary Bliss asked.

"A little of everything. Some drinking, some drugging. He was sleeping with his girlfriend, who was only fifteen. Christ, he could have been arrested for statutory rape!"

"How'd you find out?" Mary Bliss asked.

"How do wives and mothers always find out what everybody's up to?" Katharine asked. "His laundry. I borrowed the Jeep one day while the Mercedes was in the shop. His gym bag was in the back, full of nasty football clothes. I decided to be a good mom and clean it out and wash everything."

"What did you find?"

"Not what I expected," Katharine said. "Just like Erin's room. No beer cans or anything like that. These kids are too smart for their own good. They watch too much television. All I found was a key."

"A motel key?"

"The key to the lake house," Katharine said. "Which he was not supposed to have."

"Did you confront him?"

"Uh-uh," Katharine said. "It's like you said. At that age, they won't listen."

"What did you do?"

"I called the girl's daddy," Katharine said. "Told him what I thought was going on. The very next weekend, Charlie and I were supposed to go down to Jekyll Island for the state bar association meeting. I sent Charlie on down without me. And that Friday afternoon, Heather's daddy and I took a ride up to the lake. Sure enough, there was Chip's Jeep parked around back."

"Oh God." Mary Bliss covered her face with her hands. She could picture it all too clearly.

"I had my own key," Katharine said. "So we snuck in real quiet like."

"Oh God," Mary Bliss repeated. She was playing the scene in her own mind as Katharine told it, only instead of Chip and Heather, the scenario starred Erin and Josh Bowden.

"They were in *my* bed," Katharine said, still indignant over the memory. "The two of them, naked as jaybirds. On my good Ralph Lauren bedspread that has to be dry-cleaned."

"Eew," Mary Bliss said. She looked down at Erin's comforter, which, thank heavens, was machine-washable.

"Did I forget to mention that Heather's daddy picked up Charlie's twenty-gauge as we were coming through the front door?" Katharine asked.

"No."

"Yeah. It wasn't loaded or anything, but Chip didn't know that. Once Chip caught sight of me, and Heather's daddy, looking down the sights of that shotgun, he was a changed man."

"I'll bet," Mary Bliss said.

"Heather's daddy had her transfer schools the next fall, to some fundamentalist Christian school out in Gwinnett County," Katharine continued. "And Chip promised to straighten up. He promised never to take another drink, or smoke another joint, or mess with another underage girl, if I would just please not tell his daddy on him."

"He was that worried about what Charlie would say?"

"Yeah," Katharine said, gathering up the basket of dirty laundry she'd picked up in the closet. "Charlie's a very moral man. He wouldn't stand for his son having premarital sex."

48

Bargain Bonanza had chicken breasts on special, eighty-nine cents a pound, in five-pound packages. On Thursday, after she finished handing out free cups of Mango-ade ("a sure pleaser for our Latin customers," Imogene Peabody assured her), Mary Bliss loaded up a shopping cart with the chicken breasts, twin packs of Duke's mayonnaise, bottled Italian dressing, and sour cream.

She winced when Mimsy Reed, the cashier, announced her total, $367.48. "You havin' a party, hon?" Mimsy asked, gesturing toward the mountain of chicken on the check stand. "What time you want me over there?"

"It's not for a party for me," Mary Bliss said. "I'm doing a little catering for a wedding."

"A little!" Mimsy exclaimed. "That's enough damn chicken breasts to feed the Russian army. What all are you making?"

"Just chicken salad," Mary Bliss said.

"That's all? Just chicken salad? Sounds like kind of a boring party."

"It's for a wedding," Mary Bliss said. "The real caterer is doing everything else. I'm just fixing my chicken salad."

"Whooo-eee," Mimsy said. She was tall and thin, with thick-lensed glasses; thick, dark eyelashes; and straight, blonde hair that fell in her eyes all the time. In her six weeks at Bargain Bonanza, Mary Bliss had learned to avoid long conversations with Mimsy, who tended to get into everybody's business.

"That must be some world-class chicken salad if somebody's hiring you to make it for a wedding."

"It's pretty good," Mary Bliss said, loading the chicken as quickly as she could.

"My mama makes wonderful chicken salad," Mimsy volunteered. "She uses pistachio nuts and sour cream, and them little canned Mandarin orange slices. Including the orange juice. That's the secret to her success, the orange juice. What all's in yours?"

"Oh," Mary Bliss said, waving her hand vaguely, "a little of this and a little of that. I just tinker around with it, 'til I get it right."

"Mama's recipe was printed up in *Southern Living*," Mimsy said proudly. "July of 1987. 'Wonderful Ways with Chicken,' that was the headline on the story. Listen! Why don't you print up your recipe for me, and I'll get her to send it in for you. She's got kinda an in with them over there in Birmingham now."

"I don't have any set written recipe," Mary Bliss said. She shoved the cart away from the check stand and headed for the door.

At home, Mary Bliss went out to the garage to get her mother's old blue enamelware canning vat. It was the biggest pot she owned, so big that she normally stored it on a shelf above Parker's workbench.

After she'd retrieved the vat, she glanced over at Erin's car. The doors of the Honda were unlocked. Erin had come home early from work, complaining of menstrual cramps, and had gone straight upstairs to bed, refusing her mother's offer of aspirin or ginger ale.

Mary Bliss set the vat on the garage floor and opened the Honda's passenger-side door. The car's interior was immaculate. She ran her hand under the seat and came up with nothing more than the flashlight Parker always insisted Erin keep there. She opened the glove box and found a map of Georgia, a package of breath mints, and a small box of tissues.

The driver's side of the car was just as spartan. Mary Bliss could see at a glance that the backseat was empty. She bent down and pulled the latch to open the trunk.

But first she ran inside the house and tiptoed up the stairs. Erin's bedroom door was open, and Mary Bliss could hear her talking on the phone.

She slipped back downstairs and out to the garage. Flipping up the trunk, she saw only the small "Roadside Emergency" kit she'd given Erin for her sixteenth birthday, and Erin's soccer bag. She was about to close the trunk when she remembered Katharine's story about her discovery in Chip's gym bag.

Her heart pounding, she unzipped the bag and quickly unloaded it. A pair of mud-caked cleats wrapped in a plastic bag sat on top of a pile of neatly folded clothes. Shorts, T-shirts, socks; she set them on the floor of the trunk. Under the soccer gear, she found a white plastic grocery sack. Her hands shaking, she reached inside. Her fingertips touched a froth of silky fabric. A black lace teddy. Not exactly standard-issue soccer equipment. There was more. A brown paper sack. Inside it, a box of condoms. The package had been opened. Mary Bliss wanted to scream. There was something else in the bag. A small vial of KoKo-LoKo coconut-flavored massage oil.

"Are you happy now?"

Mary Bliss whirled around. Erin stood in the doorway from the kitchen. She wore an old flannel nightgown and threadbare white socks. Her hair was pulled into a ponytail. She looked about twelve.

"See what you wanted to see?" Erin asked. Her voice was icy. She stalked over to the car and slammed the trunk shut, missing Mary Bliss's hand by a millimeter.

"Just a minute," Mary Bliss cried. "We need to talk about this, young lady. I won't have you sleeping with boys at your age. You're too young."

Erin stomped over to the side of the car, produced her keys, and locked the car with a flourish.

When she turned around, all traces of the twelve-year-old had vanished. Mascara was smeared under her eyes, which were lined with dark circles, and her chin had a hard set to it. "Sleeping? Mama, it's not about sleeping. It's about fucking. Yeah, I'm fucking. So what?"

"You're too young," Mary Bliss protested, grabbing for Erin's arm. "You're not even out of high school. It's immoral. It's wrong."

Erin laughed bitterly and brushed her hand away. "Immoral? You're calling me immoral? That's a good one. You telling me you didn't screw Daddy before you were married? What a bunch of shit! Meemaw told me all about it. She told me you and Daddy *had* to get married, because you were knocked up. So don't go giving me that immoral shit, Mama."

"I was twenty-one," Mary Bliss said. "Out of college. Your father and I were engaged. We were old enough to take responsibility for our actions. You're not even old enough to make your bed in the mornings. You're a child!"

"You'd like to think that, wouldn't you?" Erin said, taunting her now. "You'd like to keep me in knee socks and little dresses, keep me locked up in this house. Keep telling me my daddy's dead? Well, fuck you, Mama. I'm all grown up. Grown up enough to know the truth. Grown up enough to know what a hypocrite and a liar you are."

Her eyes narrowed to small slits. Mary Bliss could almost feel the heat emanating from them.

"I fuckin' hate you!" Erin screamed. She whirled around, unlocked the Honda, and slid inside. The echo from the Honda's little engine seemed deafening. The automatic garage door slid open and the Honda shot backward, out and down the driveway, tires squealing as Erin threw the car into drive and sped down the street.

Mary Bliss's hands were trembling. For the first time, she noticed she was still holding the paper bag containing the oil and the condoms. She twisted the bag closed, walked outside to the garbage cans, and tossed the bag inside.

She picked up Nina's canning vat and took it inside. She ran hot soapy water in the vat and scrubbed it until her hands were red and raw.

When it was clean, she set it in the dish rack to dry. She got a jug of Clorox from the laundry room, filled a dishpan with warm water and bleach, and proceeded to wipe down the kitchen counters, the stove top, and even the floor.

The kitchen smelled like an indoor swimming pool.

Mary Bliss thumbed through her recipe file box until she came to the card for Mamie's Chicken Salad. She set the dressing ingredients out on the kitchen table. Then she started opening the packaged chicken breasts. She could fit ten pounds at a time in the kettle. She filled the vat with water to cover the chicken, added her seasonings, and turned the stove top on simmer.

She finished poaching the chicken breasts at ten o'clock. Her head throbbed and her back ached. The phone did not ring. Erin's car did not reappear in the garage.

While the chicken cooled, Mary Bliss mixed the marinade. Every fifteen minutes or so, she walked to the front door and looked out. The lights were on at the Bowdens'. She would march right over there and let

Randy in on what their kids had been up to. Maybe take the condoms over there so that he could fathom the seriousness of the situation. She would give Josh a lecture on the evils of premarital sex, cite statistics on teenaged pregnancy, appeal to his basic decency to break off this dangerous relationship with her daughter.

She did fetch the paper bag out of the trash. And she squared her shoulders, marched herself across the street to the Bowdens' house, and rang the doorbell.

Randy answered the door himself after a few minutes. His hair was tousled. He had a sleeping Jason, dressed in Spiderman underpants, draped across his shoulder.

"Hey there, neighbor!" Randy said, his thin face lighting up with a smile. "I was just putting this little guy to bed. Go on in the kitchen and pour yourself a drink, and I'll be down in a minute."

Randy's kitchen broke her heart. Or maybe her heart was just permanently in a fractured condition. The dinner dishes still sat on the Formica kitchen table. Yellow plates smeared with bright-red spaghetti sauce, glasses half full of milk, a small dish with carrot sticks and cucumber slices and cherry tomatoes.

Mary Bliss ran water over the dishes and loaded them in the dishwasher, which was already nearly full. She put the burned spaghetti pan in the sink to soak, and for the second time that day, she set about cleaning a kitchen.

"Oh no," Randy said, coming into the room. "Now you think I'm just a big jerk slob." He took a plate out of her hand. "You don't need to be doing that. I was going to clean up after I put the boys to bed."

"Here," he said, pulling out a chair for her. "At least now you have a clean place to sit."

"I don't mind," Mary Bliss said quietly. All the fight had gone out of her.

He went to the refrigerator, looked in, and frowned. "All I've got is some apple juice. Looks like Josh drank all the Cokes. And I've quit keeping beer in the house. You know, with him home alone most of the day, I don't want to put temptation in his way."

"Yeah," Mary Bliss said. "That's probably a good idea. About the beer."

How? she wondered. How would she tell this decent man that she was pretty sure his son was sleeping with her daughter?

"So. What's up with you?" he asked. "We missed you at the dance."

"Maybe next time," she said. "I know it's late. I just saw your light on, thought it might be a good time for a little visit. I can't stay, though, I'm in the middle of a big project."

He poured two glasses of apple juice. Then he raised his own glass and clinked it next to hers. "To friends," he said.

"To friends."

They chatted aimlessly for a while. He filled her in on the gossip from the dance. Who left with whom. Who fell off the wagon, who was wearing a toupee and thought nobody knew.

"The kids sure must have had a good time that night," Mary Bliss said. "I wanted to kill Erin for coming in so late."

Randy blushed. "I had a talking-to with Josh. He knows he's not supposed to stay out that late. I hope he didn't get Erin in trouble."

"Erin gets herself in trouble," Mary Bliss said. "She doesn't need any help from Josh."

"You two getting along any better?" he asked, sipping his juice and searching her face for answers.

"No," Mary Bliss said. Short and sweet. "How about you guys? Does Josh talk to you?"

"Sometimes," he said. "Not very often. He's always been a quiet kid. We talk about music. He really knows a lot about music. And not just rock and roll. He's into progressive jazz and funk. And sometimes we talk about school."

"Do you ever . . . talk about the heavy stuff?" Mary Bliss said, hesitating.

"Like what?"

"You know. Sex. Drugs. Booze."

"We've talked about it. He knows where I stand. And he knows my rules. He may not agree, but I think he respects me." Randy looked down at the kitchen tabletop. He scrubbed at a spot of spaghetti sauce with his thumbnail. "He knows about Nancye. He knows his mother's sleeping around. He won't talk about it, but I know he knows. Hell, everybody in town knows. The poor kid. It's just eating at him."

"It's a small town," Mary Bliss said. "How did that song go? It's just a little Peyton Place?"

"I remember that one," Randy said. "Peyton Place. Fair Oaks. Not much difference."

49

By her own estimates, Mary Bliss had shredded seventy pounds of poached chicken breast. Foil trays of the finished chicken lined her kitchen counter, because she'd run out of room in her own refrigerator, and the old refrigerator in the garage where they kept beer and soft drinks.

It was nine in the morning. She'd stayed up the rest of the night, cooking and worrying. At midnight, she'd had a call from Jessica's mother, telling her that Erin was there and was planning to spend the night.

"I take it you two are having some problems," said Jessica's mother, a slight, quiet woman whose name Mary Bliss couldn't remember. "She was pretty upset when she got here. I told her she could stay tonight, but she had to let you know where she was. She doesn't feel quite ready to talk to you just yet."

"That's fine," Mary Bliss said, relieved to know where her daughter was. "Thanks for letting me know. And thank you for letting her stay."

"It's no problem at all," the woman assured her. "I'll try to have her call you in the morning."

"Good luck with that," Mary Bliss said. "She's really angry with me."

"It'll blow over," Jessica's mother said. "Jess has two older sisters. When they were this age, we were always fussing at each other. Now they're just fine. They call me every day. We're best friends."

"I look forward to that time," Mary Bliss said fervently.

At ten o'clock Friday morning, Mary Bliss picked up the phone and called Katharine.

"I need to borrow your refrigerator," she said. "I've run out of room in mine and I've still got thirty pounds of chicken to go."

"Good Lord," Katharine said. "Are we having another funeral?"

"It's a wedding," Mary Bliss said. "And I've got to make a hundred pounds of Mamie's chicken salad."

"Who do we know that's getting married?" Katharine asked, puzzled. "Seems like everybody we know is getting divorced."

"Ain't that the truth," Mary Bliss said. "This is for a total stranger. Braelynn Connors."

"The blonde chick on channel eleven? That's supposed to be a really big society wedding. I've been reading about it in the *Constitution*'s 'Peach Buzz' for weeks. How'd you get hooked up with Braelynn Connors?"

"Her caterer's grandmother was Meemaw's old cook. She took care of Parker when he was a little kid. The grandson, Gerran Thomas, came to Parker's memorial service. He had some of the chicken salad and decided he absolutely had to have it for this swanky wedding. So I agreed to make it for them. A hundred pounds. I must be out of my mind to even try."

"How much are they paying you?" Katharine asked.

"Twenty-five dollars a pound," Mary Bliss said. "After this is over I'll never look at another piece of chicken again. So, how about it? Do you have room in your fridge?"

"Sure," Katharine said. "Bring it on over. Just don't ring the doorbell when you get here. Charlie had kind of a rough night."

"Charlie? He's there? So you worked things out?"

"He's here, sort of," Katharine said. "It's a long story. I'll tell you when you get here."

By noon she'd finished shredding the rest of the chicken and had poured the Italian dressing marinade over everything. Her fingers were red and shriveled. She was hungry, but the thought of food made her nauseous.

Mary Bliss was picking at a plate of cottage cheese when her own doorbell rang.

Damn. Good news never came to her front door. It was probably a bill collector. Or worse, Matt Hayslip again.

She stepped out the kitchen door and peeked down the driveway. A dark-green SUV was parked there. Not Hayslip's black cop-mobile. And her own car was now blocked in. She would have to answer the door.

The woman standing on her front porch was a massive black woman with arms like tree trunks. She wore a tentlike navy-blue dress and a stern expression, and she was clutching a thick briefcase under her arm.

"Mrs. McGowan?" the woman said sternly.

"Yes?" Mary Bliss said, taking a step back.

The woman produced a business card and handed it to her.

"I'm Quiana Reese. With Southern Mutual Insurers. I wonder if I could have a few minutes of your time?"

Mary Bliss felt the blood drain from her face. She stared down at the card, trying to think of something to say. QUIANA REESE. CASE INVESTIGATOR, the card said. This was the person Charlie had warned her about.

A fraud investigator. He hadn't told her the investigator would be a huge, intimidating woman named Quiana Reese.

"Just a minute, please," Mary Bliss said, taking yet another step back. "I've got something on the burner in my kitchen, and I'm afraid it's boiling over. I'll be right back."

She closed the door and ran to the kitchen. She picked up the phone.

"Katharine? Is Charlie awake yet?"

"I think so," Katharine said. "I heard water running down there a few minutes ago."

"Down there?"

"In the basement. You didn't think I'd let the lying, cheating scumbag sleep upstairs with me, did you? I fixed him up a bed in the playroom."

"You're keeping him down in the basement? That seems a little drastic to me," Mary Bliss said, forgetting for a moment just how drastic her own situation was.

"He's lucky I didn't make him sleep out in the garage," Katharine said tartly. "He's got everything he needs down there, no stairs to contend with, as long as he stays put. Now, why are you so interested in Charlie's living arrangements?"

"I need to talk to him," Mary Bliss said. "There's a fraud investigator from the insurance company standing on my front porch. She says she has a few questions to ask me. The last thing Charlie told me was that I was absolutely not to talk to anybody from the insurance company unless he was with me. I need to know what I should tell her."

"Stall," Katharine said. "I'll run downstairs and give Charlie the phone. He can call you and tell you what to do."

"He doesn't have his own phone down there?"

"So he can call the BW whenever he feels like it?" Katharine said. "Fat chance. He stays in the basement. And he doesn't use the phone unless I'm standing right there."

"Well, hurry," Mary Bliss said. "This woman looks like she means business."

Mary Bliss raced back to the front hall. "Just a minute, Ms. Reese," she called. "I've got a tiny little grease fire. I'll be right back."

She stood over the phone in the kitchen, willing it to ring.

"Mary Bliss?" Charlie's voice sounded thin and weak. No match for the bulldozer cooling her heels on her front porch.

"Charlie, I hate to bother you," Mary Bliss said. "But that fraud investigator is here. She wants to ask me some questions. What should I do?"

He sighed. "Let her in. Stall her some more. I'll see if I can get my jailer to bring me over there."

"No, Charlie," Mary Bliss said. "You just got out of the hospital. Katharine said you're not supposed to have any stress. Just tell me what to do. You don't have to come over here."

"I don't want you talking to anybody unless I'm sitting right there," Charlie said. "Hang on, sugar. I'm a-coming."

After she hung up, Mary Bliss took some of the fat she'd strained off the chicken broth, put it in a black iron skillet, placed it in the sink, and set a match to it. Flames shot up, singeing her eyebrows. She leapt backward, fanning her face, then reached forward and turned the faucet on. A cloud of smoke filled the kitchen.

She sighed and marched herself out to meet the enemy.

"Good heavens," Quiana Reese said as Mary Bliss led her down the hall to the living room. "You really did have a grease fire, didn't you?"

"I'm afraid so," Mary Bliss said. "I've been cooking chicken. I guess I got a little careless. That happens sometimes."

"You don't have a home-owner's policy with us, do you?" Ms. Reese asked, alarmed.

"No, ma'am," Mary Bliss said. "We're State Farm all the way. Except for that life insurance policy my aunt gave us for a wedding gift, all those years ago."

She seated the investigator on the sofa and pulled up a wing chair to sit opposite her.

Ms. Reese started unfastening the brass buckles on her briefcase.

"Let me get you some iced tea," Mary Bliss said, jumping back up. "All that smoke is making your throat itch, I'll bet."

"I'm fine," Ms. Reese protested. "Now, if we could just get down to business . . ."

"I'll be right back," Mary Bliss said, rushing from the room.

She boiled water for the tea, added the Luzianne bags and the sugar, then let it steep while she dialed Katharine's house again.

The phone rang, but nobody answered. "Hurry," Mary Bliss urged aloud.

She was just taking the tray of iced tea and sugar cookies into the living room when the doorbell rang again.

Quiana Reese's hamlike hand was hovering over the cookie plate. She snatched it back. "Were you expecting company?" she asked, frowning.

"I wasn't expecting anybody today," Mary Bliss said pointedly. "But people just keep showing up. Haven't you ever had a day like that? When people won't seem to leave you alone?"

Charlie's face was pale and his neck seemed suddenly too small for his white golf shirt. His blue blazer hung from his shoulders.

"Hey, shug," he said, stepping inside.

"Charlie," Mary Bliss said, hugging him gingerly. "You shouldn't be out of bed yet."

"Hush," he said. "I was going stir-crazy down there in the basement. You know that woman doesn't even get cable down there?"

She showed him into the living room.

Quiana Reese had a clipboard in her lap, and she was busy reading some kind of document. "Hello," she said, glancing up at Charlie, visibly surprised.

He walked haltingly to the wing chair Mary Bliss had pulled up and gripped the arms as he lowered himself into it.

"Hi there," he said when he'd made himself comfortable. "I'm Charles Weidman. I'm an old friend of Mr. and Mrs. McGowan's. And Mrs. McGowan's attorney, of course. I've been in contact with your people out there at Southern Mutual, but I wasn't aware you'd be visiting my client today."

"I'm Quiana Reese," she said. "And I wasn't aware it was necessary to notify you of my intentions. This is strictly an informal inquiry. And I'd prefer to talk to Mrs. McGowan in confidence."

Mary Bliss shivered. She'd known Charlie for years but had never seen him doing the lawyer thing before. She was impressed. And glad he was on her side.

"Anything the two of you discuss is in strictest confidence," Charlie said pleasantly.

"All right, then," Quiana Reese said, pursing her lips. She looked down at her clipboard again, then reached into her briefcase and brought out a small silver tape recorder, which she set out on the coffee table.

"You don't object to my taping our discussion, do you?" she asked, looking at Mary Bliss.

Charlie reached into the inside pocket of his blazer and brought out a black, slightly smaller tape recorder. "I don't mind if you don't mind," he said, setting his machine right next to hers.

Quiana Reese started off with the easy stuff.

"For the record, this is the home of Mrs. Mary Bliss McGowan, and this is the fifteenth of July," she said stiffly. "Mrs. McGowan has agreed to answer questions pertaining to the apparent death of her husband, Parker McGowan, in Cozumel, Mexico, on or around June fourth."

"Not an apparent death," Charlie said, interrupting. "The police in Cozumel ruled his death an accident, and after a thorough investigation issued a death certificate for Parker McGowan. Your company has been furnished with copies of that certificate, as well as the pertinent police documents."

"Mexico," Ms. Reese said. The way she said it, Mary Bliss thought, it was like it was a dirty word. Like *phlegm*. Or *vagina*.

"It's your statement that you and your husband traveled to Cozumel for a vacation, is that correct?"

Mary Bliss looked at Charlie for approval. He nodded his head.

"Yes," she said.

"You traveled separately?"

Charlie nodded again.

"Yes. Parker was away on a consulting trip. He asked me to fly down to Cozumel and meet him there. Which I did."

"And where was your husband traveling from?"

Mary Bliss bit her lip. Charlie nodded. She bit her lip again. "You know, I don't believe he said where he was traveling from," she said. "His business took him all over the country, and I guess I kind of lost track of where he was the week before. Dallas, maybe. Or Phoenix."

Quiana Reese scribbled a note on her clipboard. "Kind of unusual, isn't it? Not knowing where your husband is?"

"It wasn't unusual for the McGowans," Charlie pointed out. "Anyway, I don't see why that's pertinent to your investigation."

"Everything about them is pertinent," Ms. Reese said. "And you checked into your hotel, the Casa Blanca, on June third?"

"I believe so," Mary Bliss said.

"And your husband had already checked in?"

"Yes," she said, clasping her hands tightly in her lap.

"Has your husband always been a heavy drinker?" Quiana Reese asked, switching gears. "Has he ever sought treatment for substance abuse? To your knowledge, had he ever been arrested for possession of a controlled substance?"

"What?" Mary Bliss asked, her voice shrill. "What are you talking about?"

"Don't answer that, Mary Bliss," Charlie said calmly. He leaned forward and shut off both tape recorders.

"I wish you wouldn't interfere with my investigation," Quiana Reese said, frowning.

"And I wish you wouldn't ask my client insulting, immaterial questions," Charlie said.

"It's not immaterial," Ms. Reese retorted. "I've been to the Casa Blanca. I've talked to hotel employees. Mr. McGowan was seen several times in the hotel's beach bar, consuming large amounts of beer and tequila. I also learned he may have purchased marijuana from one of the hotel's maintenance workers."

Dinky Davis, Mary Bliss thought. If he wasn't already dead, she would surely have to track him down and kill him for real this time.

"Parker McGowan?" Charlie said, laughing. "That's ludicrous. Parker detested tequila. Couldn't stand the stuff. And he never did drugs. Of any kind. He wouldn't even take an Ibuprofen for a pulled back muscle. You'd better check your sources more carefully, Ms. Reese. I knew Parker for ten years before his untimely death. Obviously, you're talking about somebody other than Parker McGowan."

Quiana Reese thumped her clipboard for emphasis. "I have signed affidavits from all the people who witnessed your client's behavior. I have the copies of the McGowans' hotel bill—he charged two fifths of Tecate to his room, as well as a case of Dos Equis beer. That doesn't sound like a case of mistaken identity to me."

Charlie held up his hand. "That's enough. We're done here, Ms. Reeves. Mrs. McGowan lost her husband less than six weeks ago. She's still in mourning.

I won't let you sit in her house and slander her husband. If you have any other questions, you can submit them in writing to me, and we'll review the situation at that time."

Quiana Reese stood up suddenly, smoothing the voluminous folds of her navy-blue tent over her hips. She grabbed her tape recorder and stuffed it in her briefcase. Then she pulled out a pamphlet and flung it on the coffee table.

"What's that?" Charlie asked, reaching for it.

"'Timely Tips for Home Fire Safety,'" she retorted. "Your client should read it—before she burns this house down."

50

Charlie followed Mary Bliss into the kitchen, his gait halting. While she busied herself putting away the tea glasses and the cookies, he lifted the foil covering on one of the trays of chicken and helped himself to a handful of poached chicken breast.

"Stop that," she said, popping his knuckles with the back of a wooden spoon. "That's my mortgage payment you're eating."

"No, it's my legal fee," Charlie said. "What is that smell?" he asked, sniffing and glancing around the kitchen.

"Burnt chicken grease?" she said. "You told me to stall the insurance investigator. So I staged a little kitchen fire."

"What else did you stage?"

Mary Bliss stood with her back to the sink, her arms crossed over her chest.

"What's that supposed to mean? The fire was strictly a diversionary tactic. It was your idea, Charlie Weidman."

He took a saucer from her dish drainer and began spooning poached chicken onto it. Then he opened the refrigerator and got out one of the jars of Duke's, adding a huge dollop. He liberally salted and peppered the chicken, sat down at the kitchen table, and calmly tucked into it like one of the starving Armenians Mary Bliss's mother had always taunted her with.

"You shouldn't eat that," Mary Bliss scolded. "You've just had a heart attack. You've got about a cup of mayonnaise there. And all that salt! Are you trying to kill yourself?"

He continued eating. "Katharine won't feed me anything but red Jell-O and plain white rice," he said. "I'd rather die of a heart attack from eating mayonnaise and red meat than live on that crap."

He looked up at her again. "Stop playing dumb, Mary Bliss. I know you two are up to something. But I can't help you unless you tell me the truth."

"I'm telling the truth," she said stiffly. "I can't believe that woman went down to Mexico and found out about Parker's drinking. It's so embarrassing. And the drugs. I swear, I didn't know he was doing drugs too."

"All right," Charlie said wearily. "You just stick to your story, then. But I warn you, Mary Bliss. It sounds fishy even to me—and I'm your lawyer and your best friend's husband."

"I can't help it," Mary Bliss said. "It's the truth. But listen, Charlie. What that woman said about Parker contributing to his own death. If they prove he was drunk when he was driving that boat, can they refuse to pay my claim?"

Charlie took a forkful of chicken and dabbed it into the mayonnaise. "That depends," he said, chewing slowly.

"On what?"

"On how good your lawyer is," he said, scraping the last of the chicken from the plate. "You got any white bread laying around here? Sunbeam, somethin' like that? If I have to litigate this thing, I'm thinking I'm gonna have to up my fee to include a chicken sandwich. And a dill pickle would be nice too."

The back door opened and Katharine walked in. Charlie slipped his saucer under the pile of bills on the kitchen table.

"Hey, honey bun," he said, smiling warmly. "You didn't have to rush back here for me so soon. Mary Bliss and I were just discussing this man-eatin' insurance investigator of hers."

"Don't honey-bun me," Katharine said. She shoved the bills aside and retrieved the mayonnaise-smeared plate. "Is this what you do when I'm not around? Deliberately clog your arteries with enough cholesterol to choke a goat?"

"Now, baby doll," Charlie said. "Calm down. That's low-fat mayonnaise. See? Ask Mary Bliss. It's got the good cholesterol."

"There is no good cholesterol where you're concerned," Katharine said. "And let me tell you another thing, Charles Weidman. Don't come crying to me next time you have another heart attack. You want to kill yourself, go on ahead. Try calling that Bitch-Whore of yours, see if she'll stay at your bedside in the hospital night and day like I did."

"Katharine!" Charlie said. "This is neither the time nor the place to discuss our private lives. Mary Bliss doesn't want to hear all that."

"Pooh," Katharine said. "Mary Bliss knows all about your little girlfriend. For that matter, half the town knows."

"For the record, she is not my girlfriend," Charlie said. "She is my associate."

"Okay, you two," Mary Bliss said, stepping between them. "I'm calling a truce. This is an officially demilitarized zone. Like Switzerland. If the two of you want to spend the day bickering, take it on back to your own house."

"My house," Katharine corrected her, glowering at Charlie.

"Which I pay for," Charlie added.

"Enough!" Mary Bliss stacked two of the foil trays of chicken on top of each other. "Here," she said. "Katharine, help me load this stuff in the car to take over to your place. It's got to chill for at least eight hours before I can mix in the dressing and the other ingredients."

"What's this stuff for?" Charlie asked, picking up one of the trays.

Mary Bliss popped him on the arm with her wooden spoon again. "Put that down," she ordered. "It's your mother-in-law's chicken salad. I'm helping cater a wedding."

He held the kitchen door open. "I think I just heard my fee go up again."

At Katharine's house, Charlie held the doors while they ferried all the trays inside and stashed them in Katharine's big Sub-Zero refrigerator.

"I'm whipped," Mary Bliss said, sinking down into a chair.

Charlie sat down beside her, dabbing his glistening forehead with a handkerchief. "Me too," he admitted. "I guess I'm not quite ready to run a marathon yet."

"You need to be in the bed," Katharine told him.

He snaked his arm around her waist, then slipped his hand down to rest on her butt. "Whatever you say, honey bun. I'll get the sheets warmed up, then as soon as Mary Bliss is gone, you can slip in there beside me."

"You're incorrigible," Katharine told him. But she didn't move away, and Charlie's hand stayed where it was.

"Guess I'll hit the road and let you two be alone, then," Mary Bliss said.

"I don't want to be alone with this old goat," Katharine said. "Anyway, I want to hear about the insurance investigator. What kind of things did she ask you?"

"Later," Mary Bliss said, trying to give Katharine a silent warning that she didn't want to discuss it in front of Charlie.

"Ms. Quiana Reese seemed reluctant to believe Mary Bliss's account of Parker's accident," Charlie said.

Katharine frowned. "Why? It seems pretty cut and dried to me. They went out on the boat, it hit a wave, the boat capsized. Parker wasn't wearing a life jacket, so he probably drowned. End of story."

"The insurance company doesn't find it cut and dried at all," Charlie said. "That investigator took a trip to Cozumel. She talked to some people at the hotel.

Seems like Parker was cutting up pretty good down there. Drinking a case of beer at a time. Swilling tequila like it was water. Why, that old rascal even bought himself some Mexican mary-ja-wana," Charlie said, deliberately deepening his already deliberate drawl.

"Really?" Katharine seemed perplexed.

"Yeah, really," Charlie said. "Ms. Reese thinks it's pretty likely Parker was impaired when he and Mary Bliss rented that boat. That means drunk in insurance talk. And she seems to think Parker's negligence contributed to his own death."

"So what?" Katharine said. "Even if it was his own fault, they can't get out of paying Mary Bliss's death benefit, can they?"

"That's what I was just starting to explain to Mary Bliss earlier today," Charlie said. "Something she didn't know about. Hell, I didn't know it until I started doing some research. This ain't exactly my kind of specialty, you know."

"You're a lawyer," Katharine said. "The smartest one I know. You can run circles around that pissant little life insurance company."

"I'll take that as a rare compliment, darlin'," Charlie said. "But the fact remains that no matter how damn smart I am—and you're right, I am pretty damn smart most of the time—I can't run circles around the law."

"What are you talking about?" Mary Bliss asked. She didn't like the direction this was going in. Not at all.

"Just this. Even if Parker was negligent, even if he committed suicide, the insurance company would still have to pay his death benefit."

"Good," Katharine said, beaming.

"Not so fast," Charlie said. "Georgia statute provides that in the case of a questionable death—such as we have here—what with the body never being found and all, the insurance company can delay paying death benefits for up to as much as four years after the time of that death," Charlie said.

"You never told me that before," Mary Bliss cried.

"I didn't know for sure," Charlie said. "Had to get my law clerk to look it up."

"Four years," Mary Bliss said softly. "I'll be living on the streets by then."

"You might be living in the jailhouse," Charlie said, glancing from Mary Bliss to his wife. "Unless the two of you come clean and tell me exactly what kind of stunt you're trying to pull."

"That heart attack must have stopped the blood flow to your brain," Katharine said. "I don't know what you're talking about."

"I'm talking about the two of you being in cahoots to stage Parker's death," Charlie said calmly. "And don't bother denying it, Katharine. Your bank records are still mailed to me, remember? I saw all the cash withdrawals you made at the automatic teller in Cozumel. And I checked the airline records too. You were there, all right, and you were in it up to your eyeballs."

"I might have taken a trip to Cozumel," Katharine said. "But that doesn't prove anything."

"I've got some of it figured out," Charlie said. "But the one thing that scares me to death is that boat accident. I can't figure out how you pulled it off. I can't figure out how you got an authentic death certificate when Parker McGowan was nowhere near Cozumel that weekend."

51

Mary Bliss felt a muscle in her jaw twitch. One eyelid fluttered up and down like a wounded butterfly.

"You're good, Mary Bliss," Charlie said. "You had me completely snowed. I bought the whole thing, hook, line, and sinker. Until the day before I had my heart attack."

"And just what happened the day before your heart attack to make you think Mary Bliss is a liar?" Katharine demanded.

"Matt Hayslip came to see me," Charlie said.

"What does Matt Hayslip know about anything?" Mary Bliss said, her voice nearly a whisper.

"You'll have to ask him what all he knows," Charlie said. "The day he came to see me, he showed me a photograph. A grainy black-and-white photograph. I reckon it was taken off one of those closed-circuit cameras they have at all the banks now. The quality was poor, but I could tell right off that it was Parker McGowan."

"Where?" Mary Bliss asked. "Where was it supposedly taken?"

"Some bank in Columbus, Georgia," Charlie said. "And it had a time and date stamp across the bottom. It was taken at two P.M. the day you say Parker checked into the Casa Blanca hotel in Cozumel, Mexico."

"That's not possible," Mary Bliss said. Her throat felt dry. "Parker was with me. In Cozumel."

Charlie shrugged. "Okay. Whatever you say. I'm too tired to argue with you right now. I think I better do as my bride suggested, and go down to my dungeon and take a nap. But you think about this. All right? Because I've got a feeling things are gonna start getting pretty hairy with Quiana Reese and that insurance company."

Mary Bliss stared at him.

"I don't know the whole story, obviously," Charlie said. "But it looks to me like Parker handed you a raw deal. I'd like to help you if I can, Mary Bliss, but I won't lie for you. And I won't get disbarred for you, and I definitely won't go to jail for you. Understand?"

Mary Bliss blinked, then nodded. "I understand."

"Good," Charlie said. He patted Katharine on the ass again. "Sorry, darlin', but that romantic interlude you been pining for is gonna have to wait until I've had my beauty rest."

Katharine pushed his hand away. "Come on, Mr. Big Talk. You better just crash in the den. I don't want you climbing up or down any more stairs today."

Mary Bliss planted a kiss on Charlie's forehead. "Feel better. And thanks. For everything. I'll call you later, Kate," she added.

"Think about what I said," Charlie repeated.

Mary Bliss drove home slowly. She was visualizing the photo of Parker that Charlie said he'd seen. Parker. In a bank in Columbus, Georgia. Was he wearing one of those L.L. Bean golf shirts he'd ordered? And dark glasses? Had he looked directly at the camera? She wondered if he'd been frowning or smiling. Come to think of it, Parker rarely smiled when he had his picture taken. Even in their wedding photos, he'd looked serious; that little wrinkle between his eyebrows creased, eyes looking somewhere just beyond the camera lens.

It was one of the things Mary Bliss had loved best about Parker—that he took life so seriously. Her own daddy had been a clown, the life of the party, always a joke on his lips, until the day he'd suddenly wandered away to a party she and her mama had not been invited to.

Her daddy loved riddles and limericks and silly songs. Parker liked things he could touch or see. Facts and figures. Bank balances.

A bank in Columbus, Georgia. Mary Bliss didn't know a soul in Columbus. She'd never even been to Columbus. But obviously Parker had been there. And Matt Hayslip had followed him there.

Why? Suddenly she wanted desperately to know how Matt Hayslip had gotten hold of that photo. She wanted to know a lot more about Matt Hayslip and his interest in the McGowan family. And she wanted to know right now.

She pulled her car into her own driveway, but instead of getting out, she rummaged around in her wallet. He'd given her his business card the first time he'd come sniffing around over here. She'd shoved it in her wallet, where she kept odd receipts and cents-off coupons she knew she'd probably never use.

Here it was. Matthew Hayslip. Southern Utilities Corp. There was a phone number. Should she call it? Or should she follow his example, go snooping around at *his* house? He'd told her he lived in the Oaks. She could just look up the exact street number in the Fair Oaks city directory. Then she frowned. The Oaks was gated. With a security booth and a uniformed guard who had to call ahead and get the home owner's approval before he'd let any visitors through those hallowed gates. It was the thing that set the newest, chicest part of Fair Oaks apart. In the rest of the town, if you wanted to go see somebody, you simply walked over and went around to the back door. You knocked if it was somebody new, otherwise you'd just poke your head in and holler, "Hey! Anybody home?"

She could just drive in to downtown Atlanta, park in a pay lot, ride the elevator up in that big gray glass Southern Utilities skyscraper, walk right in, and demand some answers from Matthew Hayslip.

But not like this. She was still dressed in cutoffs and a T-shirt. She hadn't showered yet, she probably smelled like a reject from a poultry-plucking plant. It was Friday afternoon. By the time she could shower, change, and drive downtown, chances were good that he'd already have clocked out for the day.

Later, she promised herself. She would clean herself up, do a little checking of her own. And once she had the goods on Matthew Hayslip, she'd call him at home. Invite herself over. Get some answers.

She towel-dried her hair and dialed the Fair Oaks Country Club's pro shop. The phone rang several times. "Hiya," a British-accented voice said. "Andrew here."

Andrew Ames was South African, with a deep cara-mel tan, sun-bleached hair, and amazingly knobby knees. He'd been the pro at Fair Oaks Country Club for three years. Mary Bliss had heard rumors that his popularity with the tennis community had nothing to do with tennis and everything to do with his bedside manner. And she knew, from firsthand experience, that he was a dedicated gossip.

"Andrew," she said. "It's Mary Bliss McGowan."

"Oh, Miz McGowan," he said, his voice saddened. "So sorry about Parker. Meant to drop you a card, but it's our busy season, you know?"

"Thank you for your kind thoughts," Mary Bliss said. "You were one of Parker's favorite people. He gave you all the credit for his ability to play the net."

"Well," Andrew said. "We worked on that a lot. That husband of yours was quite a perfectionist."

"How well I know," Mary Bliss said, chuckling ruefully. "Listen, I've had a phone call from a fellow who was Parker's doubles partner. He was asking a lot of questions about Parker, and it's made me a little nervous. You know, living alone like I am now."

"Yeah, sure," Andrew said. "I'm trying to think who you'd be talking about."

"Matt Hayslip," she said. "I'd never met him until after Parker's accident. And suddenly, he seems to be turning up everywhere I look."

"Hayslip?" Andrew said. "Matthew Hayslip, did you say?"

"Yes. He told me he was Parker's doubles partner. And since I didn't keep up with Parker's tennis buddies, I didn't really know him."

"Just a minute," Andrew said. "That name sounds familiar, but I don't know why. I know he's not one of the regular guys, always hanging around here looking for a game."

Mary Bliss was doodling on a legal pad she kept by the phone. "Not a regular!" she wrote.

"He told me he was Parker's regular doubles partner," Mary Bliss said. "That they were signed up to play in some tournament at the club."

"Nooo," Andrew said, drawing it out. "Parker played a lot with Owen Claire, but Owen tore his ACL around Easter and he's not up to snuff for tennis yet. Come to think of it, I hadn't seen Parker on the courts that much in the spring. And he wasn't signed up for our member-guest tourney either."

"He was traveling a good bit," Mary Bliss said. How stupid. She hadn't seen Parker pick up a racket for months before he disappeared. Maybe not since last fall. "So you don't know Matt Hayslip? And you don't think he played with Parker?"

"Now, I couldn't swear to it," Andrew said. "Wouldn't want to take an oath or anything. But no, this fella isn't a regular down here."

"Thanks," Mary Bliss said.

"Say," Andrew said. "You used to play, didn't you? Why don't you come round and let me give you a lesson someday? Gratis, of course. We've got quite a good ladies' program going. They play Wednesday mornings. Bloody Wednesdays, they call it, because, of course, Bloody Marys are the refreshment of choice."

"I'm pretty busy right now," Mary Bliss said. She cringed at the thought of becoming a number in Andrew Ames's black book.

She hung up the phone and scrawled another note. "Not a tennis player! Didn't play with Parker!"

Matt Hayslip lived on Live Oak Circle, according to the city directory. She dialed the number, got his answering machine.

"Hi, Matt," she said, trying to sound all warm and friendly. "This is Mary Bliss McGowan here. I wonder if you could call me. I've been rethinking your offer of dinner."

She hung up the phone and headed for the shower, to get ready to go into battle.

MARY KAY ANDREWS

52

Matt Hayslip was practically panting when he called back thirty minutes later. "Dinner? Tonight? Yeah. That would be great. What time should I pick you up?"

"Why don't I come over there and cook for you?" Mary Bliss asked, trying to sound seductive. It had been a long time, so she wasn't sure it was working. "With Parker gone, and Erin in and out so much, it seems like I never get to cook anymore. And I really miss that."

"Damn. You sure you wanna stand over a hot stove and cook? There's a great new Italian place over in Brookwood that we could try. Do you like French? Ever been to Babette's Café? I used to work with the owner's husband. It's a super little place over on Highland," he said.

"I'll cook," Mary Bliss said firmly. "You can clean up. How does that sound?"

"Like the best offer I've had all year. Do I need to run out to the store? There's not much in the house, to tell you the truth. Unless you like stale English muffins and good red wine."

"I'll bring everything," Mary Bliss said. "Just tell me how to get there."

He gave her directions she didn't really need. "I'll call up to the security gate and leave your name," he said. "They'll let you right in."

"See you at eight," Mary Bliss cooed. Or she meant for it to sound like a coo.

She took a big wicker basket and went out to the garden. Her tomato plants were nearly bent double with the weight of all the ripe fruit. She picked half a dozen of the biggest, ripest tomatoes, then added some small bell peppers and a fistful of basil leaves.

Back in the kitchen, Mary Bliss peeled the tomatoes and chopped them roughly into a colander set over a plate. She sprinkled kosher salt over the tomatoes and added half a dozen grinds of black pepper, then chopped the basil and added it to the tomatoes, along with some finely chopped garlic. This was her favorite summertime pasta sauce, a quick, uncooked tomato sauce that depended upon dead ripe tomatoes and the freshest basil, which meant she usually only made it from July through September.

She had a box of good imported fettucine in the pantry, and plenty of salad makings in the refrigerator. There wouldn't be time to make a dessert, but she could stop at La Piccolina on the way to the Oaks and pick up a loaf of fresh peasant bread, and perhaps some biscotti or, if she were in luck, some cannoli.

Just before eight, she changed into what she thought of as her Mata Hari outfit: slim black capri pants and a stretchy black wraparound top that left her shoulders mostly bare. She was searching for the right bottle of perfume on her dressing table when she found a tiny white cardboard box she hadn't remembered seeing before. She lifted off the top. Inside, nestled on a bed of white cotton, was a pair of silver hoop earrings. A tiny silver heart with a jagged rip through the middle dangled from each hoop. A scrap of paper fluttered from the box when she lifted the earrings out of the cotton.

She picked it up. "Remember Cozumel!" was written in familiar handwriting. Katharine's.

"As if I could forget," she muttered, fitting the earring post to her earlobe.

She was halfway down the stairs when she remembered. The chicken salad! She had a hundred pounds of poached, shredded chicken that needed to be mixed with the salad dressing in time to chill overnight. Gerran Thomas would be here at nine tomorrow morning to pick it all up.

"God," she groaned. The chicken would just have to wait. Right now she had a more important mission.

She called Katharine's before she left the house.

Katharine picked it up on the first ring.

"Hey, Mary Bliss," she said softly. "I was hoping you'd call before it got too late."

"You knew it was me?" Mary Bliss asked.

"I've got caller ID," Katharine said quickly. "If that BW calls here, I wanna know it before Charlie beats me to it."

"Modern technology," Mary Bliss said. "I wish I'd had some of that before Parker took off. Listen, I can't talk right now. I'm going over to Matt Hayslip's house."

"A date?" Katharine squealed. "That's wonderful, M. B. But aren't you scared?"

"It's not a date. At least, not as far as I'm concerned," Mary Bliss said. "I'm going over there to find out what he knows about Parker, and why. And also, to cook dinner."

"So it is a date," Katharine insisted.

"It's a mission," Mary Bliss corrected her. "But when I get done over there, I need to stop by your house and add the dressing to all that chicken salad in your fridge. So leave the back door unlocked, will you? I won't disturb you, I'll just slip in and out, and you won't even know I've been there."

"Don't you dare," Katharine said. "I want a blow-by-blow description of your date. All the gory details."

"It's not a date," Mary Bliss repeated. "But leave the light on, okay?"

When she got to the faux-Tudor security hut at the Oaks, she leaned out the window to speak to the guard, who was ensconced in air-conditioned comfort.

He slid a window open.

"Mary Bliss McGowan. To see Matt Hayslip."

He checked a clipboard, nodded, and opened the elaborate wrought-iron gates.

Mary Bliss drove slowly down White Oak Boulevard, which was the main drag for the Oaks. Although the subdivision had been completed nearly three years ago, she'd never been inside.

Nice, she thought. The homes were large, all pseudo Tudor or pseudo Craftsman, of earth-colored stucco, river rock, and dark beams, and they were large, much larger than Mary Bliss's house.

She found Live Oak Drive with no problem, and 325, Matt's address, which was the third street on the right. This one was pseudo Craftsman, a deep caramel color, with dark-green trim and a two-car garage where a real Craftsman house would have had a porte cochere.

Mary Bliss gathered her groceries and her courage and rang the doorbell. Matt opened the door even before her hand had moved from the ringer.

His hair was damp, and he had a towel draped over the shoulders of his plain white T-shirt. His wash-worn blue jeans were fastened, but his hands were fumbling with the belt.

"You caught me," he said, grinning and taking the grocery sack from her. "After you called, I was about to jump in the shower, but then I had a business call and couldn't get the guy off the phone."

"I'm sorry," she said, feeling shy and nervous. He wasn't even fully dressed. She found herself staring at the unfastened belt, at the way his shoulder muscles strained against the white cotton T-shirt, at his tanned, bare feet.

"I haven't even had a chance to shave," he said, ushering her into the foyer, where moving boxes were stacked chest-high.

"Oh, don't go to any bother on my account," she said lightly, inhaling the scent of Irish Spring soap. The faint stubble on his chin shone pale gray against his tan.

His eyes crinkled. "I intend to go to a lot of bother on your account. And it's entirely my pleasure."

She felt herself blush. This was going too fast. She gestured to the boxes.

"Going somewhere?"

"Nope. Just never quite got the time to unpack when I moved in," he said. "Let's go in the kitchen. At least most of the stuff there is unpacked."

She glanced through open doorways at a living room and a dining room as she followed Hayslip to the back of the house. The living room had a black leather sofa and a big-screen television, the dining room had more packing crates.

The kitchen, as promised, seemed to be where Matt had set up housekeeping—or at least his version of it.

The builders had put in every high-end convenience: cherry cabinets, black granite countertops, stainless-steel appliances, including a commercial range, and a high-beamed ceiling. There was an eating area too—furnished with a battered card table and two metal folding chairs.

But Matt had set the table with care: straw placemats, thick white china, and cut-glass wine goblets.

"Very nice," Mary Bliss said, glancing around.

"You mean, for a bachelor," he said, as he set the grocery bag down on the countertop.

"Well . . . ," she said, letting it trail off. "It's quite a kitchen. Do you cook?"

"I'm hell with the microwave, and I do wonders with a George Foreman grill," he said, starting to unload the bag.

"So," she said, leaning against one of the counters. "Have you always been a bachelor?"

"I was married for nine years," he said. "But it didn't take. We split up a few years ago. It was friendly enough. She went her way, I went mine. No regrets."

"A friendly divorce?" she said, raising a questioning eyebrow. "I never heard of such a thing."

He shrugged. "She had a good job, her own friends, her own interests. We got married when we were both in our mid-thirties. Never wanted kids. I guess that makes it easier, not having kids."

"Kids and money. That's what my friends fight over when it's time for a divorce," Mary Bliss observed. "Doesn't look like you came out of the divorce in bad shape, finance-wise."

"I did all right," he said. "What's for supper?"

"Pasta," she said. "And I hope you're hungry."

"Always," he said.

She set him to work making the salad while she boiled water for the pasta. He poured the wine. She took a sip and pronounced it drinkable.

They fell into an easy rhythm, chatting while she explained the premise of an uncooked pasta sauce, and he explained his theory of choosing wine.

"There's this great store, Lee's Candler Park Market," he said. "I got to know the owner years ago when I was a cop. I worked an armed robbery there. The place looks like a glorified convenience store, but you can't let that fool you. The owner really knows good wine. I just go in there, tell him the occasion and what I want to spend, and he picks it out. He's never let me down yet."

"What did you want to spend tonight?" Mary Bliss heard herself asking him. How awful! A lady did not ask prices.

"Mmm. Forty bucks," Matt said. "Nice, but not pretentious." He grinned again. "Like me."

"And what did you tell him the occasion was?" she asked. Again, horrifying, ending a sentence with a predicate?

Matt poured more wine into her glass, which was still a quarter full. "I just said I was having dinner with a beautiful woman. And that I thought the evening had the potential for some interesting developments."

She sipped the wine slowly. It was, as promised, very, very nice. But really, he was standing entirely too close. And he was still only half dressed. And barefoot. She found herself wanting to comb his still-damp hair.

Suddenly, a loud hissing filled the room. She whirled around. The pasta was boiling over, sending cascades of water sheeting over the sides of the pot and all over the top of the restaurant range.

"It's ruined," Mary Bliss said, poking at the limp fettucine with a wooden spoon.

"Why?" Matt wanted to know. "It looks all right to me. It's not burned. It looks like all the spaghetti my mom ever made."

"This is not your mama's spaghetti," she informed him. "It's imported fettucine. It's supposed to be al dente." She held up one of the noodles, which broke in half. "This is way overcooked. And I used the whole box." She sighed. "I don't suppose you have any fettucine, do you?"

He opened a cupboard door and waved at the contents. "You got your peanut butter, your canned sardines, your canned tomato soup, your canned ravioli, your canned tuna, your minute rice, and your Kraft original mac 'n cheese. The Kraft dinner was buy one, get one free.

"And that's it," he said. "I went to the store right after I moved in, and this is pretty much what I've got."

"No pasta?" she asked, moving cans and boxes around.

"Nope."

She picked up the boxes of Kraft dinner and ripped off the tops.

"You like Kraft dinner too?" he asked. "My kind of girl!"

"Not that powdered orange cheese stuff," she said, tossing the sauce packages in the trash. "I'm just gonna cook the noodles. It's the best I can do."

This time, she had Matt set the timer on his digital watch. They ate their salads while the pasta cooked, and when exactly eight minutes was up, she drained the noodles and plated them up, adding a large dollop of the tomato sauce and a few grates from the hunk of Parmesan cheese she'd brought along.

"Let's eat," Matt said. He poured more wine, then waited for her to sip again.

"At least the wine's good," she said.

He tasted a forkful of the pasta. "This is even better," he said, smacking his lips in exaggeration. "Even if you did forget to cook the sauce."

She made a wry face and tasted. "You're right," she said, nodding in agreement. "Kraft dinner's not all that bad, if you leave out the Kraft part."

"And what's this green stuff?" he asked, poking at a bit of herb clinging to his fork. "I like it. Sort of fresh-tasting."

"Basil," she said. "I grow it in my garden. I grew the tomatoes too." She liked watching him eat. He was clearly a man of big appetites. Not so scary really, if you could just overlook the fact that he was some kind of cop with enough evidence to possibly put her in jail for the rest of her natural life.

"Where'd you learn to cook like this?" he asked, really shoveling into the noodles and sauce now.

"Here and there," she said, deliberately noncommittal. "My mom was a good ol' southern cook, and I've just picked up a lot of recipes and things over the years. What about you?" she asked. "You mentioned being a cop. I guess that was pretty exciting work."

"Some days exciting, some days boring," Matt said. "Can I have some more of that grated cheese stuff?"

She got up and shaved more Parmesan onto his plate.

"So, were you with the Atlanta Police Department?" she asked.

"In the beginning," he said. "I went in right after I got out of the Marines."

"But you said you retired from the GBI," she said.

"Yeah. I did." He took another piece of bread and wiped the rim of his plate clean with it.

"What did you do with the GBI?" Mary Bliss asked.

"Fieldwork."

"Cotton fields or cornfields?" she asked.

He looked up, quizzical.

"That was supposed to be a joke," she said. "What exactly is fieldwork?"

"You know, I was out in the field. I was down on the coast for a few years, working on a drug task force. Then I got transferred back to Atlanta. Working cases. Detective stuff, mostly. Public corruption, some white-collar stuff. The last five years, after my promotion, I did mostly administrative work. Trust me, you wouldn't be interested."

She propped her chin on her clenched fist. "Try me. I'm interested in lots of stuff."

"Well, I wrote a grant proposal to get federal funding for enhanced spectrometer microscopes for the state crime lab. That took about a year. And then I disseminated guidelines for uniform firearm purchases for the entire agency. Eighteen months. Oh yeah. During that same time, I went back to school. Took me five years, but I got my master's in criminal justice."

"Fascinating," Mary Bliss said. "Why'd you really get divorced?"

He sighed. "My wife didn't like being married to a cop."

"Why'd she marry one?"

"I think she thought it was just a phase I was going through. Like when I let my sideburns grow out. After

I started work on my master's, she thought I'd quit the agency and get a 'real' job."

"She didn't consider being a GBI agent a real job?"

"Not her kind of real job. See, she was a mortgage broker. She hung out all day with people who wore suits and played racquetball and drank Scotch. I worked with people who wore shoulder holsters and drank beer and went bowling."

"You don't like Scotch?" Mary Bliss asked.

"Generally speaking, I don't even like people who like Scotch," Matt said.

"Parker drank Scotch," Mary Bliss said. It just sort of slipped out.

"See what I mean?" he said.

"Where is she now?"

"Who?"

"Your ex-wife. You said you were friends. Is she still in Atlanta?"

"I said the divorce was friendly. She's still around, I guess, but I've lost track. Why are you asking all these questions about my ex-wife?" He leaned across the table and looked directly into her eyes.

She looked down at her plate. "You've been asking a lot of questions about my late husband, I just thought it was polite to ask about your wife."

"Ex. So you're just being polite. That's all?"

She stood up abruptly and took her plate and scraped it into the sink, then did the same thing with his plate. She started running water into the sink.

He reached around her and turned off the faucet. "Come on. I'll get these later. Let's go sit in the living room."

She followed him down the hall to the living room, dreading it all the way, walking as slowly as she could. Twice he turned around to see what was taking her so long. "You feeling all right?" he asked.

"A little tired," Mary Bliss said. "Maybe I should make an early night of it."

His face fell. "You're not leaving already? You just got here."

"I guess I could stay a little while."

She got uneasy again when she got a closer look at the living room. That leather sofa she'd glimpsed was really only a loveseat. And there was no place else to sit in the room.

Matt gestured toward the sofa. "Be right back," he said. "I forgot our wine."

She winced. She'd already had two glasses, and she was beginning to feel the way she always felt when she drank red wine. Sort of melty around the edges.

Mary Bliss avoided the sofa. Instead she walked around the room, looking at the only other furnishings besides the entertainment center and the coffee table: stacks of record albums leaning against the walls. There were hundreds of them. She rifled through the stacks. The Doors. Jefferson Airplane. The Kinks. The Allman Brothers. Blind Faith. Cream. Jethro Tull. She was in a living rock-and-roll museum.

She was reading the liner notes on the Allman Brothers' *Eat a Peach* album when he walked back in with a newly opened bottle of wine.

"One more glass, then I really need to go home," she said, reluctantly accepting the glass he offered her.

"You like redneck rock?" he asked, taking the album from her and slipping the record out.

"I guess," she said. "I wasn't much of a record buyer, but I used to listen to the radio."

"Here in Atlanta?" he asked. "I bet you listened to Quixie, huh?"

"Actually, I grew up in Alabama," Mary Bliss said. "I don't even remember what station we listened to."

He opened the door of the entertainment center and put the album on the turntable. Suddenly the room was flooded with "In Memory of Elizabeth Reed."

Matt pulled her over to the sofa, sat close beside her, with his arm companionably over her shoulders. She closed her eyes, put her head back, and listened.

"That's a funny song," she said when it was over. "Not sad really, but wistful, sort of. And yet, I always think of the Allman Brothers as sort of a good-times boogie band."

"You don't really know the Allman Brothers," Matt said. "They wrote some soul-scorching blues. Like 'Tied to the Whipping Post.'"

"I guess," Mary Bliss said. "Anyway, who was Elizabeth Reed?"

"According to what I heard, it was a name on a headstone in Rose Hill Cemetery down in Macon," Matt said. "Gregg told me he and the brothers were sitting around the cemetery, smoking dope and drinking liquor, and the name sort of intrigued them."

"You know Gregg Allman?"

"Met him a couple times. I worked security at their first concert in Atlanta, back in sixty-nine," Matt said. "It was this free music festival, held in Piedmont Park."

Mary Bliss gave him a long look. "You don't strike me as the kind of person who'd like this kind of music."

"Why not?" he asked.

"I guess I associate rock and roll with rebellion. Hippies, that kind of thing."

"I wasn't always a geezer," Matt said, laughing. "And maybe I still have a little of the rebel in me. Don't you?"

She shook her head vigorously. "Afraid not. I've always been the good little girl from lower Alabama."

He traced her hairline with his finger, slowly. "I don't buy that."

"It's true," Mary Bliss said. She felt herself blushing.

Matt drew her closer. His lips brushed against her cheek in the lightest of kisses.

"You're not nice at all," he said, and the airlike kisses were inching their way toward her lips.

"Yes, I am," she said feebly. But now she was turning toward him, and his kisses were so sweet, so warm. And he was pulling her closer, so their bodies were touching in all the right places. His hands were tight on her back, pressing her toward him. And then he was kissing her neck, and her throat. "Not nice," he muttered. "But delicious. Very delicious."

This wasn't fair. It wasn't right. It wasn't the plan. She hadn't come over here to be seduced. To be touched and kissed like this . . . like that. She shuddered as the tip of his tongue flicked against her collarbone, and then her breast, which seemed to be working its way out of her top of its own accord. But she couldn't pull away. Wouldn't. His mouth nipped and teased, and his hands were busy, and she felt things she'd forgotten feeling before.

"A nice girl wouldn't wear a top that comes untied like this," Matt said, demonstrating his prowess, cupping his hand under a breast. His beard scratched a little. She felt friction. And heat. She shuddered again. Maybe he was right. Maybe there was a smidge of rebel beaten down inside her. Maybe Parker's leaving had unlocked this side of her. Or maybe Matt Hayslip had stirred her in a whole new way. Maybe she really was a wild thing, a wicked, wanton woman who took pleasure whenever and wherever she wanted it. God, she hoped so!

Parker. An image flashed in her mind. Parker, in that grainy black-and-white bank photo. She'd begun to believe her own lie. That he was dead, drowned down in Mexico. Out of her life. But he wasn't dead. And he definitely wasn't out of her life. Not just yet.

"No," she whispered, pushing Matt away. She reached for her top, wrapped it awkwardly around her shoulders. "I can't. This isn't right."

He groaned. "I'm too old to be playing games like this."

"I'm sorry," she said, trying to work her arms into the sleeves, wrapping the ends around her midriff. "I never should have come over here. I never should have let things go this far."

He sat back and threw both arms over the sofa back, watching her intently.

"Why did you come over here tonight, if you didn't want this to happen?"

"I don't know," Mary Bliss said. She couldn't make the damn top wrap right. It was falling off her shoulders now. "Maybe I was lonely."

"You've been lonely before," Matt said, his voice even. "Tell me the truth now. Why did you invite yourself over here tonight if you didn't intend to go to bed with me?"

She blushed to the roots of her hair. "I can't figure you out."

He laughed. "I could say the same thing about you. Come on, now, be straight. What's this come-hither act all about?"

She felt a sudden flash of anger and embarrassment. "You tell me," Mary Bliss said, leaning forward, staring into those dark gray eyes of his. "You come around my house on false pretenses, asking all kinds of questions. You come to my husband's memorial service, show up at my house. Act like you want to be my friend."

"I do want to be your friend," Matt said, caressing her face. "More than a friend, actually. I'm nuts about you, Mary Bliss McGowan."

"You're a damn liar!" Mary Bliss cried, pushing his hand away. "You never played tennis with Parker. I checked. I don't think you even knew Parker. And

I know you told Charlie Weidman that Parker isn't
dead. You showed him what you said was a picture of
Parker, taken in Columbus, Georgia. You've been sniffing around here for weeks on totally false pretenses. I
want to know who you really are and what you really
want."

She jumped up and ran into the dining room. She
attacked the first packing crate she saw, ripping it open.
"I don't think you live in this house at all. This is all
just a sham. This house isn't real. I don't believe you
ever met Gregg Allman. You aren't real, damn you."

He just sat there, she could see him through the
arched doorway, sitting on that loveseat, looking dazed
and angry.

The box was full of file folders. She grabbed one,
held it up for him to see. "Am I in here? Is this what
you do? Keep files on people?"

"You're not in that box," he said calmly. "And if
you'll come in here and stop acting like a maniac, I'll
tell you what you want to know. What you came over
here to find out."

"You will?"

She dropped the file.

He nodded. "What about you? Are you capable of
telling the truth?"

53

"You first," she said, perching on the edge of the loveseat, as far away from him as she could get and still be seated in the same room.

He sipped his wine. "What do you want to know?"

"Is your name really Matt Hayslip?"

He nodded.

"And you really live here?"

He nodded again.

"But you don't work for Southern Utilities." She made it a statement.

"Not really," he agreed. "I borrowed that sedan from a buddy who does security work for them. I made the business cards on my PC."

"What do you really do?" she asked. "Why are you so interested in us? In Parker?"

"I'm a private investigator, I guess you'd say. I really did retire from the GBI a couple years ago. Towards the end of my career there, I sort of developed a specialty. White-collar crime. Financial fraud. I worked some cases that turned out well. Put some bad guys in prison. Met some important people. After I took early retirement, I decided that was the kind of work I'd pursue. Nice, clean, white-collar crime. No homicides, no maggots, no gunplay. But it wasn't all that easy. I'm not a CPA, not a forensic accountant. I couldn't get any assignments."

He glanced at her to see if she was paying proper attention.

She gave him a withering look. "Poor you."

"Until this May," he said. "I got a call from a guy who knew a guy who knew me. My first big client."

"Whoopee," she said.

"My client runs a company that provides human-resource services to firms that don't want to handle that themselves. He does all the payroll work, taxes, benefits, all of it. He had billings of fourteen million dollars last year. He was thinking of going national, franchising."

"I take it back," Mary Bliss said. "This isn't that fascinating."

"I'm getting there," Matt said. "A year ago, my client, Jerry, hired this brilliant software consultant. His name was Parker McGowan."

Mary Bliss's eyes widened.

"Parker was going to supply him with new software that would streamline all the billing functions," Matt said. "He had impeccable credentials, referrals out the ying-yang, all of it. And things were going gangbusters."

"Until," Mary Bliss said.

"Until Parker McGowan disappeared. Into thin air."

"He drowned. In a boating accident in Mexico," Mary Bliss said.

Matt put his fingers to her lips. "Shh. It's not your turn yet.

"Parker disappeared. But even before he disappeared, Jerry started having some doubts. Revenues weren't what they should be. Something was off. Jerry's a bright guy. He has good instincts. He took a closer look at his software, and he found out Parker's little secret."

Mary Bliss raised one eyebrow.

"Ever hear of a practice called graveyarding?" Matt asked.

"No."

"Parker knew all about it, which kind of surprised me," Matt said. "It's been around a long time. I used to do it myself, back when I was a rookie patrolman. Here's how it works. Say the lieutenant gives you a quota—write six traffic tickets today, or don't come back. It's a slow day. You maybe only catch two or three lawbreakers. So you take a drive over to the nearest cemetery. Find a recent headstone. Copy down the name and date of birth and death. Take a run over to the library, look up the name in the phone book or a recent city directory. Write up a ticket for the dead guy, take it back to the lieutenant. Everybody's happy."

"Parker was never a cop," Mary Bliss said.

"No," Matt agreed. "But he was a criminal. And he was real good at graveyarding. Here's what he did. For every one of Jerry's clients, Parker set up two or three graveyard employees. He even gave 'em fake social security numbers, and mailing addresses, all of them at post office boxes. So every pay period, those ghost employees were getting paid, and their paychecks were being sent out—to post office boxes rented by your husband."

"I don't believe it," Mary Bliss said. "Parker never so much as ran a red light. He wasn't capable of something like that."

"Really?" Matt looked amused. "He was capable of stealing your marital assets, capable of refinancing your house and potentially leaving you and his daughter homeless, but he wasn't capable of something like that?"

Mary Bliss pressed her lips together tightly. "He was my husband. He's dead. I can't dwell on the mistakes he might have made."

"You better start dwelling on them," Matt said, leaning forward until his face was only inches away from hers. "Because, lady, you're making some big mistakes of your own."

Mary Bliss stood up and paced around the room. "I don't know what you're talking about."

He stood up himself, strode out of the room, and came back a minute later, holding out a piece of paper.

She took it and looked at it. It was a picture of Parker. Grainy and black-and-white, as Charlie had described it. This one appeared to be taken outside. Parker stared straight into the camera, his dark glasses flipped up. He wore a sleeveless white T-shirt, and a chain with a medallion on it. She'd never seen Parker wearing any jewelry other than his wedding ring and a wristwatch. The front of a car was barely visible over his right shoulder. There was a time and date stamp on the bottom of the photo, indicating it had been taken the day Parker should have died in Cozumel, Mexico.

"Where did you get this?" she whispered, handing the photograph back.

"It was taken at an ATM machine in Macon," Matt said. "The one I showed Charlie was taken in Columbus, the day before. Parker McGowan. In the flesh. Looks pretty lively to me."

"It's somebody else," Mary Bliss said. "It has to be."

"It's him," Matt said flatly. "He had accounts in banks all over the state. We've found three so far, all in the names of those ghost employees he created. There are more too. We just haven't tracked 'em all down yet. All together, we figure he ripped off Jerry and his clients to the tune of about four hundred thousand dollars."

"He, he couldn't," Mary Bliss said, faltering.

"He did," Matt said. "He's a thief. And I aim to catch him."

She shook her head. "I still don't understand. You're not with the police? What do you want from me?"

"I'm not a cop," Matt repeated. "My client doesn't want the police involved. Not yet. He's shut down the graveyarding operation, notified his clients that he was defrauded, and has made restitution. He wants what I want. Parker McGowan."

"I don't know anything," Mary Bliss said. "I had no idea. Parker never talked to me about business."

Matt grabbed her wrist. "You must know something. He must have said something, left a note, some records, something."

She yanked her hand away. "Leave me alone. I told you. I don't know anything. Parker's dead. I'm sorry he stole from your client. He stole from me too. I don't know what else to tell you."

"Let me help you," Matt said. "Drop this insurance claim. Trust me. If I figured out it's bogus, the insurance people will too. My God, this is a felony theft, Mary Bliss. You could do real jail time. Is that what you want? Parker's gone, you'll be in prison. What will happen to your daughter then?"

She felt tears rising in her eyes, but she blinked them back. She was tired of crying, tired of feeling helpless, of being trapped.

"Trust me," Matt was saying. "Let me help you. Tell me the truth. I'm gonna find Parker, and when I do, we'll make him pay. For deserting you, and Erin. For lying and stealing. He'll pay for all of it."

She was so tempted. Let somebody else take care of things. She wanted to go work in her garden. Paint her kitchen, read a book. She wanted to be taken care of.

What had her mama told her when they'd gone down to Florida to bury her daddy? Nina had held her hand tightly all through that brief service but never shed a tear. The preacher who preached her daddy's funeral gave them a ride back to the bus station. He acted like he liked Mama, wanted to give her money for dinner.

A love offering, he'd called it. "Let me know if I can help," he'd said before letting them out at the station.

Nina had just nodded, her face expressionless. "The Lord helps them who help themselves," she'd told that pastor. Her mama watched the car drive away. "We'll do for ourselves now," she'd told Mary Bliss. "Don't never depend on somebody else to take care of you, sugar. Trust in the Lord, and then you just take care of yourself, and things will work out fine."

"You want to help me?" Mary Bliss asked Matt. "Leave me alone. You say you care about me. If you do, you'll tell your client what I already told you. Parker is dead."

"He knows Parker's not dead," Matt said, impatient now. "He's seen the pictures, seen the banking records. Parker is out there, somewhere, living the high life. You saw that picture. He's on permanent vacation. While you're pawning your family silver and hiding from bill collectors. He's laughing at us. Laughing at you. Because he fooled everybody. The liar."

"Who's the liar?" Mary Bliss asked, whirling around. "You know about the silver? You've been following me? For how long? Have you had my phones tapped too? All of this," she said, sweeping her hand around the room, "all of it was part of your game plan. You thought I knew something. Had something you wanted. So you went after it. You pestered me and petted me. You knew I was vulnerable. And God help me, I was. Another five minutes here and I would have been naked. I would have done anything you wanted, just to have somebody hold me and touch me."

"That's not what this was about," Matt said. "I was telling the truth about caring for you. I started out looking for Parker, yeah. But then I met you. In that damned wet nightgown of yours. You've been lying through your teeth since the day we met, but I didn't care. I couldn't stay away. And then, tonight, you called. I knew something was up. You were the one who came over here, lady. You knew exactly what you were doing."

"No," Mary Bliss said. "I didn't understand the kind of person I was dealing with. But now I do. You're like every man I ever met. It's all a game to you. Like with Parker. You're like him, aren't you? Because you'll both do whatever it takes to win."

He didn't have an answer for that. She found her purse in the kitchen and walked straight out the front door without looking back.

54

Mary Bliss had all the trays of poached chicken lined up on Katharine's kitchen counter. The house was so quiet, all she could hear was the ticking of the kitchen clock.

She was mixing the dressing with the sour cream and honey, letting the wire whisk clang satisfyingly against the glass bowl, when the overhead lights switched on.

"Well?" Katharine hopped up on one of the bar stools at the island. "How was your fact-finding mission?"

"Awful," Mary Bliss said. "He's a private investigator. Parker ripped off his client for about four hundred thousand dollars, and now he won't stop until he catches Parker and makes him give back the money."

"Maybe he can make him give back your money while he's at it," Katharine said, dipping her pinkie in the mixing bowl. "Hmm. Good. Just like Mamie used to make. You've got this all written down?"

"It's all in my head," Mary Bliss said, tapping her forehead. "Listen. If Matt Hayslip finds Parker, I'm cooked. He can't be alive—because I already had him declared dead. Remember?"

"Oh yeah," Katharine said. "Details. Forgive me. It's a little late in the evening for me to be figuring out all this strategy of yours."

"I'm sorry," Mary Bliss said. "Go on back to bed. I'll be out of your hair just as soon as I get this chicken mixed together."

"Bed," Katharine said, making a face. "Bed's no fun. And anyway, I can't sleep."

"Why not?" Mary Bliss asked.

"The usual. Charlie. I don't know what to do with that man, I swear."

"Is he having chest pains again?" Mary Bliss asked.

"No, it's not that," Katharine said. "It's him. And the BW. And me. Us. Everything. God. Just when I think I have everything figured out, he has to go off and have a heart attack."

"Is that what this is all about?" Mary Bliss asked. "You're worried about losing him?"

"I don't know," Katharine said, twisting to and fro on the bar stool. "Everything would have been fine if I'd just let things alone. If I hadn't dragged him back here and seduced him the other night."

"He had a heart condition," Mary Bliss reminded her. "It probably would have happened sooner or later anyway. Maybe with the BW. And he would have died."

"But I was over him," Katharine said. "Really and truly. And now everything's all stirred up again. And I hate it. And now Chip's involved. And it's making me crazy."

"What does Chip think?"

Katharine sighed. "He's still a kid. He just wants Mommy and Daddy to get back together and take him to Disney World. He's completely unrealistic."

"And Charlie?"

"He's scared. He won't admit it, but he is. And I won't take him back just because he's scared. It's not a good reason to stay married. I already promised myself, I'm not going through this shit again. I can't."

"Charlie's a good guy," Mary Bliss said. "Not perfect, but neither are you. And he loves you. I know he does."

"He loved me so much he had an affair," Katharine said dully.

"He screwed up," Mary Bliss said. "What does he say about the BW anyway?"

"That it's over. He turned fifty and he was looking for a thrill. Only it turned out not to be all that thrilling. So it was all a horrible mistake."

"That should count for something," Mary Bliss urged.

"Yeah," Katharine said, twisting a strand of her hair. "The question is, how much does it count?"

"It's everything," Mary Bliss said. "A good guy, with decent intentions? Look at all the creeps and liars running around. Look at Parker. The bastard. And Matt Hayslip." She shuddered thinking about it.

"What about Matt Hayslip?" Katharine said. "He's got a thing for you, doesn't he?"

"He was just trying to get to Parker. Through me. Using me."

"He can use me anytime he wants," Katharine said. "The man is totally hot. And you know it too."

"He's repulsive," Mary Bliss said. She was pouring the dressing over the chicken, mixing in the water chestnuts and the chopped pecans.

"So. Nothing physical tonight?"

"Nothing at all," Mary Bliss said firmly. "We had dinner, I told him what I thought about him and left."

"I see," Katharine said. "I guess you were in a hurry when you left."

"I was steamed," Mary Bliss agreed.

"So steamed you didn't notice you'd put your top on inside out," Katharine said.

Mary Bliss looked down and blushed.

The doorbell rang and they both jumped, startled.

"It's one in the morning," Katharine said, wrapping the belt of her robe tighter. "Who in the hell could that be?"

"Chip?"

"He's got a key, and anyway, he's down at St. Simon's for the weekend. I better see who it is before Charlie wakes up."

The bell rang again, and Katharine started down the hall with Mary Bliss right behind her. "I'm coming," she called softly.

Katharine peered through the peephole, then jumped back. "Jesus!" she said. "I don't believe it."

The doorbell rang again. "Hey, Katharine," a man's voice called. "Lemme in. Okay?"

"Shhh!" Katharine hissed, her lips to the door. "Go away or I'll call the cops."

"Who is it?" Mary Bliss asked.

"See for yourself," Katharine said, gesturing toward the peephole.

Mary Bliss pressed her eye to the door and took a look. "Jesus," she said, her voice shaky. "You better let him in before he wakes up the whole neighborhood. Including Charlie."

Katharine opened the door a scant four inches, leaving the security chain fastened.

"What do you want?"

Dinky Davis beamed back at her. "Heya, Katharine. I mean, *buenas noches*, Señora Weidman."

55

"**W**hat do you want?" Katharine asked, leaving the chain in place.

A horn honked and Dinky glanced back over his shoulder, in the direction of the curb.

"Cab fare, to start," he said. "You know it costs sixty bucks to get a cab out here from the airport? Man, that is fucked."

"Wait here," Katharine said, closing the door in his face. She turned to Mary Bliss. "Now what?"

Mary Bliss took another look through the peephole. Dinky was dressed in a loud orange Hawaiian shirt, dirty khaki-colored shorts, and a pair of worn rubber flip-flops. He clutched a wadded-up pillowcase in his left hand.

"He's dead," Mary Bliss said. "I saw him being thrown from the boat. He's dead. He has to be."

"He's like a cockroach," Katharine muttered. She'd gotten her billfold and was extracting twenties from it. "You ever try to kill a roach? You can't do it. You hit one with a shoe, twenty minutes later it gets up and scuttles away."

She opened the door again and thrust a wad of twenties at him. "Here, take it," she said. "That's two hundred dollars. Go away and don't come back."

Dinky nodded thoughtfully. He turned and walked toward the cab. A minute later the cab rolled away. And Dinky was back at the door.

"No," Katharine said, furious. "That wasn't the deal."

Dinky looked sad. "Deal? What deal?" He pointed at his forehead, which bore a vivid scarlet scar that ran from his right eyebrow to his hairline. "Man, this wasn't in the deal either. Come on, Katharine, just let me in. I just wanna talk. Okay?" He slapped at his bare calf. "You people got some vicious mosquitoes here, you know? Come on, now, I'm getting chewed alive out here."

Katharine looked at Mary Bliss, who merely shrugged. She took the chain off the door. Dinky walked in, looked around at the marble-floored hall and the crystal chandelier. "Nice," he said, nodding his head in approval. "Where's the shitter? I been in a cab, for like, an hour."

She showed him the maid's bathroom, which was off the kitchen. When he emerged five minutes later, his hair and face were glistening with water, and he was toweling off with a wad of toilet paper.

"Just wanted to freshen up a little," he explained.

Katharine waved him into the kitchen and shut the swinging door.

"What are you doing here?" she demanded. "We settled up with you in Cozumel. You can't just show up here like this."

"I came for a visit," Dinky said. "That's all."

"How did you find me?" Katharine asked.

He smiled. One of his front teeth had a fresh chip. "I know the desk clerk at the Casa Blanca."

"I registered under a fake name," she reminded him.

"Yeah, but you used your real address. And you left a big tip. People remember a lot about big tippers. I looked in your mailbox when I got here. You got the new Victoria's Secret catalog. Addressed to Katharine Weidman."

Katharine sighed loudly. "All right. Let's get down to business. What do you want?"

Dinky seated himself on one of the bar stools. "You got any beer?"

"No," Katharine said firmly. "No beer. You can have a glass of water, and that's it."

"Water!" He looked insulted. "Man, that's not very friendly."

"We're not in a friendly mood," Mary Bliss put in. "State your business."

"Geez," he said, wounded. "I just want a new start. Is that too much to ask? After I got out of the hospital, I said to myself, 'Dinky, you need to get the hell outta Dodge. You need some new scenery.' And I thought about my friends up here in Atlanta. And I thought, what the hell? Why not?"

"The hospital?" Mary Bliss said, horrified.

"I had, like, a major concussion," Dinky said. "My head was split open. I was all fucked up."

"Don't you dare feel sorry for him," Katharine said fiercely. "That was his own fault. He was stoned, drunk, whatever. And he didn't wear a life jacket. So that's entirely his fault and not ours. We are not liable!"

"Oh, man!" Dinky winced. "I get these headaches now. I get dizzy, can't see. Pretty soon I'm pukin'. I think I feel a headache coming on."

"No puking!" Katharine said sternly. She found two aspirin, went to the refrigerator, got him a Coke. "Here. Take the aspirin. I'll call you a cab."

He looked at the white tablets. "Aspirin? You don't got any Percocet? Dilaudid? Somethin' like that?"

"Take them!" Katharine ordered. "Now. What else? Money? I'm not a rich woman, you know. This house belongs to my husband. He's a cheap bastard."

"Money?" Dinky rubbed his scar. "Is that what you think? That I'm blackmailing you?"

"Aren't you?" Mary Bliss asked.

Dinky took a swig of the Coke. "Naw, man. Blackmail, that's not cool. I just need a coupla favors. A job. A place to stay 'til I get my feet on the ground."

Mary Bliss and Katharine looked down at his feet. Simultaneously. Dinky Davis's feet were filthy, with long, curving yellow toenails.

"You can't stay here," Katharine said quickly.

"He can't stay at my place," Mary Bliss said. "What would Erin say? What would the neighbors say? Hayslip is already watching me like a hawk. And that insurance woman . . ."

"Hey, chill," Dinky said. He got up and walked around the kitchen, running his fingertips over the white marble countertops. "Man, this is a nice place. Like a mansion, right? Big old house like this, you gotta have, what? Six, seven bedrooms?"

"It's only four bedrooms," Katharine said. "There's a lot of wasted space. And my husband is here. He's recuperating from a heart attack. So you can see, it's impossible."

"Husband?" Dinky looked interested. "I thought you were divorced."

Katharine's face flushed. "We've reconciled. He's not a well man. He can't have any stress."

"No stress," Dinky agreed. "You won't even know I'm here." He walked over to the basement door. "Hey. Is this a basement? Cool. I can sleep down there."

"No," Katharine said, closing the door and locking it. "My husband's down there."

"In the basement? Damn." He looked at Katharine with newfound respect. "You're a hard woman."

"You don't know how hard," Katharine said, her eyes narrowing. "You can stay in my son's bedroom. He's away for the weekend. But he'll be back Sunday. And then you've got to go."

"Where am I gonna go?" Dinky whined. "I got no job, no money."

"We'll find you a job. But you're out of here on Sunday," Katharine said.

"Sunday," Mary Bliss repeated.

"Fine. Whatever. Where did you say my crib was at?"

"Upstairs, last door on the right," Katharine said, pointing toward the stairs. "And don't come out until I tell you to. If my husband gets a look at you it could be fatal."

Dinky picked up his pillowcase and headed up the stairs. He stopped on the top landing.

"Hey, Katharine," he called.

"Quiet!" She glared at him.

"You guys got any rolling papers? ZigZags, something like that?"

"No smoking!" she yelled, taking the stairs two at a time. "No smoking. No drugs, no drinking."

"Fuuuck," Dinky said. "Forget Sunday. I'm outta here after tomorrow."

56

There was a message on Mary Bliss's answering machine. It was from Erin, but Mary Bliss did not recognize her daughter's voice. Her child's voice should be warm, full of love, familiar as an old sweatshirt. The voice on the machine was so chilly that it made Mary Bliss shiver.

"Mom. It's me. I'm staying at Jessica's for a while. I came home and got my things. Bye."

Mary Bliss stared down at the answering machine, but really that was a lie. The answering machine had no answers. She went upstairs and crawled into Erin's bed. She buried her nose in her daughter's squishy pillow, inhaled the scent of her shampoo, laid her cheek against the cotton pillowcase worn smooth by so many washings.

She tried to think how she could fix this thing with Erin. Maybe the rip between them was too big to patch.

How had she done this? How had she allowed her husband and daughter to drift so far away? Parker had been living a secret life, all these months, becoming someone she never knew. And now Erin. Her daughter was sleeping with Josh, making decisions that could change her life forever, and Mary Bliss had been completely in the dark.

Mary Bliss rolled over. She scrunched her eyes tight. Sleep. Maybe sleep would change things.

She slept badly. Made lists of things to worry about, checked them off as the list unspooled in her mind. At seven o'clock she'd had enough.

Mary Bliss showered and dressed. She drove over to Katharine's house, cursing herself for forgetting to tell Kate she would come over early to retrieve the chicken salad. There was a key hidden near the back door. But Katharine was always forgetting her own key, retrieving the spare and forgetting to replace it.

The newspaper was still in the Weidmans' driveway. Damn. She'd been hoping Charlie, the early riser in the family, had gotten up and would have coffee brewing. She needed to talk to Charlie. Ask him about Parker, sound him out, see if he could be trusted with the details of Mary Bliss's secret.

She picked up the newspaper and walked around to the back of the house. Dew clung to her sneakers. An orange tabby cat, a stray, mewed at Katharine's back door. Katharine claimed to hate cats, yet there was always a bowl of cat food by the back door, an invitation to all the strays in Fair Oaks.

Mary Bliss scratched the cat's ears as she searched under the doormat for the key. It was there!

As she was standing up, the back door opened. Dinky Davis yawned, blinked, scratched his crotch. He was wearing a pair of faded gray boxer shorts and a pair of orange-and-black tiger-striped bedroom slippers that must have been Chip's.

"Hiya," he said, reaching for the paper. He turned and went back inside the house. Mary Bliss followed him in.

One of the foil pans of chicken salad was sitting on the kitchen counter. A large fork was stuck in the pan, which was now only two-thirds full.

"You ate the chicken salad!" Mary Bliss said, staring down at the pan in disbelief.

"Yeah," Dinky said. "Not bad. If you like chicken salad."

"That pan had twenty pounds of chicken salad in it," Mary Bliss said. "How could one person eat that much food in one sitting?"

He grinned. "Hey. I didn't eat it all. Man, I had a bitchin' case of the munchies. You wanna Bloody Mary?"

"No. I want my chicken salad back. That's two hundred and fifty dollars' worth of food you helped yourself to. I've got a wedding to cater today, and they're expecting a hundred pounds of chicken salad. Now, thanks to you, I've only got about ninety pounds."

"Tough shit." Dinky smirked. "What are you gonna do? Arrest me?"

She felt the blood rush to her head. And suddenly, it wasn't just Dinky Davis giving her a bad time. It was Parker McGowan, and it was Matt Hayslip. It was the pawnshop guy who'd ripped her off, the mechanic who'd overcharged her for a lube job, and it was the air conditioning guy and the bill collectors who kept leaving threatening messages on her answering machine.

One minute she was a reasonable, sane suburbanite. The next she was a screaming whirling dervish.

"I want my chicken salad, goddamn you," she screamed. When he laughed, she picked up a wooden spoon and started beating him on the head with it. He laughed again, as though it were hilarious. She picked up the next thing at hand, which happened to be the rolled-up *Atlanta Journal-Constitution*. She slapped him flat across the face with the newspaper, slapped the smirk clean off his face.

"Hey!" he said, throwing his arms up to ward off her next shot. "That ain't funny, man."

She slapped him with the paper again. He snatched it away and threw it down. She picked up something else, a full liter bottle of Diet Coke, cocked her arm, and pounded him square on the skull with it.

"Cut it out," he screamed, cowering on the kitchen floor.

She had him cornered by the kitchen table. He scooted underneath, and her arm wasn't long enough to reach him with the soda bottle. She whirled around and found Katharine's broom. She held the bristle end and stabbed blindly at him with the broom handle.

"Stop," he screamed. "Ow. Fuck. I think you fuckin' pierced my fuckin' kidney."

He scrambled out from under the table and was headed for the back door. "Help," he hollered. "She's fuckin' killing me. Jesus, somebody help."

She had never once raised a hand to anyone in anger in her life. But now she fully intended to beat this man within an inch of his life.

Suddenly, somebody was holding her, pinning her arms to her side.

"Mary Bliss. Stop. Mary Bliss. Get ahold of yourself."

It was Charlie. He was barefoot. Dressed in baggy blue pajama bottoms and an undershirt. His hair was mussed and he was unshaven. He had his arms wrapped around her, pushing her gently away from her victim.

She was so blind with pent-up rage, she hadn't even seen him run into the room.

"Come on, now," Charlie said soothingly. "Leave him be. Leave him be."

"He's ruined everything," she said, dissolving into tears. "He was supposed to be dead. And now he ate the chicken salad. Let me kill him, Charlie. Just please let me kill him."

"No, no," Charlie said, gently stroking her hair. "No killing. Killing is bad."

He looked over at Dinky, who was standing by the back door, dabbing at his bloodied face with a kitchen towel.

"Who the hell are you?" Charlie asked, his voice cold and imperious.

"Hey, man," Dinky protested. "Who are you? I'm a friend of Katharine's. This chick came in here this morning, and she freaked out. She beat the shit out of me. For nothin'. She's fuckin' nuts. I want her arrested."

"I'm Katharine's husband. This is my house," Charlie said. "I think you'd better leave."

"No way," Dinky said, his voice menacing. "Katharine invited me. She's gonna help me get a job. I ain't going nowhere."

Charlie's eyes hardened. He looked around the room, his eyes lighting on a bottle of Smirnoff vodka sitting on the kitchen counter. V8 juice was spilled on the countertop. Nearby, an elaborate waterpipe rested atop a plastic bag of dried leaves.

"What's that?" Charlie asked, pointing at the bag and the pipe.

"What?" Dinky said, wide-eyed. "That ain't mine."

Charlie released Mary Bliss, walked over to the counter, and picked up the pipe and the bag. "This. Marijuana and drug-related paraphernalia." He held the bag in one hand, hefting it, giving it some thought. "Probably about six ounces, I'd say. In this state, that amount will get you possession with intent to distribute."

He reached for the phone. "On second thought. Stay right there. I'm just going to give the police a call. See what they think." He pointed at the back door. "And that door looks like it's been jimmied. So that's breaking and entering."

"Hold on, dude," Dinky said. "Let's talk about this. I never broke in here. Katharine invited me in. See, me and her got a deal. And this chick, man, she's the one you wanna talk to the cops about. The chick's working a scam. Plus, she tried to kill me. That should count for something."

"Mary Bliss," Charlie said, his face stern. "Have you ever seen this man before?"

"No," Mary Bliss said, her voice faint. "Never."

"And did you try to kill him just now?"

"Not really," Mary Bliss said. "I was coming over this morning to pick up my chicken salad. For the wedding I'm catering. And he was here. He must have broken in, because he was right here in this kitchen. I think he must be drunk. And on drugs. Because he attacked me. I was trying to fight him off when you came downstairs."

"She's fuckin' nuts," Dinky wailed. "See? I'm the one who's bleeding. The chick tried to kill me."

"In self-defense," Charlie said. "So, let's see. I can have you charged with breaking and entering, aggravated assault, and possession with intent to distribute."

"And don't forget the chicken salad," Mary Bliss said. "He ate two hundred and fifty dollars' worth of my chicken salad."

"Felony burglary," Charlie said, nodding with satisfaction. He picked up the phone again.

"Fuck it," Dinky said, throwing down the bloodied kitchen towel. "I'm outta here."

57

Mary Bliss collapsed onto a kitchen chair. Charlie sat down beside her. A short time later, Katharine drifted in, fully dressed, and began making the coffee.

"Well," Mary Bliss said, exchanging worried looks with Katharine. "I guess I better load up what's left of my chicken salad and head home."

"What's your hurry?" Charlie asked. He was trying to smooth out the pages of the morning paper.

"The caterer is coming at nine to pick it up," Mary Bliss said. "And he's going to write me a check too."

Charlie checked his wristwatch. "It's only quarter of. Plenty of time to fill me in on who that man was and what the hell he was doing in my house."

Katharine switched on the coffee grinder and let it run a minute longer than was absolutely necessary.

Charlie folded the newspaper into a neat rectangle. "I'm waiting," he announced.

Katharine shot Mary Bliss a look.

"All right," Mary Bliss said. "I'm the one who got us into this, so I guess I'll be the one to explain."

"All of it," Charlie prompted.

"His name is Dinky Davis," Mary Bliss started. "And we thought he was dead. But he's not."

"I see," Charlie said. "There seems to be a lot of reincarnation around here."

"You can't blame it all on Mary Bliss," Katharine said. "I'm the one who hired him to impersonate Parker."

"But I'm the one who went out on the boat with him," Mary Bliss said. "And I'm the one who paid for the death certificate."

"I gave her the money," Katharine said.

Charlie's head swiveled from left to right. From Katharine to Mary Bliss.

"Let me get this straight," he said. "You went down to Cozumel, wandered around, hired a complete stranger, that degenerate, to impersonate Parker? Then you staged some botched-up boating accident, all in an effort to collect on Parker's life insurance?" He shook his head. "I'm stunned. I really am. I knew there was something going on, but I never dreamed the two of you would attempt something as imbecilic—not to mention criminal and downright dangerous—as this."

Mary Bliss hung her head. Katharine sipped her coffee for a minute.

"It almost worked," Katharine said finally. "And it would have worked. How did we know he would get drunk and crash the boat? It was a really beautiful plan, Charlie. Mary Bliss was going to let him off the boat—"

Charlie stopped her. "I don't want to hear another word. I'm an officer of the court. And what you're talking about is fraud. You could both go to prison."

Mary Bliss sighed. "I'm sorry I got Katharine mixed up in this, Charlie. And I'm sorry you got mixed up too. And I'm really, really sorry Dinky Davis showed up here last night." She raised her chin. "But I'll tell you what I'm most sorry about. I'm sorry it wasn't really Parker on that boat."

"You don't mean that," Charlie said, patting her hand. "You're just upset."

"No," Mary Bliss said. "Parker took everything. Robbed me. Robbed Erin. If he wanted a divorce, I think I could have handled that. But he didn't do that. He snuck out in the middle of the night. Like a common thief. I guess I made some stupid choices. But I didn't know what else to do. He didn't leave me any choices."

Charlie folded the newspaper and set it aside. "I wish you'd talked to me. You could have told me the truth. We would have figured out something."

"Like what?" Mary Bliss asked. "Parker did a great job. He put me in a hole so deep, I could never dig myself out. Not legally, anyway."

"*Legally* is the key word," Charlie said. "Parker didn't defraud just you. He defrauded the mortgage company when he did that refinance. He falsified your signature on that power of attorney, so it's not a valid document."

Mary Bliss did a double take. "You mean, I don't owe them the whole seven hundred thousand dollars?"

"That's exactly what I mean," Charlie said. "I should be able to get the company to stop the repossession action, after I present them with your affidavit about the phony power of attorney. The signature on it definitely isn't yours."

"That's it?" Mary Bliss said, her voice rising. She giggled. "That's all it takes? I get to keep my house?" She jumped up and kissed Charlie on the top of the head.

"Charlie Weidman, if Katharine doesn't take you back, I'll marry you my own self."

Charlie pushed his glasses back to the bridge of his nose. "Aren't you forgetting something? You're still married to Parker McGowan. And he's out there. Somewhere."

That sobered her up again.

"God, what a mess I've made of things," she said, slumping down into her chair. "Even if I get to keep the house, how do I undo everything else? How do I tell Erin the truth? That her lying, thieving daddy isn't dead after all. He's just on the lam."

Katharine poured Mary Bliss a cup of coffee. "Guess what my mama always said was true."

"What did your mama always say?" Charlie asked.

"That it's easy to squeeze the toothpaste out. It's gettin' it back in that's the killer."

"That may be the only thing Mamie was ever right about," Charlie said. "That and her chicken salad. And her martini. Mamie could mix a mean dirty martini."

"The chicken salad!" Mary Bliss jumped up again. "I almost forgot. That caterer will be at the house any minute. And I'm ten pounds short. What'll I do?"

Katharine didn't miss a beat. "Do what Mama did. One time, Daddy came home from work and he saw a bowl of that chicken salad in the icebox. He ate half the bowl, not realizing Mama was having bridge club the next day. She liked to have killed him."

"But what did she *do*?" Mary Bliss asked.

"She got out her best silver platter and loaded it up high with pretty lettuce leaves. Then she threw in a lot more mayonnaise and chopped pecans and green grapes and sliced water chestnuts. Nobody knew the difference."

Mary Bliss thought it over. "That would work, I guess. Or, I could just tell the caterer the truth—that I'm about five pounds short."

"The truth," Charlie said dryly. "That would be a novelty for you. What about the real issue, Mary Bliss? Are you ready to come clean about Parker? With the insurance company? And Erin, of course."

Mary Bliss had taken a head of lettuce from Katharine's refrigerator and was already slicing it into thin ribbons. "I can't talk to Erin. We had a huge fight after I went through her things and found out she's been sleeping with Josh Bowden. She left and she hasn't been back, except to pick up clean clothes. She blames me for everything, including losing her daddy."

"You know what the answer to all this is, don't you?" Charlie asked. "We have to find Parker. Make him come home and deal with this mess he's created."

"How?" Mary Bliss asked. "Just tell me how to find him."

"Matt Hayslip," Charlie said. "He's a smart sumbitch. He's got a couple of leads. He tracked down those bank photos, and he's established a money trail. I really believe he can find Parker."

"No," Mary Bliss said flatly. "I don't want anything to do with that man. I mean it, Charlie. I'd just as soon leave things the way they are. I don't want that man messing in my business."

"That man?" Katharine said, raising an eyebrow.

"I mean it, you two," Mary Bliss said, giving them both a stern look. "Leave Matt Hayslip out of it."

"You may not have a choice in the matter," Charlie pointed out. "He doesn't work for you, remember? And I get the feeling he is a very determined kind of guy."

58

The days thudded by. Mary Bliss worked every shift she could get at Bargain Bonanza. One day she demonstrated Frozen Tooty-Frooty Tofutti, which went over like a screen door in a submarine; the next day, she cooked so many boxes of Microwave Ginger-Honey Chik'n Bitz that she lost count.

She'd fixed two more fifty-pound batches of chicken salad for Gerran Thomas's weddings. She promised herself she'd never eat chicken again.

After a week Erin reappeared at home. Just like that. One morning, Mary Bliss came downstairs and Erin was sitting at the kitchen table, drinking a Coke.

"Hey!" Mary Bliss said, swooping down to kiss her daughter.

"Hey," Erin said quietly. She did not return the kiss.

"Honey, we need to talk," Mary Bliss started. "I'm so sorry I've made such a hash of things. I hate fighting with you. I hate having you mad at me. You're all I have left. We girls have to stick together . . ."

Erin shoved her chair back abruptly. "I gotta go. I'm late for work. And I've got soccer camp after that."

Mary Bliss caught hold of Erin's pocketbook as she was swinging it onto her shoulder. "Erin, just give me five minutes. We really need to talk. It's pretty important."

Erin stopped dead in her tracks. "There's nothing to talk about," she said flatly. "I live here. You live here. That's it. Just leave me alone and we'll get along fine. Okay?"

"It's about Daddy," Mary Bliss started.

"Just shut up!" Erin screamed. "No more goddamned lies! I won't listen to you. I won't."

She stomped out of the kitchen and a minute later Mary Bliss heard the Honda screech out of the driveway.

The phone rang. Mary Bliss let the answering machine pick up.

It was Matt Hayslip. Again. He'd called every day for the past two weeks. The message was the same. He wanted to see her. He needed to talk to her. He wanted to help.

"No more help," Mary Bliss told the machine. "Not from you, anyway."

But she would take all the help she could get from Charlie Weidman. He was still staying at Katharine's house. Mary Bliss knew he'd moved out of the basement and back into the master bedroom, but Katharine was staying uncharacteristically quiet about the nature of their relationship.

Charlie had started to put weight on again. His color was better, and he was going in to his law office four days a week now. He'd been in negotiations with the mortgage company. Mary Bliss had signed depositions stating that she'd never given Parker her power of attorney, and that she never would have consented to a cash-out mortgage on her house.

The bankers seemed to believe her. There was just one hitch. Parker had their money. And they wanted it back.

"Join the club," Mary Bliss had told Charlie. "I want my money back too. But I don't have a clue where Parker could have gone."

She didn't, either. The only person who might know was her mother-in-law.

But her last visit with Eula had been truly awful. Eula was really sick this time. The doctors said she was in kidney failure. They wanted her to undergo dialysis, but Eula wasn't about to spend her last days hooked up to a machine.

"Probably pump me full of poisons," she said, glaring maliciously at Lillian King, who was attempting to coax Eula into taking her medicine.

"Now, Miz Eula, you know that's not true. Your doctors want you to feel better, that's all," Lillian King said.

"The new doctor's an Ay-rab," Eula told Mary Bliss. "That's all they get working in here. Ay-rabs and nigger girls and Chinks."

Mary Bliss was mortified, but Lillian King just laughed off the insult. "You callin' me a girl, Miz Eula? That's mighty good of you."

When the nurse was gone, Mary Bliss closed the door to the hallway.

"Meemaw," she said, taking a seat close to the bed. "I need to talk to you. About Parker."

"He's dead," Eula said. "Or so you say."

"He stole a lot of money from some people," Mary Bliss said. "Not just me. Other people. A mortgage company. His business associates. There are detectives looking for him."

Eula snorted. "Detectives? Do they think they can outsmart my boy? You know what Parker was famous for when he was just a little boy? Hide and seek. He could hide so good, none of the other children could ever find him. They'd just give up and go on home. Anyway, my son is no thief. That's just more of your lies. To try to get money out of me."

"No," Mary Bliss said, shaking her head. "It's not about the money. It's about Erin. I'm worried about her. Since Parker disappeared, she's different. Moody, sullen. She won't even talk to me."

"The child is fine," Eula snapped. "I'm the one who's dying. And nobody around here seems to give a hoot and a holler. I hurt all the time. My bowels are either locked tighter than Dick's hatband or I'm spewing all kinds of nasty stuff. You know they got me wearing a diaper? A grown woman wearing a diaper!"

"I'm sorry you're in pain," Mary Bliss said simply. She got up to leave and felt she'd aged ten years since she'd walked in the door of Meemaw's room. She squeezed Eula's hand, tried to plant a kiss on her cheek, but Eula turned away.

"I'll see you next week," Mary Bliss said.

"If I'm still alive," Eula shot back.

Mary Bliss drove home holding her breath. They'd had no rain in two weeks. It was in the upper nineties, and heat shimmered off the asphalt pavement. She didn't dare turn on the air conditioning. Her car was making a whirring sound under the hood, but she didn't get paid until Friday, and all her credit cards had long since maxed out. She patted the dashboard. "Stay with me, baby. Don't you quit on me too."

As she coasted into her driveway, the whole car seemed to shudder, and then it stopped. All the lights on the dashboard lit up.

"Shit," she said. The car shuddered again. She stroked the steering wheel. "I didn't mean that. Don't mind me. I'm just mad at the world."

"You always talk to your car?"

Mary Bliss startled. Matt Hayslip was standing right beside the car.

"Only when I've given up on talking to humanity," she said.

He poked his head in the window, ignoring the cold stare she was giving him.

"Try and start it up again," he said.

She turned the key, but the engine did not respond.

"Alternator, I bet," Matt said. "Has your warning light been coming on?"

"All my warning lights are lit up when you're around," she said, "but yes, the lights on the dash were flashing. I never can tell what all those symbols mean."

"It's the alternator," he said, as if that settled it. "What model year is this?"

"It's a ninety-three," she said.

"Does your husband keep any tools in the garage?"

"Tools?"

He shook his head impatiently. "Automotive tools. Was Parker the mechanical type?"

She laughed. It was the first time that day. Possibly that week.

"Parker didn't even like to change lightbulbs," she said. "There are some tools on the workbench in the garage, but I think they're pretty basic stuff, like hammers and pliers and stuff."

Matt said, "We'll stop by my place on the way."

"On the way to where?" Mary Bliss asked.

"Pep Boys," he said. "Unless this car of yours is the self-healing type. Or you have a mechanic you really trust."

She sighed. "The car has been dying in stages all week, I think. I have a mechanic, but I still owe him money from doing a tune-up on Erin's Honda last month. I don't dare call him until I can pay him something."

"Then I guess you're left with ole Matt the Mechanic," Hayslip said, giving her a wink. "Cheap, and reliable."

"No, thanks," Mary Bliss said, slamming the car door. "I'll just have to see if I can use Erin's car."

He followed her to the back door. "You're still pissed at me. I'm a detective. I can sense these things."

"I'm not pissed at you," Mary Bliss said, unlocking the back door. "I don't care enough about you to be pissed."

"As much lying as you've been doing, you'd think you'd be better at it," Hayslip said. He pushed the door open for her. "But you're not that good a liar, Mary Bliss."

"I'm not inviting you in," she said, trying to pull the door shut before he could walk in. But he walked in anyway.

"I'm not waiting for an invitation," Matt said. "I've been doing too much waiting as it is. So here's the thing. Let's start over, okay? I'll be straight with you, and you can be straight with me."

"I've been straight with you," she said, crossing her arms over her chest.

"No. You've been lying through your teeth. About Parker, anyway. Don't you want to know what I've found out in the past two weeks? That's why I came by here today, to fill you in, since you won't answer my phone calls."

"No," she said. "I don't want to talk to you."

He waved a finger. "See? There you go, lying again."

"All right. What have you found out?"

"Are you gonna let me fix your car for you?"

She shrugged. "I don't have too many other options."

"And buy you dinner?"

"No. Dinner is not part of the deal."

"All right, lunch. It's close to lunch right now. And I'm starving. We can pick up the parts at Pep Boys. There's a deli right around the corner from there. I'm in the mood for corned beef and rye. What about you?"

"I'm not hungry," Mary Bliss said. She was starving. Her stomach had been growling nonstop since she'd left the nursing home.

"Chicken salad," Matt said. "I'll bet you're a chicken salad person. Most women are."

It was Mary Bliss's turn to shudder. "No. No more chicken salad."

"Tuna, then," Matt said. "Or egg salad. Whatever you want." He took her hand in his. "Come on, Mary Bliss. Let's have a truce. All right?"

His gray eyes were pleading. She felt her resolve collapsing. She could hear Mama's voice telling her about how the Lord helps those who help themselves. Maybe she was helping herself by allowing Matt to help her.

59

"**W**ell?" Matt said, putting his sandwich down on the plate. "Come on. Quit with the silent treatment. Talk to me."

The deli was crowded, and the tables were packed tightly together. A mother at a table next to theirs was trying to coax a preschooler into eating his peanut butter and jelly sandwich. Two elderly women to their left were complaining loudly about the deli's lack of a senior citizen discount.

Mary Bliss twisted her paper napkin into a tight roll. She had been concentrating on her lunch, tuna on rye, listening, nodding.

"It's not that I don't want to know," she said slowly. "Maybe I just don't trust myself to ask the right questions. Or maybe I don't know what I'll do once I know something."

Matt took a gulp of iced tea. "My investigation isn't that far along yet," he said. "I'll find Parker. But I haven't yet. He's still two or three steps ahead of me."

"What do you know?" Mary Bliss asked.

A muscle in Matt's cheek twitched. "While you're riding around in a half-dead ten-year-old sedan, Parker has bought himself a new car. I did a title search. He's driving a brand-new black Range Rover. And he paid nearly seventy-three thousand dollars cash."

Mary Bliss stared down at her plate, picked at the potato salad with the tip of her fork. "When was this?"

"Three weeks ago. He bought it at a dealership in Jacksonville."

She nodded. "What else?"

"He's moving around a lot. I've found two more bank accounts for his graveyard employees—one in Birmingham, another in Orlando. I've got photos from ATMs in both places. It's Parker, all right." He reached for the briefcase he'd brought into the restaurant.

"No," Mary Bliss said. "Don't show me. I don't want to see."

"He's grown himself a cute little mustache," Matt said. "And he's wearing a gold chain with what looks like a diamond ring around his neck."

"Maybe it's my engagement ring," Mary Bliss said.

Matt gave her a sharp look. "He took that too?"

She nodded. "He told me he was having the prongs on the setting tightened. I didn't know until I called the jeweler that he never took it in there."

The muscle in Matt's cheek twitched again. "The next thing is something you're not going to want to hear."

She gave him a sad smile. "I don't really want to hear any of it, you know. But I guess I need to, don't I?"

"Yeah," he said. "You do. So here it is. Parker's not traveling alone. He's got somebody with him."

Mary Bliss raised one eyebrow. "So there is somebody else. Katharine is right. She said a man never runs off by himself. There's always another woman involved. Do you know who it is?"

"Not a clue," Matt admitted. "But in two of the five ATM photos we've recovered, there's somebody waiting in the front seat of the car parked directly in back of Parker. The car is the Range Rover. All we can see of the passenger is a silhouette. But it's the same silhouette in both photos. Both times, the passenger is wearing a white baseball cap, with chin-length blonde hair visible. The rest of the face is hidden under the ball cap."

"A blonde," Mary Bliss said. "Why is it that the other woman is always a blonde? Is she young?"

"Hard to say. The ball cap shades all the facial features."

Mary Bliss pushed her plate away. She felt nauseous. "Where do you think he's going? What's he done with all that money?"

"I don't have any idea where he's going. But at least he hasn't left the country. Yet. And I don't know what he's done with the money, either. The graveyard bank accounts only have a few hundred apiece left in them."

"What would you do?" Mary Bliss asked. "Where would you run if you were Parker?"

"Me?" Matt grinned. "I would have stayed home with my beautiful wife. And if I had run off, I would have taken her with me."

"That's not fair," Mary Bliss said, twisting her napkin again.

"You said you wanted me to be straight with you. I'm being straight. If I were running away with you, we'd go somewhere beautiful. Tropical, remote. Ever been to Hawaii?"

She shook her head. "Parker never liked to travel that much."

"Until now," Matt said. "I think you'd like Hawaii. Gorgeous flowers, beaches, waterfalls. Great deep-sea fishing. Do you like to fish?"

She smiled. "The last time I went fishing was with a cane pole on the banks of a creek back in Alabama. I guess I liked it. I was probably six or seven years old.

My daddy showed me how to bait my hook, and how to take the fish off and let it go, so it wouldn't get hurt and die."

He cocked his head. "Are your folks still around?"

"No," she said lightly. "Mama died when Erin was a baby. Daddy died when I was just a kid. He'd been out of our lives a long time by then."

"Divorce?" Matt asked.

"No. He just up and left us. Daddy wasn't real big on paperwork."

"I see," Matt said. She could tell he did.

"Can we change the subject, please?" Mary Bliss asked. "You've told me what I needed to know about Parker. I hope you catch him, I guess. But I can't think that far ahead."

"Does the insurance company know? That he's really alive?" Matt asked.

"Charlie is handling that," Mary Bliss said. "Let's talk about something else. Something pleasant."

"Us?"

She clamped her lips together, tried not to smile. "There is no us."

"Yet."

"I'm legally married to Parker McGowan."

"You could get a divorce," Matt suggested.

"I wouldn't know where to start," Mary Bliss said. "How can I divorce somebody I can't even find?"

"Ask Charlie," he said. "He's the man with all the answers."

"I've been depending too much on Charlie. He's been so wonderful to me. And he's not out of the woods yet, you know. He looks a lot better, but you never know."

"All right," Matt said slowly. "Forget the divorce. Everybody thinks Parker's dead. As far as the world is concerned, you're a widow. You can do as you please."

"But I'm not a widow," Mary Bliss said. "You know it, and I know it. And so do Charlie and Katharine. And there's Erin to consider too."

"Excuses," Matt said. "You keep coming up with excuses to stay away from me. Am I that ugly?"

"No," she said. "That's not it and you know it."

"Give me another chance," Matt said. "We'll take it slow, I promise. Just one night out. Please? You won't even have to be alone with me."

"I can't," she said reluctantly. "It just wouldn't look right."

"To who?"

"Whom," she said, automatically correcting him. "To the world."

"The world can take a flying leap," Matt said. He leaned across the table and kissed her gently on the cheek. "I want to spend time with you. Is that so wrong?"

The two blue-haired old ladies the next table over had been staring and actively eavesdropping. Now the older of the two started to giggle. Mary Bliss felt herself blush.

"You're making a spectacle of me," she protested. "Please behave."

"No," he said. He pushed his chair back. "If you don't agree to go out with me, I'm going to get up and come over there and give you a bend-over-backward Rhett Butler–does–Scarlett O'Hara kiss. And the whole joint will see it. It'll be all over Fair Oaks in no time at all."

"All right, all right," she said hastily. "But no more intimate dinners at home. No more red wine and candles."

"I've got just the place," Matt said. "The country club dinner dance is Saturday night. What do you say?"

"I don't know," Mary Bliss said, biting her lip.

He pushed the chair out a little farther, stood up and walked over to her, pulled her out of the chair.

"Yes," she said, laughing, pushing him away. "I give in."

One of the blue-hairs at the next table beamed at her. "Good for you, dear," she said. "He seems nice. Give him a chance."

60

August 15. Mary Bliss had been avoiding the kitchen calendar all week long. She had tried to put it out of her mind. Saturday night was no big deal. A dance at the country club. No big deal. She had been to dozens of country club dances.

But not with a *date.* And the fact was, she had a date. She was a married woman, and she was going out on a date. She was ashamed and terrified and wild with a kind of electric anticipation she hadn't felt since she was a teenager.

At ten o'clock Saturday morning, Katharine appeared at her house, unannounced. She was carrying a stainless-steel thermos bottle and two matching pairs of hot-pink flip-flops.

"What's up?" Mary Bliss said warily, putting down her first Diet Coke of the day.

"Let's go," Katharine said.

"Where? What's in the thermos?"

"Our destination is on a strictly need-to-know basis," Katharine said. "The thermos contains a morning's worth of Bloody Marys. Now put on the flip-flops. We're on a tight schedule here."

"What kind of schedule? I can't just leave. Erin isn't up yet. I want to talk to her about . . . tonight. About Matt."

Katharine winced. "Maybe you should just tell her a little bitty white lie about tonight. Tell her you're going with us."

"No," Mary Bliss said. "No more lies. I can't expect her to tell the truth unless I tell it myself."

"Have you told her the truth about Parker?"

"She won't discuss it with me," Mary Bliss said. "But I know she's been spending some time at the nursing home with Meemaw. I have a feeling Meemaw's been filling her ears with all kinds of stuff about me."

"Isn't she due to die any day now?"

"Katharine!" Mary Bliss said. "It's true she's not well. The doctors want her to go on dialysis, but she's adamantly refused, so far. To tell the truth, the nurses tell me they're amazed she's lived this long without it."

"She's an evil old hag," Katharine said. "She's probably hanging on just to spite you."

"I feel sorry for her," Mary Bliss said. "The only person she ever really loved is Parker, and he's gone. She's cut herself off from all her old friends, and she's made it very clear that Erin and I are not big priorities with her."

"But she loves Erin, right?"

"I guess so. I think she sees something of Parker in Erin. But Eula was never the adoring grandmotherly type. You know what she gave Erin for her sixteenth birthday? An Abs-R-Cizer."

"Like they sell on TV?"

"I swear to God," Mary Bliss said. "She saw an infomercial for it and sent away. Gave it to Erin, no card, no gift wrapping. All she said was, 'Here. You don't wanna get a spare tire now, do you?'"

"Sweet," Katharine said.

"And the funny thing is, Erin adores her grandmother. She calls her on the phone, goes over there, takes her funny little presents."

"Amazing," Katharine said. "Now let's go."

"Just let me leave a note."

"Let's go!" Katharine ordered. "Right now. My car is running, and we've got a lot to accomplish this morning."

Mary Bliss followed Katharine out to the Jeep, her pink flips making slapping sounds against the pavement.

Mary Bliss was halfway through her Bloody Mary by the time Katharine wheeled into a Buckhead shopping center, the centerpiece of which was a pale-pink stucco wedding cake–looking building called Spa Serenity.

"No," Mary Bliss said, setting her drink in the cup holder. "No spa."

"Yes. Spa. Good," Katharine said, ignoring her. She got out of the car and headed for the door, but Mary Bliss didn't budge.

Katharine backtracked and yanked open the passenger side door. "You might as well come in," she told her best friend. "I've booked us the full package. It'll take three hours at least. And I'm not leaving."

"This is ridiculous," Mary Bliss said. "I'm going to a simple little dance. It's not the senior prom. I don't want all this fuss. I don't need it."

Katharine gave her a long, withering up-and-down full-body scan. "Have you looked at yourself lately, M. B.? I mean, please. If this were the emergency room instead of a spa, you'd be in the intensive care unit. Split ends, lackluster color, raggedy-ass nails, chewed-down cuticles, enlarged pores. And don't get me going on your eyebrows."

Mary Bliss grabbed the sun visor, pulled it down, and stared in the mirror there. "What's wrong with my eyebrows?"

"One word," Katharine said. "Unibrow. Now let's go."

A tiny, wizened Asian man sat behind the stark smoked-glass reception desk in the lobby of Spa Serenity, yelling nonstop into a cell phone in a language Mary Bliss didn't recognize.

"Hon," Katharine said politely. The man didn't look up. "Hon!" Katharine repeated. The man looked up, held up a finger in the "one minute" gesture, and continued gabbing.

"Hon!" Katharine screamed. "Get off the phone!"

He looked wounded, but pressed a button and set the phone on the glass-top desk. "What you want?" he snarled.

"We have an appointment," Katharine said. "The works. And we're on a tight schedule."

He glanced down at the open appointment book in front of him. "No. No appointment. You come back. Very busy today."

Katharine walked around the desk, grabbed the book away from him, and jabbed her finger on the line where somebody had written "Weidman (2)."

"Right there," she said. "I'm with Ruby, and my friend is with Pearl."

He frowned, but walked behind an elaborate pink-and-gold dragon screen that divided the reception area from the salon.

"You were so rude to him," Mary Bliss said. "Really, Katharine. There's no excuse for rudeness."

"Hon thrives on rudeness," Katharine said. "He's Gena's father. She owns the place. Hon thinks everybody is out to cheat them. So if you're not rude, you'll never get your nails done on time. It's expected."

"Who are Ruby and Pearl?" Mary Bliss asked.

Katharine waved her hand. "They say they're Gena's cousins. I don't think those are their real names, but who cares? Wait 'til you get your sea-salt rubdown. You'll swear you're having an orgasm."

"Katharine!" Mary Bliss said.

Hon reappeared with two Vietnamese women in tow, both dressed in pale-pink Spa Serenity jumpsuits. One was tiny, no bigger than an American preschooler. The other was muscular and had a blonde crew cut and a nose ring.

"Kaffrin," cooed the butch one.

"Ruby!" Katharine exclaimed. She enveloped the crew-cut woman in an expansive hug, saying a few words in Vietnamese.

"Hello," Mary Bliss said, extending a hand to the other woman. "I'm Mary Bliss."

Pearl took her index finger, spit on it, and rubbed it across Mary Bliss's forehead. "Oh yeah. You the one with the eyebrow. Kaffrin tell us. You come."

Before she could protest, Mary Bliss had been wrapped in a pink duster and was lying back in a chair, having her scalp massaged with something that smelled like a combination of mango and Coppertone suntan lotion. It felt heavenly. Maybe Katharine was right. Maybe she could use a little harmless pampering.

Five minutes later, another Vietnamese woman dressed in a Spa Serenity jumpsuit entered the mirrored cubicle where Mary Bliss had been seated. This woman was also petite, but she had waist-length black hair and wore four-inch stiletto heels.

"This Gena," Pearl said.

Gena circled the chair three times, yanking at strands of Mary Bliss's damp hair and clucking her tongue in deep disapproval. She spoke to Pearl in rapid-fire Vietnamese. Pearl nodded several times, and Gena disappeared.

"What did she say?" Mary Bliss asked.

Pearl sighed. "She never see hair the color of yours before. Who do that to you?"

Mary Bliss stiffened. "I do my own hair color. I always have."

Pearl shook her head. "You got job?"

"I'm a schoolteacher," Mary Bliss said.

"Good," Pearl said approvingly. "You stick to kids. Let Pearl do hair color. Okay?"

A few minutes later Gena was back, holding a plastic bottle of bright-orange goo in her plastic-gloved hands.

"What's that?" Mary Bliss asked.

"New color," Pearl said, beaming. "Gena invent for you."

Gena lunged at her and started squirting the dye on Mary Bliss's scalp.

"Wait," Mary Bliss said, ducking, trying to fend off the dye bottle. "I don't want a new color. I like my own color. Miss Clairol. Luxe Lynx."

"Lynx stinks," Pearl opined. "You like this. Wait and see."

It was too late. Gena had already doused her head with the dye and was vigorously working it into her hair, muttering dire words in Vietnamese.

"What color is this?" Mary Bliss asked. "It looks awfully orange."

Gena said something else.

"She call it Sunflower," Pearl said, grinning broadly. "She invent for you. Big honor."

"Sunflowers are yellow," Mary Bliss said. "I'm a brunette. I can't have yellow hair."

"Blonde," Gena said, speaking her first words of English. "You a born blonde."

Mary Bliss shut her eyes. She was going to be blonde. A year ago she would have fainted at the suggestion.

But too much had happened. Maybe it was time to go with the flow.

Half an hour later, she was seated under a massive hair dryer in the communal dryer room. The room was lined with a dozen dryers, and each of them held a pink-clad woman in its clasp.

She was given a magazine and a glass of chardonnay. She took a sip and had begun to doze off when she felt something jabbing her in the eye.

She sat up. Pearl was squatting before her, brandishing what looked like a Popsicle stick full of Silly Putty.

"Now what?" Mary Bliss asked.

"First wax, then dye," Pearl said. "No more unibrow. No more lynx."

Go with it, Mary Bliss told herself. She took another sip of the chardonnay. Pearl continued to poke at her eyebrows with the applicator of hot wax. After a while she gently laid little strips of fabric over the wax and patted them into place. She could get used to this, Mary Bliss told herself.

Suddenly, Pearl grimaced and yanked the fabric.

"*Owww!*" Mary Bliss screamed. Her flesh was being ripped from her face by this Vietnamese maniac.

The other dryer women looked up, smiled, then looked back down at their issues of *Vogue* and *Architectural Digest*.

"That hurt," Mary Bliss whined.

Pearl smiled, nodded, and pointed to a sign at the front of the room. It was written in Asian symbols.

"What's it mean?" Mary Bliss asked.

"Beauty is pain. Pain is beauty."

61

"Oh. My. Gawd."

Katharine blinked several times. She made Mary Bliss twirl around so that she could get the full effect. Then she made all the dryer women look too.

"Stunning," was Katharine's verdict.

"Perfect." The pink-clad dryer women put down their magazines and gave Mary Bliss polite applause, using only the palms of their hands so as not to smudge their manicures.

"Not so bad," Pearl said, lifting up a lock of Katharine's sunflower-hued hair. "Better than brown. Huh?"

Mary Bliss herself was speechless. She did not recognize the woman in the mirror. Her hair was a warm-toned blonde, not yellow at all. It had been cut and softly feathered so that it hugged her head, and she had new wispy bangs that brushed the tops of her newly arched eyebrows. The last time she had bangs she was seven years old. Pearl had insisted on a new hot-pink lipstick color to go with the sunflower. The lipstick, which came in a shiny black phallic-looking tube, was called Hysteria.

Pearl made Mary Bliss hand over her old lipstick, the one she'd worn for the past seven years. "Look like baby food," Pearl pronounced, flipping it into a trash can.

"Well?" Katharine was waiting for her toenails to dry. "What do you think?"

"I don't know," Mary Bliss said slowly. "I guess I'm shell-shocked. It's not what I expected."

"You were attractive before," Katharine said. "In a schoolteacherish kind of way. Now you're a bombshell. You know that, right? You're a bona fide bombshell. You look like somebody's second wife."

"I feel like somebody's second wife," Mary Bliss admitted. She was staring down at the long acrylic nails Pearl had painstakingly applied to her own bitten-down fingernails. The new nails were slightly squared, and painted a pale seashell pink that made her hands look long and tanned and elegant.

"I feel like I should be smoking a cigarette or drinking a martini, or doing something . . . naughty," Mary Bliss said, a note of wonder in her voice.

"Not a martini, sweetie, a cosmopolitan," Katharine said kindly. "And that's the whole idea. Starting tonight, you are going to cut loose. And I'm not just talking about a new lipstick color. Remember back at the beginning of the summer? You made me run through the sprinkler with you? And you said we were being baptized. A whole new you. Well, I'll grant it, you've changed on the inside. You've boldly gone where you never dreamed of going before. But your exterior was holding you back. All we've done today is finish the transformation. It's the all-new, improved Mary Bliss McGowan."

"You think?" Mary Bliss asked, blushing.

"I know," Katharine said firmly. She stood up and heel-walked over to the reception desk, where Hon was again screaming into the cell phone. She reached into the pocket of her smock and brought out a platinum American Express card.

She waved it under Hon's nose until he looked up.

"Hon!" she yelled. "Get off the phone!"

62

Mary Bliss's hands shook as she fastened the single strand of fake freshwater pearls around her neck. She had refused Katharine's offer of a new outfit. Her pink spaghetti-strap sundress was only two years old, and she'd never worn it to a club function before. It would be just fine. She would be just fine.

If only.

If only her heart weren't racing, and her mouth weren't cotton-dry. Her hands wouldn't quit shaking and she kept having to pee every fifteen minutes. All the women in Mary Bliss's mama's family had nervous bladders.

High-strung, her mama had called her. Right now she felt like a live electric wire was running the length of her body. She could generate power for all of northeast

Georgia with the electricity running through her body right now.

"Mom?"

Mary Bliss turned slowly away from her dressing table. Erin stood in the doorway of her bedroom, wide-eyed.

"What do you think?" Mary Bliss asked, fluttering her eyelashes in what she hoped was a comic effect.

"What have you done to yourself?" Erin asked. "Now you're a blonde? Oh my God, what is going on with you?"

"Nothing," Mary Bliss said. "It's just hair color, honey. It's a color wash. Nothing permanent. Don't you like it?"

"You've gone nuts," Erin said. "I don't even know who you are anymore. Why have you done this to yourself?"

Mary Bliss felt a switch thrown. All the electricity stopped flowing. She felt cold and old again. Suddenly, the Sunflower had faded and the Luxe Lynx was back. Pearl was right. Lynx did stink.

"I wanted a little change," she said quietly. "We've gone through so much this summer. I was tired of looking at the same old me."

"Well, I wasn't," Erin said hotly. "Did you ever think of that? I liked the old you. I liked having a mother and a father, and a normal life and a normal family. But you've gone and fucked that all up, haven't you?"

Mary Bliss stood up and walked over to Erin, to hold her, to reassure her that they were still family. But Erin backed away from her.

"And why are you all dressed up like this?" Erin asked. "Like some kind of, of, hooker or something? Where do you think you're going?"

What was this, Mary Bliss wondered. Why was she being interrogated like a child, like a criminal, by her own daughter?

"I'm going to the dance at the country club," she said, trying to sound dignified. "You've seen this dress before. It's two years old. And I don't think it's very nice of you to talk to me like this."

"Nice?" Erin shrieked. "Oh my God. Nice? Who are you going to the dance with? Don't tell me you've hooked up with somebody. Oh my God. Don't tell me you have a date."

"I'm going with a friend," Mary Bliss said. "It's not really a date. His name is Matt Hayslip. He lives in the Oaks. We're going to ride to the dance with Katharine and Charlie. It's perfectly innocent."

"You've hooked up with somebody," Erin cried, running her hands through her hair until it stood on end. "You've hooked up with an Oakie. I can't believe it. You fuckin' give me all moral outrage when you find out I'm having sex, then you fuckin' run around like a damn slut!"

"Erin," Mary Bliss said, grasping her daughter's arm. "Stop it. Stop it right now. I won't have you talk to me this way. I'm your mother. And I won't have it."

"Oh. You won't have it," Erin said, her voice mocking. "You'll have anything you like, won't you? Meemaw was right. She said this is all a big act you're putting on. She said Daddy left you because you weren't sexy enough for him. Meemaw says she knows where Daddy really is. He's got a girlfriend, and a boat and a beach house, and pretty soon he's gonna send for me, and I'll get the hell out of here. I'll get the hell away from you!"

"Erin!" Mary Bliss raised her hand to slap her daughter, but she wasn't fast enough. Her daughter was gone. Running down the stairs, down the hall. "I hate you," she called to her mother. "I hate you."

Somehow, Mary Bliss stumbled downstairs to the phone. She called Katharine. "I'm not going," she said when her friend picked up. "Call Matt for me, please, tell him I can't talk right now. You explain it. He'll understand."

"Understand what?" Katharine asked. "Charlie's out getting the air conditioner running in the car to cool it down. We're just leaving to come get you."

"It's Erin," Mary Bliss said. "We had another horrible fight. She was right. I don't have any right to act like this. I'm a married woman."

"I'm not calling Matt," Katharine said firmly. "I'm sorry, Mary Bliss, but your daughter is a spoiled little bitch. You shouldn't have to apologize to her for having a life. You've sacrificed everything for her. Now it's time for you to get on with your life."

"I can't go," Mary Bliss said. "I'm so upset, I'm shaking."

"You're going," Katharine said. "If I have to carry you there on my back. Now put on your lipstick and your boogie shoes. We'll be there in five minutes." She hung up.

Mary Bliss didn't know whether to laugh or cry. So she did as she was told. But first she went out to the kitchen and polished off the rest of Katharine's thermos of Bloody Marys.

When the doorbell rang she was in the downstairs powder room, gargling with Listerine. The vodka seemed to have switched the current back on in her body, and she'd managed to apply a fresh coat of Hysteria to her lips.

Matt stood in the doorway. He was wearing a pink Polo golf shirt, khaki slacks, and an aged white dinner jacket. He was holding a cellophane florists' box out in front of him.

He said what Katharine and Erin had said.

"Oh my God." But he was smiling as he said it. "Have you entered the witness protection program?"

"Should I?"

"Katharine told me you'd had a do-over," he started.

"Makeover," Mary Bliss corrected him.

"Whatever. Wow. I had no idea."

She blushed. "Do you like it?"

"I'm getting used to it," he said. "I like it a lot, I think."

She pointed at the box. "Are those for me?"

"Yeah," he laughed. "Something came over me. I thought, it's a dance. I should get her a corsage. I called Katharine, and she said your dress was pink, so I should get something that goes with pink."

"How sweet." She opened the box and found a bracelet of pale-pink roses nestled on a bed of white excelsior.

"I love this shade of rose," Mary Bliss said, fastening the corsage around her wrist. "I love roses, period. But now I feel bad because I don't have a boutonniere for you."

"That's okay," Matt said. "I'm just glad you decided to come out tonight. Katharine told me you were pretty upset."

"I was," she said. "I still am." Her eyes lit on the shrub by the front door. It was still covered with gardenia blossoms. She reached down and picked the largest, freshest one on the bush.

"Hold on a minute," she said, disappearing back inside the house.

When she came back a moment later, she was still carrying the florist's box.

"Hey!" Matt said. "I was afraid you'd changed your mind and decided to stay home."

"No," she said, her voice level. She held out the box to Matt. "This is for you."

He lifted the homemade boutonniere from the box. "Great," he said. "Where does it go? I haven't worn one of these things since my wedding."

"Let me," she said. And as she pinned the gardenia to the lapel of his dinner jacket, she noticed with surprise that her hands had stopped shaking. Her face was directly under Matt's chin. He kissed the top of her head, nuzzled her neck a little.

From behind them a car beeped its horn. Katharine leaned out the window of Charlie's Lincoln. "Get a room, for God's sake," she called.

63

They were standing by the bar, waiting for the men to bring them their drinks. Katharine nudged Mary Bliss. "Do you see who I see?"

The Acorn ballroom at the country club was packed. The room was dimly lit to begin with, and tonight it seemed darker than usual, which Mary Bliss decided was a good thing.

She scanned the room until her eyes lit on a beautiful strawberry blonde who was flirting with the deejay the club had hired to provide music for the dance. Mary Bliss hadn't seen her in months. "Who? You mean Ava Grace Samford? I thought they were spending the summer up in Highlands this year."

"It's not Ava Grace I'm talking about," Katharine said. "You're looking in the wrong direction. Look over there. Under that big bunch of silver balloons hanging by the ceiling."

Mary Bliss spotted the balloon bouquet. Directly beneath it she spotted Nancye Bowden, who was doing a wicked shimmy to "Louie Louie." Nancy was wearing a strapless, ruched silver lamé sheath that reminded Mary Bliss of aluminum dryer vent hose. With every slither Nancy made, the bodice of her dress slipped a little further south, and her surprisingly full breasts were a little more exposed.

"I can't believe it," Mary Bliss said, her jaw dropping open.

"Can't believe what?" Charlie asked, rejoining them with the drinks and Matt.

"Nancye Bowden," Katharine said.

"Where?" Charlie asked. He knew all about Fair Oaks's biggest summer scandal.

"Check the balloons," Katharine said.

Charlie had found Nancye Bowden. "Literally," he said dryly.

"The woman in the silver dress?" Matt asked, handing Mary Bliss her glass of white wine. "I've seen her around town. What's her name?"

"Nancye Bowden," Katharine said. "The town tramp. Will you look at that outfit she's wearing? And those honkers which she is happily exposing to God and everybody? Isn't that amazing?"

Charlie was openly staring at Nancye, grinning in appreciation. "Amazing. Yessir."

"You're drooling," Katharine said, dabbing at Charlie's chin. "Anyway. They're store-bought. You know, a boob job."

She had Matt looking too. "Is that right?" he asked. "Women still do that kind of thing? They go through that kind of thing, just to get bigger breasts?"

"Pain is beauty," Mary Bliss said, quoting the Spa Serenity slogan. "Anyway. It's not nice to stare. And I should know."

People had been staring at Mary Bliss all evening, or it felt like it anyway.

She'd made Charlie drive twice around the parking lot at the club, just trying to delay making an entrance at the dance. Still, heads had been turning and jaws had been jabbering since they'd walked in the door.

"They're staring because they don't recognize you, and they're trying to figure out who you are," Charlie told Mary Bliss.

"No, they're staring at you because they can't believe what a knockout blonde you are," Matt said proudly.

Katharine clutched Matt's arm in a chummy gesture. "Or they saw the four of us come in together and they think I'm with Matt, and you're Charlie's new girlfriend." She gave Matt a noisy kiss on the cheek.

"Or they can't believe you and Charlie are back together again," Mary Bliss said, feeling better about things.

"We're just the biggest scandal in town." Katharine giggled, loving the idea. "Nancye Bowden is yesterday's news."

The deejay had slowed down all the southern frat party music and was playing a Johnny Mathis song, "The Twelfth of Never."

"Come on," Katharine said, edging Charlie toward the dance floor. "This one is just our speed."

Matt looked expectantly at Mary Bliss. "Is dancing allowed? Was that part of our agreement?"

Mary Bliss had been hoping for something a little more up-tempo for her first dance.

"I guess," she said, giving him a tentative smile.

He led her onto the dance floor and put a chaste hand on her waist. "See?" he said, gliding her easily around the floor. "I'm not so bad, am I?"

"No," she said, smiling up at him. She remembered something Nina used to say. "Better than a poke in the eye with a sharp stick."

It truly wasn't awful. Matt was an easy, relaxed dancer. It was strange, though. Strange dancing with somebody who wasn't Parker McGowan. Strange catching on to another man's rhythm.

They danced that dance and sat out a cartoonish Macarena, because Matt said he didn't do the Macarena. Then the deejay started spinning "The Tennessee Waltz" and Matt nodded at her; she nodded back, and then she saw him.

Randy Bowden hovered near the bar, sipping a bottle of beer and staring balefully in his estranged wife's direction. He looked pitiful, his face pinched, his dinner jacket ill-fitting. He broke Mary Bliss's heart.

She kept seeing him over Matt's shoulder as they waltzed around the waxed country club dance floor. She saw that he saw her too. She gave him a generous, beaming smile and an encouraging wave.

When the dance was over, Randy materialized at her side.

"Mary Bliss? Is that you?"

She nodded. "All my life I've heard blondes have more fun. I decided to give it a shot."

"It's wonderful," Randy said. "You were beautiful before. But now . . ."

She noticed Matt's amused smirk.

"Randy, this is Matt Hayslip," she said, gesturing in his direction. "Matt lives in the Oaks. And Matt, this is Randy Bowden. He's sort of the boy next door."

"Across the street, actually," Randy said, taking a long swig of beer.

"Randy's son Josh is Erin's boyfriend," Mary Bliss explained. Randy gave her a funny look, then finished off his beer. Was it possible that he was tipsy? He was always so serious, it was hard to tell. "Josh is a great kid," she added. "A talented musician."

The deejay was changing the tempo again. It was "Double Shot," the old Swinging Medallions song, a country club anthem for middle-aged people who liked to think they could still party hearty like they had in college.

Randy glanced over his shoulder toward Nancy, who was thrashing around the dance floor with a different man than she'd been dancing with earlier.

"Come on," he said, grabbing Mary Bliss's hand. "How 'bout a dance with the boy next door?"

They had to fight their way onto the dance floor. Along the way Randy picked up a fresh bottle of beer.

"Woke up this morning, had a headache so bad," he shouted, off-key, moving his arms but not his feet to the music.

Mary Bliss sang along, too, laughing. Randy really was tipsy. He was adorable. He apparently hadn't learned any new dance steps since seventh-grade cotillion, because he was gyrating his arms in something approximating a dance Mary Bliss had always called "The Robot."

"It wasn't Budweiser that I had too much of," Randy hollered, waving the Budweiser bottle over his head.

"It was a double shot of tequila!" everybody screamed in unison.

They went on like that, screaming the words to the song, adding silly improvised verses, until Mary Bliss was laughing so hard that she could hardly dance.

She was standing still, trying to catch her breath, when the deejay switched tempo again.

His choice brought howls of approval: "With this Ring," another southern frat house standard.

Randy caught her up in his arms and they were dancing again, this time not so frenetically, and much closer.

He was tall, much taller than Parker, taller even than Matt. And the beer had given him the courage to hold her tight against his dinner jacket.

He was very sweet, Mary Bliss decided, much better at slow dancing. But she worried about the words to the song, which promised "I'll always love you," over and over again. He had probably danced to this song with Nancye a hundred times, sung the words, promised the promise. And she had probably promised back, the little liar. How humiliating to have her here, flaunting herself and those silicone boobs with every man in the room. Randy Bowden was a wounded bird, and she felt an urge to bandage him up and put him in a shoe box and feed him milk through an eyedropper.

He didn't smell bad either. She inhaled and had a sudden sensory overload.

"Brut!" she said, surprised.

He stepped back a little. "I'm sorry. Did I step on your feet? I haven't slow-danced in a long time."

"No," Mary Bliss said, patting his sleeve. "It's all right. I meant Brut, the aftershave. Aren't you wearing Brut?"

"A little," he said apologetically. "The kids made me wear it. They gave it to me for Father's Day. The little guys put it on me. I guess they overdid it."

"I like Brut," Mary Bliss said dreamily. "The first boy I ever dated wore Brut aftershave."

The song ended then, and Randy gave her a deep, courtly bow.

"Thank you," he said, kissing the back of her hand. "For the dances. And for everything."

"You're welcome," Mary Bliss said. "Anytime at all."

He drifted away then, and later in the evening Mary Bliss saw him, standing by the bar, drinking another beer. She smiled, he waved. Then Matt and Katharine and Charlie dragged her off to the midnight supper being served in the men's grill, and before she knew it, the deejay was breaking down his sound system and the dance was over.

"That wasn't so bad, was it?" Matt asked. They were sitting in the plush backseat of Charlie's Lincoln, Matt's arm thrown casually across her shoulders. Katharine was up front, driving, because she claimed Charlie had disgraced himself with one too many Manhattans.

"It wasn't bad," Mary Bliss said. "But it was an adjustment."

They were two blocks away from Mary Bliss's street, and Katharine was laughing wildly and driving way too fast, careening around corners, going up over the curbs, actually trenching old man Kirby's grass at one point.

Matt saw Mary Bliss's alarm. "Hey, Katharine," he called. "Why don't you just let us off here? It's cooled off a lot. I'll walk Mary Bliss home and then walk home from there."

Katharine slammed on the Lincoln's brakes, sending Mary Bliss nearly airborne. "Sure," she cried gaily. "We get it, don't we, Charlie?"

Charlie's head was slumped to the side. He snored loudly.

"You guys want to be alone," Katharine said. "I can take a hint."

Mary Bliss still had one leg in the car when Katharine screeched off.

"Charlie wasn't the only one dipping into the Manhattans tonight," Matt said. "Think she'll make it home all right?" he asked, watching the Lincoln's taillights disappear.

"It's all a show," Mary Bliss said. "I was watching her. She sipped the same club soda all night. I think she wanted you to do something like this."

"So we'd be alone?" he asked, reaching out to take her hand. "Isn't that against the rules?"

"I forgot to tell her the rules," Mary Bliss said.

64

They walked back to Mary Bliss's house hand in hand. It had rained sometime earlier, and steam still rose up off the cooling pavement. She could smell wet earth and flowers, and off in the distance she heard the fleeting hoot of a train whistle. It was only a little past midnight, but most of the lights of Fair Oaks were dimmed. The town had gone to bed.

"It's a nice place," Matt said, stopping to admire a neat white brick cottage on the corner of Mary Bliss's street. "I can see why you like it so much. How long have you been here?"

"Eighteen years," Mary Bliss said. "We bought the house when we were newlyweds and spent years fixing it up. How long have you been in the Oaks?"

"Seven, eight months," Matt said. "It's not like here. It's just a bunch of houses. Not a community, like Fair Oaks. I would have preferred to buy a house over here, but I couldn't find one in my price range."

"We could never afford our house now," Mary Bliss agreed.

"Parker managed to take out a whopping new mortgage on your house. Somebody must have thought it was worth that."

Mary Bliss felt her face warm. "I still can't believe any of this has happened. I can't believe he was capable of any of this. It's all like a really vivid bad dream."

"You had no idea he was planning any of it? The marriage wasn't in trouble?"

"I was blind and stupid," Mary Bliss said, her voice dull. "Running around, worrying about Charlie and Katharine's marriage, and Randy and Nancye's. I was obsessed with divorce. You know, I even plotted a map, of all the marriages in the neighborhood that had broken up. I didn't have a clue in the world that my own marriage was dissolving."

"He was a sneaky bastard," Matt said. "You shouldn't blame yourself."

"Who else can I blame?" she said lightly.

They had arrived at Mary Bliss's doorstep. They walked up onto the porch, and Matt pulled her into the shadows and kissed her. She kissed him back, long and deep. Full of regrets, she pulled away. From the corner of her eye she saw a flicker of movement. Heard the faint hiss of water running.

Across the street, Randy Bowden stood in his front yard, a hose trained on his shrubbery. He was staring in her direction. Mary Bliss waved. He turned away, pretending not to notice her.

"I can't ask you in," Mary Bliss told Matt. "Erin had a fit when I told her I was going out tonight. She called me awful names. She says my mother-in-law told her Parker really isn't dead. Erin says Meemaw told her her daddy is living on a beach somewhere, with a girlfriend and a boat. And that he's going to send for her."

"Is that right?" Matt asked, his interest piqued. "Do you think the old lady is telling the truth?"

"I don't know," Mary Bliss said. "She's gotten kind of senile. She claims the CIA is sending her coded messages through the fillings in her molars."

"Was Parker close to his mother?"

"Very," Mary Bliss said. "The only decent thing he did before he took off was to pay up her nursing home bill in advance."

"Meemaw won't tell you anything?"

"Not a word," Mary Bliss said, sighing.

He kissed her again, briefly. "Can I call you?"

She sighed again. "Better not. I've got to patch things up with my daughter. I can't stand living like this, with her hating me."

"You could call me."

"Maybe."

She went inside and locked the front door behind her. The house was quiet. Erin's room was empty. It was past curfew.

Enough, Mary Bliss thought. She dialed Jessica's house. The phone rang several times before a sleepy female voice picked up.

"Jessica? It's Mrs. McGowan. Is Erin there?"

The teenager yawned loudly. "No, Mrs. Mac."

"Was she there earlier?"

The girl hesitated.

"Jessica, I really need to know where Erin is," Mary Bliss said. "It's after midnight and I'm worried about her." She paused. "We had a bad fight. She ran off and I haven't seen her since."

"She came over around eight," Jessica said finally. "But I had a date tonight, so she left."

"Where was she going? Was she planning on coming back to spend the night with you again?"

"No," Jessica said. "My mom kinda kicked her out. She told Erin she can't stay here anymore until you guys make up."

"Your mom is a smart lady," Mary Bliss said gratefully. "Tell her I said thank you for putting up with us. Do you have any idea where Erin might have gone?"

Mary Bliss peered out the window at the Bowdens' house. All the lights were out.

"Could she be with Josh?"

"Josh? I don't know."

"Another girlfriend's house, maybe?"

"She didn't say," Jessica said. "Most of the kids we hang out with went down to the beach this weekend. The only reason I didn't go was that I had to work today."

"All right," Mary Bliss said. "Thanks."

"Wait. Mrs. Mac?"

"I'm still here. What is it?"

"Sometimes, Erin stays with her grandmother."

"Meemaw?" Mary Bliss was stunned. "You think she spends the night in the nursing home with Meemaw? In her room?"

"She sneaks in through the window," Jessica said. "She says she sleeps in a chair, and then she leaves in the morning, before the nurses come in to give her grandmother her medicine."

"Good heavens," Mary Bliss said.

65

Mary Bliss waited until nine Sunday morning before depositing herself at the Bowdens' front door. She'd been up since six, drunk a pot of coffee, washed and folded laundry, and started looking at her lesson plans for the coming year. She had to report back to school in two weeks.

Randy answered the front door, wearing loose pajama bottoms and a washed-out cotton undershirt. His hair hadn't been combed, and his eyes were slightly red-rimmed.

"Oh," he said, taken aback. "Come on in."

She followed him inside the house. The front hall was strewn with toys and books and magazines. Josh's guitar was laid across a living room chair, and there was a greasy pizza box on the coffee table.

"Coffee?" Randy asked when they got to the kitchen.

"No thanks, I've already had six cups this morning. I'm about to jump out of my skin."

Randy blinked. "What's up? You look kind of upset."

"It's Erin," she said. "We got into it again last night, and she took off and never came back home. I was wondering if she spent the night over here?"

"Here?" Randy looked around the room, as if he expected to find Erin McGowan hiding under the kitchen table. "Why would she spend the night here?"

"With Josh," she said firmly. "I know they've become really close. Inseparable."

"I was at the dance last night," Randy said. "You saw me there. Josh stayed home with the little guys."

"Was Erin here when you got home?" Mary Bliss asked.

"No," Randy said. "Everybody was asleep. I think they sent out for pizza and watched videos 'til late."

"Where's Josh?" she asked.

Randy ran his fingers through his hair. It didn't improve things. "Upstairs. He's still asleep."

"Can I talk to him?"

"You want me to wake him up?" Randy asked.

"I'll wake him up," Mary Bliss volunteered. "If you don't mind."

"Okay," Randy said reluctantly. "But he's kind of a bear in the morning. He usually doesn't get up 'til noon on weekends."

"I'll risk it," Mary Bliss said.

Upstairs, she pounded purposely on Josh's bedroom door. "Josh? Wake up, Josh."

She heard a muffled noise. "What the . . . ? Who's that?"

"It's Mary Bliss McGowan," she called. "I'm coming in. All right?"

"Huh?"

She pushed the door open. Josh's room looked remarkably like a male version of Erin's. The walls were covered with posters of race cars, rock groups, and half-naked women. The floor and every piece of furniture in the room was covered with clothes. Josh lay swaddled in a green plaid sleeping bag that lay on top of his bedspread. A large orange pillow covered his head.

"Mrs. Mac?" Josh slid the pillow off his head. "What's up?" he said groggily. He was wearing a set of earphones. He took them off and tossed them on the floor.

"I'm looking for Erin. She never came home last night."

"Oh."

He didn't sound surprised. Or concerned.

"Do you have any idea where she might have gone?"

Josh half sat up, pulling the sleeping bag over his bare chest in a touching display of modesty. "No."

"I called Jessica," Mary Bliss said. "Erin wasn't there. And the rest of her girlfriends are down at the beach."

Josh shook his head, not disagreeing.

"That just leaves you," she said pointedly.

He rubbed his eyes. "You think she was here?"

"Was she?"

"No. I was watching my little brothers all night."

"Has she spent the night over here before?"

"No. Why would she?"

She gave him a level look. "What do you think?"

He rubbed his eyes again. "I think you're messed up," he said finally. He turned over and put the orange pillow back over his head. "Go away. Okay?" The pillow muffled his voice, but Mary Bliss got the meaning.

Randy met her at the foot of her stairs. "Find anything out?" he asked. "Was Erin hiding in the closet up there?" He seemed vaguely amused.

"It's not funny," she snapped. "You've got sons. You wouldn't understand what it's like to have a daughter. To wonder where she is, and what she's doing, and who she's doing it with." Angry tears sprang to her eyes.

"What's that supposed to mean?" Randy asked.

"Never mind," she said, brushing the tears away and heading for the door.

At noon, she drove over to the Fair Oaks Assisted Living Facility. The lobby was crowded with families there to make their weekly visit with the elderly.

Mary Bliss brushed past them and headed toward the memory-impaired unit.

Lillian King was leafing through some charts at the nursing station, sipping a can of Diet Dr Pepper.

"Hey, Miz McGowan," she said, surprised. "We didn't expect you today."

"I didn't expect to be here," Mary Bliss said. She tossed her head in the direction of Eula's room. "How's she doing?"

"'Bout the same," Mrs. King said. "Ornery. Bossy. She say she in a lot of pain, but the doctor upped her medicine, so I swear she shouldn't be feelin' nothing."

"No changes in her condition?" Mary Bliss asked. "Is she any more focused? Does she seem to recognize people?"

"She can focus plenty good when she want to. You know how she is. Like an old she-possum."

"Isn't that the truth," Mary Bliss said fervently. "Is she awake?"

"Oh, yeah. Had her breakfast and been fussin' about not having a BM. And then, her newspaper didn't have no TV guide in it. You know how she is about that."

"Let me ask you something, Mrs. King," Mary Bliss said. "Have you seen my daughter around here this morning? Or last night?"

"Erin? Hadn't seen her today."

"Do you know anything about her sneaking into her grandmother's room and spending the night?"

"You kiddin'?" Mrs. King asked. "Why would the girl do something crazy like that?"

"We're not getting along. Since her father's accident. I know she's been visiting Meemaw a lot, and now, one of her girlfriends says Erin sometimes spends the night, sleeping in the chair beside her grandmother's bed."

"If she is, I hadn't caught her," Mrs. King said. "That ain't allowed, you know."

"I know," Mary Bliss said. She started toward Eula's room but turned around and came back.

"If you see Erin, would you call me?" she asked, shamefaced. "I'm really worried about her."

Mrs. King enveloped Mary Bliss in a hug. "Sure you are, baby. If I see that child, I'll call you right off. I promise."

For the first time in weeks, Eula was sitting up in her wheelchair when Mary Bliss entered her room.

She was staring at her television, pointing the remote control at it, swearing.

"Dammit," she muttered. "Damned cable."

"Hello, Meemaw," Mary Bliss said.

Eula looked up and frowned. "What are you doing here? It's Sunday, isn't it?"

"I'm looking for Erin," Mary Bliss said, deciding to get right down to business. "We had a fight last night. She's been really difficult."

"She's been difficult?" Eula said, laughing. "That's not the way she tells it."

"So you have seen her."

"She came over here last night," Eula said, finally clicking the remote. "Madder than spit."

"Did she tell you what the fight was about?" Mary Bliss asked.

Eula nodded. "I hear you got yourself a boyfriend."

"He's not a boyfriend," Mary Bliss said. "He's a neighbor. A friend. I went to the dance with him and another couple. It was all very innocent."

"Hah!" Eula said. "While the cat's away, the mouse will play."

"What's that supposed to mean?" Mary Bliss asked. She was about out of patience.

"Just what it sounds like," Eula said. "Did you bring any pudding today?"

"It's just barely noon. I haven't had time to cook. Anyway, I need for you to answer some questions for me."

"Maybe I will, and maybe I won't," Eula said, her voice a singsong. "How about gin? Did you bring me any gin?"

"No," Mary Bliss said. "You're not allowed to drink alcohol with the medication you're on."

"Bullshit," Eula said. "Erin brings me gin. Brings me olives too."

"Where would a seventeen-year-old girl get a bottle of gin?" Mary Bliss demanded.

"I don't ask," Eula said smugly, "and she doesn't say."

"What else have you put her up to?" Mary Bliss asked. "Is it true she spends the night over here sometimes? Was she here last night?"

"She's here sometimes," Eula said, lapsing again into singsong. "And sometimes she's not."

"What about last night?" Mary Bliss repeated, kneeling down in front of Eula. "Tell me, Meemaw. She didn't come home. I'm worried sick. Where was she?"

Eula just shook her head vigorously. "It's a secret."

"I've had enough of your secrets," Mary Bliss said, her voice harsh. "Was she with a boy? Is that it?"

Eula shrugged wordlessly.

"I know she's having sex with her boyfriend," Mary Bliss said. "Surely you don't condone that. She's just a child, for God's sake."

"What makes you think she's having relations?"

"I found condoms in her gym bag," Mary Bliss cried. "She admitted it to me. I know she's sleeping with Josh, across the street, but I can't talk sense to her."

"Josh?" Eula looked puzzled. "What was that name?"

"Josh. Josh Bowden. Did she tell you about him?"

"She told me she's in love. But that wasn't the name she called. The name she called was some other name. A Bible name."

"Joshua is in the Bible," Mary Bliss reminded her.

"That's not the name," Eula said sharply. "She's been asking me a lot of questions. About relations. Things like that. I told her she should save herself for marriage, but she just laughed. Headstrong, that one. Just like her mother." Eula gave her a bitter look.

"What kind of questions?" Mary Bliss asked. "Oh God. What was she asking about?"

"I told you," Eula said, her voice weak. "Relations. *Intercourse!*" She shouted the word. "She asked me what would happen if the boy didn't use protection.

She said it was just the one time when her friend's boyfriend didn't use protection, but she was kind of worried for her."

Mary Bliss buried her face in her hands. "Dear Lord. She had sex without protection. What did you tell her?"

Eula smiled coyly. "In my day, a girl who was having relations douched with Coca-Cola. Not that I ever did it, mind you. I was saved at church camp as a young teen. But I heard all about it from some bad girls."

"Coca-Cola?" Mary Bliss wanted to scream. Actually, she was screaming. "Coca-Cola can't keep you from getting pregnant. It can't keep you from getting herpes or VD or, God forbid, AIDS."

"You don't need to shout," Eula said. "I'm sick, but I'm not deaf. Not yet, anyway."

"All right," Mary Bliss said. "You say she was here last night. What time did she leave?"

"We watched *Love Boat* together," Eula said. "That's our favorite program. She made me a martini, then she said she had to go. She was waiting on her boyfriend to call her. She climbed out that window over there, and she was gone."

"What time?" Mary Bliss repeated.

"Maybe eleven o'clock," Eula said. "You say she didn't come home? How would you know, running around in the streets all night with some strange man?"

"I was home right after midnight," Mary Bliss said, gritting her teeth to keep from lapsing into the screaming meemies again. "Where does the boyfriend live, did she tell you that?"

"Maybe a ways away from here," Eula said. "She asked me for gas money for her car. So I gave her twenty dollars. And the thirty for the gin. Beefeater's. I always pay for my own gin."

Mary Bliss's molars were grinding themselves into a powder. Erin had a full tank of gas. She could be anywhere. Or nowhere.

"Meemaw," Mary Bliss said. She grasped both the old lady's hands in hers. Eula fidgeted, but Mary Bliss held tight.

"Last night Erin said you know where Parker is. She said he's living on a beach somewhere, and he's going to send for her. Is that true? Do you know where Parker is? Has he talked to you? Has he talked to Erin?"

Eula snatched her hands away and buried them in the sides of her wheelchair. She grinned maliciously.

"Maybe so. Maybe not. That's for me to know and you to find out."

66

Erin still wasn't home.

Mary Bliss called every friend she could think of. She drove by the mall to see if the manager at the Gap had seen her. She hadn't.

By five she was frantic. Her daughter had been gone nearly twenty-four hours. Where? Where would Erin go? As far as Mary Bliss knew, she had only her car and her pocketbook. Should she call the police? She sat at the kitchen table and picked at the long acrylic nails. They were driving her crazy. They itched. She couldn't even dial the phone properly with the damned things.

Finally she went back upstairs and tore into Erin's room. The place was a land mine. Somewhere in there, there must be a clue to her daughter's secret life.

This time, she didn't bother to fold or neaten. Mary Bliss dumped out the dresser drawers and combed through their contents. She emptied the closet, dug under Erin's bed, even tossed her trash can on the floor and picked through the discarded Coke cans and used tissues.

Nothing.

In desperation, she stripped Erin's bed, throwing the sheets and quilts and pillows to the floor. When she'd removed the mattress pad too, she noticed a slight lump in the mattress. She slid her hand under the mattress, dreading what she would find. Her fingers closed around something small, smooth, and plastic.

A cell phone. It was a tiny Nokia, smaller than Mary Bliss's own bulky old phone. Mary Bliss turned it over. She'd never seen it before. Erin's own cell phone was just like Mary Bliss's, but since she couldn't afford to keep up the cell service, both phones were in the kitchen, still plugged into their chargers.

Mary Bliss carried the Nokia downstairs. She tried turning it on but got only a digital readout that said "Low Battery."

Neither of the old cell phone chargers fit this one. She chewed on one of the ragged acrylic nails. Where had Erin gotten this phone? Was this how she was conducting her clandestine affair? And if she wasn't sleeping with Josh, who was she sleeping with? She turned the phone over and over again, hoping it would suddenly come to life and start providing answers.

Josh. He knew something, she was sure of it. He'd become Erin's most trusted confidant. She picked up her own phone and called the Bowdens. No answer. She got up and looked out the front window. No cars were parked in the driveway. Sunday. Was this Nancye's day to have custody of the kids?

She had to do something. This inactivity was driving her nuts. But driving around in circles wasn't the answer.

She went to the refrigerator to look for something to eat or drink, something to calm her nerves. The pink wrist corsage sat in the middle of the top shelf. Mary Bliss took it out. She put it on her wrist and held the roses up to her nose and inhaled. Last night seemed a world away. Last night she had allowed herself a few hours away, to laugh and dance. She thought of one of the songs she and Matt had danced to. "Be Young, Be Foolish, Be Happy." She'd been all of that, and where had it gotten her?

She ruffled the roses with her fingertips. Already the pink petals were tinged with brown.

Call me, Matt had said last night. She bit her lip. She needed help. She'd been trying to deal with her family secrets all summer, and she'd made a mess of it. Maybe, she thought, it was time to let go. Time to get help.

He answered on the first ring.

"Matt?"

"Hey there," he said warmly. "Did you change your mind?"

"No. Yes." She hesitated. "Erin never came home last night. I think she's run away."

"I'll be right over," he said.

And he was. She told him again about the fight, about Erin's movements the previous night.

"So," he said, taking notes. "She was at Jessica's at eight. Then she went to the nursing home. She left her grandmother around midnight. And nobody's seen her since?"

"Nobody that I can find," Mary Bliss said. "I talked to Josh this morning. He says he didn't see her last night, but I think maybe he knows something. He's her best friend."

"Did she have any money?"

"Her grandmother gave her fifty dollars," Mary Bliss said. "But she doesn't get paid until this Friday."

"What does she do with her paycheck?" he asked.

"She puts it in the bank," Mary Bliss said. "She's had her own checking account since she was thirteen."

"So she could have, what? Several hundred dollars?"

Mary Bliss's face paled. "I don't know. I tried not to talk to her too much about money. I didn't want her to know just how tight things have been."

Matt picked up the Nokia. "I'll be right back."

She followed him out to the car. "What are you doing? Where are you going?"

He was driving his own car, a black Explorer. He slid into the driver's seat, turned on the motor, and plugged the little Nokia into an adapter mounted on the dashboard. "This is the same kind as mine," he said. He let the motor run for ten minutes, and when he was satisfied the battery had charged enough, he unplugged the phone and she followed him back inside.

He sat down at the kitchen table again and began pushing buttons on the Nokia.

Mary Bliss leaned over his shoulder to watch, but his fingers moved so fast that they were a blur. She saw him punch the "Menu" button, and then select "Messages." He paused. "I need a code to get in here. Does she have a special or lucky number?"

"Her birthday is nine fifteen," Mary Bliss suggested. He tried it but shook his head. "We'll come back to that," he said. He pushed some more buttons, then got a list of what appeared to be phone numbers.

"What are those?" Mary Bliss asked.

Matt was jotting down the list of numbers. "This is the call log. It lists all the numbers dialed, either in or out, on this phone. It also lists missed calls. You recognize any of these?"

Mary Bliss scanned the list. "No. It looks like most of them are local area codes, though."

"Only three or four numbers," Matt pointed out. "She's been dialing them over and over again." He pointed to another number with an area code Mary Bliss didn't recognize. "This is a South Florida exchange."

"A lot of her girlfriends are at the beach," Mary Bliss said. "I guess they could be down in Florida. Now what do we do?"

"First, we dial the numbers, see who picks up," Matt said.

He dialed the number, listened, frowned, then handed the phone to Mary Bliss.

"Hey," a man's voice said. "Hit me back later."

"You recognize him?" Matt asked.

"No," Mary Bliss said. "It's not Parker, if that's what you were wondering. And it's not Josh either."

He dialed the next number and handed it to her. This time it was a woman's voice. "We can't come to the phone right now, but leave a name and number and we'll call you back," she said.

Mary Bliss shook her head again.

He dialed the next number. She listened, confused.

"It's just the school," Mary Bliss said. "Fair Oaks Academy. Erin's school. She was probably calling about soccer practice."

Matt punched in the last number. He listened, but didn't hand the phone to Mary Bliss this time.

"What?" she asked. "Who was it? What was that last number?"

"It was for a hotline," Matt said.

"What kind of hotline?" she demanded. "Tell me. I need to know."

"It was for a pregnancy support hotline," Matt said.

Mary Bliss's nails itched unbearably. She pulled the right thumbnail off.

"It's what I was afraid of," she said, choosing her words carefully. "She was asking Meemaw questions. About birth control. She had unprotected sex. She's pregnant. And now she's gone."

"You don't know that," Matt said firmly.

"It's why she ran away," Mary Bliss insisted. "I let her down. She needed me to be strong, to be there for her, and I just . . . wasn't."

"If she were pregnant, where would she go?" Matt asked. "What would she do?"

"I don't know," Mary Bliss said, biting her knuckle. "We don't have any other family. Just Meemaw and Parker."

"And the baby's father," Matt reminded her. "If there is a baby."

He kept looking down at the phone. "AirOne is the provider," he said, tapping his pen on the edge of the table. "We need to find out who this phone is billed to."

"Will they tell us if we ask?" Mary Bliss asked.

"Probably not. Privacy is a big issue these days. The companies guard that information like it was Fort Knox."

"But we know who she's calling," Mary Bliss said, feeling more hopeful. "I can just call them back and ask them to call me. Right?"

"You can ask, but that doesn't mean they'll do it," Matt said. "Also, this log only lists the last ten calls received or dialed. If Erin was upset, and calling the same numbers, this might only reflect a day or so of phone calls."

"Can we get all the phone records?" Mary Bliss asked.

"It's tricky," Matt admitted. "Legally, you need a subpoena. And that takes time." He took a deep breath. "I think maybe you should file a missing persons report. With the police. It's been twenty-four hours, she's a minor. They have resources to look for her that we don't."

Mary Bliss chewed her thumbnail. She looked over at Matt.

"I can't call the police," she said, her voice low. "What if Erin's just hiding out with a friend I haven't thought of? If I call in the police, she'd never forgive me. Anyway, I can't really call the police, after what happened with Parker, can I?"

He winced. "Good point."

"Isn't there another way to find out more about this phone?" she asked.

"I could call in a favor," he said slowly. "I know a guy. He used to work at AirOne when I was with the GBI. He left there a few months ago, but maybe he could pull some strings for me."

"Can you call him?" Mary Bliss asked. "I hate to ask, but I have to."

"I'll have to track him down," Matt said. "It's Sunday. He's a big golfer. No telling where he is this time of day."

"We've got to find her," Mary Bliss said. "We've got to."

67

Katharine came over at six, with a casserole and a copy of a Meg Ryan movie Mary Bliss had never seen.

"Matt called," she said, putting her arms around Mary Bliss. "He didn't think you should be alone."

"I shouldn't," Mary Bliss agreed. She held up her right hand. She had methodically yanked off every one of the acrylic nails.

Katharine put the casserole in the microwave. "Have you called all her friends?"

Mary Bliss nodded. "Jessica's the only one who's in town. I called her mother a little while ago and explained the situation. She had a talk with Jessica, who then called me back. The child swears she has no idea who Erin was sleeping with. All she knows is that Erin has been really secretive about it, and that she was crying when she went over there Saturday night."

"Her best friend doesn't know who her boyfriend is?" Katharine sounded skeptical.

"Erin's like that," Mary Bliss said. "Buttoned up. She takes after Parker that way. She has friends, but she never lets them get too close."

"What about Josh?" Katharine asked.

"Nobody's home," Mary Bliss said. "I think Nancye must have the kids today. I saw Randy this morning when I went over there to look for Erin, but he left shortly after that, and he hasn't been back since."

"You're positive Josh isn't the boyfriend?" Katharine asked.

"That's what he says," Mary Bliss said. "And Meemaw swears Josh wasn't the name Erin mentioned to her. She says it's something from the Bible."

"Aaron? David? Esau? Jacob? Abraham? Simon? Did she specify whether it was New or Old Testament?"

"She can't remember," Mary Bliss said. "She can remember her winning hand from a bridge tournament six years ago, but she can't remember the name of the boy her granddaughter is sleeping with."

The microwave beeped and Katharine lifted the steaming casserole out with pot holders. She spooned the chicken and rice mixture onto a plate and set it down in front of Mary Bliss. "Eat," she said.

Mary Bliss shook her head. "I don't think so."

"Just a little," Katharine said. She picked up the fork, loaded it with food, and did a little loop-de-loop with it, making whooshing airplane noises. "Come on," she coaxed. "Open the hangar."

Mary Bliss took a bite to appease her friend, then another bite, because she couldn't think of anything else to do. Little by little, Katharine spoon-fed her almost a cup of chicken and rice.

"Good girl," Katharine said approvingly. "You're a member of the clean-plate club. You get a prize."

She went to the wicker basket she'd brought over and picked up a prescription pill bottle. She shook a white capsule out into her palm and offered it to Mary Bliss.

"Ta-da!" she said gaily. "The grand prize."

"What is it?"

"It's a chill pill," Katharine said. "My doctor gave them to me when Charlie first left. It's just to take the edge off. It won't make you woozy or anything."

"I don't think so," Mary Bliss said. "I need to be alert. I can't be doped up looking for my daughter. But thanks anyway."

Katharine frowned but put the pill back in the bottle. "Let me ask you something," she said. "Just what do you plan to do next?"

"Find my kid," Mary Bliss said. "Bring her back here. Love her, take care of her. Fix her."

Katharine gave her a long, level look. "What if she really is pregnant? What if she doesn't want to come back? What if she doesn't want to be fixed?"

"That won't happen," Mary Bliss said. "I won't let it."

They watched the Meg Ryan movie in the den, and Mary Bliss kept the phone in her lap the whole time, waiting for it to ring.

At ten they heard a knock at the back door. Mary Bliss flew to open it.

Matt came in, holding a flat manila envelope.

"What took so long? Did you get it?" Mary Bliss asked, clutching his arm. "The phone records? Did he get them for you?"

"Yeah," Matt said. "It took some doing. I had to meet him at the Krispy Kreme out in East Cobb, and drink coffee and talk over old times. I owe favors to three guys I've never even met, but I got 'em. I made some phone calls and found out some stuff too. That's what took so long."

Katharine came in from the den. "Tell," she said, hoisting herself up and sitting cross-legged on the kitchen counter.

Matt slid three sheets of computer printouts from the envelope. "The phone is billed to Isaac Brownlee," he said, looking straight at Mary Bliss.

"Erin's soccer coach?" Mary Bliss said immediately. "Oh my God. Isaac. Right out of the Bible." Her face went pale.

"Her soccer coach?" Katharine said. "Why would he buy a cell phone for Erin?"

"I can't believe it," Mary Bliss moaned.

Matt showed them the printouts. "These are the call records for that phone—incoming and outgoing. Dozens of calls—lots of them late-night calls, to and from Isaac Brownlee. He has his own cell phone too, but my guy wouldn't pull those records. Doesn't matter anyway, we've got what we need with this."

Mary Bliss's face crumpled. She started to cry. "Her soccer coach? He's the boyfriend? It can't be. He must be close to thirty years old."

"He's thirty-two," Matt said grimly. "Married, no kids. I've checked him out. Isaac Brownlee is a real piece of work."

"Oh God," Mary Bliss moaned. "You're positive, then? He's the one? They've been . . . together?"

"Those other phone numbers, the ones we found on Erin's call list, one was Brownlee's cell phone, the other was his home phone. I imagine the woman's voice on the answering machine is Mrs. Brownlee," Matt said. "Erin was also calling him at school."

"He's her coach," Mary Bliss said weakly. "Erin's the starting goalie on the team. She was calling him about soccer."

"Why would he buy her a cell phone and get her to keep it a secret?" Matt said, his voice gentle but insistent. "Think about it. It's the perfect setup. And it's not the first time he's done something like this."

"What do you mean?" Mary Bliss asked.

"I told you I did some checking," Matt said. "Isaac Brownlee used to teach science at a public high school in Dayton, Ohio. He was terminated two years ago. They have strict personnel confidentiality rules, but I went back to the office and ran a computer search of back issues of the *Dayton Daily News*. They did a big story about a popular male high school teacher there who left the school under a cloud after accusations were made about 'improper behavior with female students.' The newspaper story didn't mention the teacher's name because no criminal charges were ever filed. I called the reporter. She hemmed and hawed and wouldn't volunteer any names, but when I mentioned Isaac Brownlee, she let me know I was right on target."

Mary Bliss's hands were shaking uncontrollably. "Oh God. Soccer camp. Erin told me it was a special soccer camp for goalies. That's why none of the other girls were going. Coach picked her up himself. It was down in Jekyll Island. Four days they were gone. Back in June. Right after Parker left. I was so distracted, so upset. It never dawned on me that something was wrong."

Katharine clamped her own hands over Mary Bliss's. "Stop that. You're not to blame. That bastard took advantage of Erin. Of both of you. It's not your fault. It's not Erin's." She looked at Matt. "Where is this bastard Brownlee? Do you think Erin's with him?"

Matt shrugged. "No way to tell. I checked Brownlee's house. There are a couple of days' worth of newspapers in his driveway, and a stack of mail in his mailbox. It looks like he's been out of town, at least two days."

"Maybe Erin went to meet him somewhere?" Mary Bliss asked.

"I called the principal at Fair Oaks Academy," Matt said.

"You called Anne Harris? What did she say?"

"According to her, Brownlee went to Panama City, Florida, on Thursday, for a long weekend."

"You didn't tell her about Erin, did you?" Mary Bliss asked.

"No. I just said I was a soccer coach from Alabama and I wanted to talk to him about a tournament coming up. She says she doesn't know where he's staying."

"Do you think Erin is with Isaac Brownlee?" Mary Bliss asked.

"Maybe," Matt said. "It's a possibility. But there's another possibility too. I checked the phone company records on that number I thought was a South Florida listing. I was right. It's a public phone booth. In Key West."

"We don't know anybody in Key West," Mary Bliss said automatically. She looked over at Katharine. "Do we?"

"Maybe you do," Hayslip countered. "Parker."

"No," Mary Bliss said quickly. "It can't be Parker."

"I think it is," Matt said. "Erin made the call to that number. It's a phone booth on Duval Street. I think Parker is somewhere down in the Keys. Somehow, Erin found that out and tried to call him."

"It couldn't be," Mary Bliss said. "She would have told me."

"No. You said it yourself," Katharine reminded her. "Erin's all buttoned up. She keeps secrets. Just like Parker."

"The call was only a few seconds long. It never connected," Matt said. "Maybe that's where Erin's gone. Her lover has left town. As far as she's concerned, there's nobody left to turn to. Nobody but Daddy."

68

"What now?" Katharine asked.

"That depends on Mary Bliss," Matt said. "I think she should bring in the police. They can do more than we can. You've got Erin's license plate number—they can put out an alert on that. They can try to find Brownlee down in Panama City."

"No," Mary Bliss said adamantly. "No police. Erin's not a criminal. She's already in trouble. She'd be terrified if the cops stopped her. There's no telling what she'd do."

Mary Bliss walked quickly to the living room and looked out the window. Randy Bowden's car was in the driveway. It was past eleven, but there were still lights on.

"I'm going over to the Bowdens' to talk to Josh," Mary Bliss called over her shoulder. She was out the door and across the street before her own front door had closed.

She walked around to the back of the house and knocked on the kitchen door. She could see Josh through the glass. He was standing with his back to the counter, eating a huge slab of pizza. She rapped sharply on the glass.

"Josh! I need to talk to you."

He rolled his eyes, put down the pizza, and let her in.

"What's up, Mrs. Mac?" he asked.

"You know what's up. Erin's run away. I found her cell phone. The one Coach Brownlee gave her. I know all about them, Josh. Is that where she's gone? Is she with Coach Brownlee?"

Josh squirmed and looked around the room. Just then, Randy walked in.

"I thought I heard voices," he said. "Did you find Erin?"

"No," Mary Bliss said. "I was just asking Josh to be straight and tell me what he knows."

"He told you everything he knows this morning," Randy said, sounding annoyed. "Didn't you, Josh?"

Josh squirmed again. He picked at the cheese topping on the pizza.

"Didn't you, son?" Randy repeated, his voice stern.

"Is she pregnant?" Mary Bliss asked.

Josh blushed. "She thought she might be. But it was a false alarm." He still wouldn't meet her eye.

Randy clapped a hand on his son's shoulder. "Josh! What the hell are you talking about? Who got Erin pregnant? Was it you?"

"No, sir," Josh said, his face sullen. "It wasn't me. I told you that."

"She's been sleeping with Isaac Brownlee. Her soccer coach up at the high school," Mary Bliss said. "I imagine Josh was the only one who knew about it."

"Is that true?" Randy was incredulous.

"Yessir," Josh said. "I told her it was a bad idea. But she says she's in love with him, and he's in love with her. Ha!"

"Where did Erin go when she left last night?" Mary Bliss asked. "She didn't take the cell phone. She had her car and a little money her grandmother gave her. Have you talked to her at all?"

Josh's face was getting red. He looked up at Mary Bliss. "You lied to her," he said, furious. "How could you tell her he was dead? How could you? What the hell kind of bitch are you?"

"Josh!" Randy said.

"Ask her, Dad," Josh said. "See if she'll tell the truth now. I bet she won't. She's as big a liar as Mom. She told Erin, she told me, she told everybody Mr. Mac was dead. It was all a big, stinking lie."

"Mary Bliss?" Randy looked from his son to her. "Is he making this up? Is Parker alive? Are you really capable of something like that?"

"You have no idea what I'm capable of," Mary Bliss said, a threat implied in her voice. "Josh. Tell me where Erin has gone. I know you know. Is she with Coach Brownlee?"

"That prick?" Josh said, contempt dripping from his voice. "Hell, no. He left town. Erin told him she was late. That she might be pregnant. He didn't care. He and his wife went down to Panama City. He doesn't give a shit about Erin."

"Then where?" Mary Bliss said. "Where did she go?"

"Key West," he said finally. "To see her dad. She came by here last night. She needed money. I couldn't leave my brothers alone, so I gave her my ATM card. She took fifty dollars. It's all I had."

"Where in Key West?" Mary Bliss asked. "What makes her think Parker is down there?"

"He is," Josh said. "She talked to him."

"When? Where is he? Does she know for certain?"

"He's somewhere in the Keys. He calls her from different phone booths. On her cell phone. She tried calling him back, but he never answered."

"When did this start?" Mary Bliss demanded. "When did she first hear from Parker?"

"Like, last week, I think. When she thought she was pregnant. She told her grandmother she was in trouble. I think Mr. Mac calls the old lady sometimes. Erin gave Meemaw her cell phone number, and he called her, like, earlier in the week. But he made her swear not to tell anybody. Especially you."

"She told you," Mary Bliss pointed out.

"I'm her best friend," Josh said. "The only one she trusts."

"God," Randy said disgustedly.

Mary Bliss kept on ignoring him. "Does Parker know Erin is coming down there? How does she plan to find him?"

"I told her, it's a big place down there. You don't even know where he is. Or if he'll help you. She didn't care. She was outta here."

"She hardly has any money," Mary Bliss fretted. "Maybe a hundred bucks. That won't even cover gas and food."

Josh laughed bitterly. "She'll be okay. She took your Visa card. Last week. You know, when she thought she was pregnant. I think she was maybe planning this all along. Even before you guys had that fight last night."

"My Visa? It's no good," Mary Bliss cried. "It's two months in arrears. If she tries to use it, they'll take it away and cut it up."

Josh shook his head. "Man. I thought my mom was fucked up."

"Josh!" Randy warned.

"Has she called you at all?" Mary Bliss asked.

He shook his head. "I was at work all day. Just got home. Anyway, she doesn't have her cell phone with her, right?"

"That's right," Mary Bliss said. She'd made up her mind. "Listen, Josh," she said. "I know you hate me right now. But I need a favor. For Erin. I'm going after her. Tonight. To Key West. Can you stay over at my house tonight? And bring your cell phone, all right? In case she tries to call you that way. If she calls, try to get her to tell you exactly where she is. Tell her I'm sorry. Really, really sorry. Make sure she stays right where she's at. Then call me. On her cell phone. I'll have it with me the whole time. All right? Can you do that?"

Josh looked away, still angry at her.

"He'll do it," Randy said.

Mary Bliss put both hands on Josh's shoulders. He tried to twist away from her, but she held on tight. "Promise me, Josh. Erin could be in a lot of trouble.

Anything could happen to her. I mean it. Promise me you'll help me find her."

"Whatever," he mumbled.

"What can I do?" Randy asked. "Shall I go with you?"

"I'm fine," Mary Bliss said reflexively. "But thanks."

She ran back across the street. Matt was talking on the kitchen phone. He put his hand on the receiver. "Did the kid talk? What did you find out?"

"It's like you thought. Erin's gone to Key West to find Parker. I'm going after her."

Mary Bliss ran upstairs to her bedroom, with Katharine not far behind. She got an overnight bag out of the closet and threw in a change of clothes and a toothbrush. She hesitated a minute, then went into Erin's room and got a change of clothes for her daughter and added it to the bag.

"Just like this?" Katharine asked. "You're going to take off in the middle of the night?"

"Yes," Mary Bliss said. "Don't try to talk me out of it."

"I won't," Katharine said. "Do you have any cash?"

"No," Mary Bliss admitted. "Maybe five bucks. And my credit cards are useless."

"I've got cash at the house," Katharine said. "Maybe five hundred bucks. You can follow me home and get it. Take my American Express card too. I'd go with you, but I don't want to leave Charlie home alone this soon."

"I'll be fine by myself," Mary Bliss assured her. "But the money will help. Thanks. You really are the best."

"Don't try to drive all night," Katharine warned her. "Stop at a hotel. Not some fleabag either. Do you have any kind of a plan?"

"Yeah, do you have a plan?" The women looked up. Matt Hayslip stood in the door. "Don't tell me you're planning on driving to Key West tonight."

"That's just what I'm planning," Mary Bliss said.

"You can't go off half-cocked like this," Matt said. "Let me do some legwork. I've put in a call to the sheriff's office, asked them to put out an APB on that Range Rover of Parker's. They're going to send patrols by that phone booth on Duval Street. If Parker's down there, they'll find him. And they'll find Erin too."

Mary Bliss pushed a strand of hair out of her eye. "I told you, I don't want the police scaring Erin. Why can't you let me do this my own way?"

"Because you don't know what you're doing," Matt retorted. "You're scared and you're panicky, and you're not thinking things through clearly."

"I've thought it through very clearly," Mary Bliss said, her teeth gritted. "I'm going over to the nursing home right now. Eula knows where Parker is. She gave Erin his phone number. And now I'm going to go over there and wake her up, and if she doesn't tell me every damn thing she knows, I swear to God, I'll twist her head off with my bare hands."

Katharine gave her a wan smile. "I'd pay money to see that. Come on, then, let's get your cash and get you going."

Matt shook his head in disbelief. "You're just going to let her go like that? Alone?"

Katharine was already out the door, tagging after Mary Bliss. "You don't know Mary Bliss very well, do you? Nobody *lets* that girl do anything."

"At least let me go with you," Matt called, hurrying down the stairs after the women. "It's eight hundred miles to Key West. That's a sixteen-hour drive, Mary Bliss. We'll get there quicker with two drivers."

"No way," Mary Bliss said. "You just want Parker. So you can get your client's money back. This isn't about Parker anymore. It's about my child. And me. And if she sees you, she'll take off running in the opposite direction."

Mary Bliss hefted her overnight bag onto her shoulder. "I appreciate everything you've done, Matt. Really. But I've got to do this alone."

69

Midnight. The front door of the Fair Oaks Assisted Living Facility was locked. Through the glass Mary Bliss could see a large middle-aged black man. He was asleep, with his chins resting on his gray uniformed chest.

She rapped on the glass. He jumped up, startled, stared at her as if she'd just been beamed down there by an alien life force.

"I need to see Mrs. McGowan," Mary Bliss called. "It's a family emergency."

He walked over to the doors and continued to stare at her.

"Let me in," Mary Bliss insisted. "It's an emergency."

He wavered, then unbolted the doors and opened them. "Everybody's sleeping. Visiting hours aren't until morning," he said.

She brushed right past him. "I told you, this is an emergency. Anyway, she hardly sleeps at all these days. I'm sure she's still awake."

The security guard trailed after her, past the abandoned nursing station, past an aide who was coming out of one of the rooms, 'til finally, she paused outside Eula's room.

"I'll just be a few minutes," Mary Bliss said, opening the door.

The room was dark and quiet, not what she expected. Even when she was sleeping, Eula left the television on and the overhead light blazing. That way, she said, she could see who was stealing from her.

Mary Bliss felt in the dark for the light switch. The overhead light snapped on. The room was empty. Eula's wheelchair was empty. Her bed was unmade, the covers shoved to one side. The television had been turned off.

"She's gone," Mary Bliss told the security guard, who stood there, openmouthed, his hand on his holster, which held only a two-way radio. "Call somebody," Mary Bliss said loudly. "My mother-in-law is missing."

The guard switched on his two-way radio and Mary Bliss followed him back to the nursing station. "Hello," she called, until a night shift nurse she didn't recognize emerged from a supply closet.

"Mrs. Eula McGowan," Mary Bliss said, a little breathlessly. "My mother-in-law. She's not in her room. I'm very concerned."

"Let me call the supervisor," the nurse said. Mary Bliss stood by the station and drummed her fingers on the countertop until the nursing supervisor came hurrying down the hallway toward them.

"Mrs. McGowan?" she said when she got closer. This was a woman Mary Bliss had seen before. She was tall and thin with strangely colored red hair. Her name badge identified her as Mrs. Shoemaker.

"I'm Mary Bliss McGowan. I came looking for my mother-in-law. We've got sort of a family emergency. But she's not in her room."

"We've been trying to call you for the past hour," the woman said, a note of reproach in her voice. "But we kept getting a busy signal. Mrs. McGowan's doctor was in this afternoon. Her blood pressure had dropped noticeably, and her heartbeat was irregular. She was complaining of dizziness and chest pain. The doctor ordered a new medication on Friday; we think maybe she's had some kind of reaction to it."

The gin, Mary Bliss thought. Eula had been mixing martinis with whatever medication she'd been given.

The nurse was talking rapidly, her face flushed. "We sent your mother-in-law over to Piedmont Hospital's emergency room, not thirty minutes ago."

"It's that bad?" Mary Bliss asked. "Is she conscious?"

"She was highly agitated," the woman said. "At one point, she pulled out the IV the doctor had ordered. So she's been sedated. You'll have to speak to her doctor if you want any more information than that."

The nurse stood back and watched to see Mary Bliss's reaction.

"Are you talking about Dr. Hansen? Dick Hansen?" Mary Bliss asked. "Her regular doctor?"

"No," the nurse said. "This was Dr. Katz. Sheri Katz. She was on call this weekend. I can give you her beeper number. We called the service and let her know we were sending your mother over there."

"Mother-in-law," Mary Bliss automatically corrected her. The nurse wrote down the number. Mary Bliss tucked it in her pocket and said a quick prayer that this would not be Eula's time. Not yet. Then she went back to Eula's room.

She'd gotten very good at ransacking, she thought, as she opened drawers and cupboards. Eula's room was much neater, an easier job. She searched under the stacks of cotton nightgowns, thrust her hand into the cartons of adult diapers on the floor of Eula's closet, opened the medicine cabinet in the bathroom, looking for something.

She plunged without guilt into Eula's pocketbook. Her billfold held an expired Georgia driver's license, her social security card, a Kroger discount card, and a dog-eared snapshot of Parker. There was a key ring, an address book, a checkbook, and a package of tissues. Mary Bliss checked every page of the address book but found nothing out of the ordinary.

On a shelf under the windowsill, Mary Bliss went through the half dozen books stacked there. A Bible—untouched, Mary Bliss noted. Two Eugenia Price paperback novels. A paperback book about prescription medications. The last book was one of inspirational poetry by a Methodist minister's wife. Mary Bliss riffled the pages until something fell out.

She picked it up and looked. A thin rubber band–wrapped package of postcards. All the scenes appeared to be of tropical beaches. Florida beaches. She turned them over and recognized Parker's handwriting immediately.

"Hope all is well at home. Weather wonderful." All were signed "Your loving son."

There were four of them. The postmarks were from Fernandina Beach, Cocoa Beach, Orlando, and Fort

Lauderdale. The most recent card had been mailed nearly three weeks earlier.

Mary Bliss put the books back on the shelf and walked quickly back to the nursing station. Luckily, Mrs. Shoemaker was still there, checking something on the computer monitor there.

"Mrs. Shoemaker," Mary Bliss said, willing herself to be calm. "I'm sorry you weren't able to reach me tonight. As I've said, we've had another family emergency. I was wondering, who else did you call tonight? To notify family about Mrs. McGowan's transfer to the hospital? Doesn't somebody have to give you permission to do that?"

Mrs. Shoemaker drew herself up indignantly. "This was a medical emergency. We sent her on the physician's order."

"I'm sure you were right to do so," Mary Bliss said, trying to placate the woman. "But did you call anybody else in the family? It's really important that I know."

Mrs. Shoemaker allowed herself a slight smirk. Mary Bliss decided to let it go. For weeks now, Eula had been telling everyone within earshot that Parker was definitely alive—even though his widow had supposedly "buried" him in June.

"Did Eula give you another family member's name?" Mary Bliss repeated.

"Mrs. McGowan did give us a new emergency contact number two weeks ago," Mrs. Shoemaker relented. She opened a drawer and pulled out a metal file box. She leafed through the index cards until she'd found the one she wanted and extracted it.

"Alvin Bayless," she read. "Is that a nephew or something?"

Mary Bliss snatched the card out of her hand and ran for the door with it.

Alvin Bayless. She couldn't believe Parker had been so obvious. Alvin was Parker's first name, a name he hated so much, he'd had it legally changed as soon as he turned twenty-one. Bayless was Eula's maiden name.

When she got to the car, she looked at the writing on the card. The area code was the same one she remembered from Erin's cell phone log. She picked up the Nokia and dialed.

"Hello?" A man's voice, not Parker's.

"Let me speak to Parker McGowan, please," Mary Bliss said, crossing her fingers.

"Who?" the man said. But he'd waited a beat too long. He knew who she was talking about.

"Parker McGowan," Mary Bliss repeated. "It's urgent that I speak to him tonight."

"I don't know a Parker McGowan," the man said. "I think you must have the wrong number."

"All right," Mary Bliss said, deciding to play along. "How about Alvin Bayless. Is he around?"

"He's gone," the man said.

"When did he leave?"

"Who's calling, please?"

"His wife," Mary Bliss said.

"Right." The man laughed and hung up.

Mary Bliss redialed. The phone picked up on the first ring.

"Listen, I told you he's not here. He left an hour ago. Who is this really?"

Mary Bliss felt helpless. "It really is his wife. Don't hang up, please. Listen. Parker's mother, I mean, Alvin's mother, is in the hospital. She's very ill. She might not live out the night. His daughter has run away from home. I think she's headed down there to see her father. Now, I have got to talk to him. Tonight. Right away."

"Like I said, he left here an hour ago. He got a phone call. Something important, I guess, because he just took off. Without saying a word about what was going on. Of course, he never tells me anything, anyway."

"Where does he live?" Mary Bliss asked, crossing her fingers.

"You're his wife, you tell me," the man said, laughing at his own joke.

This time it was Mary Bliss's turn to hang up.

She was headed for the Amoco station near the interstate when she saw a red light blinking on the dashboard.

"No," she said, pounding the steering wheel. "I fixed you up last week. No more red lights."

The light kept on blinking. Was it the one telling her she needed more coolant? Or more oil? She couldn't remember which. Maybe somebody at the gas station could help. As she was pulling into the station, her heart sank. The old gas station office, which had for years housed two homely but competent attendants, both of whom were named Buddy, now featured a minimart convenience store, a cappuccino counter, and a Burger King.

But no Buddys.

Erin's cell phone rang. Mary Bliss snatched it up, praying it was news about Erin.

"Mary Bliss?" It was Matt. "I'm still at your place. The nursing home called right after you left. Your mother-in-law is in the hospital . . ."

"I know," Mary Bliss said. "Is there any more news? Has Erin called?"

"No," Matt said. "Listen, I really think you should reconsider driving down to the Keys by yourself. That car of yours is on its last legs. The tires are bald and it's burning oil. Not to mention the air conditioning. Come on back here. We'll take my Explorer. And I swear, I won't turn it into a manhunt for Parker. We'll find Erin and bring her home. That's it."

Should she tell him about Parker? While she considered, Mary Bliss looked over at the dashboard again. A second blinking red light had joined the first. It was like the car had a nervous twitch.

"If you break down in Hahira, you'll never find her," Matt pointed out.

"All right," she said. "You can come. But I'm driving first shift."

"Pick me up at your place," he said.

70

Matt was sitting in the Explorer, with the motor running, when she pulled into the driveway. She hopped out of her own still-sputtering car and gave the balding right rear tire a vicious kick. "Thanks for nothing," she whispered.

As she walked to the Explorer, she heard water running. She glanced across the street. Randy Bowden stood in the dark, a garden hose clutched idly in his right hand. Water puddled around his bare feet, totally missing the dried-up shrubbery near the front door. "Bye," he called out. His voice was soft, defeated. "Call if you need anything."

"I will," she promised.

She went around to the driver's side and tapped on the window. "Shove over," she said. "I'm driving, remember?"

Matt looked annoyed, but he got out and switched seats.

Driving the Explorer was like driving a big, air-conditioned battleship. It had tinted windows and leather seats and the new-car smell, and every car-type gadget known to mankind. She steered the thing onto Interstate 75, headed south. The radio was tuned to a classic rock station. They were playing "Rambling Man" by the Allman Brothers.

She waited until the song was over to speak.

"I went through Eula's things at the nursing home. I found some postcards Parker had sent her. All from Florida."

"Any news?" he asked eagerly.

"'Weather wonderful. Your loving son,'" she quoted, her lips twisted in a bitter smile. "He gave her a phone number too. I called it."

"And?"

"Some guy answered. He claimed Parker had gotten a phone call an hour earlier and taken off. He said he didn't know where Parker had gone."

"What do you think?" Matt asked.

"I'm wondering if the phone call was from the nursing home, telling him Eula was being taken to the emergency room," Mary Bliss said. "I'm wondering if he's heading back to Atlanta—at the same time Erin is headed down there to find him."

"What a mess," Matt said, shaking his head. "Did the guy tell you anything else?"

"No," Mary Bliss said. "He wouldn't even tell me where Parker's been living. I can't stand it, Matt. I can't stand the idea of Erin wandering around South Florida, looking for her dad. She's so young. Anything could happen. You said it yourself, it's eight hundred miles. What if her car breaks down? South Florida is full of homicidal maniacs. What if—"

"No more of that," Matt said gently. "We'll find her."

"How?" Mary Bliss asked.

"We'll work as a team. You know your daughter. You know her habits. I know police work. I have a cop's instincts. Do you still have that number Parker left at the nursing home?"

Mary Bliss handed him the index card. He pulled out his cell phone and made a call. He listened, then left a message.

"By morning, we'll have an address for that phone number," he promised her. "We'll start there."

That seemed to satisfy her. She put the Explorer on cruise control and adjusted her seat back. She and Matt talked a little bit about not much of anything.

Mostly they listened to the music. It started to drizzle before they passed the Atlanta airport, with the rain growing more intense as they headed south. They lost the classic rock station just south of Macon, right after they heard a tornado warning issued for all of central Georgia. "We were watching the Weather Channel before you picked me up. It's a tropical storm," Matt told her. "Moving up from the gulf. Ought to help with our drought." Instead of being comforted, she pictured Erin, alone in the little Honda, swamped by the torrential downpour. She kept her worries to herself. The radio played mostly static until they picked up a decent country station just over the Florida line in Perry, where Matt insisted that she let him drive.

She gave in gratefully and dozed off as soon as she climbed into the passenger seat.

It was still dark and still raining when she felt the Explorer come to a stop. Mary Bliss yawned and stretched. They were in a motel parking lot. A neon vacancy light splashed a pink pool of light over the flooded-out pavement.

"What time is it?" she asked. "Where are we?"

"It's five o'clock," he answered. "We're right outside Ocala. I can't see for shit through this rain, and I'm beat. We'll get a few hours sleep and hit the road again."

"I can drive," Mary Bliss objected.

"It's just for a few hours," Matt said. He had one foot out of the car. He turned and fixed those gray eyes on her. "You're not afraid to be alone with me, are you?"

"No," she said warily. "I'm a big girl. I can take care of myself."

She watched him splash through the parking lot into the motel office, saw him through the rain-streaked picture window, standing at the check-in desk. He emerged a few minutes later and was soaked by the time he'd run back to the Explorer. He shivered in the cool of the air conditioning and drove around to the back of the horseshoe-shaped motor court. The buildings were typical Florida fifties construction, concrete block slathered with some kind of fake stucco painted a shrimpy orange. Faded green canvas awnings covered each doorway.

Matt grabbed a canvas duffle bag and her own overnight bag. He ran to the door and unlocked it quickly, standing aside to let her enter.

It had only been a quick sprint from the car to the room, but now Mary Bliss was drenched. Her T-shirt clung to her back, her hair was plastered to her head. The room seemed to be left over from an old *Laugh-In* set. The wallpaper was metallic gold with huge abstract Day-Glo pink and orange daisies, set off with pink-and-gold striped drapes, and orange shag carpet. A window air conditioner sent arctic blasts into the room.

"Groovy," Mary Bliss said, rubbing her arms for warmth. She stared at the bed. It was a king-sized water-bed covered with a shocking pink fake-fur bedspread.

Matt saw the expression on her face change. "It's all they had," he said, peeling his wet polo shirt over his head and draping it over the back of an orange vinyl chair. "There's a girls' softball tournament this week-end. Every room in town is booked."

She looked quickly away, but not so quick that she couldn't appreciate his tanned, well-muscled chest and the flat belly with dark hair that thickened below his exposed navel. She shivered involuntarily, then tried to cover with an exaggerated yawn. "So you rented the love shack," Mary Bliss said. She took her overnight bag from him and headed into the bathroom. "At least the ceiling doesn't leak. Anyway, I'm too wet and too tired to argue right now."

She dried her hair with a threadbare towel, then brushed her teeth and washed her face, peeled off her bra, and stuffed it into the overnight bag. She had a nightgown in her bag but decided to change into a clean T-shirt and jeans. She'd sleep in the same bed with him, but just for a few hours. And as far as he knew, she'd be fully clothed.

He was hanging up the phone on the bedside table when she emerged fully clothed from the bathroom. He frowned but said only, "I left us a nine A.M. wake-up call." He looked just fine without a shirt. She was running out of places to look, so she watched while he took his wristwatch off and laid it carefully on the nightstand on the right side of the bed, leaving it near the clock radio. He took his wallet out of his pants pocket and laid it beside the watch.

Mary Bliss frowned. She'd always slept on the right side of the bed. Always.

"Bathroom's free," she said, gesturing toward the door. As soon as he'd closed the door, she picked up his watch and wallet and relocated it to the left-hand nightstand. She peeled the fake-fur spread off the bed, folding it neatly at the foot. She carefully inspected the sheets. They appeared to be clean, if somewhat faded. She climbed into the right side of the bed and set up an immediate wave action that sloshed her gently into the middle.

She frowned and worked herself back to the right edge. But that set up the wave action again, and soon she was marooned again—back in the middle.

Mary Bliss looked suspiciously at the bathroom door. She could hear water running from inside. He was a cop. He had connections. Had he somehow planned this? No, she decided. Nobody deliberately planned a seduction in the middle of a tornado watch in Ocala, Florida.

She got out of bed, scooped up the fake-fur spread, and rolled it up like a rug. She placed it squarely down the middle of the bed, like a gigantic curb. She smiled with satisfaction, patted the bumper, and got back on her side. She still rolled into the middle, but now she had a distinct boundary. She squished the pillows to fit her head, turned off the lamp, and tried to relax. She yawned, closed her eyes, but every muscle in her body was tensed. The waistband of her jeans cut into her flesh. She sighed, peeled them off, then climbed back under the covers in her T-shirt and panties, pulling the sheet up to her chin. Better. She closed her eyes again and finally fell asleep to the sound of the water running.

Sometime later, she was vaguely aware of a door opening. She heard a puzzled "I'll be damned," felt the wave action setup when he collapsed onto the bed. Her body tensed, then floated gently toward the middle, then stopped. She didn't dare open her eyes. Was he naked? She held her breath and listened. Matt was right beside her; the only thing separating them was the fake-fur bumper. She smelled his deodorant, felt the heat of his bare shoulder inches from her own.

There was that humming feeling again. Very distinct. And very weird. She hadn't really slept in twenty-four hours. And now she was in bed, mostly undressed, in a motel with a strange man. She'd slept alone for three months, and before that, with Parker McGowan for nearly twenty years. She was acutely aware of Matt's closeness. She was cold and scared, and face it, she yearned to have somebody hold her close, to tell her it would be all right. He was so close. Right beside her.

But she was so tired. And married, technically. Fortunately, Matt was apparently as exhausted as she was. She listened to the reassuring rise and fall of his breathing, letting its rhythm lull her back to sleep. The last thing she remembered was wondering: boxers or briefs?

It seemed like only minutes later the phone was ringing. The phone was of the same vintage as the rest of the room's furnishings, and the ring was sharp and insistent. Before she could open her eyes and reach for it, she heard the bathroom door fly open. A figure hurtled across the room. Matt dove for the phone, landing nearly on top of her.

"Hello?" he whispered. "Yes. Thank you." He put the phone back in its cradle. She opened her eyes. He looked down at her. He was soaking wet, with a towel draped around his middle. "Wake-up call," he explained. "I thought I'd let you sleep a little longer."

"I'm awake now," she said, trying to scoot out from under him. But the waves were building. She rolled and he rolled with her.

"You're getting me wet," she whispered.

With a finger, he traced a droplet of water from the corner of her eye to the corner of her mouth.

"You talk in your sleep," he told her.

"What did I say?" she asked, alarmed.

He grinned. "You said, 'Matt. Matt. I want you, Matt. Take me, Matt.'"

She tried to sit up. "In your dreams." He leaned hard on his elbow, and she rolled back into him. He fitted his arms around her waist. He really was dripping wet. She was shocked to find herself wondering what was under that towel. He kissed her neck. She flicked a speck of shaving cream from the tip of his earlobe.

"We better get going," she said, trying to scoot away.

"That's what I was thinking," he murmured in her ear. He slid his wet hands under her T-shirt, up her back. She shivered slightly, which he totally misinterpreted, because in another instant he was pulling her T-shirt up over her head.

"That's not what I meant," she protested, but he was butting her gently with his hips, kicking the covers aside. That set up another wave action, but he locked her in his arms and they rolled the crest together. What with all that rolling, the towel came undone and Mary Bliss's questions were answered. Very shortly after that, they were both quite wet, and quite naked. Somehow, she forgot to be shocked. Somehow, having outlived its usefulness, the fake-fur bumper rolled off the other side of the bed.

At one particularly vigorous point in the proceedings, the waves sent Matt rolling off too. He sat up, roared with laughter, and climbed back onto the bed. "I feel like a pirate," he told her, catching her to him and kissing her with Crest-scented breath. "I've never made love in a waterbed before, have you?"

"Mmm-mmh," Mary Bliss breathed. She'd never done a lot of things before that she was doing this morning. She was going to chalk it all up to being newly blonde.

"When we get married, let's get a waterbed, okay?" he said, sliding his hands down her back. "We can play pirate every night. What do you say?"

"What?" Mary Bliss said, catching her breath.

"Pirate. You know. I board your ship, ransack and ravage you. Or we could take turns. You be the pirate."

"That's not what I meant," Mary Bliss said. "The other thing you said. When we get married."

He stopped kissing her and propped himself up on his elbow.

"You know. I meant, after all this business with Parker is settled. After we get Erin home safely, and after you divorce his sorry ass. Not right away. After."

"Oh," she said. She sat up and pulled the sheets over her breasts. She took a deep breath. "This is all going kind of fast for me, Matt. I mean, we only met two months ago."

"It's been longer than that," he said, frowning. Now he got out of the bed and pulled the towel back around his waist. He disappeared into the bathroom and came back out dressed, his hair neatly combed. He picked up his wristwatch and put it on, took his wallet and put it back in his pants pocket.

"You go ahead and shower," he said curtly. "I'll go get us some coffee and gas up the Explorer. Try to be ready in fifteen minutes."

"Okay," she said, weak with disappointment. She'd really blown it. Now she might never find the answer to that burning underpants question.

71

"This is a bad time for me," Mary Bliss said quietly. Matt had turned the Explorer's radio to an all-talk station. The woman host was excoriating working mothers, deadbeat fathers, and everyone everywhere who talked on a cell phone in a restaurant.

Matt kept his eyes on the road. "I know that," he said finally.

"I haven't started a relationship with a man in more than twenty years," she said. "Parker was the first man I was ever with, you know, sexually. To tell you the truth, I always thought he would always be my only."

He glanced over at her. "You really thought that?"

She sighed. "I was naive. But that's how I was raised. All of this is so new to me . . ."

He gripped the steering wheel, his arms locked as though he were trying to push it away. "This isn't a casual thing for me, you know. I've tried to tell you that from the start. I'm not a casual person. I don't really . . . date. I want to be with you. I want to be part of your life. Is that so hard?"

She sighed. "I'd like to be with you too. But my life is such a mess . . ."

Mary Bliss had put Erin's cell phone on her lap. It rang, surprising her so she jumped slightly.

She fumbled with the right button, finally connecting on her second try. "Erin?" she said breathlessly.

It was Josh. "Mrs. Mac? It's about Erin."

"Did she call? Where is she? Is she all right?"

"She's all right," Josh said quickly. "She called your house last night. We tried to call you, but I guess maybe you were out of range or something. Anyway, she's okay. She was at a police station, way down in Waycross, Georgia. She tried to use your Visa card at a gas station there, and like you said, it was no good. And Erin got upset and tried to drive off without paying, so the gas station guy called the cops, and they arrested her."

"Dear God," Mary Bliss cried. She turned to Matt. "Erin got arrested for trying to use my credit card at a gas station in Waycross. She spent the night in jail."

"Josh, is she all right?" Mary Bliss asked.

"I guess," Josh said. "Mr. Weidman talked to the sheriff, and he was wiring the money Erin owed to the gas station people this morning. Once they get it, they'll drop the charges and the sheriff says Erin can go. He said he'll put Erin on a Greyhound bus back home."

"A bus?" Mary Bliss tried to picture Erin after a night in a South Georgia jail cell. "I don't want her riding a bus back home after what she's been through."

Matt's jaw tightened. "I'll turn around at the next exit. We can make Waycross by noon. I used to know a deputy in Ware County. I'll call, make sure they take care of her."

"That would be wonderful," Mary Bliss told him. She closed her eyes and said a silent prayer of thanks.

Matt nodded and put on his turn signal.

"Mrs. Mac?" Josh said, his voice hesitant. "You had another call this morning, just a little while ago. It was Mr. Mac. He said I should tell you the hospital called. It's kinda bad news. He said I should tell you Erin's Meemaw died."

Tears sprang to Mary Bliss's eyes. "When was this?" she asked, her voice nearly a whisper.

"He just said it was early this morning. He asked to speak to Erin, but I told him she wasn't here."

"Did you tell him where she was?"

"No, ma'am," Josh said. "I just said you guys were out of town, and I'd come over to pick up the newspaper."

"Good," Mary Bliss said. Josh was an excellent improvisationalist. Were all teenagers that accomplished at lying?

"Did Parker leave a number where he could be reached?" she asked.

"No, ma'am," Josh said. "He just said I should tell you he wasn't dead after all."

She nearly laughed. It was so perverse. So insane. Such a relief.

"All right, Josh," she said, dabbing at her eyes. "You did well. We're down in Ocala, so it'll take us maybe five or six hours to get back there, after we get Erin bailed out. If Mr. Mac calls back, try to get him to leave a number, will you?"

"Uh," Josh started.

"I'll talk to Erin when we get to Waycross," Mary Bliss said, her voice firm. "I'll tell her the truth. I won't keep her from seeing her dad if that's what she wants. I promise."

When she turned off the phone, Matt was in the process of heading the Explorer back north.

"Eula died this morning," she said simply.

He winced. "I'm sorry."

"I guess it was for the best. She hated being sick. Hated the doctors, hated feeling so powerless. I just wish things had gone differently. I wish . . . I wish she could have seen Erin one more time. I wish I could have told her that Erin wasn't pregnant. That she was okay. That we'd all be okay."

"What about Parker?" Matt asked.

"He's the one who called the house to say she died," Mary Bliss said. "Josh actually talked to him. Parker called to tell Erin her grandmother was dead."

"And that he wasn't?"

"I guess," Mary Bliss said. She tilted her head back against the headrest and massaged her temples. "Parker didn't tell Josh where he was. I know the nursing home contacted him last night to tell him Eula was in bad shape. I just hope he made it to the hospital in time to see her. I'd hate to think she died all alone."

Matt shook his head in disgust.

"What?" Mary Bliss asked.

"Her son treated you like dirt. She treated you like dirt. Called you names, refused to help you. She knew where Parker was all along, and she wouldn't tell you. Seems to me, she doesn't deserve any of your sympathy."

"I can't help it," Mary Bliss said simply. "She wasn't much, but she was family. My own mama's been dead a long time now. I guess I just never took Eula personally. It wasn't just me that she was mean to. She was mean to everybody. Except Parker. She never gave up on him. He was her son, and to her, he could do no wrong."

"Love is blind," Matt observed.

Or maybe just stupid, Mary Bliss thought. She glanced surreptitiously over at the man sitting beside her. For some crazy reason, this gorgeous, sexy man seemed to think he loved her. But what did Matt Hayslip really know about Mary Bliss McGowan? They had done everything backward. He knew the intimate things. That she had a small mole beneath her right breast. That she talked in her sleep. That she slept on the right side of the bed. And where she liked to be touched. But he knew nothing about her politics, her past, her passions.

He reached over and took her hand, as though he could read her thoughts. He put the back of her hand to his lips and kissed it lightly. A chill ran down her spine. It was a good kind of chill.

"Quit it," he said.

"Quit what?"

"Quit coming up with reasons why it won't work between us."

"What makes you think that's what I'm doing?"

"Aren't you? You're frowning. And you keep looking at me funny."

"You don't know me as well as you think you do," Mary Bliss said.

"Fine," Matt said. "You're a woman of mystery. I like that. In fact, I love it. It's a major turn-on for me."

"You've got to stop talking like that," Mary Bliss ordered. "And stop looking at me that way too."

His lips twitched. "What way?"

"Like you've seen me naked."

"That's asking too much. I'm gonna carry you naked around in my head for a long, long time. And there's nothing either one of us can do about that."

"We'll be in Waycross pretty soon," Mary Bliss said, blushing. "It's going to be bad enough explaining to Erin why you're with me. If she sees you looking at me like that, she'll know."

"I don't mind her knowing," Matt said. "I'm not ashamed of how I feel about you. Are you ashamed of me?"

Mary Bliss bit her lip. "It's complicated. Right now, I need to concentrate on Erin. On fixing things between us."

"And what about us? You and me?"

She sighed. "Just let me get my child out of jail. All right?"

72

The Ware County Jail was a squat, buff-colored concrete block box. Matt had called his deputy friend from the car. Her name was Olivia, and she was Hispanic, in her early thirties. She buzzed them back into the booking area, where she and Matt talked in low whispers, and then Olivia took her to a buff-colored visitor's room, where Erin sat alone on a plastic chair, in a bright-orange jumpsuit. Her hair was dirty, matted to her head, and she needed a bath.

"Mama!" Erin jumped up. She looked so small, like a little girl.

Mary Bliss wrapped her arms around her daughter and held Erin tightly, afraid her little girl might turn back into the sullen teenager who'd stolen her credit card and run away from home just twenty-four hours earlier.

"I'm sorry, Mama," Erin said, starting to weep.

"You better be," Olivia said. She touched Erin gently on the shoulder. "Come on, now, let's get you out of orange and into your own clothes."

Matt was waiting in the lobby when they emerged, Erin dressed in the clean clothes Mary Bliss had brought her.

Erin scowled and looked from her mother to Matt, a question in her eyes.

"This is my friend, Matt Hayslip," Mary Bliss said. "My car quit. Matt was driving me down to Key West to look for you when we got the word that you were here. He used to be in the GBI. He's been a big help to me, tracking you down."

"A big help," Erin said, letting the words hang there. "Your friend."

"Hi, Erin," Matt said, extending his hand to shake Erin's. She kept her fists clenched, at her side. "You had us pretty worried," he said.

"I'm fine," Erin said. "It's no big deal."

Mary Bliss put an arm around Erin's shoulder. "It would be nice if you thanked Matt for bringing me to get you. So you didn't have to take the Greyhound bus back home."

Erin shrugged. "Whatever. Thanks."

"You're welcome," Matt said, ignoring Erin's rudeness. "Olivia has to take a class in Atlanta this weekend.

She's offered to drive Erin's Honda up for us, and she can catch a ride back with one of the other deputies. So Erin can ride back home with us. I'm guessing she's pretty tired."

"I can drive," Erin said.

"No," Mary Bliss said, surprised at the firmness in her own voice. "You'll come back with us. You gave us a terrible scare. I don't want you out of my sight for a while."

Erin folded herself into the backseat of the Explorer and fell asleep almost immediately. She slept the whole way back to Atlanta, even while they stopped for lunch in Warner Robbins.

It was late afternoon by the time they pulled into Mary Bliss's driveway in Fair Oaks. Mary Bliss saw a flicker of movement in her downstairs window and wondered, idly, if Parker might be waiting for them.

She turned to Matt, covered his hand with hers. "I'd better go in. We've got a lot to do."

She leaned across the console and kissed his cheek. "Thank you. For everything."

"Everything?" He smiled despite himself.

"All of it," she said. "I'll call you."

"You better," he said.

Mary Bliss shook Erin awake and walked her still-woozy daughter into the house and upstairs to her room.

Someone, Katharine, she guessed, had straightened up. Erin tumbled into the bed without a word.

She found Josh Bowden downstairs, a look of anxiety on his face.

"She's exhausted. She slept the whole way back," Mary Bliss said. "We haven't really had a chance to talk."

"Tell her to call me," Josh said. "As soon as she wakes up."

"I will," Mary Bliss promised. "Were there any phone calls for me?"

"Just Jessica," Josh said. "No word from Mr. Mac."

She gave him a quick hug. "You've been a good friend to her, Josh. And I'll never forget that."

She called Katharine, got her answering machine, and left a quick message. "We're home. We're all right. I'll call you later."

When Mary Bliss looked in on Erin two hours later, she found her daughter awake, flopped face-down on her unmade bed, listening to a country music CD.

Mary Bliss walked over to the stereo and turned the sound down. Erin sat up and frowned.

"I was listening to that," she started.

"You can listen to it later," Mary Bliss said. "We need to talk."

"I don't feel like talking," Erin said, rolling over again. "There's nothing to say."

Mary Bliss sat down on the bed beside Erin. She ran her fingers through Erin's fine brown hair. Touching her child seemed to help her find the words she needed.

"I'm sorry," she started. "Sorry I lied to you. I was wrong. But I was scared, and I didn't know what to do. I should have told you the truth. About Daddy. And me. I thought you were too young to understand, but I was wrong about that too. I underestimated you. You're a young woman now."

She felt her daughter's shoulders shake, heard muffled sobs. Mary Bliss stroked Erin's arm.

"You've made some mistakes, sweetie," Mary Bliss continued. "I wish I could have talked to you about that, but we were both hurting. Instead of trying to help each other, we've just been at cross-purposes all summer. I wanted to help you, and all I've done is hurt you."

"It's not all your fault," Erin said chokily, lifting her face from her pillow. "I was a bitch. Mama, I was awful to you. It was like I wanted to hurt you as bad as I could. I was mad at Daddy, but it was like, if I hurt you, I could get back at him."

"I know," Mary Bliss said, her voice even. "But that's all done with now."

"I know where he is," Erin said, sniffing. She sat up, scrunched the pillow in her lap. Her face was red and tear-stained. "Mama, he's down in Key West. Meemaw knew it all along. She kept telling me he wasn't really dead. She even showed me postcards she said he sent her. I didn't know what to think. I didn't want you to be a liar, but I didn't want Daddy to be dead. She gave me his phone number. I talked to him. Only for a minute. He told me to be nice to you." She sniffed loudly.

"Did he?" Mary Bliss got up and went to the bathroom and got a handful of tissues. She handed them to Erin. "Blow, baby."

Erin blew her nose loudly.

"I wanted to go live with him," Erin said. "At the beach. But Daddy said I couldn't. He said there was no place for me to stay. I went anyway. I can't go back to school, Mama. Isaac's there. Everybody will know."

Mary Bliss felt a familiar stabbing sensation in her rib cage at the mention of Isaac Brownlee's name. She took a deep breath.

"We'll figure out what to do about Isaac. But running away from your problems won't fix them."

"I loved him," Erin said tearily. "I loved him so much, Mama. I would have done anything he wanted. He said I was special. Not like anybody else. I told him about Daddy. He was the only one I could talk to. He treated me like a woman, not like a little kid."

Mary Bliss took one of the tissues and dabbed at Erin's chin. "He let you down, didn't he? I could kill him. For what he did to you. A grown man. Sleeping with a teenager."

Erin shook her head. "It wasn't all his fault. I wanted to have sex. With him. It was my idea, to go down to Jekyll. Just the two of us. And then, I thought . . . I was late. And I was so scared. I kept calling him. I left messages on his cell phone. I called his house, but his wife kept answering, so I hung up. I even called him at school, in his office. He never would call me back. And I was so scared! One night, when I was supposed to be at Jessica's, I slept in my car. Outside his house. And when he came out in the morning, I followed him. I followed him all the way to the soccer field, honking my horn at him, trying to get him to stop. I just wanted to talk to him. Finally, he pulled into this gas station. He got into my car, and he was so mad, he was shaking! He screamed at me, Mama! He said it was over, and I better stop bothering him. I told him I was late, and he was so mean. He said I was making it up, to try to get him back."

She was sobbing now. "He said if I got pregnant, it was my own fault. He said it probably wasn't even his kid! And then he said if I told anybody about us, he'd get me in real trouble. And then he left! He went to the beach. Josh called the school and asked, and they said he went to the beach with his wife."

Mary Bliss wrapped her arms around Erin. Her whole body convulsed in sobs. "It hurts so much. I can't stand it. I wanted to die. And then Meemaw told me where Daddy was. And I stole your credit card, Mama. I stole money from you too, out of your pocketbook. I'm sorry, Mama."

"Hush," Mary Bliss said, rocking her daughter back and forth. "Hush now. You were scared. Everybody you loved let you down. You didn't know what else to do."

"Not you," Erin said, hiccuping loudly. "You tried to help me. But I wouldn't listen."

"Shh," Mary Bliss said. "Stop crying now, can you? I need to tell you some things."

Erin blew her nose again. She pushed her soggy hair out of her eyes. "I'll be all right. What do you want to tell me?"

"It's a lot," Mary Bliss said. "Can you handle all this right now?"

"Sure. I thought I was pregnant and I wasn't. I thought my dad was dead, and he's really alive. My boyfriend dumped me, and I ran away and got arrested," Erin said shakily. "I guess I can handle anything now."

"All right," Mary Bliss said. "Here it is. Meemaw died."

Erin's face crumpled. "What happened?"

"I don't really know," Mary Bliss admitted. "She'd gotten pretty sick in the last few weeks, you know. Her kidneys weren't functioning properly. And then she got much worse Sunday. The doctors moved her to the hospital early in the morning. I'm so sorry, sweetie. She died Sunday morning."

"Poor Meemaw," Erin said. "I knew she was sick. Saturday night, I made her a martini, and then I got into bed with her and we watched *Love Boat*. And she kissed me. Meemaw hardly ever kissed me."

"She hardly ever kissed anybody," Mary Bliss said. "You were pretty special to her, you know. She was worried about you."

"Do you think she knew she was gonna die?" Erin asked suddenly.

"Maybe," Mary Bliss said. "Maybe that's why she told you how to reach Daddy."

"Daddy!" Erin exclaimed. "Poor Daddy. Do you think he knows about Meemaw?"

"He knows," Mary Bliss said. "The nursing home called him to tell him she was going to the hospital. And the hospital notified him . . . later."

"Where is he?" Erin asked. "Have you talked to him?"

Mary Bliss shrugged. "He called the house while I was gone, trying to catch up to you. Josh was here.

Daddy told Josh to tell us Meemaw was dead. And that he was alive."

Erin's brown eyes searched her mother's face. "What's going to happen now? With you and Daddy? Will you be in trouble?"

Mary Bliss lay down on the bed beside her daughter and looked up at the ceiling.

"I don't know what will happen," she admitted. "Remember how scared you were when you thought you might be pregnant? That's how scared I was when I found out Daddy was gone. He took all the money. We were so broke, and I was so scared and ashamed. I didn't want anybody to know the truth. I was afraid we'd lose the house. And I couldn't pay your tuition. And everything just seemed to pile up on top of me."

"And I was being a bitch," Erin added remorsefully.

"It wasn't your fault," Mary Bliss assured her. "I'm a grown-up. I'm supposed to be able to handle all this stuff. But I'd never been alone before. Ever. I didn't know what to do. So I told a lie. And when that lie seemed to work, I told some more. And then I got so I couldn't tell the truth. Not even to myself."

"That's the thing about lying," Erin said. "The first time I lied to you, about staying late for soccer when I was really with Isaac, I was so scared, I threw up. But the next time, it was easy. And then it was easier to lie than it was to tell the truth."

"We made a big mess of things, didn't we?" Mary Bliss asked, reaching for her daughter's hand.

Erin's fingers curled around hers. "We screwed up. Big-time."

73

The phone rang most of the day Wednesday. She let the answering machine pick up, or Katharine.

Erin slept until noon. When she came downstairs her face was pale and swollen. She wore an old soccer T-shirt over a pair of faded blue shorts and she was barefoot. She poured herself a bowl of cereal and sat at the kitchen table, staring at the cereal box.

"Has Daddy called?" she whispered.

Mary Bliss shot Katharine a panicky look.

"No, baby," Katharine said, ruffling Erin's hair. "But he's probably had a lot to do, arranging the service for your grandmother."

"Will he be there?" Erin asked. "Can I see him?"

"I hope he'll be there," Mary Bliss said. "He loved Meemaw very much. I'm sure he wants to be at her service. But your daddy's in some serious trouble, Erin."

Erin's face clouded. "He is?"

"Business trouble," Mary Bliss added. "He made some bad decisions and he broke the law. Some of his former clients are really angry with him. I don't understand all of it, but I think that's one reason he went away down to Florida, without telling anybody."

"I thought he just hated us," Erin said, propping an elbow on the table.

"No," Mary Bliss said. "I don't think he hates us."

"Will he have to go to jail?"

"Honestly? I don't know."

Later in the afternoon, Katharine took Erin shopping for a dress to wear to Eula's funeral. Soon afterward, Charlie arrived at the house with a briefcase full of papers.

"Have you talked to him?" Mary Bliss asked, seating Charlie in the den.

"I have," Charlie said, his face grave. He didn't have to ask to whom Mary Bliss referred. It was understood that they were talking about Parker McGowan.

"What's going to happen?" she asked. "Now that he's back? Have you talked to the insurance company people?"

"Nothing's going to happen right away," Charlie said. "You know I've been negotiating with the insurance people. They're aware that you've withdrawn your claim on Parker's life insurance. And I think they're inclined to let the whole thing drop."

"Really? That's the best news I've had in weeks."

"There's some paperwork," Charlie said, opening his briefcase and sliding out a sheaf of paper. He fanned the documents out on Parker's desktop. There were yellow Post-it notes attached to all the documents. "They're waivers," Charlie explained. "You'll be waiving your right to ever make a claim on those policies, in exchange for the company's agreement not to prosecute you for fraud."

She scribbled her name on every document he presented. Satisfied, he clipped the papers together and put them back in the briefcase.

Mary Bliss put her arms around Charlie's neck and hugged him. "You're a good old bear," she told him.

"Stop," Charlie protested. "You'll ruin my reputation as a curmudgeon and a rake."

"You were never a rake," Mary Bliss said, straightening the collar on his golf shirt. "So, it's all over?"

"For now," Charlie said.

"What next?" Mary Bliss asked. "What do I do about Parker?"

Charlie looked distinctly uncomfortable. "I can't advise you about Parker," he said finally.

"Is he in town?"

"I believe so," Charlie said. "I talked to him on the phone, but I haven't seen him."

"He's afraid he'll be arrested," Mary Bliss said, guessing.

"That remains a distinct possibility," Charlie agreed. "Matt Hayslip called me. He wanted me to set up a meeting with Parker."

"Did you?"

"No," Charlie said. "I respect that Matt has a job to do. But I'm not going to help him get one of my oldest friends arrested, and I told him that. Anyway, I'm not representing Parker."

"So. The police are involved now?"

"I assume so," Charlie said. "I've advised Parker to hire a criminal attorney. From what Matt's told me, he's going to need one."

"Katharine says you made the funeral arrangements for Eula," Mary Bliss said.

Charlie nodded. "She left very specific instructions on what she wanted. Right down to the Beefeater's gin at the funeral luncheon."

Mary Bliss gave him a funny look. "You talked to Eula?"

"She called and summoned me to the nursing home the week before she died. Wanted to talk about her will, and her funeral arrangements. And give me a copy of her obituary. Which she wrote out herself on Blue Horse notebook paper."

"You never said anything to me about that, Charlie," Mary Bliss said.

"I'm just following my client's instructions," Charlie said. "And believe me, I'm not about to cross Eula McGowan. Dead or alive."

"That's probably wise," Mary Bliss said.

She woke up early Thursday. Six o'clock. She wandered downstairs in her nightgown, went outside to pick up the newspaper. She stared at the Bowdens' driveway. A new car, a shiny black PT Cruiser, was parked there. The lawn had been mowed, and the sprinklers were running. A FOR SALE sign was stuck in the middle of a bed of red petunias that hadn't been there until very recently.

Randy hadn't mentioned wanting to sell the house, Mary Bliss thought. But then, she'd been so wrapped up in her own dramas lately that she hadn't been attuned to the Bowden family soap opera. For Erin's sake, she hoped Randy wouldn't move too far away. Erin was going to need Josh's friendship in the coming months.

She took the newspaper inside and sat down with a cup of coffee to read it, starting with the obituary section.

Eula McGowan's obituary merited ten inches above the fold on the obituary page of the *Constitution*. "Eula McGowan, Bridge Champion," read the headline. Mary Bliss skimmed over it, laughing. The obituary made Meemaw seem like a cross between Mother Theresa and June Cleaver. The black-and-white photograph was an old one, probably taken in the fifties. In the photo, Eula had marcelled blonde hair, cat-eye glasses, and a polka-dot dress. She was smiling down at the playing cards fanned out in her white gloved hands. "She is survived by a son and daughter-in-law, Parker and Mary Bliss McGowan, and granddaughter, Erin Marie McGowan, all of Fair Oaks, Georgia," the obituary said.

The mention of Parker as a survivor should set Fair Oaks spinning, Mary Bliss thought. Gossip was the number one spectator sport in this town. Before this summer, she would have been quivering with anxiety over the prospect of being the object of all that chatter. Now gossip was the least of her problems.

She glanced at the kitchen clock. It was still early. Without even meaning to, she found herself busy, chopping onions and celery, adding them to a kettle full of boiling water, along with a bay leaf, salt, pepper, chicken bouillon cubes—and five pounds of chicken breasts.

While the chicken was poaching, she threw together some batter for banana bread from some blackened bananas she'd put in the freezer days earlier. She turned on the radio and listened to the early morning news on WSB, then ran out to the garden to pick some tomatoes.

The grass was still wet with dew. The tomato vines had started to turn yellow in places, and the Early Girl vines looked completely played out. But the Better Boys were still loaded with fat, misshapen fruits that fell into her hands when she touched them. She gathered an armful of tomatoes, some so ripe that they split open and spilled seeds down her front.

When she got back to the house, Matt Hayslip was sitting at the kitchen table, sipping a cup of coffee. He was wearing a black golf shirt and neatly pressed chinos. A large brown grocery sack was placed on the chair next to his.

"Hey there," she said, dumping the tomatoes in the sink. She quickly finger-combed her hair and tried to straighten the neckline of her tomato-stained cotton nightgown.

"I rang the doorbell," he said, "but when you didn't answer, I came around back. I saw you out there in the garden. Is it all right for me to be here?"

She nodded. "Erin's still catching up on her sleep. She probably won't wake up for another couple of hours."

Matt smiled. "That's the same nightgown you were wearing the first time we met."

She looked down and blushed. "You always seem to catch me at my worst."

"That's not true," Matt said, stirring his coffee. "And you know it."

He gestured toward the kitchen counter, which was lined with spoons and bowls and pans. "You catering another wedding?"

She made a face. "It's for Meemaw's funeral luncheon, actually. Nothing much. Just some chicken salad and some banana bread. I was so antsy this morning, I needed something to do."

"I saw the obituary," Matt said.

"You and all of Fair Oaks," Mary Bliss said. "That funeral ought to be quite the social event."

"Will Parker be there?"

"I don't know," Mary Bliss said. "I haven't talked to him."

"Oh?"

Mary Bliss sat down opposite him at the kitchen table. "Will you do something for me, Matt?"

"If I can," he said, choosing his words carefully.

"Don't come to the funeral. Don't come looking for Parker. I know it's your job, but think of Erin, please. It's her grandmother's funeral. And she still hasn't seen or talked to Parker yet. Don't spoil that by making a scene at the church."

He frowned. "You think I'd do something as crappy as that? Crash a funeral and arrest somebody?"

"I don't know," she said, feeling helpless.

"You don't know me very well," he said. "I didn't come over here looking for Parker today. I came to talk to you. You haven't been answering your phone, and I didn't want to leave a message, in case the wrong person was listening."

"It's been a madhouse," Mary Bliss said. "What did you want to tell me?"

He scooted his chair over so that his knees were touching hers. "That I'm here for you. And I'm in for the long haul. No matter what." He picked up her hand and kissed the back of one. He smacked his lips. "Tastes like bananas."

"What about Parker? He's still my husband. Technically. Although, if I see him, I may kill him for real this time. I'm so angry at him, it terrifies me."

"You're angry? That's good. That's a start. Stop making excuses for him. Stop being so goddamned nice, why don't you?"

"I dream about hurting him," Mary Bliss whispered. "About tracking him down on that island Eula talked about. And in the dream, I just keep punching him and kicking him and hurting him. And I'm enjoying myself. It feels good. Isn't that sick?"

"It's normal," Matt said.

"I don't think so," Mary Bliss said, shaking her head. "What's going to happen to me? And what's going to happen to Parker?"

Matt's face hardened. "He's going to jail, if I have anything to do with it. My client has decided to press charges. He's talked to the police, and the district attorney's office is involved now."

"What'll I tell Erin?" Mary Bliss asked. "No matter what else he's done, Parker is still her daddy. She's been through so much this summer, Matt. First this, this teacher preys on her, seduces her, and drops her, then her grandmother dies. She's already lost Parker once this summer. If he goes to jail, I don't know what she'll do."

"Stop trying to shield the kid from the truth, why don't you?" Matt said, impatient now. "You said it yourself. She's no virgin anymore. And you're not doing her any favor by making her mother a martyr, or her father a saint." Matt's eyes narrowed. "Parker's a criminal. He's a con artist and a thief. Even if I walk away from this case, somebody else is going to pick it up. And sooner or later, the law is going to catch up with him. You can bet on it."

Mary Bliss stood up abruptly. "I can't talk about this anymore. It's too painful."

Matt took his coffee cup and put it in the sink. He turned around at the kitchen door and gestured at the paper bag on the chair.

"I almost forgot. That's for you."

"For me? What is it?"

"Nothing. Just something I picked up at a pawn-shop. See you."

She pounced on the paper bag. A gift-wrapped box was inside. It was heavy. She set it on the kitchen table and pulled away the wrappings and ribbon to reveal a heavily carved wooden case. Mary Bliss held her breath and opened the lid.

The sterling silver glittered against the black velvet lining. She didn't bother to count the pieces. It was all there, she knew. Twelve place settings of Frances I, plus serving pieces and demitasse spoons. She felt flooded with warmth. With hope, really. Matt Hayslip had given her a present, of her past.

424 • MARY KAY ANDREWS

74

Mary Bliss and Erin sat in the front row at Fair Oaks First United Methodist Church. The scene was eerily reminiscent of the last service they'd attended here, Mary Bliss thought.

Mr. Isler was playing soft, soothing organ music. The altar was banked with dozens of floral arrangements, including one large floral blanket covering Eula's casket. The blanket was made of sprays of white chrysanthemums, red carnations, and dyed black statice that was an exact replica of a playing card—a queen of hearts, to be exact. It had been sent by the surviving members of Eula's bridge club.

People were filing quietly into the pews. Katharine and Charlie sat to her left, Katharine's arm thrown protectively over Erin's shoulder. Erin kept glancing toward the back of the church. They all knew who she was looking for.

Mary Bliss glanced at her watch. The service was scheduled to start in less than five minutes. Old Reverend Strayhairn, Eula's pastor, had cautioned her that he intended to be prompt today, because he had another appointment down in Griffin, an hour south of Fair Oaks.

"Psst!"

Mary Bliss glanced at Katharine. "What?" she mouthed.

Katharine jerked her head to the right, and Mary Bliss looked in that direction. Randy and Nancye Bowden walked quickly up the right side aisle, holding hands. Josh, wearing an ill-fitting suit, his hair wet-combed, followed behind, along with his two younger brothers, who were pushing each other to get into a pew first.

"Do you believe it?" Katharine whispered loudly.

Erin turned and looked too, smiled and waved at Josh, who waved back.

But Mary Bliss was staring at the figure right behind the newly reunited Bowden family.

He was deeply tanned, wearing a light tan suit, summer sandals, and an open-collared light-yellow sport shirt. The chain around his neck glinted in the morning sunlight, and she could just catch a glimpse of the ring—yes, it was her engagement ring, dangling from the chain.

Erin caught sight of him at approximately the same time. "Daddy!" she squealed. She scooted past Charlie and Katharine and threw herself into Parker's arms.

Mary Bliss heard a faint buzz rising from the pews.

Parker, blushing, seated himself at the far end of the front pew nearest the aisle, with Erin clinging tight to his arm. At one point he leaned over and shook hands with Charlie. He tried to buss Katharine on the cheek, but she turned away, stony-faced.

The organ music swelled and Reverend Strayhairn walked onto the altar and leaned on the lectern. The microphone crackled and he started to speak, his voice deceptively deep and booming, despite his advanced age.

Mary Bliss heard little of what he said, although she thought it had probably all been scripted by Eula herself. She was aware that Katharine had scooted over to fill the void left by Erin, and that her best friend was clutching her hand tightly. She was aware of Charlie's concerned glances in her direction, and she had a fuzzy, out-of-focus impression of Eula's old neighbors and friends, pressed into the pews beside and behind her.

She allowed herself just one more look at Parker. He sat slumped in the pew, eyes straight ahead, watching Reverend Strayhairn, listening intently. His hair was longer than she'd ever seen it, the back curling over the collar of his shirt, and he appeared to be wearing blue contact lenses. If he was aware that his wife was staring at him, he gave no notice. His eyes moved only once, when he seemed to be looking at someone sitting in the pew directly behind theirs.

Mary Bliss felt cold. Her bare arms were covered with goose bumps. She shivered, even heard her teeth chattering. "Hang in there," Katharine whispered in her ear.

Eventually, Reverend Strayhairn ran out of Bible verses and plaudits for the deceased. The organ music swelled again. A soloist started a mournful version of "How Great Thou Art." Parker slipped out of his pew and walked to the front of the church, where he took up one of the handles of his mother's mahogany and bronze casket. He was joined by five dark-suited men whom Mary Bliss did not recognize. She supposed they were employees of the funeral home.

Suddenly, Erin darted out of the pew too. She ran to the front of the church and grasped the same casket handle that Parker was holding. Parker frowned, but slowly the group moved the casket down the aisle, toward the back of the church.

As the organ music wound down, Mary Bliss was aware of another buzz arising from the congregation. People were walking up to her, kissing her on the cheek, offering hasty greetings and hushed expressions of sympathy.

She stood like a statue, enduring the hugs and kisses, the gentle pats on the shoulder. Randy and Nancye Bowden edged toward her. Nancye hung back, but Randy enveloped her in an embrace. "Call me," he whispered. "I've got news."

After fifteen minutes, Katharine gave her a nudge toward the aisle. "Let's go," she said loudly. "I need fresh air."

The church was nearly empty, but Erin was nowhere in sight. Mary Bliss craned her neck, trying to see over the backs of the departing funeral-goers. "Where's Erin?" she asked anxiously.

Charlie took her arm. "I saw her get in a car with Parker. She'll be all right."

"No," Mary Bliss said, feeling panicky. "Not with Parker. Where were they going? I don't want her to go with him."

"It's all right," Katharine said soothingly. "They're going over to our house. For the luncheon. Charlie talked to Parker this morning. He'll be at the luncheon. He promised. On Eula's grave."

"Are you sure?" Mary Bliss asked, her voice frantic. "Are you sure he won't take off again? He won't be arrested? I don't want him arrested in front of Erin."

"It'll be fine," Charlie assured her. "Parker has hired Mike Payne. He's one of the best criminal lawyers in town. I know for a fact that Payne has talked to the district attorney's office. They're not going to come near Parker until after the funeral is over."

"How do you know?" Mary Bliss asked. "How do you know Parker won't run and take Erin with him?" She sprinted down the aisle, toward the back of the church. But Katharine was quicker. She caught up to Mary Bliss and tugged her arm, hard.

"Don't!" Katharine said, her voice sharp. "Don't you dare go running after him. Not after what he's put you through."

"It's not him I'm after. It's Erin. I can't let her go with him."

"He's not going anywhere," Katharine said. "Didn't you see those pallbearers? Don't you get it?"

"No," Mary Bliss said. "Those men? They work for the funeral home."

"Actually, they don't," Charlie said calmly. "They're cops."

"Now will you relax?" Katharine said. "Come on. I've got a flask of Bloody Marys waiting out in the limo. We'll hoist one to the memory of Eula McGowan. The meanest woman who ever drew breath."

"To Meemaw," Mary Bliss repeated.

75

C ars lined both sides of the street in front of the
Weidmans' house. Mary Bliss sat in the back-
seat of the black limo, clutching her untouched Bloody
Mary.

"I thought I was done caring what people think,"
she said, leaning forward to look out the tinted glass
window. "But now I'm not so sure. I'm not sure I can
do this. Not again. Everybody knows. They know I
lied. They know Parker's back. They probably even
know cops were swarming all over the church during
the funeral."

"Oh, who cares?" Katharine said briskly. "Don't
make yourself so important. Sure, everybody's talking
about you right now. But that'll be over in five minutes.
As soon as the next scandal du jour hits the street."

"A scandal bigger than my faking my husband's own death?" Mary Bliss asked. "What's bigger than that, in Fair Oaks?"

"Take a look over there," Katharine said, pointing to the black PT Cruiser edging into a spot at the curb. "Nancye and Randy Bowden are together again. That's quality gossip right there."

"What about us?" Charlie asked, nuzzling Katharine's ear. "We could make an announcement at the luncheon. That'd take some of the heat off Mary Bliss."

"What announcement?" Mary Bliss asked.

Katharine blushed. "It's too soon yet. I can't talk about it."

"Katharine!" Mary Bliss screeched. "What kind of an announcement? Are you and Charlie getting remarried?"

"We already did," Charlie said proudly. "We got hitched in Judge Waller's chambers on Wednesday."

"I would have told you," Katharine said apologetically. "But Charlie made me keep it a secret. Chip's the only one who knows—other than you."

"That's wonderful," Mary Bliss said, beaming. "Then, what else can it be?" She grabbed Katharine's arm. "Tell me you're not moving. Anything but that. You can't move away. I won't allow it."

"Go on," Charlie said, laughing. "Tell the woman. She deserves some good news. You know you want to tell it."

Katharine's grin matched Charlie's. "All right," she said. "Promise you won't make fun of me."

"I swear," Mary Bliss said quickly. "Now tell me before I die of curiosity."

"Okay," Katharine said. "It's the most ridiculous, outrageous thing you ever heard. Even I can't believe it's true. But it is. I made the doctor run the test twice to be sure."

"Test?" Mary Bliss furrowed her brow. She glanced over at Katharine's plastic Bloody Mary cup in the armrest holder, which was also untouched. "Are you telling me . . ."

"I'm *pregnant!*" Katharine screamed, throwing one arm around Charlie and the other around Mary Bliss. "Can you believe it?"

Now it was Charlie's turn to beam. "She's six weeks pregnant as of Saturday. As far as I'm concerned, it's official. Isn't it amazing?"

"That's why he had to marry me," Katharine said. "Otherwise, I would have been the world's oldest unwed mother."

"That's not true," Charlie said quickly. "I never wanted a divorce in the first place. And I'd been begging you to marry me again way before we found out about the baby."

"Amazing," Mary Bliss repeated, looking from Charlie to Katharine. "But when? Charlie's been so sick. I can't believe . . ."

"Do the math," Katharine said, giggling. "The Fourth of July dance, you fool."

"Oh my God," Mary Bliss said, her eyes widening.

"Oh my God is right," Katharine said. She planted a kiss on Charlie's forehead. "The old fool nearly killed himself doing it, but he managed to knock me up that night. Can you believe it?"

"That's amazing," Mary Bliss said. She felt her mood lifting. Katharine and Charlie were holding hands, laughing their heads off, like a couple of high school kids who'd just let the air out of the principal's tires.

"Here's the part you'll love," Charlie said, a twinkle in his eye. "The baby's due April first."

"April Fool's Day," Katharine chortled. "Isn't it too delicious?"

"It's the best, most wonderful news I've heard all summer," Mary Bliss said. She was choking up with happiness. "And I can't believe you tried to keep it a secret from me," she added, giving Charlie a playful punch on the arm.

"Oh, he's full of secrets," Katharine said, squeezing her husband's knee. "But I'm surprised you didn't notice something was up with us. Charlie's been strutting around like the cock of the walk ever since we found out. And I've been green every morning."

"But you were drinking wine with me, just the other night," Mary Bliss objected.

"No. You were drinking, I was just swirling it around in my glass, inhaling the bouquet, enjoying it vicariously," Katharine said. "That's the only thing I mind about being pregnant. Do you realize I'll have to get through Christmas and New Year's without a drink?"

"I'm your best friend," Mary Bliss said loyally. "I'll drink enough for both of us."

They heard a polite tapping on the limousine's window then. Charlie pushed the button and the window slid down noiselessly.

It was Carol Kuhn, small, blonde, perturbed. She was holding a plastic-wrapped bundt cake in her hand. "Aren't you people coming in yet? My sour-cream cake is starting to curdle in this heat."

"You ready?" Katharine asked Mary Bliss.

Mary Bliss picked up the Bloody Mary and chugged it down. "I am now," she said grimly.

Katharine's house was full of flower arrangements that had been brought over from the church. Her massive cherry dining table had been pulled out to full banquet size and the white damask cloth was barely visible under the bowls and platters of food that had been arriving steadily all morning.

Mary Bliss gritted her teeth and waded into the crowd.

"Mary Bliss!" cooed Nancye Bowden, stopping her cold in the doorway to the living room.

"Hello, Nancye," Mary Bliss said. "Thank you for coming."

Randy hovered right behind Nancye, his hand gripped firmly in hers.

"We're so sorry about Parker's mama," Nancye said. She let go of Randy's hand just long enough to readjust the black bra strap that was sliding down her shoulder. "I know Parker was totally devoted to her. Is he around? We want to give him our condolences."

"I'm sure he's here somewhere," Mary Bliss said, her voice flat. "We came back from church in separate cars."

"So I noticed," Nancye purred. "He gave us quite a shock, turning up today the way he did. But I have to admit, he looks marvelous. So tan and fit. Death really becomes him."

"Nancye!" Randy's face went gray. Nancye shot him an evil look and drifted away.

"I'm sorry," Randy mumbled, staring down at his shoes. "She doesn't mean anything by it. That's just the way Nancye is. She's got this weird, sick sense of humor."

"It's all right," Mary Bliss said. "I brought it on myself. So I deserve to be the brunt of people's jokes."

"No, you don't," Randy said quickly. "None of this was your fault. You've been magnificent, if you ask me. It's been the summer from hell, yet you've managed to survive. I wish I had your . . ." He shook his head, as if hoping to shake the right word loose. "Your survivor's skills. I guess that's what I'm looking for."

"You survived," Mary Bliss said. "The kids are okay. You're okay. And you and Nancye?"

"We're going to try and make the marriage work again," Randy said. "For the sake of the little guys. And Josh. I've been offered a job down in Macon, and I've accepted it. Nancye agrees that we probably need to make a complete break from our past here. So we've put the house on the market."

"I saw the FOR SALE sign," Mary Bliss said. "I understand, but it still makes me sad. And Erin will be devastated to lose Josh just now."

"She won't lose him," Randy said. "We promised him he could finish his senior year at Fair Oaks Academy. My younger sister just got transferred to Atlanta. She and Josh will stay in the house until it sells, then he'll move in with her until May. Until graduation."

"I'm glad," Mary Bliss said. "For Josh and for you guys. And see? You're a survivor after all. At least, your marriage is."

"But not yours?" Randy asked. "What about you and Parker?"

Mary Bliss wasn't looking at Randy. Her eyes were scanning the room, looking for that carefully coiffed hair, the myopic now-blue eyes, and the gold chain gleaming against the deep tan. She saw him finally, scrunched into a corner, deep in conversation with a blue-haired woman of at least eighty who must have been one of Eula's buddies. He looked perfectly miserable.

"What?" she asked, looking back suddenly at Randy. "What did you just ask me?"

"I asked about you and Parker," Randy said. He'd seen where Mary Bliss was looking. "Whether or not you'll stay together after all this."

"Together?" Mary Bliss seemed to find that funny. "How could that be? I killed him off. And he came back a different person."

"Oh." Randy shifted uncomfortably. "Well, I better find the kids, before they mow their way through the dessert table. See you."

"Yeah," Mary Bliss said vaguely. "See you."

When she looked back at the corner where Parker had stood only moments earlier, he was gone. She elbowed her way into the living room, but he wasn't there. A group of men were clustered around the big-screen television in the den, watching the Braves game, but Parker wasn't with them. Finally, she worked her way back into the dining room, over to the corner, where she found the blue-haired woman picking at a plate of squash casserole and deviled eggs.

"Excuse me," she said. "I'm Mary Bliss McGowan."

"Darlin'," the old woman said, beaming up at her. "Don't you remember me? I'm Joyce Boore. I was at your wedding to Parker. Don't you remember? Eula and I were roommates at church camp."

"Oh yes," Mary Bliss said. "So nice of you to come. I do remember you now. Do you know where Parker went? I really need to speak to him for a moment."

She raised one blue eyebrow. "He said he had to see about something in the kitchen. But, sugar, I was just out in the kitchen, looking for some more iced tea, and I saw him slipping out the back door."

"When?" Mary Bliss asked. "How long ago?"

"Just now," Mrs. Boore said. "Not two minutes ago."

Mary Bliss rushed through the dining room and into the kitchen. Katharine's longtime maid, Valeria, was at the sink, rinsing off dishes.

"Valeria," Mary Bliss said sharply. "Have you seen my husband?"

"Yes, ma'am," Valeria said, not bothering to look up from the sink. "He came in here and made a phone call a little while ago. Called a cab, I believe. He waited a little bit, then he scooted on out of here not even a minute ago."

Mary Bliss sprinted for the back door. Her heels sank into the Weidmans' plush grass. She kicked off her shoes and ran around to the front yard. A yellow cab was just pulling into the circular drive. She saw a man, dressed in a tan suit, half hidden behind one of the entry columns.

"Parker!" she yelled.

He turned, saw who was yelling for him, then darted over to the cab.

"No," she yelled, running to the drive. "No!"

76

The cab pulled forward, then stopped, because a black Explorer with tinted windows had pulled into the other side of the drive, blocking it.

Now the cab was backing up, but the driver had paused long enough for Mary Bliss to catch up to it.

She wrenched the back door of the cab open. Parker was huddled in the backseat, his hand on the door handle.

"Where are you going?" she demanded, sliding into the seat beside him.

He shrank away from her. "Back to the hotel. I had to get out of here."

"Is that true?" she asked the driver. "Were you taking him to a hotel?"

The driver, an emaciated-looking Ethiopian man, shrugged. "Hotel at airport?"

"You were running away again, weren't you?" Mary Bliss said.

Parker stared out the window.

"Weren't you?"

Finally, he turned to face her. "All right," he snapped. "You're right again, Mary Bliss. Yeah, I'm leaving, if you'll get the hell out of this cab."

"No," Mary Bliss said. "Not again. Not before you talk to your daughter. And me. You owe us that much."

"Come on," Parker said, his voice wheedling. "Those guys in the house are gonna notice I'm gone pretty soon, and they'll come looking for me."

Mary Bliss pointed at the Explorer. "Too late," she said. "That's a private detective. He was hired by one of the companies you bilked. He's not about to let you waltz away from here. And neither am I. I want some answers, dammit. I want to know why."

"Why not?" he countered. "You can take care of yourself. You're the most competent person in the world, Mary Bliss. And I was entirely superfluous to your existence."

"That's not true," she said.

"I had to get out," Parker said, ignoring her. "I was buried alive here. I was going crazy, day by day, and you never even noticed, you were so busy being the world's most perfect wife and mother and neighbor."

"Why?" Mary Bliss pleaded with him. "Why did you leave like that?"

"Because I could," he said simply. "Once Mama was in the nursing home, once I knew she'd be taken care of for the rest of her life, I knew it would be okay. It was like I had the weight of the world lifted off my shoulders. That's when I started tunneling my way to freedom."

"You mean stealing," Mary Bliss corrected him.

"I didn't hurt anybody," Parker said. "A little money from a lot of people, that's the way it worked. Nobody went out of business, nobody went hungry. But I got a new life."

"What about us? Erin and me? We nearly lost the house. You could have talked to me, told me you wanted out. I would have given you a divorce."

"You would have wanted half of everything, and I couldn't afford that," Parker said. "It was my money in the first place. I was entitled to it. All of it."

"We would have been homeless!" Mary Bliss said. "I couldn't pay Erin's tuition. All those bills you left. I was wild with worry. And what was I supposed to tell Erin?"

"You figured it all out," Parker said, laughing. "I gotta hand it to you, M. B., killing me off was brilliant.

I never figured you'd pull a stunt like that. Of course, you forgot to take Mama into account. You should have known she'd never accept that I was dead."

"And you drove me to it," Mary Bliss said, clenching her fists in rage. "I'll never forgive you for that. I lied to my daughter to protect you. We nearly lost her, did you know that? She ran away because she thought she might be pregnant. She was scared to death, and you turned her away. Do you have any idea of what she's been through this summer?"

"She'll be fine," he said. "She's upset about Mama, sure, a little angry with me, maybe, but Erin's a great kid. Nothing fazes her. She's like you that way."

Mary Bliss hauled off and slapped him then.

"Christ!" Parker exclaimed. A trickle of blood oozed from the corner of his lower lip. "You see? I could never talk to you."

"Why don't you talk to me now?" Mary Bliss asked, her eyes blazing. "Tell me about your new life that you bought for yourself. You were living in Key West, right?"

"That's right," Parker said. He reached into the inner pocket of his jacket and brought out a neatly folded handkerchief. At least that hadn't changed about him. He was still meticulous with his appearance. He dabbed at his lower lip.

"I've got a new business. A bed-and-breakfast. That's why I needed all that money. Real estate prices are astronomical in the Keys. But I don't care. This is something totally new for me. A real adventure. Something you'd never understand."

"An adventure." Mary Bliss stared at him. "What makes you think I wouldn't have wanted an adventure?"

"You? No way. There's no way you would have picked up and moved down to Key West. No way you would have left dear old Fair Oaks. Uh-uh," he said, shaking his head vigorously. "Anyway, it was over between us."

"I saw the pictures of your girlfriend," Mary Bliss said. "You didn't think I knew about her, did you?"

"What are you talking about?" Parker asked, clearly stunned. "What pictures?"

"The pictures of you, at the ATMs. Of your new car, and the blonde, sitting in the front seat of the Range Rover. So don't give me any crap about wanting a new life and a new adventure. You just wanted somebody new to screw, you shit!" She was screaming again, and striking out at him. He put his arms up, batting away her blows.

She saw the glint of gold at his neck then, and she reached out and yanked, as hard as she could. Mary Bliss held up her engagement ring, the broken gold chain dangling from it. "You took everything else. I'm taking this back."

"You're crazy," Parker yelled. Now he dabbed at his neck, and the handkerchief came away bloody. "Look what you did. You ruined my Escada suit."

"Uh-oh," the Ethiopian said, looking at them in the rearview mirror, his high, bald forehead knit with worry. "I don't want any trouble. Maybe you get out now."

"Shut up!" Mary Bliss snapped.

"A girlfriend?" Parker said, his laugh nasty. "That wasn't a girlfriend in the Range Rover. That was Russell."

"Russell?" Mary Bliss was remembering the photos. The blonde shoulder-length hair nearly hidden by the baseball cap.

"My business partner," Parker said smugly. "I met him in the real estate office. He's the one that found the bed-and-breakfast for me."

"Russell?"

"You talked to him when you called down there the night Mama went in the hospital," Parker said impatiently. "He was sitting in the pew right behind you in church today."

"Your partner? Parker, are you telling me you're gay now? Is that what this is all about?"

"Uh-oh," the Ethiopian said quietly. "This is very bad. You get out now. No charge. Okay?"

"Shut up!" Parker screamed. "Turn around and shut the fuck up." His tan had turned to a mottled purple. "You see!" he yelled at Mary Bliss. "That's why I had to get out. You take things and you just twist them around. You have no idea who I really am."

Mary Bliss clenched and unclenched her fists. She was angrier than she'd ever been in her life. But she spoke calmly, quietly. She didn't want to spook the cab driver again.

"I think I deserve some answers here, Parker. I was married to you for twenty years. Just tell me the truth. I deserve that. Which is it? Did you leave me because you hate me, or did you leave me because you found out you're gay?"

"I am *not* gay!" Parker shouted. "Did you tell Erin that? Did you tell my daughter I'm gay? Is that why she's so angry with me?"

"I told her nothing," Mary Bliss shouted back. "I hid everything from her until after your mama died."

"You'll turn her against me. She'll think I'm a fag."

"No," Mary Bliss said. "She's just going to think you're a sorry excuse for a man. I think she could deal with your being gay, if you could be honest about that."

"I am *not* gay!" Parker screamed, pounding the back of the driver's seat.

The Ethiopian turned around. "No more hitting seat. Okay?"

"I was so dumb," Mary Bliss said, shaking her head in wonderment. "So dumb. I tried to keep Erin from learning the truth about you. But she's going to be eighteen pretty soon. She's a woman. She's loved a man and been left brokenhearted. She found out all by herself how sorry a man can be. And I hate that. Not all men are like Isaac Brownlee. Or even like you. There are fine, decent men in the world. I know that now. That's one favor you did me, Parker, by leaving. You didn't leave me any options. I had to find out about myself. And about you. I had to find out what marriage really was and wasn't. I got smart in a hurry. You forced that on me."

"Hooray for you!" Parker said, clapping his hands in mock glee. "Hooray for brilliant, wonderful Mary Bliss McGowan. But don't think I haven't heard what's been going on around here while I've been gone. I heard you found a new man already."

Mary Bliss pressed her lips together to keep from screaming again.

"Okay," the Ethiopian said. He'd turned all the way around and was facing them now. "Everything settled. You go, lady. I take man to airport. Okay?"

"No," Mary Bliss said. "We're not done here yet."

"What do you want?" Parker asked, staring nervously at the Explorer, whose motor was still running.

"I want the title to the house," she said. "I want you to pay it off with all that money you stole. It's the least you can do. I've got lawyer's expenses, and I'm still paying off all that debt you've saddled me with. But the most important thing is Erin. I need money to pay her tuition. You owe her that."

Parker laughed. "Money. I should have known that's what it all comes down to. Well, you're shaking the wrong tree, Mary Bliss. I've sunk every damn dime into the bed-and-breakfast. And it's all in Russell's name. So even if I do get arrested, you won't be able to get your hands on it."

He laughed again. He was actually enjoying himself. "But don't worry, there's always good old Meemaw."

"What's that supposed to mean?" Mary Bliss asked. Her head was starting to pound. She shouldn't have chugged that Bloody Mary.

"Charlie called me this morning. About Mama's will."

"Let me guess. She left me the dusting powder and Erin the martini shaker."

"That and the house down in Griffin, a trust fund for Erin, and some assorted stocks and bonds. In short, everything."

"I don't believe you," Mary Bliss said, her head throbbing. "Eula was broke. She ran through her granddaddy's money years ago."

"Actually, she was loaded. Charlie says there's a couple million just in mutual funds. Mama was just testing us. To see if we really loved her. If we'd take care of her 'til the end. Another one of her goddamned games."

"So you're a rich man," Mary Bliss said. "How does it feel?"

"I wouldn't know," Parker said, his smile bitter. "She left me exactly zip. Nada. It all goes to you and Erin."

"You're such a liar. I was just with Charlie. He never said a word."

"Mama's instructions. He only broke the bad news to me today when I asked him for an advance on my inheritance. To pay for my lawyer. Charlie says Mama called him late last week, insisting he come over to the nursing home. She wanted to amend her will. Up until then, I was her sole beneficiary. Right up until last week. She told Charlie she'd changed her mind. She told him as far as she was concerned, I was dead."

"But she knew you weren't dead," Mary Bliss said, interrupting. "She never believed me. She kept all your postcards. I found them in her room, after she'd gone to the hospital."

Parker kept dabbing at his lip, even though the blood had dried now. "Control. Mama was all about control. She called me, to tell me Erin was in trouble. 'You've had your fling,' she said. 'You've had three months now to get it out of your system. Come on home, boy.' That's what she called me. Boy. 'I'm sick. I'm dying,' she said. 'Erin's in trouble. Time to do right by your family.'"

"Why didn't you come?" Mary Bliss asked wearily.

"Mama didn't sound all that sick. And as far as I could tell, you were handling things just fine. Anyway, she was wrong about me. It wasn't just a fling. I'd changed. I couldn't be married anymore. I couldn't even be the old Parker McGowan. I tried to tell Mama that, but she wouldn't listen. She pitched a hissy and then she hung up on me."

"And then she died," Mary Bliss said. "She died alone. Erin ran away to look for you, and I went after her, and Meemaw died while we were both gone. Did you know that? She died wondering when you were coming home."

Parker smiled. The purple rage was gone. He was tan and poised again. "It won't work. No more guilt.

Mama's dead. You're fine. Erin's fine. And I'm out of here."

He pounded on the driver's seat back again. "Let's go, buddy," he called. "Time to move out."

The Ethiopian's war-weary eyes lit up. "What about that car? He's blocking the way."

They both looked at the Explorer. It had pulled within inches of the cab's front bumper.

"Your boyfriend, there," Parker said. "The detective. Is he gonna arrest me?"

"Eventually," Mary Bliss said.

Parker reached into his breast pocket and brought out a wad of bills. He peeled off some twenty-dollar bills and handed them to the driver. "Back up. Lose him, and you keep the money."

"Good deal." The driver gestured to Mary Bliss. "You go now, lady."

Parker sat back in his seat. "Tell Erin I'll call her."

"When?"

He looked annoyed. "On her birthday. September fourteenth, right?"

"Fifteenth," Mary Bliss said, opening her door. "What about the rest? I want a divorce, you know."

"Fine. Talk to my lawyer. He'll know where to find me."

Parker glanced at the black Explorer, and then at the house. The plainclothes cops began spilling out of the Weidmans' front door, running now, dropping the pallbearer's ruse.

From off in the distance, she heard the wail of police sirens. The cab's motor raced, and it jerked backward. Mary Bliss had to jump for the curb to keep from being run over. The Ethiopian gunned the motor again, and the cab shot backward out of the Weidmans' driveway, grazing the rear fender of Charlie's Cadillac.

Out in the street, the driver threw the cab into gear and screeched off in a cloud of burning rubber. The Explorer roared to life and went careening out of the driveway and down the Weidmans' street, in hot pursuit of the cab. Three police cruisers joined the race.

Mary Bliss stood in the driveway, watching until she could no longer see any of the cars. She was putting her engagement ring on her right-hand ring finger when she felt an arm wrap around her shoulders.

She looked up. Matt Hayslip stood beside her.

"I thought . . . you were in the Explorer. Going after Parker."

"No. Not my job. Not anymore." He squeezed her arm, kissed the top of her head.

"What is your job?"

"Taking care of you. And Erin. If you'll have me."

She looked down at her engagement ring, the diamond sparkling in the late afternoon light.

"Guess what? I'm an heiress. Eula left us two million dollars."

"All right," Matt said agreeably. "Then you can take care of me."

BEYOND THE GRAVE CHICKEN SALAD

5 lbs. chicken breasts
2 qts. water
Parsley sprigs
1 large onion, quartered
1 tsp. seasoned salt
2 chicken bouillon cubes

In a large pot, bring water and seasoning to a boil, add chicken, lower heat, and simmer 40 minutes. Remove from heat, cool. Shred chicken and refrigerate.

Dressing

½ cup bottled Italian salad dressing
1 cup Duke's mayonnaise
1 tbsp. white vinegar
1½ tsp. celery seed
2 tbsp. sugar
⅛ tsp. salt
Dash paprika

Blend well together.

Salad

Toss shredded chicken with one cup of dressing and let stand one hour to marinate.

Combine remaining dressing with:

½ cup sour cream
1 tbsp. honey

Add to chicken and mix well. May add canned water chestnut, blanched almonds, or chopped pecans.